STORMFORGED

Also by Eric R. Asher

Shop ebooks, audiobooks, and paperbacks at ericrasherstore.com

The Theme Park at the End of the World

The Steamborn Series

Steamborn

Steamforged

Steamsworn

Skyborn

Skyforged

Skysworn

Stormborn

Stormforged

Stormsworn

The Vesik Series
(Recommended for Ages 17+)

Days Gone Bad

Wolves and the River of Stone

Winter's Demon

This Broken World

Destroyer Rising

Rattle the Bones

Witch Queen's War

Forgotten Ghosts

The Book of the Ghost

The Book of the Claw

The Book of the Sea

The Book of the Staff

The Book of the Rune

The Book of the Sails

The Book of the Wing

The Book of the Blade

The Book of the Fang

The Book of the Reaper

Dreams of the Forgotten Dead

Garden Gnome Graves

The Vesik Series Box Sets

Box Set One (Books 1-3)

Box Set Two (Books 4-6)

Box Set Three (Books 7-8)

Box Set Four: The Books of the Dead Part 1

Box Set Five: The Books of the Dead Part 2

Mason Dixon: Monster Hunter

Episode One

Episode Two

Episode Three

Episode Four

Want to receive an email when one of Eric's books releases?

Visit ericrasher.com to get started.

STORMFORGED

THE STEAMBORN SERIES, BOOK EIGHT

By

ERIC R. ASHER

We cannot always be ready for what must come.

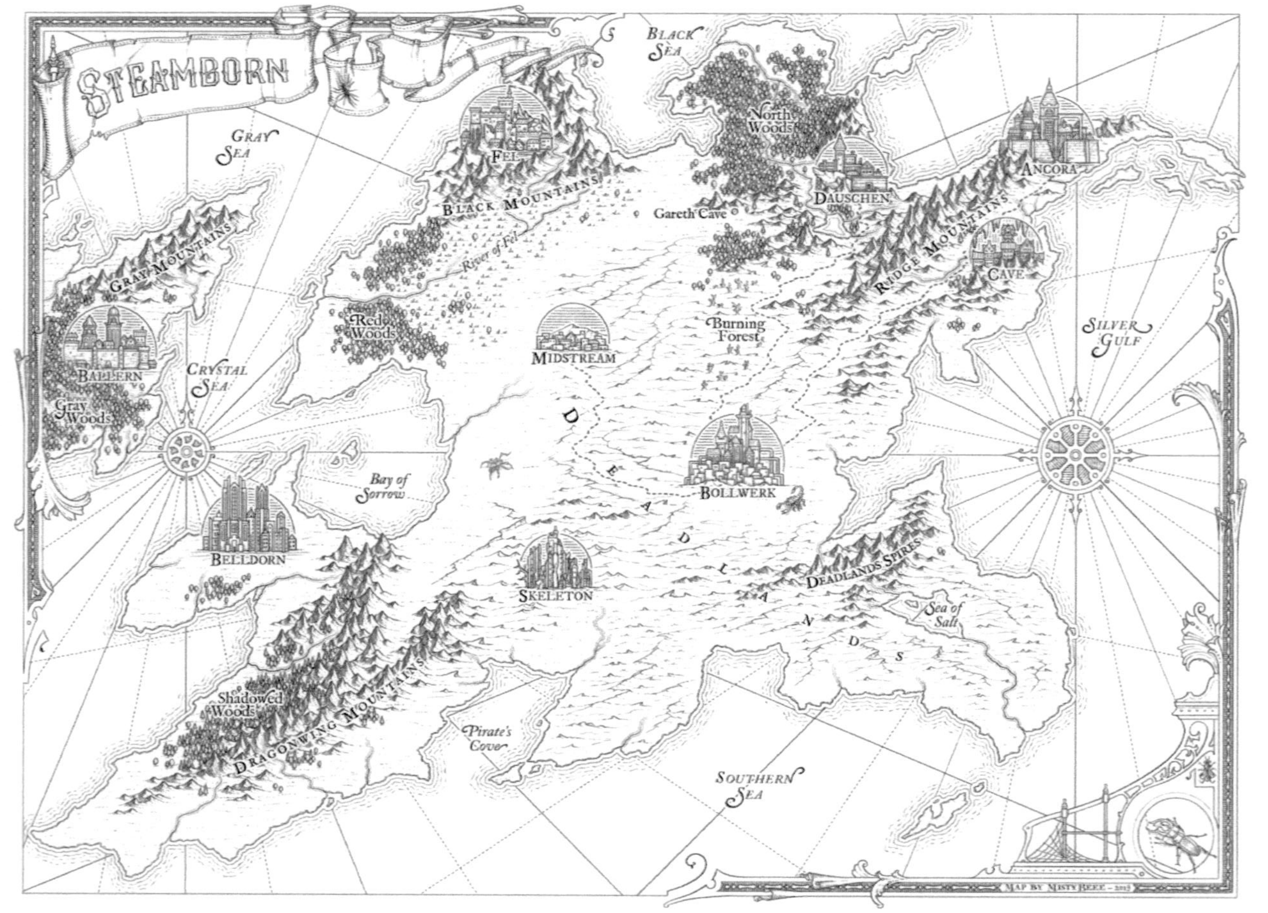

STEAMBORN
GRAY SEA
BLACK SEA
NORTH WOODS
ANCORA
FEL
DAUSCHEN
RIDGE MOUNTAINS
BLACK MOUNTAINS
Gareth Cave
CAVE
GRAY MOUNTAINS
River of Fel
Red Woods
Burning Forest
SILVER GULF
BALLERN
Crystal Sea
MIDSTREAM
D E A D L A N D S
Gray Woods
BOLLWERK
Bay of Sorrow
BELLDORN
SKELETON
DEADLANDS SPIRES
Sea of Salt
Shadowed Woods
DRAGONWING MOUNTAINS
Pirate's Cove
SOUTHERN SEA
MAP BY MISTY BEEE - 2015

CHAPTER ONE

J ACOB STOOD IN the secondary pilot house above the deck of the carrier. Excitement warred with dread as workers scattered across the metal expanse like so many mites. They swept debris as they went, tying down anything that might cause injury should it fall from the platform.

Four Titan Mechs surrounded the massive ship, ready to redirect the monstrosity if things went bad. And Jacob knew if things went bad, it could cost them far more than the labor and materials of the carrier. He clenched his fists as the first pontoon rose in the west, knuckles whitening as the consequences of failure loomed overhead.

Frederick leaned forward over the control panel. Levers and switches stood out from the rough metal plating like the spines of a Stone Dog. The older tinker nodded to himself, brushing gray hair back behind his ear before making small adjustments to the ballast valves.

A distant hiss rumbled below them, and Frederick tapped the gauges. He cast Jacob a sideways glance and smiled. "It'll fly, son, but it's an ugly bastard."

"Let's see if it gets off the ground before we say that," Jacob muttered. It wasn't the prettiest ship he'd ever seen, that was certain. But Jacob was proud of what they'd built in a matter of weeks. Where Ballern's carrier had been graced by enormous hangers, Belldorn's had little more than reinforced tents to offer shelter. But those tents had been gifted to them from Canopy, built of the same materials that held a city in the trees. Cables spun from the strongest spider silks, woven so tight as to be their own sort of armor.

The bolt cannons had come from Ancora on the first supply ship. Ambrose thought they'd be needed more in Belldorn now that Ancora's wall was done, and so the same cannons that had helped protect Jacob's home now drove bolts into the steel of a carrier.

Bollwerk provided what the crews couldn't salvage from the ruins of Belldorn and Ballern's temporary docks.

Ballern. Alice was there, waiting with the Skyborn. The Stormborn. Some of Bollwerk's citizens thought this wasn't their fight because it was across the Crystal Sea. It had fractured their city, but Archibald understood. Archibald risked his own power base to set these carriers in motion, and that was something Jacob hadn't thought the Speaker would do. Alice believed it was a calculated gamble. A way to gather even more power after the war.

Maybe it was. But Jacob was certain they couldn't defeat Mordair without him.

A Titan Mech on each side raised its left arm. All thoughts of their allies fled Jacob's mind. This was what they'd been working toward, day and night, with far too little sleep.

The transmitter crackled to life, and Smith's voice filled the cabin. "Ballast clear on all sides. Cargo is locked. On your signal."

Jacob leaned toward the transmitter. "Carrier One lifting off."

"Together," Frederick said. He didn't count down, only waited for Jacob to grab the second of the largest levers on the control panel.

The metal felt cold beneath Jacob's sweaty palm. He eased it forward, impressed by the smooth path Frederick had built into the system in such short time. There was no roughness to the switch or its gears, but the roar they summoned jarred Jacob.

The boilers came to life in full, and in each quadrant, a dull orange glow lit beneath the deck. Jacob cringed at the sight, knowing they'd need to address the heat rising from those areas. That concern faded as the floor shifted under their feet, and the entire expanse of the carrier lifted into the air.

It was only a short distance at first, and there wasn't much cargo left to speak of, but it was a test that needed to happen. An unbalanced load that would help them determine how to configure a whole fleet across the carriers.

The sole Titan Mech remaining on deck sat on the opposite side, daring the carrier to rise higher. But its movement couldn't have been more level, as if the gargantuan machine was no more than a single dockhand.

A minute passed, and the carrier rose above the highest roofs of Belldorn, leaving those around the docks far below.

Frederick turned to Jacob. "It'll fly."

Jacob breathed out, releasing something between a sigh and a laugh.

"Commence landing sequence," Smith said across the transmitter. "Get anchored and we will begin the load tests."

Frederick flipped a dozen switches before clicking the transmitter. "Ballonets inflating. Descent in five minutes."

"This is what I never understood about airships," Jacob said. "There are gas chambers *inside* the gas chambers?"

"More or less, that is correct. We installed ballonets throughout the ballast chambers as well. It allows us to compensate if some are damaged. Inflated, ballonets displace the lifting gas of the chamber, and without that volume, the ship descends."

"But the gas itself is never vented?"

"Never is a strong word, Jacob. It isn't *supposed* to be vented, but valves degrade over time. Nothing we should need to worry about until the carriers are much older."

The carrier stopped hovering and started a slow descent back to the ground.

"Give me gears and steel and bronze," Jacob muttered. "Just the thought of trying to balance those gas chambers makes me nervous."

"It's not as bad as it sounds. One could argue it is far less dangerous than working on a Titan Mech."

"But Titan Mechs don't fall out of the sky when you get it wrong." He shivered at the idea of it.

Frederick grinned at Jacob. "A fair point."

Smith's voice crackled as he spoke. "Stern is two degrees lower than the bow. Still within tolerances. Prepare for docking."

Docking felt like an optimistic word to Jacob. There wasn't a dock on the entire continent where a carrier could settle in. It would simply land where it could fit, and that was that. And that's exactly what it did, touching down on the earth with a crash of metal against stone and dirt. But the vibrations that ran along the deck and up through the pilot house were minimal. None of the plates separated. No ballast split, and every gas chamber remained inflated.

Jacob looked up at Frederick. "It worked?" He didn't mean for it to be a question, but with all the worries he'd had, it felt like something *should* have gone wrong. "It worked."

"Quite well!" Frederick squeezed Jacob's shoulder and gave it a short shake.

The Titan Mechs around the perimeter moved, anchoring the carrier before the workers returned to the deck. A small group of people walked in unison, a single figure surrounded by four guards. Jacob grabbed a pair of binoculars from the side of the control panel.

"Lady Katherine's on deck."

"Best not to keep the lady waiting." Frederick pulled the switches to cut off the boilers, and two pillars of smoke rose from the edges of the carrier. They hurried out of the pilot house and down the stairs that would take them to the deck.

✧   ✧   ✧

SMITH WAS ALREADY at Kat's side by the time Jacob and Frederick made it to the carrier's center. It was easy to forget just how long the deck was until you had to traverse it on foot.

"And you were able to launch with only two boilers?" Lady Katherine asked as Jacob and Frederick joined Smith.

"Yes. Slowed the pumps down a bit, but it was good enough. We can lose four boilers and still stay in the air."

Lady Katherine turned her attention to Frederick. "Perhaps your idea of repurposing the boilers from the old factory was not so misguided."

Frederick gave a small bow. "Thank you, My Lady. We'd done much the same in Bollwerk for the warships when they needed a critical repair, and I thought it would work for the carrier, as well."

Lady Katherine looked back toward the main pilot house of the sprawling ship. "Show me a carrier in the sky with a Porcupine on board and you'll truly impress me."

"We plan to load test later today," Smith said. "Tomorrow at the latest. They're preparing the ramps for crawlers and Titan Mechs." He glanced at Jacob before standing a little straighter. "Do we have your permission to load a Porcupine?"

Lady Katherine blinked at that. "Are you … serious, Smith?"

"Damn right, he is."

Jacob startled at Mary's voice right by his ear. He squinted and stared at the shadowed helmet of a Royal Guard. "Mary?" He was about to ask more, but the memory of the assassins in the throne room answered any question he could have asked. Mary was one of Kat's closest friends, and who better to vet your guards than a paranoid pirate? It also explained the utter lack of surprise on Kat's face.

Jacob grinned at Mary with the unspoken thought.

"What?"

"Nothing, nothing at all."

Mary turned back to Smith. "Once this thing is load tested, we're ready to strike out at Ballern?"

"Mary," Lady Katherine said, a warning tone in that name.

"It's time you told them, Kat." Mary gestured to the expansive deck. "This is as alone as any of us are going to be if you want to keep it under wraps. Though I think the fact you're building a carrier makes it rather obvious."

"Fine, Mary. Fine." Kat rubbed her neck and studied the group. "If we can't breach the walls of Ballern, any response we offer will be a worthless gesture. An unnecessary loss of life."

"Are you saying we aren't going?" Jacob couldn't hide the anxiousness in his question.

"With Bollwerk's warship and two carriers, we can cross the sea in force, Jacob. Then the bolstering of our forces will fall to Furi and Alice's efforts with the Skyborn." Kat clenched a fist. "The city is screaming for a response to the invasion that stole so many lives and homes in Belldorn. And a response they will have."

A weight lifted from Jacob's mind. The thought that Kat might try to back out of an attack on Ballern had been worrying him. He knew she didn't want a war, but Mordair had miscalculated. Smith believed because of the assassination attempt, Kat would be more committed to the idea than ever. It looked like he might have been right.

"I spoke to Archibald about the fractures forming in Bollwerk. He sent Lady Grey to engage with the factions, but I do not know if even she has the sway to quell the masses. It is a nightmare I wanted to avoid in Belldorn. It is why I opened more shelters than were needed. Why I am providing food and care at no cost to those who need it. Dissent has quieted on the streets, but the call to arms has not. So we are in agreement. The reconstruction will be swift, but justice more so."

"Bollwerk will heal in time," Frederick said. "We have been through worse than the unrest we have now."

"Perhaps if Archibald had spent more time healing his own city than rebuilding Ancora, it could have been avoided."

Jacob stood up a little straighter. "And leave them all to die?"

"There are hard choices, Jacob." Kat looked away for a moment. "There are always hard choices. You cannot save everyone."

"I can try." There was a terrible heat in his words. An anger he hadn't meant to let slip. But it was raw, and it was real, and it was there.

CHAPTER TWO

CAGE RUBBED HIS chin and studied Owen. "You're talking about taking on Mordair in a foreign city. You don't know the alleys and byways, much less the people."

"We know them well enough, and we only need one ocean liner." Owen gestured out to Fel's docks, far below them. "Hoist our fishing vessels up like lifeboats. Once we're past the worst of the Crystal Sea, we can deploy our own boats and slip into Ballern's docks with little fanfare. I don't need to know the city to sabotage his ocean liners, Cage."

"You risk much. What if no one is left in Fel who can get one of those ocean liners running? What about Vaughn and Hefina? You don't want to leave them alone in Ancora if you don't come home."

"If we fail, they won't have a home anywhere." Owen's lip curled. "Mordair will come for Ancora, Cage. You know that as well as I do. In the end, either he dies, or the rest of us do."

Cage sighed. "I wish I could say I didn't agree with you about that." He squeezed Owen's shoulder before stepping away, heading for Nora's clipper. He paused before the gangplank. "The fisherfolk are with you, Owen. Your speech saw to that. Rally them at The Crooked Blade. Others will come. Mordair made more capable enemies here than he likely knows."

"Look after Ancora while I'm gone, will you?" Owen reached out and squeezed his cousin's shoulder.

Cage blew out a breath and smiled at him. "I'll do what I can. Vaughn and Hefina are safe behind those walls, Owen. Worry about yourself out there. Until the seas bring us together once more."

"Peace, cousin."

Cage didn't respond to Owen's words. Perhaps peace would one day find them again. But for a time, the world would be anything but peaceful.

✧   ✧   ✧

WITHOUT OWEN ON board to talk to, Cage opened up Nora's clipper in earnest. The tiny airship cut through the air like a ballista bolt, and he had to admit he enjoyed the clipper far more than he would have expected. It felt cramped with only enough seating for two, but its maneuverability was stunning.

The North Woods passed below in short hours before he guided the clipper between the peaks of the Ridge Mountains. Dauschen's damaged skyline graced the horizon, slowly vanishing behind the taller peaks, staying in sight for nearly an hour. The flight grew far less relaxed in the more violent winds of the passes before finally relenting as Cage rocketed out over the Black Sea.

He followed the railroad for a time, catching glimpses of smoke billowing out from the trains before Ancora came into view. He slowed the clipper's thrusters, nearly overshooting the city through inertia alone. Cage guided the clipper into Ancora's new docks, letting the ship drift into the docking clamps where the springs released and locked the ship into place.

Cage hopped out and tossed a coin to the dockhand, who hurried over to engage the remaining clamps. "Fuel her up for Nora, would you?"

"Of course, sir. Right away."

"Do you know where I can find her by chance?"

"Nora? At the stables, I assume. I served under her during the reconstruction of the wall. She's always in the stables."

Cage inclined his head and struck out to the north. He studied the completed walls around the Lowlands as he went. Only one of the cranes worked along the top edge that afternoon, moving backward as it positioned plates of inverted spikes and spears to crown the wall. It would offer protection from invaders and soldiers alike. Something that should have been built for the Lowlands long ago.

Dauschen could have benefited from much the same, but that was a line of thought with no end. One did not always know what would help prevent a disaster in a city until the moment had long passed.

Cage turned his attention back to the road ahead. Once, the city walls had towered without peer. Now, the Lowland walls threatened to overshadow them, and Cage didn't stop the small smile that crossed his lips as he entered the Highlands, mulling over that change.

The courtyard was nearly empty, where just two weeks before it had teemed with refugees. The new apartments had drawn a good deal of people back to the Lowlands, and Cage wondered how much the dynamic would shift between the two areas of Ancora now. How much it already *had* shifted.

He headed northwest, keeping close to the wall until the entrance to the stables came into view. It was an odd thing, seeing them so bare. Only a handful of mounts remained—two Jumpers and some older beasts that bore scars from carrying heavy armor.

Cage made his way to the end, where a small cluster of offices were embedded into the wall itself. The musty scent of Sweet-Flies and old hay didn't lessen as he stepped into the hallway, finding Nora in the first office, where she studied a teetering pile of maps.

He knocked on the doorframe to get her attention before stepping inside.

Nora glanced up, a familiar look of concentration furrowing her brow. A look Cage had seen many times in Dauschen. "Is she still in one piece?"

"Of course." Cage smiled and crossed his arms. "The dockhands are refueling her too, so she'll be ready for you."

"Good, that's good. Owen stayed in Fel?"

He nodded.

"I wondered if he would. He truly means to go to Ballern?"

"I don't think anyone could change his mind at this point." Cage glanced at the door. "The mounts. I noticed several of the stables were empty."

"On their way to Canopy." Nora pushed her chair back and rose. She'd looked like little more than skin and bones toward the end of her stint in Dauschen. Now, whipcord muscles stood out on her arms, and the sleeves of her jerkin pulled tight against a powerful frame. "Cave sent their soldiers to defend Ancora. Only a half dozen Spider Knights remain in the city now. The others will train with Canopy to face Ballern, Cage. You know what Ancorans are capable of. They'll end Mordair."

Cage sighed. "Good. I think they can do the best there. We have enough beds for the Cave Guardians?"

"The new apartments have been completed, so there are enough at the inns for now. Though I believe some of them were more excited to find Branddur had opened a restaurant in the Lowlands than they were to have a bed to sleep on."

A low chuckle escaped Cage's lips. "There's something about having a taste of home. That I can understand. Are there any more supply ships leaving for Canopy?"

"One tomorrow. Do you intend to join them?"

"No. I gave my word to too many that I would look after those who remain in Ancora."

"Good. Then help me with these maps. We have scouts covering most of the walls, but there *is* a small drawback to the new Lowlands defenses. It created a handful of blind spots."

Strategy was something familiar to Cage. Familiar to all of Bollwerk's spies, if he was being honest. He walked to the other side of the table to see things from Nora's perspective. Food could be a reminder of home, but keeping your friends and family protected was far more satisfying.

✧   ✧   ✧

OWEN RECOGNIZED MANY of the faces who joined him at The Crooked Blade. Fisherfolk had turned out in numbers, but what surprised him was the number of others who wandered in. If many more arrived, they were going to have a hard time fitting inside the bar.

Fiona and Trevor spoke to a trio of city folk closer to the door. Trevor was easy to recognize by his reedy, towering frame and thinning hair, while Fiona stood out because she looked like she could split logs with her bare hands.

None of this was of concern to the barkeep, who poured beers and spirits as fast as the swarm of patrons could order them. Owen waited until the hour struck four and then stepped up on the short ladder the barkeep lent him.

"Thank you all for coming!" Owen's voice had always carried, and when he made an effort to project it, there were few who could ignore him. "I asked you here so I could tell you my plans to strike back at Mordair. I never want our king to return to this place. And I believe if he is given enough time, solidifies his alliance with Ballern, and perhaps, more critically, with the Children of the Dark Fire, he will return."

A few mutterings sounded in the bar, but most had turned their attention to Owen.

"I'm not here to tell you anyone *must* join this fight. But I won't turn away volunteers. We need fisherfolk and dockhands who know their way around the ocean liners. If any of you are left from the crews who helped build them, we need you most of all."

A few hands rose in the back of the bar, and a knot of dread unwound itself in Owen's gut. Dread that Cage would have been right and no one could make the remaining ocean liners seaworthy.

"You are our key to this operation." Owen nodded to Fiona and Trevor, who moved toward those who had raised their hands. Owen wasn't taking chances. Not so close to bringing his plan to action. Fiona and Trevor's movement left an opening in the room, clearing a line of sight that had been obscured.

There, in the corner, waited two dark cloaks. Owen had little doubt who they were. Two of the Children of the Dark Fire. Bold enough to wear cloaks inside the tavern? Or had they donned them after entering?

They held his gaze. Long enough Owen grew uncomfortable, so instead, he turned his attention back to the crowd at hand. But he wasn't the only one who had noticed their presence. The barkeep appeared below, speaking just loud enough for Owen to hear.

"My boys have them cornered, Owen. They can't draw a blade without consequence. Speak your piece."

Owen nodded. "Three days. I want to sail into the ports at Ballern in three days' time."

"To be immediately sunk to the bottom of the sea?" one attendee shouted.

"No. I want to strap our fishing vessels to the sides of the ocean liner in place of lifeboats. I want to cross the heart of the Crystal Sea, through the expanse, and drop anchor before arriving in our own boats. The smallest vessels of the fisherfolk will blend in. They will not expect us."

"And what do you mean to do once we're there?" Trevor called out.

Owen steeled himself. "I mean to fight."

Another cloak fluttered. This one far too close. Far too … high.

"Be you blessed by the Dark Fire!"

A shout preceded the glint of metal in the shadow. The thrown cloak meant to hide the assassin behind it. The assassin who had come far too close to Owen, and had far underestimated the mood of the crowd.

He'd scarcely finished his shout before a heavy glass pitcher crashed into his face. The fool had given them warning with that battle cry, and the barkeep had taken care of the rest.

"Grab the other two," the barkeep growled over the rising voices. "Take them to the prison and we can decide what to do with them from there."

"Hang them from the walls!" one of the townsfolk shouted.

"No," Owen's voice thundered through the room as his hand smacked down on the bar. "Those days are *done.*"

Every eye in the bar turned toward Owen while the barkeep dragged the would-be assassin toward the door and his men.

"I never want to see another man, woman, or child hanging from those walls. Leave the gate buried in the earth. Open our city to the world beyond. We will all be the better for it, my friends. But it is a dream that cannot be if Mordair ever returns to our city. And it is *our* city." Owen's voice had fallen to a deadly whisper, a promise to fight, a promise of what might come to be. "Fight with me to keep it that way."

There was no breaking of blades in that bar. Only the solemn nods of his fellow fisherfolk and townsfolk who had already decided to join the fight, long before they ever set foot inside The Crooked Blade.

CHAPTER THREE

L ADY GREY ADJUSTED the wide-brimmed leather hat on her head. It provided a good amount of protection from the sun, but the reinforced leather offered far more protection than that. Her father had been a paranoid man in the days he'd worked for Archibald. But it hadn't saved him in the end.

As paranoid as that man had been, he'd raised his daughter to be both paranoid and prepared. It had served her well, and while the stories of her would-be assassins had grown into tall tales in Bollwerk, there was a kernel of truth to them.

They *had* tried to kill her. She'd killed them first. There hadn't been nearly so many assassins as the stories said, but an opportunity was an opportunity. Lady Grey had leaned into her own mythology, and as the decades passed, her infamy grew.

Now she worked side by side with Archibald, as her father once had. Whether he would be proud or enraged, she couldn't be sure. Either way, she figured the old man would have been worried. He'd never been fond of Archibald.

"I cannot thank you enough for joining me, My Lady," Natalia said.

"Of course, dear. And call me Liz when we're alone. Your grandfather fought in the Deadlands War beside my father. Even if keeping the riots away from the factories wasn't in my best interest, I would not leave you and yours without allies."

Natalia offered her a broad smile before turning her attention back to the streets and alleys ahead.

Those streets were oddly empty two blocks from the factory. Archibald's doing, Lady Grey presumed. She followed Natalia's casual stride, admiring the woman's confidence in such a trying time as black smoke twisted with white in the distance.

Natalia ran her fingers through her brown hair and blew out a breath. "I spoke with Frederick this morning. They already tested their carrier."

"So Archibald has told me."

"Of course he did." Natalia didn't hide the irritation in her voice. "We have an *actual* factory here, one large enough to build our carrier, and Frederick built his faster in the mud. I can't even explain how annoying that is."

"Frederick didn't have rioters intercepting his workers, though, did he?" Lady Grey slowly raised an eyebrow.

"No …"

"Then perhaps give yourself a little grace. Unless you'd prefer to force your workers to live inside the factory?"

"Absolutely not, Liz." Natalia frowned as if the name felt wrong on her tongue, and Lady Grey found that quite amusing. "Tobias and I had a hard apprenticeship. I understand working long hours when it's critical, but we should have been able to finish before Frederick."

"You still could. Test flight done or not. Did Frederick tell you they have almost none of the hangars built on their carrier yet?"

Natalia blinked.

"I take it he did not. And how are your hangars coming along, dear?"

"They're … they're almost finished. Are you telling me he tested the gas chambers before they even …" Natalia's jaw flexed, and she rubbed at her temples. "It is infuriating how well that man knows me."

Lady Grey could hear the crowds clearly when they rounded the next corner. Floating bits of ash and embers from the bonfires drifted past, leaving a layer of gray dust over the streets. The factory loomed ahead, its giant doors pulled closed, hiding the progress within.

Brick and brass rose behind the soldiers keeping the entrance free of rioters. The simple clean lines of the factory walls a contrast to the broken bottles and rotten vegetables smeared across the soldiers and grounds before them.

Lady Grey grimaced and stepped ahead of Natalia. She recognized faces from her own faction, and it kindled a low anger in her gut. She thought she had led her citizens better than that, but perhaps she had left them too much to their own devices.

"Is the transmitter active at the podium?" Lady Grey asked of Natalia.

"It is. Archibald had us set it up before he lost his nerve to come down here himself."

"Don't be too hard on the Speaker, Natalia. We all have our gifts." She offered the smallest hint of a smile before she approached the line of soldiers, focusing on a stern-looking pair with rotten fruit dripping down their breastplates. One of them started to speak and then froze.

"Thank you for protecting the factory. Times are hard for us all, and your service has not gone unnoticed. May I have passage to the podium?"

"Of course, Lady Grey."

The second soldier stiffened at the mention of her name, immediately shuffling to the side to let her pass.

Lady Grey glanced back at Natalia. "I can join you inside later, if you prefer. It would be nice to see the factory floor, if I may."

"I'll tell Tobias you're here." Natalia whispered a set of orders to another guard. The guard slipped away, his space in the blockade soon filled by another.

Lady Grey turned her attention to the podium and mounted the stairs without fanfare. She stood in that place and waited. There was a method to dealing with unruly crowds. Well, there were the tried-and-true methods, and then there was *her* method. And in the end, Lady Grey always found a sympathetic ear garnered far more allies than an iron fist.

It started as a whisper at first. Disbelief and excitement that warred with disgust as more and more rioters took notice of who she was. The transmitter could have drowned out every voice in that place, but instead she waited for the mumbled curses and shouts of support to evolve into something else. Something far more direct that eclipsed the quieting buzz of the crowd.

"How can you support another war?" The voice was high, angry, and drew many calls of agreement.

"My dear people," Lady Grey said, "this isn't another war. This is the same war that has come to our doorstep, brought buildings to the ground in Belldorn, crushed Dauschen, and leveled half of the mountain city of Ancora."

"You're talking about a war across the bloody sea!"

"Yes, but it is a war that will return to us tenfold if we do not end it. A war that will come for your children and leave your grandchildren to toil under the iron fist of Gregory Mordair. I see you, many of you from my faction. I know you've been to Fel. You've seen the bodies hung from those walls. Do you wish the same of Bollwerk?"

"Only if it's the warmongers like you!" another voice cried out.

Lady Grey smiled and looked away from that speaker. Their mind was made up. They were kindling to those she needed to reach, and to engage with them would only drive the wedge deeper between the factions.

"You can take risks now, or fight for your lives after Mordair consolidates power. He has already destroyed two cities. Do you think him incapable of striking another?"

"We're safe here. There's no need to put our families at risk. It's an unnecessary risk."

"I must strongly disagree with you, dear. Mordair assassinated the queen of Ballern. Do you believe yourselves better protected than her?"

Stunned silence evolved into disgusting shows of glee and others of disbelief. If Archibald had told these people the same, they never would have believed it was anything but political maneuvering. Archibald's citizens were far savvier than he gave them credit for. Most of them, anyway. Acknowledging that more often would have gone a long way to healing the rifts between factions.

"I hear your celebrations, but know that she was an ally to us against Mordair. Understand that he struck down someone who protected her citizens the same as Archibald does, the same as I do. It is no different than if Mordair had struck me down. Remember that. Remember that he will come for you and your families. If we do not fight, our factions will be at their end. As will we all.

"I do not expect you to celebrate this war. But do not stand in the way of this factory. The ship our tinkers are constructing here may be our only chance to keep Mordair's fleet from turning its full force against Bollwerk. We are all family behind these walls. Families fight and scratch and scream, but we stand together when it matters most." She paused and waited for the shouts of dissent to be swallowed by those most loyal to her.

"Know what I have said here I believe to be true with all my heart. I would not lie to my own faction, and I gain nothing by lying to the rest of you. Go in peace. Speak with your families and friends, but let the good people trying to protect you *protect* you."

She turned away from the podium then, leaving the transmitter to buzz and click with the ambient noise of the square. Few shouts of protest rose into the air, and Lady Grey didn't turn around to look at the gathered crowds. It showed both a trust in the guards at her back, and a trust that the crowds would not come for her directly. She might have been known for fending off assassins, but that was far different than being swallowed by a riot. Lady Grey was well aware turning her back was a calculated risk.

✧   ✧   ✧

LADY GREY FOLLOWED Natalia through a small door that led to the entrance hallway of the factory. Offices lined the hall, each showing a massive floor-to-ceiling blackboard with a cacophony of diagrams, equations, and symbols she failed to recognize. It was a place filled with the madness of tinkers, and that was before they'd even set foot on the factory floor.

"Ask your questions," Lady Grey said.

Natalia's back straightened, and she glanced at the lady. "What do you mean?"

"I mean, it looks like you're going to fall over and die from curiosity if you don't ask whatever is on your mind."

Natalia smiled and hesitated. "I don't want to offend you."

"You won't." She offered a brief smile.

"Okay, it's just …" Natalia wrung her hands together, and her steps slowed. "Do you think that was the best approach with the crowd? It seemed like a lot of people were still angry, and you didn't really address that."

"Dear, you can't tell someone not to be angry. All that will do is make them angrier. I've seen that time and time again. It is the surest way to drive factions apart, or split a faction down the middle." She gestured with an open palm. "It is why some of our leaders focus on anger and outrage. Keep the less fortunate despising each other and they will dance to any tune you play."

"I never thought about it like that. That's … horrible."

"Yes, one of many reasons I hate politics, dear. We'll see how the crowd evolves as the days go by. I hope they will calm. Enough about that. Show me your works, if you would."

Natalia smiled and led the way to the end of the hall. She pushed open a pair of tall double doors, revealing the cavernous factory floor beyond.

All Lady Grey could do was stare at the behemoth being constructed in that space. Words escaped her at the sheer length and breadth of the deck. She'd been in that factory before, when the massive warships that protected Bollwerk were being constructed. They'd filled the space, or so she'd thought.

The carrier was something far different. Perhaps not as tall as the warships, with their huge gas chambers, the carrier stretched nearly from wall to wall, and those walls were farther apart than a city block. A Titan Mech worked on the deck nearby, repositioning a thin metal sheet that served as a hangar. The sheet bowed and crashed like thunder as the pilot set it in place.

In the distance—far in the distance—Lady Grey could see another Titan Mech that appeared no bigger than a person from her perspective. Except the people milling about the surface of the carrier on the far side looked miniature.

"I guess she's a little impressive," Natalia said.

Lady Grey let out a quiet laugh. "I do not think that fully encompasses what you've accomplished here."

"Frederick was a great help planning the layout of the factory. We only have an eleven-inch clearance on each side. Let's hope the measurements for the roof were correct, or Archibald is going to have far more to repair than a few hostile factions."

The idea that something so massive had so little clearance for its launch left Lady Grey dumbfounded. The breeze might be controllable inside the factory, but once the bulk of that behemoth cleared the roof, how could they possibly keep the hull in line? She didn't doubt the skills of Bollwerk's tinkers, but the task looked impossible while standing at ground level, looking over the expanse of the carrier.

A ceiling-mounted crane hummed as it dragged a load of thin metal beams into the air, racing across the factory before almost disappearing in the distant shadows. It lowered the bundle to a waiting Titan Mech. She counted three of the Titan Mechs, which brought a question to her mind.

"Where are the other Mechs? I would have thought you'd be using far more for the construction."

"We don't have too terribly many of them," Natalia said. "Archibald sent a pair to assist with the reconstruction of Fel. The loss of their wall is problematic, to be sure. Theo has two more in Midstream. Or is it three now?" She tapped her chin before shaking her head. "The rest have been loaded onto supply ships bound for Belldorn."

"To reinforce the city? Or something else?"

"Both." Natalia gestured to the nearest of the Titan Mechs. "They mean to take several of them to Ballern. The battle for that city is going to be terrible, Liz."

Lady Grey grimaced as a shower of sparks lit from beneath the deck of the carrier. Tobias walked by above the workers, shouting directions as to what needed to be reinforced before they could test the gas chambers.

She focused on that conversation while, in the back of her mind, Natalia's words hung like a fog. The tinker was right, of course. All battles were terrible, but the combined might of the eastern cities had the potential to inflict bloodshed like nothing seen since the Deadlands War.

✧   ✧   ✧

HOURS LATER, LADY Grey found herself walking beneath the artfully rusted sign of The Fish Head. She recalled many a night when she'd worn a tattered old cloak to visit the restaurant. It was a simple thing to hide oneself from prying eyes when they were used to seeing you in far more regal attire.

No one was being subtle tonight, however. Two guards stood outside the door, not so much as glancing at Lady Grey as she pushed her way inside. The rich scent of long-cooking broth and bright herbs met her senses before she fully registered the perimeter of guards within.

It wasn't like Archibald to be so overly cautious. Apparently, the riots had shaken him far more than the Speaker had revealed to her. She knew he needed to keep a confident air around his citizens. Perhaps he was concerned her favor with the people would not withstand the temptation of opportunity for the worst of the city. Regardless, he stood beside a chair at his low table. Lantern light glinted through his wispy hair as he gestured for her to sit.

"Do you think you brought enough guards?" she asked.

Archibald smiled, but there was no humor in the expression. He pushed a beautifully carved ironwood bowl toward her, filled with heavily spiced roasted sunflower seeds.

She didn't hesitate to scoop up a handful of the delectable treats. She'd had seeds at a great many establishments, but whatever seasonings George imported from Midstream could not be surpassed.

Archibald gestured to the chef behind the bar.

Lady Grey recognized the man, but she didn't recall his name. It was hard to remember anyone who wasn't George in that place. His personality was larger than life, and she rather enjoyed his offbeat humor.

The chef arrived with two dark, slender glasses that smelled quite strongly of a soju infused with a floral tea. A sip told her that's exactly what it was.

"Are you preparing me for bad news?" Lady Grey asked as she leaned forward on the tall banquet table. "I must admit, this is a fantastic way to do that."

Archibald smiled again, but this time his eyes crinkled just a little bit. "No, Liz. The arrangement for the guards was twofold. One to keep us protected should the riots breach deeper into the city. And the other as a reward for keeping us safe. They will have a feast here when we are done."

"Let them feast now, Speaker," Liz said. "Unless there is some threat I am unaware of? I spoke to the masses earlier today, and I have no wounds to speak of."

Archibald gestured to a guard wearing a ten-pointed star formed from curved copper lines. "Release your men to the tables, Captain. Eat as we eat." It was a nice gesture, but Liz noted he didn't actually dismiss the guards. They'd still be at hand if needed.

The captain inclined his head, and in short order almost every table in The Fish Head was occupied, a low rumble of conversation making the place feel more like it ought to.

Liz took a deeper drink of her soju and leaned away from Archibald. "What are we *really* doing here?"

"An early celebration." He glanced at the door. "How did you come here, Liz? Did you traverse the crowds by the bonfire?"

"No, Natalia showed me to the back door, and I took the northern alleys to cut my walk somewhat shorter. Why do you ask?"

"Because you couldn't have cut through the crowds, Liz. Not as they were. Within three hours of your speech, nearly two-thirds of the gathered protesters were gone. The bonfires extinguished, and what little anger was left in those people fled in mumbled curses and quiet vendettas. The citizenry respects you in a way I can never meet."

"They'll likely be back, Archibald. Though I'm glad to hear they dispersed."

"Enough that we don't need as many guards posted at the factory. I will keep them at the ready, but the threat has receded."

Liz looked around at the guards in the restaurant with them. "These are all guards from the factory?"

"Except the two outside. They are assigned to me for the day." He tapped his fingertips on the table. "Liz, I have a favor to ask."

She took another sip of her drink. "I would expect nothing less." She winked at Archibald and then froze. It was a good sign she needed to slow down a bit on her soju. Archibald wasn't always one to take a humorous barb in stride.

"No, you're right to say so." Archibald took a deep swig of his own drink. "I need you to talk to the protesters again if they reassemble, and I'm sure they will. I need you to speak to them before things escalate."

"Tonight?"

He shook his head. "Tomorrow. And possibly each day after that. Until this carrier is deployed and perhaps until this battle is over. Most of those people have a deep respect for you, Liz. Some of the factions don't trust anything I say when it comes to the battles ahead. I hope to correct that in time, but time is something we do *not* have."

"Or the battles behind." Liz tapped her fingernail on the delicate glass. It was an interesting gamble. One that could help unite the factions under Archibald, or at least make them less openly hostile. That would be a benefit to all. It was no small thing that the Speaker would see it as a favor to be repaid in the future. "So be it, Archibald. I will do as you ask, but I have a condition of my own."

He raised an eyebrow.

"Order me some soup."

This time Archibald's smile was genuine as he laughed, and it was nice to see the relief on her old friend's face.

CHAPTER FOUR

Alice sat at an open-air bar on the Bones with Furi, Jakon, and Eva. They were a motley bunch, to be sure. Jakon closed one of the many bronze zippers open on his finest leather pilot's jacket, the collar folded over to reveal its plush wool lining. He cursed and checked another pocket before pulling out a small square of folded paper.

Eva smoothed the gray material of her own jacket, so dark it could have been mistaken for a Fel uniform, which was much the point.

Alice eyed Jakon as a boy sprinted by, snatching the paper from the chef in a move so quick Alice wasn't entirely sure she'd seen it. The fact Jakon wasn't bothered by this told Alice the boy was *exactly* who Jakon had expected to take his message.

Furi and Alice, on the other hand, looked like any other Skyborn at a glance. Alice tucked her hair under a black aviator cap Jakon had offered her. Hiding that brilliant red hair cut down on the stares and gawking almost immediately, and the insulated flaps kept her ears warm in the brisk breeze along the airship docks.

"Mordair's the best thing to happen to this city in ages!" The man gestured widely to restaurants and shops all around.

Alice tensed at the man's words. She hadn't spoken to her friends much while the other barstools were occupied, and having to listen to the nearby family praising Mordair and Fel made her breakfast sour.

"Dad, I don't think he is." The girl couldn't have been more than two years older than Alice. "There are soldiers everywhere, and two of my friends have gone missing."

The man harrumphed. "That's what you get. Carrying around those Stormborn flags like it's some kind of classroom game. When was the last time you ate so well? Food is cheap. The damn nobles are staying out of our business. What could be better? Nothing."

The girl leaned away from her father and grimaced. "They closed another hospital."

This time it was the girl's mother who answered. "Because more people are healthy and well fed. You should appreciate what you've been given."

Alice barely caught the girl's muttered response. "I could get better in prison."

And so it went from bar to bar, restaurant to restaurant. Stormborn and those loyal to the throne, side by side. But with each stop they made, Alice noted it was the supporters of the throne, of Mordair, who were most vocal. Some of the Stormborn spoke against them, but most looked the other way, as if those loyal to Mordair were already lost.

They sat and listened until that family moved on, and Furi's shoulders slumped a hair. "How can they be so ignorant?"

"That's worse than ignorant," Jakon said. "That's blatantly ignoring everything happening around you because you got *one* thing you wanted. They won't see the noose until they're hanging from it."

"The daughter sees it," Eva said. "I'm more concerned about what she said. Some of her friends are missing? Do you think it's Mordair?"

Jakon tilted his head to the side and shrugged.

"Maybe." Furi bolted upright. "Or it could be the Children of the Dark Fire."

Alice frowned at the idea. "I can't see that. All the work they've done to influence the leadership of Ballern?" She gestured to the crowds on the docks. "And they just decide to become abductors for Mordair? Maybe if they get something out of it, but what?"

"Keep it in the back of your mind," Eva said. "We'll find the pieces, eventually. I only hope it doesn't cost too many lives here. Listening to these people who are *happy* about the queen being dead. What is *wrong* with them?"

The barkeep's rag squeaked inside a clean glass as he dried it. "Things have been wrong here a long time. Furi knows. Jakon knows. You live here long enough, you see it. They might fool those willing to look the other way, but not all of us. When the happy ones are around, it's best to watch your back."

"Have you heard anything about it?" Jakon asked.

The barkeep paused and glanced away before stepping closer to Jakon and lowering his voice. "Not much more than you have, but you might want to see if they have any books on it."

Jakon nodded and slid an octagonal coin, silver streaked with tarnish, to the barkeep. It vanished in a swipe of the rag.

"Finish your drinks," Jakon said, eyeing Furi and Alice. "I have something I need from you two."

They followed Jakon to the farthest section of the Bones. As crowded as the docks were, few still ventured out onto the rickety bays where you could readily see your life flash before your eyes.

"What are we doing out here?" Eva muttered, looking over the side of the railing.

"I need Furi and Alice to go to the bookstore. Talk to William. That was no offhanded statement the barkeep gave us, Eva. He knows something we don't. Something he wasn't willing to say."

"There was hardly anyone around us," Furi said. "He could have just told us."

Jakon shook his head. "We're past that point now, Furi. Hardly anyone could be enough to get you killed. Talk to William. See what he knows about why so many Skyborn are suddenly what the barkeep called 'happy ones.'"

"It doesn't exactly sound like an issue when you put it like that," Eva said.

Alice laughed under her breath. "Not until you consider the context. Queen assassinated, nobles have gone missing, and apparently more of the Skyborn are missing as well. Skyborn who supported the Stormborn."

"Exactly," Jakon said. "Go. See what you can see and find me at Kura's."

✧   ✧   ✧

THE DEEPER INTO the docks Alice and Furi walked, the more appreciative she was of Jakon's somewhat ridiculous cap. She drew far fewer stares, and while one passerby commented on how pale she was and asked if she was ill, that was much preferable to drawing attention and muttered exclamations about the old blood.

"Do you think you have enough buckles on that cap?" Furi asked.

"Considering I'll probably have neck problems by this evening, yes."

Furi grinned and stepped into the lift beside Alice. It wasn't overly crowded, but there were enough people that Alice didn't want to say anything important while they rode to the street level. Instead, she fiddled with the straps of the cap's built-in goggles, getting them loose enough to relieve the impending headache she'd been feeling.

The gates opened with a squeak and Alice had to force her way out against a crowd of people pushing their way onto the lift.

"Must you really push?" Alice growled. "Back off. Let us out!"

There were two mumbled apologies, but it didn't stop the crush.

"Elbows up," Furi said.

Alice glanced back to find Furi with her elbows literally up, and people avoiding them as best they could. Alice mimicked the pose, and while she still got bumped a few times, enough people shifted to the side that they finally made it off the lift.

Alice shook her hands out and shivered. "What was that about?"

It was a guard who answered her. "Word is they're handing out dried meats by the warships."

"Who?"

"The Steward and some of the nobles, from what I understand. Quite a kind gesture, though it could have been organized better." The guard stiffened. "Don't mention I said that."

Alice offered him a weak smile and followed Furi away from the crowds at the lift. They didn't speak as they crossed the street and slipped into the nearest alley. Alice could tell by Furi's quick pace and clenched fists that she wasn't happy with what the guard had told them.

"Are you okay?"

Furi glanced back at another street, lined with towering buildings of pale stone and graceful arches. "No, Alice. I'm not. This city has been lied to for centuries, and now Mordair is doing the same damn thing. Offering a bit of meat for the soul of its people. I'm pretty far from okay."

They cut through a dark alley and turned right on the next street. The bookshop waited at the end of the block, its rounded entryway guarded by sleek pillars, a beacon of light in the shadow Mordair had cast on Ballern.

A muted bell sounded as they pushed their way inside. Alice couldn't remember if that was new, but the thought was lost as the scent of old paper and aged glue filled the space like a welcoming hug. Shelves spiraled up to the second floor, each with a ladder mounted on wheels, and that mass of books didn't take into account the floor-to-ceiling shelves that lined every wall.

William sat behind the counter, furiously scribbling something with a simple copper fountain pen, the nib stained with ink. He slowed when he heard their footsteps, glancing up at the pair as he slid round glasses over his nose.

"Are we alone?" Furi asked.

"As far as I know." He raised his voice. "Anyone still upstairs?"

When no one answered, Furi locked the front door. She jogged up the stairs and checked the aisles before nodding to herself and coming back down to join Alice and William.

He finished writing something before setting his pen down. "What is it?"

Furi ran her fingers through her hair and took a deep breath. "Someone mentioned you might know why folks are so happy on the docks?"

"Someone, eh?" William rolled his eyes. "Not much need to guess who that was. Haven't you noticed anything strange up there? I would have thought every last Skyborn would have grown suspicious by now."

"Why?" Furi crossed her arms. "What have I missed?"

"A guard told us Mordair is handing out dried meats on the docks," Alice said.

"Is that it?" Furi asked, focusing on William. "They're just bribing them with food?"

William laughed, but the sound had no humor. "Dried meats? No, that's the smallest part of it. Mordair's loyalists have been handing out stipends. And it's not just Mordair. The Children of the Dark Fire have been seen offering gold to the poor as well."

"Gold to the poor," Alice whispered, her voice trailing off as William's words echoed a passage she'd read. "William, I know you said the book was mostly nonsense and propaganda, but have you studied *The Great Machines and the Salvation of Karn*?"

"Of course. It was required reading for most of the classrooms in Ballern. I'm not sure if that was the case for the Skyborn, though." He raised an eyebrow and looked to Furi.

Furi shook her head. "It wasn't."

"Do you have a copy of it here?" Alice asked.

William sighed and walked back to one of the towering bookshelves. "More than I care to." He tapped a few spines with his fingers before pulling a volume down.

Alice took it from his grasp when he offered it. She flipped toward the back. "I'm certain it was in the last chapter, but I can't recall exactly where. Karn is a city not far from the Great Machine to the west, if the book is to be believed."

"*Was* a city." William looked down at the map embedded in the countertop.

"What do you mean *was*?" Furi asked. "Was it destroyed?"

"Yes. Mind you, it still exists at a much smaller scale, but it is no longer a hub for traders and travelers. That village has no love for the Children of the Dark Fire, or the Great Machines. But they are proud, and they will not abandon their home."

"How do you know that?"

Alice turned another page before glancing between the pair. She scoured the next page, reading so fast she almost missed what she'd been hunting for.

"I found it." Alice tapped the passage and started reading it aloud. "Gold was offered to the poorest families of Karn. This effort of good will saved countless children from the neglect of their families. Karn was a lost, godless abomination before the arrival of the benevolent followers of the Great Machines. Now they are loyal to the throne, as are all who bow before the Great Machines."

William's response was quieter, and he didn't meet Alice's eyes. "Karn tells that story a little differently." He glanced at Furi. "I didn't answer your question earlier. I know Karn has no tolerance for the Great Machines because I lived there for a time. When I was younger."

"In the woods?" Furi asked.

He smiled at that. "Yes, in the woods. Beside the ruins of a city that could have become a shining beacon like Ballern, but was instead bombed by the *benevolence* of the Children of the Dark Fire."

"Do you mean *literally* bombed?"

William nodded. "There are many elders who lived in Karn at the time who told that story. They didn't commit it to books for years because they feared another attack should they fall out of line with that cult again."

"But …" Alice started and then paused. "But do the Children of the Dark Fire even have the ships needed to bomb a city?"

"No, Alice. Not at the time." William hung his head. "Ballern dropped the bombs. I don't know how they were manipulated into that, but considering they joined the Deadlands War as if they were puppets of that cult, I'm not surprised.

"Where is Karn?" Alice asked.

William shifted a small pile of books across the map, his finger tracing a line through the Gray Woods before tapping a space that looked like nothing but trees.

"And the Great Machine?"

It was nearly double the distance from Ballern. A waypoint. A place that could be a strategic hold for an invading fleet. Alice's brow drew down, and she spread her fingers over the region.

"Could supply ships deliver goods to Karn? Unseen by Ballern or the Great Machine?"

William leaned back. "You want to land outsiders in Karn? That's … I can't imagine that going well, Alice. You would have to coordinate with the village. Arun, their leader, might be willing to speak, but outsiders are not welcomed in Karn. You could be killed for setting foot there. There's more than one reason Karn isn't mentioned in most of the newer textbooks."

"William, I know Lady Katherine," Alice said.

He stood up a little straighter. "You … what?"

"This is information that could change the war. You understand that, yes? Ballern tried to build docks outside Belldorn to create a waypoint. But Karn could already *be* a waypoint for Belldorn."

William clenched his teeth and ran his fingers through his hair. "You're an outsider, Alice. Even more so than Furi."

"*You're* not." Alice held his gaze. "Come with me. Introduce us. Let me talk to them."

"Rust it all," Furi said. "She's old blood. It's worth a try."

William closed his eyes and cursed under his breath. "They're superstitious about things like that. Furi, you could be right."

When he met Alice's gaze again, he looked focused, almost angry, but she didn't think that anger was directed at her. He sounded resolved. "Gather your bags. Meet me at the west gate in two hours' time. We can get to Karn before dark."

"I have a better idea," Furi said. "Meet us at The Ray in two hours."

William blinked.

CHAPTER FIVE

WHATEVER CONCERNS ALICE had about Jakon not being interested in flying to a rather remote town that was as likely to shoot them down as welcome them fled in an instant. The pirate didn't just *know* about Karn, he'd traded with them on multiple occasions. It shouldn't have surprised her as much as it did, considering how well traveled the other pirates she knew were.

Alice sank into the plush upholstery of The Ray's cabin. It was the oddest contrast of opulence and bare metal on the rest of the ship. But somehow, it fit the pirate chef perfectly.

William paged through one of the many books he'd brought with him to show Arun, studying a passage of Mokuskrit before frowning and flipping back to an earlier page.

Jakon guided them away from the docks, leaving the city to grow distant behind them as the Gray Woods overtook the horizon. For a time, Alice thought they were heading for another mountain range, but it didn't slope like the Ridge Mountains she was so used to, and the mountains weren't high enough that they'd passed the treeline.

"What kind of trees are those?" Alice asked. "How are they growing so high in the mountains?"

Furi leaned over by Alice and looked out the window. "Oh, those aren't mountains. That's just the Forest Giants, the old trees."

Alice blinked. "That's … no, surely not."

Jakon glanced back at Alice before focusing on Furi. "Did you never take her to the observatory on top of the docks?"

Furi almost cringed at the question. "We had other things going on, Jakon. You know, the war and stuff."

"And stuff," Jakon echoed with a laugh. "Well, you're about to get a much better view of the Forest Giants, anyway. But you really should see the observatory. Many of the Skyborn tinkers can be found in the area of the observatory."

"The Forest Giants look big enough to hold Canopy," Alice said. "Is Karn a treetop city?"

"Not in the slightest. Too many wild Tree Killers and Acidwings among the leaves. It's much safer on the ground. Relatively speaking."

"Speaking of Canopy, Forest Giants are close to twice the height of the woods around the Dragonwing Mountains," William said. "The tallest of them reaches nearly four hundred feet into the sky. That *is* far above average, though. Most are between one hundred and three hundred feet tall."

"Four hundred …" Alice stared at William, impressed at the recollection of those numbers, and awed that any tree could reach those heights. "How tall are the airship docks in Ballern?"

Jakon scratched the back of his head. "The tallest Forest Giants would reach about halfway to the lowest docks. Maybe a bit more."

"Wow." Alice ran her fingers over the back of her neck and looked out through the window. She was excited to see Karn, but part of that thrill had been displaced by the idea of the Forest Giants. She wished Jacob were there to see them, too.

✧   ✧   ✧

ALICE, FURI, AND William gathered around a small folding table anchored to the bulkhead. Jakon had an old map of the area held to the wall with magnets, and below that was a teetering pile of books held down with a leather strap.

"The early illustrations of the Queen's Crest are interesting," William said, turning *War! The Triumph of the Great Machines Against Heathen Aggressors* toward Furi and Alice. "You can see it wasn't always metal plates. It was separate flames grouped together. I believe it was an illustration of the Queen's Court."

"Or her alliances?" Alice said, comparing the illustration to one in the newer title *Lost Souls. The Binding of the Fire After the Death of a Lady*.

"Possible. I've never found anything old enough to really be sure."

"Why did they change it to metal-plated flames?" Furi asked. "Re-purposing the Queen's Crest as it was seems like it would have been just as effective."

"Not quite." Jakon turned away from the windscreen. "Why did you adopt a new symbol for the Stormborn, Furi? Would the emblem of the Steamsworn not have served your purpose well enough?"

Furi paused. "Do you think it's the same as that? As simple as a new symbol to rally behind?"

"I wouldn't call it simple." William's voice darkened. "It was a violent shift in leadership, even if it was spread over decades or more. The Children of the Dark Fire are masters at phasing things out they want people to forget. You burn enough books, and people will forget what they contained soon enough."

Furi sighed and leaned back in her chair. "No one should be frightened of books."

"Books hold different perspectives." Alice rubbed her forehead. "It would be easier for some leaders if those other perspectives no longer existed."

"Like Mordair," Jakon said. "The worst of both worlds. Burning books and hanging bodies."

They dug deeper into those titles, trying to pry the truth from the lies of the Children of the Dark Fire. It was an impossible task without more texts to compare them, too. Or without the stories of the people who witnessed it as so little had survived.

As much as Alice hoped Karn would allow the allied forces of Boll-werk and Belldorn to use the forest city as a base, she also hoped they might shed some light on the histories that had been lost to Ballern. As the Forest Giants grew larger in the windscreen, worry gnawed at the back of her mind.

✧   ✧   ✧

ALICE FINISHED STASHING the last of the books in a secure basket beneath her chair before William pulled the table legs up, tilted it, and slid the entire assembly into a slot in front of the bulkhead.

"Now you can really see the Forest Giants," Furi said. "Amazing, aren't they?"

Alice meant to nod in agreement, but all she could manage was a blank stare out the windscreen. The canopy had appeared solid and impenetrable from a distance, but here and there, vast openings carved a tunnel into the shadowed depths of the forest below.

It wasn't simply the height of the trees that inspired awe, but the enormity of every leaf. Some looked large enough to shelter an entire family beneath a single leaf or serve as a hangar for an airship. A small cluster of Sky Needles spiraled up from one such opening before zipping off to the south.

"You've been here before?" Alice wasn't looking at anyone in particular when she asked that question, but it was Furi who answered.

"Training drills with Fleet. We found ourselves out here on more than one occasion."

"Did they make you camp in the forest?" William asked. "I hated that when I served."

Furi laughed under her breath. "That training hasn't changed in a decade, from what I understand. Beck always hated camping. It didn't matter if we had a tent or were stuck scavenging our own shelters. He'd complain the entire time."

Alice turned her attention away from the windscreen, reaching out to squeeze Furi's hand.

"I miss him." Furi's voice was quiet, the words barely a whisper.

Alice looked back to the windscreen, not wanting Furi to feel like everyone was staring at her. The majesty of the forest, for there was no other word for it, drifted by The Ray. That isolated beauty, so far from the city of Ballern, couldn't stop the darker thoughts that sometimes crept into her mind.

Many in Belldorn had lost their lives. Many more in Ancora, Dauschen, and even Fel. But the fighting wasn't over. It was going to cost more of their family and friends. War was not done with them. And now they would ask more to join them.

The Ray slowed so suddenly that Alice's thoughts cleared, a spike of adrenaline replacing everything else.

"Hold on," Jakon said. "I almost missed it."

The ship tilted forward before leveling, and the brilliant green canopy rose outside the windscreen until they'd descended far enough that the bright sun was replaced by tinted shadows. Long stretches of white clouds vanished above, obscured by the soaring branches of the Forest Giants.

"It's beautiful." Alice reached out and placed her hand beneath the window. "I can see why they wouldn't want the Dragonwings here."

Jakon nodded as they drifted lower. "There are only a few entry points like this, made by cutting out a few strategic branches."

The area they were in was large enough for a Dragonwing to fly and hunt and rest, but tangles of vines and twisted branches created blockades nearby. For a rider to maneuver through those tight twists and turns would be an impossible task. Spiders, on the other hand, were made for that kind of terrain.

The Ray's bow turned to the east before Jakon nudged the throttle. They entered a tunnel formed between the branches that wouldn't allow passage for a much larger vessel. The leaves grew closer, the occasional branch squeaking along the armored gas chamber before it opened again, and Alice could see the ruins that waited there.

Memories of the desert remnants of the skeleton flashed through her mind. Old buildings that must have towered as high as the Forest Giants. Aged support beams reached for the canopy, rising from the collapsed rubble at their base. Brick peeked through some of the moss and fallen leaves, but much of it could have been mistaken for uneven forest terrain.

Jakon pulled the lever for the landing gear, and The Ray descended below the top of the ruins.

Alice leaned back from the window as they turned, and one of the trunks grew uncomfortably close. She expected to hear the squealing of a branch on the gas chamber or the heavy thud of impact at any moment, and the thought caused her to stiffen.

"I feel like you've done this a few times, Jakon," Furi said.

Jakon flashed her a quick smile. "Enough times. Maybe reassure Alice? She looks like she's about to grab her glider pack and jump."

Furi grinned at Alice. A second later, The Ray shook as the landing gear made contact. Jakon shut down the boiler, which brought another question to Alice's mind.

"Are we staying here?"

"For a while, yes. This isn't the kind of place you get in and out of fast, Alice. The people of Karn would take offense to that, and it's generally good not to offend people you want an alliance with." He locked two more levers down before standing and stretching. "Alright, get off my ship." He cast them a small smile. "Let's stretch our legs a bit."

Alice checked her wrist launcher before pulling her backpack on and following Furi down the hall. Their bootsteps echoed off the bare walls. Furi slid the locking bolts out of the hatch and kicked a ladder to the ground. She led the way, looking up as she cleared the ladder.

The ladder was short enough that Alice hopped past it, flexing her knees with the impact before following Furi's gaze. As large as the Forest Giants had looked from the sky, it was nothing at all compared to standing next to them. It wasn't just their height, but the massive width of the trunks themselves. The largest of them could easily hide The Ray from view. That was even before considering the expanse of branches above them.

"Sometimes I miss camping," Furi said. "You should hear these woods at night."

"Night?" Alice looked around the clearing. "It's loud enough in the day."

And it was. The scrabbling sounds and chirping. The nearby rustling of leaves that could have been the wind, or could have been a Tree Killer. It was a beautiful place, yes, but unnerving as well. History lurked there, but danger likely wasn't far behind.

Boots clicked on the ladder behind her before William and Jakon joined them.

"There's a rare mushroom that grows around here," William said. "It's a cream color and looks like a ball of hair. Quite valuable, if you can find it."

"You'll be dead before you get back to the ship if you steal their mushrooms." Jakon wasn't making a threat. His voice was calm and even, as if he simply knew those words for a fact. Considering his less-than-legal smuggling operations, Alice figured he likely knew what he was talking about.

Jakon pulled out a small copper telescope and held it to his eye, scanning the treeline. He made a quarter turn before stopping and raising his hand.

"Did you find them?" William asked.

Jakon nodded.

William turned toward the area Jakon had been facing and projected his voice. "I'm looking for Arun."

The voice that answered pierced the air, but it did not sound like a shout, as though the woman could project effortlessly. "Many seek Arun, secret keeper."

William frowned and squinted before stepping toward the voice. "I am William of Karn, keeper of truth, not secrets."

A quiet laugh echoed up from the woods. "A grand name for a librarian, William of Karn."

"Mali?"

The bark of the nearest Forest Giant shifted, fluttering back to reveal a section to have been nothing but a cloak hiding the speaker. "Yes, William, though I was surprised to see you with the pirate."

Jakon placed his hand over his heart. "You wound me, dear Mali."

William glanced back at him with an arched eyebrow. "You know Mali? Of course you know Mali. All the pirates know each other."

Mali pulled her hood back, revealing a welcoming smile that took Alice off guard. She looked kind, but no one so skilled with stealth was a stranger to fighting. It made her wonder how much of the culture had been represented correctly in *The Great Machines and the Salvation of Karn.*

What struck Alice more than anything else was how much Mali looked like the people she knew from Ballern. Her complexion might have been a little paler, but the stories of Karn and how the city was destroyed made it sound like everyone there was wildly different from

Ballern—almost alien, grotesque. While Alice had assumed that was more propaganda from the Children of the Dark Fire, she'd fallen short of understanding how grossly exaggerated the story was.

"Arun, will you come talk to your friend now?" Mali called, almost sounding annoyed that Arun hadn't made himself known.

A crumbled leaf stirred across the clearing, revealing a man floating in midair. Or so he appeared until his mount stepped forward, six spindly legs propelling his rider with an even gait. Each section of the beast was as rough and chiseled as the bark that had hidden it. Long antennae searched the space ahead until it found Mali.

"A Giant Stick!" Alice said. "I've only seen them at Festival! Oh, Jacob will be so jealous. Are they as friendly as the stories say?"

Mali tilted her head to the side, revealing a long, raised scar that ran from her hairline down to her chin. "So long as you don't have sap all over your hands." She swatted the antennae away, only to get leveled by it on the backswing. Mali scowled at the Giant Stick from her new position on the ground. She brushed herself off and stood up, gesturing to the rider before giving a deep bow.

"Almighty Lord Arun, at your service."

Alice could almost *feel* Arun's eye roll.

"Thank you, daughter. You have been most … *helpful*." Arun's smooth features gave him the presence of someone much younger than what Alice would consider an elder. Only a few gray hairs and the wrinkles along his neck gave any hint of his true age.

Arun turned his focus to William and Jakon. "Why do I suspect whatever brought the two of you together is not going to be welcome news?"

William offered a sheepish grin and Jakon scratched the back of his head.

Arun didn't wait for a response, instead turning to Alice and Furi.

"Young ones, you are welcome in Karn. But please, do not steal our mushrooms."

Alice didn't miss the wink he gave William.

William stuttered over his words before finally saying, "I wanted it for a gift, Arun!"

"Of course, of course." Arun made a circle in the air with his hand before releasing a high-pitched whistle.

The trees came alive, and Alice stared as over a dozen Giant Sticks shifted from their hidden positions. Riders removed their hoods, and as fast as they'd revealed themselves, they vanished into the denser parts of the forest. The best view of them came as they crossed the broken ruins of the old city, the Giant Sticks no longer blending in, instead revealing themselves in full.

But two riders were mounted on something else. Something deadly, and Alice shivered as she watched the pair of Tree Killers follow the Giant Sticks into the forest. Scythe-like limbs gripped bark and dirt alike, propelling them forward effortlessly. But Alice remembered what those scythes could do. She remembered the blood in the sand when a Tree Killer had taken Jacob's leg.

"Alice?" Furi whispered.

She shook herself out of the memory. "I'm fine, really."

Arun gestured to the group from The Ray. "Come, friends. But do heed the warning about theft from these woods. Mali and I may jest, but there are many whose lives depend on the bounty of the woods. They will not hesitate to strike down thieves. Now, that distastefulness aside, let me welcome you to our city, and you can deliver whatever terrible news you have brought."

Jakon hooked his thumbs in his pockets and smiled. "I missed your optimism, Arun. It's been too long."

"A pirate and a merchant traveling together of their own accord. Do you mean to say you do not have terrible news to deliver?"

"Well, no. I wouldn't say that. But it could be *quite* the opportunity."

Arun grunted and led the way into the woods with no further response.

ALICE FOUND THE forest floor to be quite spacious, as most vines didn't reach the ground. She could see a reasonable distance in most directions on the path, but she still wondered how many of the guards who had revealed themselves were following above.

It had been nearly fifteen minutes before Alice couldn't see the towering ruins anymore. There either weren't any in their location, or the forest had claimed them for its own.

Furi grabbed Alice's arm and pointed up. "Acidwings."

Far above, in the shadow of the canopy, iridescent shadows shifted back and forth, occasional shifts of wings dislodging a shower of dust that caught the trickling sunbeams.

"They won't hurt you," Mali said. "Well, usually. They hunt the Bombardiers at night, and *that* is a hunt you don't want to be caught up in."

Arun turned where the path diverged ahead, and Alice's growing comfort with the surroundings of the forest vanished. Gone were the half-buried buildings of an old city. Before them stood the restored structures of once-forgotten ruins.

"It looks like it could be part of Belldorn," Alice whispered.

Furi followed her gaze, looking at the soaring towers of glass and brick all around them. "Look down the street. The forest closes in on the other side, too."

"It closes in from all sides," Mali said. "It keeps us safe from most things that would want to attack us from the ground. Although the Tree

Killers do like to nest on the roofs sometimes. That … can be problematic."

"Still needs an airship dock," Jakon muttered.

"We have considered it," Arun said. "But to ease access to Karn would invite too many unwanted visitors, I am afraid. The Children of the Dark Fire dwell too close, and they do not forfeit opportunity."

Mali stepped up beside her father's mount, opening her arms as she faced the group. "Welcome to Karn."

One thing that struck Alice about the city was the quiet. There was still the sound of carts on the cobblestones and the click of chitinous feet on pavement, but it all felt muted. She wondered if it was the thick vegetation that not only surrounded the city, but had also been trimmed and manicured all down the streets she could see.

A city it might have been, but it was full of the greens and vibrant palettes of a hundred different plants. The closer they walked to the buildings, the more Alice realized the towers weren't quite as high as Belldorn. She suspected each would peek above the walls of Bollwerk if they were inside that city, but they did not touch the clouds like the tallest spires in Belldorn.

"I like how wide your streets are," Furi said, looking at Mali. "Ballern is cramped. Everything is built close together because we have the sea on one side and the mountains to the north. Have you been there before?"

Mali nodded. "I have, yes. It was a nice place to visit. The docks were the most fascinating place. I found the people to be far more kind in the sky."

"We don't have many nobles on the docks, so that makes sense."

Mali grinned at Furi. "I've heard many stories of your nobles. I don't always agree with the elders in Karn, but at least they are far more focused on the well-being of our people than the well-being of our leaders' coffers."

"Sounds like Midstream," Alice said. "Now *that's* a nice place to visit, if you ever get the chance."

"I'd like to see the desert one day. And it was such a pivotal place in the Deadlands War."

Mali's comment spurred another question from Alice. "Have you studied the Deadlands War?"

"We all study it here," Mali said. "Many of the elders, or their parents, fought in the war. But it wasn't only the Deadlands War. There was backlash here. You saw the ancient ruins. There are other ruins, far newer, that we let the forest bury."

Alice didn't think Mali was simply referring to the ruins of buildings. A small cadre of Pillies wandered by, herded by two boys who couldn't have been more than nine. It reminded Alice of home, of a home that wasn't there anymore. She took a deep breath and watched the group waddle by.

Arun slowed at the next intersection. A large stone fountain sprayed water into a deep pool, each spout sculpted with delicate Acidwings and oddly welcoming Tree Killers reaching to the sky.

He looked back at Jakon. "Now, old friend, tell me why you have come to our city."

Jakon didn't hesitate, as though he'd been waiting for Arun's prompt. He stayed calm, but his words were slightly rushed. "You were allied to the queen of Ballern. A bastion against the Children of the Dark Fire. The Lady of Belldorn needs a staging ground to fight the Children of the Dark Fire and the usurpers to the throne in Ballern. We all need an alliance with Karn, Arun."

Arun squeezed the reins of the Giant Stick before sliding off the saddle. He patted the bug on the side of its neck, and the beast dipped its head into the fountain.

"I appreciate you being so forward. I should have asked you in the forest, but there are many ears I do not know in the woods. Tell me of the queen's death, and perhaps we can help in some way. But do not ask to bring war to Karn, Jakon. We have had enough of betrayal and fighting in this place."

Jakon held a finger up when Furi stepped forward, as if asking her to wait.

Arun led the way to one of the smaller buildings, a simple two-story structure with wide wooden beams that could have been at home in Cave. Inside waited a round table and a massive fireplace.

The second floor stood open, tiered seating looking down on the table below. It was then that Alice realized this small building was a place of power in Karn. Perhaps not an opulent castle like they had in Ancora, or a grand hall like Bollwerk, but it was functional, humble even, and perhaps, strangest of all, Alice didn't feel intimidated in that space.

"Sit, please." Arun motioned to the heavy wooden chairs.

Alice took a seat by Furi while Mali sat between Alice and William. Alice wasn't entirely sure what the expression was that flashed across Arun's face, but the crinkling of his brow was gone as fast as it had come.

Jakon was the last to sit, taking the chair beside Arun. "I must warn you, I have a task for Kura that I cannot delay."

"Can you tell me the nature of this task?" Arun asked.

"Yes. Scouting the woods for the Children of the Dark Fire. We're worried they may come to reinforce Ballern. If they do, the damage done by a battle at Ballern could be far worse than anticipated."

"So you mean to strike Ballern in earnest? Bring a war to its citizens?"

Jakon rubbed the top of his hand. "I don't, Arun. But Belldorn is coming. Many Skyborn have pledged themselves to the Stormborn. You know of this?"

Arun inclined his head.

"War is coming to Ballern, no matter our actions." Jakon glanced away.

"Your honesty is appreciated, Jakon. What reason have we to give way to Belldorn's fleet?"

But it wasn't Jakon who answered. It was Mali's fist on the table. Mali's growl that became her words.

"What reason *don't* we have? Our queen is dead, Father. Murdered. You've heard the scouts who monitor the Great Machine. The Children of the Dark Fire are active. Something is coming, and it will cost us more of our own. Just like before. Just like the Deadlands War. You say we are loyal to the throne, and yet we do nothing."

"Mali—"

"I'll fight for Karn, *Father*. Whether the elders join us or not, we should give way to Lady Katherine. Have we learned nothing from our past mistakes?" She gestured violently around the table. "You heard the story some of the elders tell. We had a chance to join with the eastern cities before, and we didn't. We hid, as we hide today. We waited, and Ballern *slaughtered* us in our sleep. That cult stole our people. My grandmother! This is the time—"

Arun's shoulders stiffened, and his patience snapped. "Enough, Mali! I know the mistakes of our past better than most. You do not make such declarations in the company of outsiders. Our eyes have not seen what they say. We are not warmongers. We do not seek to die for glory. We are *not* them. We did not see our queen die on the blade of an assassin!"

"I did," Alice whispered.

Arun froze as the room crashed to silence.

"Tell us," Mali said, her voice cracking.

Alice didn't miss the glint of tears at the corners of Mali's eyes. Tears of rage, or sadness, or something in between. And Alice told the tale one more time. The story of infiltrating the palace. Of hearing the alarm. Of seeing the footprints made of blood in the halls. Of learning of the murder, of her hidden alliance with the dissenters, and of the lost chance to fix so much in Ballern.

William cursed and rubbed his eyes. "I hadn't heard the whole story, Alice. I didn't realize …"

But it was Furi who was in tears at the end. A harsh sob escaped her lips as she clenched her fists. "We were so close. Everything could have been different. And now Fel has warships in Ballern."

Arun sighed and studied his hands. "We were not sure the rumors of the assassination were true." He glanced at Jakon. "Give me a day. I must speak with the elders. This is not a decision that can be made by one hand. It must be made by all."

"Of course. Can you give Alice and Furi shelter for the night?"

"You're leaving us here?" Furi asked.

"I assumed you would want to stay."

"I do! I just … I thought we'd have to go back with you. How else will we get home?"

Jakon shook his head. "I'll be back. If not, Eva can pick you up with that old pile of rust."

Arun reached out and placed his hand on Jakon's shoulder. "I preferred the days when you smuggled goods and not information."

Jakon grinned. "I always smuggled information. I just didn't always tell you about it."

"Pirates," Arun muttered.

CHAPTER SIX

THEY WERE ONLY hours away from the first heavy load test of the carrier, but Jacob was tucked in at Targrove's old workbench. He almost had the leg inserts worked out for the exoskeletons, but they needed more adjustments. It technically functioned, but if someone spent more than five minutes walking around, he worried it was going to take their skin off at the contact points.

Jacob grumbled as he unwrapped the leather cushion from the brace that latched over the wearer's knee. He'd thought that would be the solution, but the leather itself was still too hard. Jacob only had one more idea to try, and as he glanced at the hands of the exposed clock on the wall, he wasn't sure he could get it done.

He finished removing the leather wrap and gathered it into a ball before moving to the back wall, grabbing a long length of rubber that was normally shaved down into thin gaskets and fittings for the hydraulic systems. Jacob took everything to Theo's workbench. Theo was a master tinker, but that wasn't all she'd accomplished in her life.

Jacob spread the leather out and laid the rubber inside it. Once it was coiled around like the handle of a Highlands briefcase, he still had a good half inch of material left. He hoped it would be enough for the stitches. Jacob clipped the rest of the rubber off. Frederick had learned many of Theo's techniques, and Jacob was happy the older tinker had shown him where to find the pricking irons.

He lined up the first iron, keeping it close enough to the rubber insert he hoped the edges wouldn't tear out. Once in position, three taps of the hammer set the hole. A few more punches done, he grabbed a needle and heavy thread to lace the edges together with a saddle stitch. It left a lip sticking out that could wear a blister into someone's leg, so he'd have to mount it carefully.

Jacob blew out a breath and headed to the exoskeleton insert. Two long screws dug into the leather and rubber, holding it firmly in the curve of the leg bracket. Everything fit, and it didn't spin with a few good twists from his pliers.

He nodded and made his way back to Theo's workbench. One insert might have been enough to test the build, but it wasn't enough to put the suit on. He was going to make a second one, regardless.

The door clicked open behind him just as he finished installing the second pad, and Jacob turned to find Smith walking into the workshop.

"It is about time to get to the carrier. How goes the work?"

Jacob held up the second insert so Smith could see the new pad. "The leather by itself was too hard, so I added some of the rubber for the gaskets."

Smith whistled. "That's an expensive addition. That rubber is hard to come by."

"I know. I stole some from the Butcher once." Jacob threw Smith a sideways grin. "I'm sure Lady Katherine will buy us some more."

Smith laughed and sat down on the stool beside Jacob. He took the leg insert and prodded at the mount. "Doesn't look like it's going to move. But it could turn over hours of use. You might want to try a corset stitch instead of a saddle stitch."

"I don't know how to do that."

"I will show you later, when we are done testing the carrier. We better go." Smith's voice trailed off as he said the last. His brow furrowed just a hair, a look of curiosity Jacob knew. "Well, I suppose we could do *one* quick test with the inserts here."

Jacob grinned and snatched the assembly out of Smith's hands. "We don't need to warm up the boilers or anything on it. The gear ratios take a lot of the weight off. That's not to say I'd want to try walking around very long in it while it wasn't powered, being so heavy, but it's a good test for the padding."

"I'd say so."

Jacob grunted and forced the insert into the braces that formed the leg of the exoskeleton. It clicked home into its brackets, and he stepped up into the foothold. Smith had come up with the idea for the anchors in the feet so a single pilot could lock themselves into the Mech without falling over, but it was still faster with help from a partner.

The metal felt cool along his forearms as he slid into the arms. The head of the Mech was just an exposed bracket, but Charles's design for the Titan Mech had given him the idea for what he intended to do. A dome of glass, the same durable material they used on the larger Mechs. It would increase the protection of the armor without nearly blinding the pilot.

"Locking up," Smith said as he swung the rear cage closed.

Jacob pushed himself against the back of the exoskeleton so he could pull his left arm out and throw the latch below the shoulder joint. He laced his fingers into the gauntlet controls, a pair of rings that loosely fit over each finger and thumb.

It felt good to close his fist. The hydraulic lines offered a satisfying resistance, and anyone who found themselves on a battlefield should be strong enough to control it.

Smith stepped away and slapped Jacob's back. "Clear."

Jacob took a deep breath and focused on the ground ahead of him. It wasn't as easy as walking. Even when it was powered, it wouldn't be that easy. But now it felt like hiking through deep snow, raising one leg against the tension in the drifts, or in this case, the gears.

He felt the exoskeleton tip forward. It was familiar to him now, and while it might have caused a brief panic the first time it happened, now he was expecting it. His leg straightened, pushing on the padded insert as the foot caught the ground and he repeated the motion with the other leg.

Jacob walked a few more steps, passing between the workbenches where Targrove and Theo's students had worked over the decades, stopping only when he reached the door.

"A little help," Jacob said. "Walking without power is one thing, but I can't turn it easily without power."

Smith let out a quiet laugh and grabbed the waist of the exoskeleton. "On three. One. Two. Three." He grunted as he twisted, and Jacob did the same until the exoskeleton was pointed back in the opposite direction. "It is a good design, but I believe we may want to revisit the joints in the hip. Turning should not be so difficult, Jacob."

Jacob muttered in agreement as he walked back across the room, each step echoing in the workshop with a metallic thud like a dropped hammer. It wasn't the stealthiest of devices, but it would do the job.

He made it back to the starting point and didn't bother turning it around this time. Smith was right. The joints needed to be replaced. It was a relatively minor change, and one he should have addressed after he'd read Charles's notes, but there were a dozen other changes he'd prioritized.

Jacob pressed himself into the exoskeleton and slid his left arm free, lifting the latch to open the back before opening the brace at the rear bands of the insert. He hopped to the ground and nodded to himself, rubbing his legs just above the knee.

"How were the pads?" Smith asked.

"Good. Really good. It doesn't look like they turned, but I definitely want to try the corset stitching you mentioned."

Smith clapped him on the shoulder. "And that we will. I can help you with the joints, too. I believe we can use something quite similar to the portable furnaces Fel uses on their fishing vessels."

Jacob frowned at that. He'd been on one of those small boats, and he couldn't think of anything that would work as the joint on the exoskeleton.

"Trust me," Smith said. "Now gather your things. We need to head to the carrier."

✧　✧　✧

Two brigs flew by overhead as Jacob and Smith made their way back to the construction site for the carrier. It hadn't registered what those ships were doing until they turned the corner, and watched as the second brig settled onto the middle of the carrier.

He glanced at Smith. "I thought we were only testing with a few Titan Mechs onboard first."

"Frederick spoke with Natalia in Bollwerk." Smith rubbed his shoulder where his biomechanics met flesh. "Apparently, she already built hangars onto their carrier and is claiming victory for finishing their carrier first."

"Did they even make a bet?"

Smith let out a low laugh. "Yes, they did. Winner gets new tensioners in their workshop first."

Jacob whistled. "That's a pretty good prize."

"Only between tinkers, Jacob. Only between tinkers."

They crossed the edge of the city proper and entered into the mostly cleared ruins over the outskirts. Not much remained that hadn't been repurposed or flattened to make way for the carrier build. But the earth was still stained with ash and cracked mud where Belldorn had once thrived.

Jacob's darker thoughts fled as they reached the edge of the carrier. Two Titan Mechs walked across the deck, positioning themselves in the far corners before crouching to be anchored beside the hangars.

Smith gestured to the nearest stairs and Jacob led the way up. His bootsteps echoed on the metal plates of the carrier, but the sound was lost to the roar of boilers and the venting of great clouds of steam. Wind ripped over the deck, pulling at the fabric hangars that gave shelter to various workshops and maintenance bays.

Cabling ran the perimeter of the carrier now, the installation finished since Jacob had seen it that morning. It doubled as a safety line and an anchor for workstations outside the hangars. Smith had insisted on it for explosives work after he heard some of the tinkers wanting to assemble bombs in the hangars. Jacob still sometimes couldn't believe how much tinkers needed a little common sense.

The workers at the far side of the carrier looked small at such great distances. The brigs were settled now, and Jacob could just make out a light line tying down the nearest of them.

"Will that line hold?" He gestured to the brig.

Smith looked at the ship and shook his head. "Not if things get rough. But this is a load test, Jacob. If something goes wrong, those brigs need to be able to release quickly, whether they're tied down or not."

A shadow crossed over them, and Jacob's steps slowed when he glanced up. Shouts and directions rose all along the carrier as the workers scattered. Drifting into their airspace was a monstrosity, a behemoth of a ship armed with so many cannons it had earned a unique name in the Fleet. Porcupine.

The transmitters in Jacob and Smith's collars crackled to life before Frederick spoke. "Join me in control tower A. We can go down together if this goes wrong."

Smith clicked his transmitter. "On our way." He turned to Jacob. "I believe that was Frederick's attempt at a joke."

Jacob grinned.

They hurried to the nearby tower. It stood on a wide base that tapered closer to the cube of the pilothouse. They'd originally planned to put one tower in the center, but that idea had obviously changed since Jacob saw the original plans.

"Did they finally decide to change to two control towers for redundancy?" Jacob asked.

"They did," Smith said and gestured to the opposite side of the carrier where the framework for the second tower had recently been enclosed. "It is more than that, though. The ship can break in two should the need arise."

Jacob nodded. "I understand. You need a pilot house on both sides because of that."

"And redundancy," Smith said with a smile. "You were correct about that as well." The larger tinker pulled the door open to the control tower, and they stepped inside. Smith led the way up the stairs. By the time they reached the fourth landing, both of their steps had slowed.

"You know what would have been nice?" Jacob muttered.

"A lift." Smith continued up without complaint, but it was a hard thing for Jacob not to embrace Samuel's penchant for complaining. Stairs were far less irritating without a Biomech leg. Not that it was a large problem, but the angle always hit the cap in his knee at a somewhat odd angle.

Six more landings, and they reached the door to the pilot house. It stood open, revealing Frederick and Lady Katherine waiting inside. Smith stepped inside first.

Jacob almost jumped when he entered the room, turning to find Mary standing guard just beyond the door.

"You awake?" Mary asked with a smirk.

Jacob let out a long sigh. "Getting there."

Frederick nodded to the group before turning his attention back to the scene unfolding before them. "Nose south fifteen degrees and you are clear for landing."

The Porcupine shifted, the edges of the forward cannons' barrels growing perpendicular to the starboard deck. The angle of descent left all the flank cannons pointed directly at them, which was quite an unsettling sight as the ship drifted closer to the deck, finally dropping landing lines.

Several crew members of the carrier raced out of the hangers and grabbed the lines, running them to the mooring masts set strategically around the hangars and landing zones. The carrier barely creaked as the Porcupine settled into place, the crash of landing gear on metal ringing out around them. Only the slightest tremor could be felt in the tower.

"We'll need to give it a few minutes for the ship to settle." Frederick clicked the transmitter on the control panel. "Power down turbines. I want the full weight of that beast on the carrier's deck."

A crackle preceded the captain of the Porcupine's response. "Do you need the gas vented fully? It will take a great deal of time to restore the system if we do."

"Negative. The weight of the cannons will be enough with the turbines shut off."

"Understood. Pending shutdown in sixty seconds. All crew clear the hold."

Jacob glanced over at Smith and whispered, "Why clear the hold?"

It was Lady Katherine who answered. "In case it collapses. It's happened before."

"Umm, what?" Jacob's eyebrows rose ever higher.

"One time," Frederick grumbled. "One time, My Lady. And we only lost two shipping crates."

"Oh, it's *My Lady* now, is it?" Lady Katherine asked. "When just fifteen minutes ago, I was a daft Pilly for joining you in the control tower."

Mary failed to hide her laugh behind a cough.

Frederick stiffened and glared at the captain of the Skysworn. "That was a private conversation, Mary."

Mary nodded. "It was much funnier to share."

"It's fine, Frederick," Lady Katherine said. "I'd have quite a boring job if the worst someone ever called me was a daft Pilly behind my back."

Frederick rubbed his forehead and muttered an apology before hitting the transmitter again. "Control tower B, begin launch. Deflate the ballonets."

"Would those really be enough to stop a launch?" Lady Katherine asked.

"Likely not, but it would certainly slow us down. The turbines provide a great deal of lift to get us into the air. Smith's design could overpower the ballonets, I am sure."

Smith stepped closer to the windscreen and frowned, studying the edges of the carrier as the gas chambers swelled and flexed. "I am not sure of that, Frederick. The sheer mass of this carrier … the weight of it is extraordinary. The gas chambers themselves weigh more than most airships."

Whatever insulation Frederick's crew had added above the boilers looked to be working. No plates glowed red hot as a familiar whine reached Jacob's ears. Like the thrusters on the Skysworn when they were first engaged, but deeper, louder, and far more terrifying. One turbine being thrown out of balance could tear a hole in the ship they'd never repair in time. The control tower tilted as the northern edge of the carrier started to rise before the southern.

Mary grabbed Smith's shoulder. "I love that sound."

Before anyone could say anything more, the control tower rocked back, shuddering beneath their feet as the turbines pulled enough air to assist the gas chambers to level the deck. Most of the sane crew members stayed near the hangars, clipped into safety lines and harnesses normally reserved for operations on the outside of an active airship.

Of course, that's exactly where they were now.

The carrier, in all its bulk, slowly rose from the dock, hardly showing so much as a curve in the deck from the weight of a Porcupine. A warship that was one of the heaviest ever to take to the skies. Until now. Until this beast, which could *transport* a Porcupine, took flight.

Jacob's excitement was slightly tamped down by the memory that Ballern had built a carrier first, but still. This was the first carrier to take flight in the east. And he was there to see it. To feel it. And the over-whelming emotion of that realization came together in one glorious shout.

Smith and Frederick joined him, clapping each other on the back. Smith grabbed Mary, lifting her into the air before setting her back down by Lady Katherine.

"And to think you doubted us," Smith said, beaming at the Lady of Belldorn.

She blew out a long breath. "I certainly hoped you'd make it work."

Frederick laughed. "To be fair, I doubted us, too."

"Thank you, Frederick," Lady Katherine said. "I do appreciate that honesty, but the work speaks for itself."

And it did. It truly did as they drifted higher than the tallest towers of Belldorn.

Frederick broadcast another command over the transmitter. "Thrusters full to starboard. Take us out to sea and back. Boilers at full. I want a full stress test of every propulsion system on this carrier. Now."

Calls of acknowledgment came back to Frederick, and the momentum of the carrier shifted. Instead of merely rising, they drifted to the west as they rose, crossing the beach and leaving the Titan Mech standing below in shadow.

"I want altitude readings at all four corners and another beneath the Porcupine. If the deck is sagging, we need to know."

Workers moved across the deck below, clipping into the outer safety lines as they dragged various equipment from station to station. It felt like he'd only been watching them for a moment, but when Jacob looked out over the starboard side of the ship, they were fully over the Crystal Sea.

"I want fifteen minutes in the air," Frederick said. "That should give us enough information to calculate fuel requirements."

"So long as we overestimate." Smith tapped his finger on the console as he nodded to himself. "You never know what else might go wrong."

"That's the truth," Mary muttered. "Well, Kat, what do you think?"

Lady Katherine watched the activity below for a time before answering Mary. "With Archibald's support, I think we have a chance. And I believe Frederick might have won his bet with Natalia."

Frederick grinned at the Lady of Belldorn as the cycle of tests began anew.

CHAPTER SEVEN

GEORGE SAT IN the corner of the watchtower. It was an ideal position, providing a view both to the north and west, the most likely sources of a strike from the warlords, or Fel loyalists, on Midstream. He'd accepted Rikken's offer to share the guard duty. It both gave him an opportunity to rest his eyes and to spend time talking to Drakkar's son.

"Have you given any thought to joining the Nameless as Drakkar did?" George asked.

Rikken turned away from the window, revealing a small patch of peeled paint that had grown quite a bit larger. "I thought about it, but it's hard on the family. When Dad was in it, I hated not being able to talk about him. You have to sever all ties. It's like you don't exist anymore. You're just a weapon for the city. It's just hard."

George inclined his head. "I have heard much the same from many in Cave. Though I admit, I was surprised to hear Drakkar had reclaimed his name."

"It's pretty rare, but it happens. Most who join the Nameless stay for a full shift of five years. In the old days, you could be exiled for leaving the Nameless. It's not so strict now. Some train the recruits after five years, but they aren't Nameless anymore. But those who stay, it's five years their family has to pretend they don't exist. No family can do that without pain, George."

"No, I don't believe they can."

Rikken's stomach rumbled, and George could hear it from his spot on the opposite side of the watchtower.

"Gladys should join us soon. And if she remembers my request for food, we will break for a time."

Rikken rubbed the back of his neck and laughed. "I guess you heard my stomach."

"In your stomach's defense, I have excellent hearing."

Rikken smiled and turned to the window. George did the same, watching the dunes for any sign of movement and the horizon for any shadows making their way toward Midstream.

✧   ✧   ✧

ANOTHER FIFTEEN MINUTES passed before George heard the knock on the hatch in the floor.

"Enter."

The wooden hatch rose in increments before flipping over on the hinges and quietly smacking into a pillow.

Gladys scowled at George. "Just 'enter' is all you say? You'd lock me in the dungeon if I were that careless about letting someone into the watchtower."

"Last I checked, you did not even bother to lock the door to our home, Princess."

Gladys huffed and finished climbing the ladder, hoisting up a covered silver bucket with steam rising from the edges. "At least I remembered your food."

George grinned at her as she set the bucket down on the table in the center of the room. "Come, Rikken. Join us for lunch. The other watchtowers can keep an eye on the city."

"It smells amazing." Rikken leaned forward before crossing his legs and taking a seat on a floor cushion. "What is it?"

"From the hint of figs and honey, I believe it is Sweetwing buns."

George smiled as he took a deep breath. "Though more often we have them for dessert, it is not uncommon for citizens of Midstream to enjoy them for any meal."

Gladys rolled her eyes. "Yes, George, we know you're a chef. And yes, they're Sweetwing buns." She tossed one to George, and he caught it easily.

She gently handed one to Rikken before taking one for herself.

George bit into the bun and chewed slowly. It had a bit too much honey for his preference, but the salt and the earthy aroma of the thyme set the flavor off nicely.

"This is amazing," Rikken said around a mouthful of bun. "How do they get the bun so doughy? It's cooked, but it's so … squishy."

"It is like the steamed buns of Cave, but we do not bake them once they're done."

Rikken closed his eyes and chewed. "I could eat four of those."

"Then I have good news for you," Gladys said with a grin, tilting the bucket toward him so he could see the pile of steamed buns waiting inside.

"Thank you for your generosity." Rikken offered a nod.

They made it through another bun before Gladys broached a topic George had been expecting. "We should be on the front lines. The fighting will be in Ballern. Our allies are in Belldorn and Bollwerk as we speak! And we're just here eating steamed buns."

George held a hand up. "We already are, Princess. We are Bollwerk's warning system, and its northernmost defense. It is why Archibald has invested in our new docks and our reconstruction. It is not merely because we are allies, but because we are of strategic use to him. But should we abandon our posts, that usefulness may lessen."

Gladys sighed, but she didn't argue the point. "That doesn't mean I don't feel like I should be helping my friends."

"You're definitely helping your friends." Rikken leaned forward and snatched up another steamed bun. "This city has nothing but kind words for you. You may have a great deal of love for your friends in other places, but don't forget about the people you lead. They're friends too, and allies, and family."

Gladys's lip twitched, and a small frown flashed on her lips. For a moment, George worried how bad the verbal assault on Rikken was about to be. It was clear Gladys didn't think they were doing enough to help their allies. Then she spoke.

"You sound like Drakkar."

Horror crossed Rikken's face, and George howled with laughter.

CHAPTER EIGHT

PATRICE EYED THE Archduke of Willett, wondering when the man might finally stop rambling about the greatness of his tower. She'd long since learned to hide her annoyance, but every time she thought the end was coming, he started again.

"I assure you, Steward, nothing can breach the airspace of Ballern without long being sighted by my people. My tower is manned from dawn to dusk, both of the upper floors, a combination of which bears no blind spots."

Mordair pinched the bridge of his nose. "Enough, Jonas. You have made your point."

"I only wish to remove any question about the strength of my house, Steward." He leaned forward, almost frenzied in his response. "I can be a strong ally. Unwavering in the face of these rebellions. These … Stormborn, as they call themselves."

Patrice cleared her throat. "Perhaps it would be best to focus on items of import, Archduke? The Steward is quite busy today, and I would not want his absence to cause controversy among the other nobles."

Jonas hesitated and then nodded vigorously. "Of course, of course. I have no desire to keep you from your duties, Steward. Please, should you have any need of me or my staff, do not hesitate to ask."

"I will keep that in mind," Mordair said, tapping the arm of his throne. "Be well."

Jonas gave something that wasn't quite a formal bow but was more respectful than a nod of his head, and then departed.

Mordair slumped into his throne when the chamber door clicked close. "These fools are worse than Newton, Patrice. At least he had *some* level of reason and compassion before he got himself killed. These … *nobles*…" He almost spat the word. "They're no better than the pirates. Gold could sway their loyalty to any whim."

"Then it is good you are not relying on whims," Patrice said.

Mordair crossed his arms and leaned back in the Steward's throne. It might have merely been a seat of power in the eyes of the nobles, but only those who willfully ignored their reality could argue against it being a throne.

"I have training with Lane and the Children of the Dark Fire at noon, Gregory."

Mordair nodded. "Then go, Patrice. Strengthen our alliance with those fools, so I may join them at the Great Machine, as I was destined to."

Patrice started to turn toward the door, but hesitated. "Do you think they'll welcome you into their halls, Gregory? They'll know you're a threat, even if they see you as an ally. Only a fool would think you abandoned Fel without intention."

Mordair gave her a smirk that made her want to strike it from his face. "I have little doubt Lane and his followers have already made up their minds, Patrice. The fact we have not been assaulted tells me that even if they do not intend to let us rule their people, they will certainly tolerate the illusion of it. And that, my friend, is more than enough for what I intend."

Patrice eyed him for a moment before nodding. The hesitation would tell him she was irritated, but she'd long ago learned to keep the extent of it hidden. "I will be in the old arena, should you need me. I understand Lane intends to train another company of his faithful before the week is done."

"By all means, tend to your flock." Mordair dismissed her with a wave, and it wasn't the first time she imagined ramming a dagger into his throat for simply annoying her.

Patrice took her leave, heading down the hall and turning toward the spiral stone stairs instead of the larger corridor that would have taken her to a lift. It was closer to the arena, and generally held far fewer citizens of Ballern. The footsteps of the nearby guards echoed all around, but the soft soles of Patrice's boots moved her in silence.

✧　✧　✧

DEALING WITH JONAS, and sometimes Gregory, if she was being honest, almost made her training sessions with Lane and his soldiers enjoyable. In fact, if they hadn't been entirely loyal to that damn cult, Patrice might have admitted she liked their company. But the Children of the Dark Fire were just as terrible and self-serving as any other religion or noble she'd encountered in her years.

Patrice watched the disciples start their drill over again as Lane walked closer to her. "They're listening. That's something, at least."

"They need time," Lane said. "None of them have ever encountered an instructor quite as demanding as you."

"They'd consider me far less demanding if they simply did as they were asked."

Lane smiled, the flesh around his pale blue eyes crinkling just a hair. "You have made a great deal of progress with them in a few short weeks, Patrice. I cannot thank you enough for that."

"I haven't done enough to keep them alive, Lane. Every one of your disciples is going to get themselves killed." There was no heat in her words, only a simple statement of fact. "You're talking about fighting a fleet who turned away Ballern's strongest, with allies who brought down the Butcher of Gareth Cave."

"You have done enough, Patrice." Lane laced his fingers together and smiled. "Every soul loyal to the Children of the Dark Fire knows their life may be extinguished in service to the Great Machines."

"Lane. Have we truly done enough? Will Mordair be welcomed at the Great Machines?" She gestured to the disciples and they started another drill before focusing on Lane. "Legacy or not, I know many will still view him as an outsider. He has lived across the Crystal Sea for his entire life. How could they possibly welcome him as one of their own?"

Lane crossed his arms, hiding his hands in the sleeves of his cloak. "That is my burden to bear, Patrice. I have given my word, and my word is sovereign."

"I hope your sovereign word holds more weight than that of the nobles in Ballern. Every one of them is conspiring behind our back, seeking ways to leverage the Steward to their advantage."

"It is their nature, Patrice. You cannot change one's nature, no matter how much you mask it."

Patrice glanced away, watching the Children of the Dark Fire across the arena floor. Some of them showed promise in their drills. A natural aptitude for combat that would have given her far more satisfaction if she had months to train them instead of weeks.

"Patrice." Lane waited for her to meet his gaze. "It has already been agreed among those who protect the Dark Fire. You are welcome at the Great Machines. Mordair is welcome at the Great Machines. Do as you will to Ballern. Our prophecies have long foretold of the return of one of our own. And those prophecies did not specify a place. A source, if you will.

"Mordair fits that description well enough. Our followers will find him as evidence of our truth, because we will tell them so. And in exchange for being that figurehead, we will share our resources with him, and you, in whatever path you choose. Long have there been docks along the northern seas. Empty and waiting for a grand fleet. Your forces in the air and the sea will find a home at the Great Machine, and the world will bow before the might of the old world once more."

It took everything Patrice had not to grimace at the ridiculous proclamations of a disciple of the Children of the Dark Fire. "Your generosity is most welcome, Lane. The Steward will not soon forget it. We'll need those airship docks as well. Once chaos is sown in Ballern, the docks here will no longer be safe. The fools who govern will be lost. Give them a month of turmoil, and they will beg for the rule of an iron hand. Mordair's hand."

"Our hand." Lane's voice took a steel tone.

Patrice smiled. "Of course."

✧   ✧   ✧

THREE MORE HOURS of drills passed, and by the end of it, Patrice could pick out who would likely survive the first encounter of a real battle, and who would be buried first. Of course, that was always a roll of the dice, as it were. Sometimes the clumsiest fool ended up being the luckiest, but that was something no one would know until the earth was soaked in blood.

She left Lane and the trainees behind once her duty was fulfilled. She'd made it four blocks before she noticed the tail. Another of Jonas's spies. Better than the last, but still not good enough to go unnoticed by her. She pondered her meeting with Lane while scouting for the best location to remove her tail.

Gregory would be glad to hear of Lane's pledge that the forces of Fel would be welcomed at the Great Machine. That might not have been exactly how Lane had stated it, but it was close enough that Mordair could easily leverage the last few measures of diplomacy on them. They were useful to each other, which meant Gregory could likely take advantage of the cult.

Of course, what Lane might not have realized was that Gregory was already taking advantage of them. Depending on how thorough Lane's spies were, they might not yet realize the full extent of Mordair's efforts when it came to the Skyborn and those outside the reach of the nobles. The promise of wealth could motivate a great many people. Tensions were rising among the lower classes, and soon the Steward would strike the match.

Patrice ducked into the iron-banded door of an armory. She hated to cause the shopkeeper any grief, considering how well kept her storefront was, and how impeccable her arms were, but when Jonas's spy turned inside the shop, Patrice hammered a blade home into his neck four times in an instant.

A perfect blow, the vocal cords ruined. The man could only gasp and hiss. The struggle lasted seconds before he fell unconscious on the floor. Sadly, the spray of blood lasted a bit longer, staining a perfectly good display of leathers lined with a weave of fine cream fabric.

"My humblest apologies," Patrice said, turning to the shopkeeper, who appeared unusually unperturbed by the dead man on her floor.

"Never liked him much," the shopkeeper said, her voice gruff.

Patrice pulled out four gold coins. Each bore the mark of the Queen of Ballern, a symbol few would dare to counterfeit. She handed them over and nodded. "For the trouble."

"Would you prefer to keep this quiet?" the shopkeeper asked.

"If at all possible, yes."

"Then go. I'll close early and clean the shop. You've paid your due, friend. That man had a history you'd have nightmares about. You did the city a service."

Patrice studied the shopkeeper before nodding and returning to the street. It wasn't the end to the encounter she'd expected. And part of her wondered if she could have saved the coin. It didn't much matter, though. Gregory had access to the treasury vaults. They had more coin than they could spend in a very long time.

She slipped back into the crowds, pulling her hood tight so no other spies might recognize her, and so it would be harder to see the blood splashed across her cheek.

CHAPTER NINE

THE RAY HAD far more instruments for distant observation than it would appear to any casual observer. Where Mary had built a gun pod onto the underside of the Skysworn, Jakon had built a concealed array of scopes and gauges ideal for detecting distant vessels and gathering information to sell.

He peered through one such scope from his position high above the Gray Woods, checking on yet another caravan moving through an open space in the canopy. If they were part of the Children of the Dark Fire, they certainly didn't look it.

Most members of that cult wore cloaks or loudly displayed flags and banners bearing the metal-plated Queen's Crest. Jakon lifted the eyepiece off one scope and moved it to a higher-powered telescope. It was harder to track the movement so far below, but he could make out more details. An odd assortment of pots and pans hung from the sides of an old cart, and Jakon could almost hear the clattering and clanging of all that loose metal. It would make for one irritating ride through the woods.

Satisfied he'd stumbled upon yet another group of merchants, Jakon turned away from the bay of scopes hidden in the floor and clicked the transmitter. "No sign of movement in the west. Heading toward the sea to find out if any have slipped past."

Kura's static response cleared as she spoke. "Or they were smart enough to stay in the denser woods."

"Unlikely if they understand Karn's prowess in the forest. At least, if they did, they aren't hauling any kind of heavy armaments. I suppose that's a good thing."

Kura was silent for a time before she asked a question Jakon had been expecting. "Are you sure about leaving the kids in Karn? It's another world inside the Gray Woods."

"Those kids have seen more in their lives than anyone should. They can take care of themselves. More importantly, Arun may be the worst dice player I've ever met. He couldn't bluff to save his life."

Kura's response came slowly. "What does that have to do with the kids?"

He smiled as he answered. "Everything. He has three tells, and the only thing he lied to me about today was that he hated my soup."

Kura erupted in a short laugh. "By the gods. You're either a genius or a fool."

"Probably both. I'll contact you again if I find anything between here and the sea. Oh, and if you could tell our mutual pilot friend the kids are probably going to need a ride, that would likely save her some stress."

"Understood. Be careful."

"You too." Jakon eased two levers forward, causing the nose of The Ray to dip. Low clouds were rolling in, and he needed to be below them if he was going to make a thorough sweep.

The other thing that struck him as he passed another clearing in the canopy was how few airships flew in the vicinity of the Gray Woods. Twice he'd seen a ship on the horizon, but they never came closer. The clear skies reminded him why trading with Karn had been so easy over the years.

It was one thing to conceal a ship when you had to dock at Ballern. It was a much simpler thing when there were no eyes to conceal your ship from. No one in Karn had ever boarded The Ray in an effort to discover all the various smuggling holds hidden around the ship, quite possibly because Jakon had never killed anyone in Karn. And while searches rarely happened on the Bones either, it was certainly a regular occurrence on the more desirable levels of Ballern's docks.

With the horizon clear and the forest too far below to be a threat to the hull, Jakon grabbed the rubber handle of a piloting switch. It was one of his favorite things he'd gotten in a trade from Smith, if he were being honest. And *that* was an impressive thing, considering the transaction was some seven years past.

The mechanism resisted as he pulled it right, releasing the locked position so he could pull it down and set it in place. Guided by a compass and a level, it would hold The Ray's course while Jakon went below deck. Of course, it wouldn't do any good if the ship was headed for a mountain, but it was the safest way to fly solo. A feat he couldn't do very well before Smith had helped him install the piloting switch. It wasn't that the switches were exceedingly rare, but a good switch was another story.

Jakon took one last look at the horizon before heading down the hall and into the main cargo hold. From there, he opened a hatch and slid down a short ladder to a much smaller hold. It gave him access to the retractable cannons that ran along the hull, but from inside the ship, they looked like nothing more than well-organized barrels.

A sudden memory of Mary and those damned pickled eggs flashed through his mind. He laughed at himself and then moved to check the cannons. Two barrels could use a reload after some test fires the day before, but the rest were ready to engage with whatever hapless target crossed The Ray.

He rolled a powder charge into the barrel and tamped it down before using a pulley to hoist one of the many rounds of shot from the smuggling hold to the end of the barrel. It made a satisfying scrape as he rammed it home with a long, padded ramrod.

The Ray shook beneath his feet as it either hit a rough patch of air, or a strong crosswind. Jakon felt the floor level, telling him the piloting switch was doing its job. He finished the reload before pausing and locking down the small smuggling holds behind the cannons.

There wasn't anything there that would get him in trouble if he was boarded, per se, but he also figured any fleet who searched the hold wouldn't be too happy about the sheer volume of ammunition he transported on The Ray.

Jakon wiped his hands on a gray towel before heading back up to the cabin. He checked every window. Both port and starboard were clear to the horizon, but he could see his next target directly ahead off the bow. Jakon disengaged the piloting switch and took control of the ship once again, angling for another wide stretch in the sparser parts of the forest. There, the road below came into view.

It wasn't caravans, but a small assembly of tents. Jakon slid the long brass tube of his scope assembly into the floor to look for any signs of who had gathered there. He couldn't help but laugh to himself when he saw the symbol painted on the canvas roof of the largest wagon.

Stormborn.

He left the scope mounted in its dock as he turned back to the windscreen. The Gray Woods weren't as tall there, and the shorter trees told him where he was. Soon enough, he crossed over the Gray River. *Quite a terrible name*, he thought. He understood *why* someone had named it the Gray River, but having worked in city planning a lifetime ago, Jakon very much thought *nothing* should ever be called a Gray River. That was a term that would never mean anything to him other than sewage.

The transmitter crackled, but no voice followed the sound for a time. When it did, it was a harsh whisper. "Jakon. Jakon, if you're there, answer me *now*. Four clippers are under attack on the southeastern coast. Scouts near the delta."

"Eva?"

"Yes! I can't talk. There are soldiers nearby. Do what you can. Please. They're ... they're friends."

Jakon cursed under his breath and eased the throttle forward on The Ray. He was already passing over another river delta, and if that wasn't where the conflict was, then he knew where it had to be. Jakon didn't dare respond to Eva again. Depending on how close those soldiers were and where she was, a transmitter could be less than subtle.

But if she was on Kura's transmitter, and soldiers were that close to the school ... Jakon's grip tightened on the lever for the thrusters and he pushed them to their max. Even at speed, it would be minutes before he reached the Crystal Sea. And minutes in an airship battle could be disastrous.

✦   ✦   ✦

JAKON INCREASED ALTITUDE when the small Sapphire River came into view. Movement dotted the horizon, and he had little doubt that was his target when the smoke materialized in the sunlight. Jakon pinched a release concealed on the underside of the console. It dropped a small panel set into what appeared to be the supports for the controls.

Behind the hidden door was a lever, then three buttons in a column, and a final lever near the floor, the perfect height for triggering with a foot. Each handle ended in an orb of blank polished brass with no identifying marks.

Perhaps more than anything else, this mechanism gave The Ray an advantage in almost any battle. Even flying alone, Jakon could deploy his cannons, trigger a mechanism to switch to a loaded barrel, and fire them without leaving the captain's seat.

Part of him hoped he wouldn't have to deploy them, but the closer he got, the more he realized how unlikely that was. Jakon clicked the top button, disengaging the locks on the cannons. Two of Belldorn's clippers wove around the sleek gray form of a Fel striker. It was a fast ship, not quite so fast as the clippers, but armed well enough to prevent almost any ship from retreating.

Judging by the smoldering debris on top of the water, the other two had tried.

Jakon cursed and pulled back on the throttle, changing his angle of attack as he grabbed the top lever and forced it down. The Ray shook as its cannons unfurled from the hull. After the initial tremors, The Ray stabilized, giving Jakon a line of sight straight through the retreating clippers.

He smashed the button for the transmitter, knowing it was a risk to contact Eva again, but he didn't have the frequency for the clippers. "Tell them to scatter!"

No answer came. He could take the shot and risk hitting the clippers, or wait and risk the striker taking notice of The Ray. Jakon lingered over the button to fire. He couldn't wait much longer.

One of the clippers shot off to the north while the other veered south. The striker moved to follow the southbound ship, and Jakon bared his teeth.

He slammed the button for the starboard cannon, then the port. Before those shots had even made themselves known to his target, he stomped on the lever to reload, waiting for the heavy thunk that told him the barrels had rotated.

Jakon fired another salvo, but as he reloaded for the second time, the third shot cut through the striker's bow. The entire cabin vanished in a ball of smoke and splinters before the gas chamber inhaled like some great beast, and detonated like a bomb.

Jakon shut his eyes and closed The Ray up. Once more, it could have been nothing but a fancy freighter, if you didn't look too closely at the smoke rising from the vents on the deck.

"It's done. Two left. I'm … I'm sorry."

The captain of The Ray watched the clippers head back out to sea. They didn't have enough fuel to return to Belldorn, so he had no idea where they were headed. But he knew this wouldn't be the last of the ships sent into the depths of the Crystal Sea. The battle was coming to Ballern, and worry gnawed at his gut.

Eva's voice came back over the transmitter, not as quiet as before. "Thank you. Skyborn out."

CHAPTER TEN

"ONE MORE TIME." Samuel gestured from Bessie's saddle. The old girl bounced on her legs a few times, clearly ready to move through the woods of Canopy again. The dragonriders behind him, on the other hand, had a rather distinct expression on their faces, that being concern.

"You're mad, Spider Knight!" Tatsu pointed at the Jumper. "You have no wings, yet you jump through the trees as if you do."

Samuel grinned at the dragonrider. "If you'd prefer to go back to train with the Stalkers, I'm sure they have extra mounts available. I don't know what Alana would think of that, though. Her bravest dragonriders, scared to ride a Jumper through the woods." He couldn't quite make out all the very creative cursing under Tatsu's breath, but it had the desired effect.

Tatsu's mount was a brownish red Jumper, a little smaller than Bessie, but just as effective in her jumps. A gust of wind ruffled the trees around Samuel, but the spiders were unconcerned. Tatsu leaned forward, and his mount rocketed into the air, tilting back so it could dig its feet into the tree, and raising her abdomen to better support her rider's saddle.

"Not so bad, was it?" Samuel asked.

The glower on Tatsu's face was all the answer Samuel needed.

"I should have stayed with Drakkar."

Rin's mount, a gray Jumper a little darker than Bessie, slammed into the tree beside Tatsu as Rin released a howl of joy. "There's nothing like it! Truly, the Dragonwings are fast, almost out of control, but these Jumpers are *powerful.*"

Samuel raised his voice to be sure not only the trainees on the tree with them could hear, but also those trailing behind by a jump or two. "Rin brings up an excellent point. Jumpers *are* powerful. They're also mindful of their rider. If they feel you slipping, they'll normally attempt to reposition so you don't fall. The only exception to that is if they feel it'll kill you both."

"That is somewhat more reassuring than the Dragonwings," Tatsu said. "I can agree on that."

Rin flashed a smile at Tatsu before turning his attention back to Samuel. "What about armor? I've heard Jumpers can carry armor like the Stalkers do."

Samuel nodded. "They can, that's true. But a fully armored Jumper won't be moving through the trees like we are now. They'll be faster than a Stalker on the ground, but only just. A full set of armor plate will add too much burden for them to jump. And even if they could, the impact would kill them. In Ancora, we rarely armor our Jumpers' legs, but if they are to be on an open battlefield, it's a good option. We'll carry extra plating with us, but it's unlikely we'll use it. But remember, the extra agility comes at too high a price if long-range weapons have a clear field of view.

"Follow me back to the stables and we'll repeat our drills with the halberds while mounted."

More than a few groans went up from the trainees, apparently still a little worn out from the morning's drills. Samuel smiled as he urged Bessie forward, remembering his own training from years before. His instructors had been merciless, but effective, and he hoped he'd sharpened some of their training skills.

Bessie shuffled from one branch to another, crouched, and launched out of the tree. Samuel shifted to the side, looking down at several dragonriders as they repositioned their own mounts, and a few who stared slack-jawed at the gray Jumper hurtling through the air.

Samuel leaned forward before they hit their target, Bessie spreading the impact out across her legs so neither of them ended up splattered across the bark. This time she didn't hurry to the trunk, instead staying in the thick outer branches, racing across them as if they were solid ground before launching forward again, angling down for a lower branch.

He glanced back to make sure his dragonriders-turned-Spider-Knights were following. And they were, with varying degrees of skill and poor landing posture, though that would improve with experience. Samuel was fairly sure there was going to be a broken nose or two by how far forward some of the recruits were leaning, but that was better than the alternatives. The net beneath Canopy might have caught them, but with a fall from their current height, the net might as well be stone.

Samuel tapped Bessie's side with his hand, feeling the rough hairs beneath his fingers. She responded to the direction, turning slightly to the south, angling for the stables. Bessie's sense of direction always outmatched his, but he'd still been worried the first time they had taken the Ancoran mounts into the woods. Strange lands could trigger long-dormant behaviors, but the mounts still had their troughs of Sweet-Flies in Canopy, and that seemed to be enough to keep them coming back, even when they decided to go exploring on their own.

The last jump loomed before them, a bit longer than the others, but Bessie didn't hesitate, scampering to the edge of the branch until it just started to bend. And then she launched.

It was the closest a Jumper ever got to feeling like a Dragonwing. The wind pulled at Samuel's armor as Bessie adjusted her legs, controlling their fall, and he couldn't help but smile. She slammed into Canopy's walkway, startling a pair of guards before racing forward to the stables.

Samuel turned back and watched his trainees make that leap of faith one after the other. Some took the impact well, and others had leaned a bit too far forward, as he feared. Tatsu looked dazed after smacking his head on the front of the saddle, but he stayed upright, and his mount followed Rin's.

Their skill with the Dragonwings gave them an enormous advantage in learning to ride Jumpers. It gave Samuel some small hope that the dragonriders would be just as formidable on the ground as they were in the air. He'd be happier if they had months to train, but he'd do the best he could with the time they'd been given.

✧   ✧   ✧

DRAKKAR RODE IN the saddle of an orange and black Stalker. As slow and plodding as the beasts appeared to a casual observer, once a Stalker had a target, they moved at unsettling speeds. But the most important thing to Drakkar was that they moved along the ground.

He did find a degree of joy in flying on the back of a Dragonwing. It was exhilarating, to be sure, but somewhat terrifying as well. And that was when things were going to plan.

Stalkers were patient mounts that followed directions better than the best-trained Walkers of Cave. Allie, one of Canopy's leaders, stood at the end of the forest path with a cluster of canvas targets. She'd proven herself proficient with the Stalkers, and a flustered instructor had sarcastically handed her authority for the day. Needless to say, the instructor probably wasn't getting their job back. She designated one target for attack, and it was the riders' job to strike only that target.

Drakkar breathed deeply when she gave the signal. He lifted the padded rod used to guide the Stalker and gently rubbed it between the spider's two largest eyes, making sure to keep the tip directed at the sole target. The spider bobbed on its legs, which was all the warning Drakkar had.

He grabbed the pommel of the saddle as tight as he could an instant before the Stalker sprinted forward. They might be large and slow compared to a Jumper, but unencumbered by armor, they were faster than any person could move.

The Stalker's feet sent leaves and detritus into the air as it closed on the targets, Allie safely tucked away behind a tree. Her mount's foremost leg rose over the closest burlap sack, the others following a neat arc as the Stalker bared its fangs and slammed them home on the designated target.

The target might have been a two-hundred-pound sack of grain, but the Stalker tossed it aside like so much wool. Drakkar patted the Stalker's head as it searched for other targets. Apparently satisfied that it had murdered the grain sack, the Stalker turned and started walking back down the forest path.

"That's enough for now," Allie called out as she stepped into view. "If the dragonriders are having half as much luck with the Jumpers as you are that Stalker, Drakkar. I think we'll be in excellent shape."

Drakkar tried to smile at that idea, but riding Jumpers … that was a whole other world. "Let us hope so, my friend."

A few more Stalkers appeared in the woods as Allie spoke. "Everyone back to the stables. The supply ships are scheduled for later today, and it'll be easier if the mounts are well fed. Once you're done, meet me up top at the stables. The Dragonwings are overdue for a parasite check."

Drakkar let out a low laugh at the groans that rose from his fellow riders. They were apparently not too fond of that task. Of course, after he found out what that task was, he might not be too fond of it either.

✧   ✧   ✧

His Stalker fed and secured in the lower stables, Drakkar headed to one of the hidden lifts that would take him to Canopy. Inside, he closed the gate and threw the switch. The lift moved in silence. There was no rumble or rattle like so many lifts in the cities. It preserved the secretive nature of Canopy, even if the Stalkers were nearby.

The doors opened on a short side path near the Dragonwing stables. He could see the Jumpers had returned, but he saw something else that caught him off guard. Drakkar made his way over to the old man with a white beard.

"Targrove?"

The tinker turned with a raised eyebrow. "I think you've mistaken me for someone else, young man."

Drakkar coughed into his hand, feeling a flush on his face. "Right, of course. How is Theo, being you are *merely* her assistant?"

Targrove winked at Drakkar and ushered him to the back of the short path, beyond the lift itself, where no ears could be seen. "She's still in Midstream. Insisted on overseeing the construction of a new shelter. *I* told her Helena was more than qualified, not to mention a dozen other people. And don't worry about using my name, Drakkar. It's likely time people found out I was still around. Something to strike fear in Mordair's shriveled little heart."

"What are *you* doing here?" Drakkar asked.

Targrove looked down at the thin wooden box grasped between his wrinkled fingers, his words sounding reserved. "I have something for Alana. I heard she was here, and wanted to be sure I saw her before … before anything else happens. There are things I need to say."

"Is everything okay? Are you well?"

Targrove barked out a laugh and suddenly sounded much more like himself. "Other than the fact I could drop dead at any moment? I am fabulous, Cave Guardian. Fabulous."

"Alana is probably with the council, or possibly the stables." Drakkar smiled at the old tinker. "Apparently it is time to see to the parasites on the Dragonwings."

"Ah, a feast then!"

"A … feast?" Drakkar asked slowly.

"Come, come, if it's time for stew, likely everyone is in the stables."

Now thoroughly confused, Drakkar followed Targrove across the path. They turned onto the main street, flanked by small shops and large multi-family homes set in the treetops before the road narrowed and flowed into the stables. The very crowded, nearly overrun stables.

Targrove led the way, moving through the mass of soldiers and spiders and Dragonwings like a stream flowing around rocks. Drakkar considered himself quite good at navigating crowds. They were a regular occurrence in the narrower intersections of Cave. But trying to keep up with the old tinker proved somewhat challenging in the denser parts of the crowd.

If Targrove hadn't turned into one of the short hallways with stairs leading to the second level, Drakkar might have lost him. The crowds thinned a bit up top, and Drakkar found Targrove making a straight line for Alana.

The sides of her shaved head stood out among the soldiers of Canopy, who tended to have longer hair, which likely helped them keep warm in the high winds of the cooler months. They didn't have to worry as much about things like that in Cave, as there wasn't a much more thorough windbreak than a mountain.

Targrove waited at the gate to the open-air stable. Drakkar stepped up beside him and glanced at the old tinker, a little surprised by his silence.

"Are you going to talk to her?" the Cave Guardian asked.

"Of course I'm going to talk to her. I'm not going to interrupt her now, though, am I? Don't want the Dragonwings to get hurt."

Drakkar frowned and looked at Alana and the Dragonwing she stood beside. She picked up a long, flat tool, something like a shovel but with no curve to the head. The more he watched, the more it reminded him of the wide paddles some of the chefs used in Bollwerk to reach into deep stoves.

Alana had her cloak tied back, revealing the decorative copper accents on the leather armor of her station. It was a rare thing to see one of Cave's leaders outside of the city with something so precious to their people, and it gave him an unexpected swell of pride to see it there.

She slid the blade of the tool between two chitinous plates on the Dragonwing's abdomen, and Drakkar cringed as she leveraged it up. The mount itself did not appear to mind, still focused on the shallow trough of Sweet-Flies.

Alana reached into the gap between the Dragonwing's plates and started yanking on something Drakkar couldn't see. A stable hand joined her, holding the tool up so Alana could use both hands. She made short work of it after that, dragging a flat, translucent white creature out of the Dragonwing. It almost looked like a Sea Claw, snapping at the air, unable to reach whatever dared dislodge it from the Dragonwing. A quick knife to its head quieted it, and Alana dropped it into a barrel with a rather nasty squishing sound.

Drakkar slowly turned to Targrove. "They make stew from those?"

Targrove nodded before laughing. "It's … well, it certainly tastes better than it looks."

Alana caught sight of them after she took the prying tool from the stable hand and set it back on the mounts along the Dragonwings' perch. She reached down for a towel, wiping her arms off before joining Drakkar and Targrove.

"What brings you two here?"

She might have asked both of them, but Drakkar was certain the question was meant for Targrove. After all, Alana knew exactly why Drakkar was there, along with the other Cave Guardians, who dotted the stables of Canopy.

"I have a gift for you," Targrove said. "It's … it's a bit more special than I realized when I took it from the Great Machines, and it should be at home with you and your people."

Alana raised an eyebrow. "The last man who told me he had a gift tried to stab me with a dagger."

Targrove threw his hand up in protest. "No, of course not. Well, it is a dagger. I mean, not for stabbing. Not for stabbing you. That … that's not what I meant to say." He pinched his forehead.

Alana's piercing amber eyes didn't leave Targrove's. She let him fumble over his words for a time before granting him the mercy of stopping him by raising her hand.

"Please, tinker. You would be no friend of Drakkar if you meant to stab me. I know who you are."

Targrove paused and glanced at Drakkar. "Did you tell her about me? I didn't say to tell anyone until today."

"I have been to Belldorn," Alana said. "Spent time in the southern markets and heard tales at the darkest bars. Long have there been rumors about you, Targrove. We have photos from the Deadlands War. Photos of allies, and enemies, and those who were something in between." She gave him a pointed look at that last.

Targrove blew out a breath that wasn't quite a laugh. "Had a lot less wrinkles back then." He squeezed the box in his hand and held it out to Alana. "For what it's worth, I am … sorry for what came to Cave in the Deadlands War."

Alana inclined her head and gently opened the box, folding a strip of velvet back to reveal the wavy blade of an old dagger.

"I thought it was a reproduction. Someone making a statement by killing with it inside the Great Machine. Took a closer look in my lab. The folds in that metal, the alloy, the shine. There's nothing like it."

Alana didn't answer. She only stared at the blade, slowly reaching out to touch it. "How ... how could you even know about this?"

"What is it?" Drakkar asked, frowning at the dagger. It was well made, that much was obvious, but beyond its age, he didn't recognize it.

Alana looked up at Drakkar, shaking her head. "It is not a story we tell, Drakkar. It is a fable passed down from one head of the Nameless to the next. The arms carried by the Founders, lost to time except for a sword, a sheath, and a pauldron. They are hidden in the temple. Silently standing guard for all of Cave."

Her eyes turned down to the blade. "And now a dagger." She rested her fingertips on the hilt before turning her focus back to Targrove.

"How did you know what it was? I do not mean the metal, Targrove. I mean the story."

Targrove took a deep breath before nodding to himself. "I'm old, Alana. But I once met a Cave Guardian who swore he was one hundred and five years young. A character, that one." Targrove laughed. "Told me he was the grandson of a Founder. Whether that was a great grandson, or several greats, I don't know. But he had stories, and one of them was about those blades."

"Wanderers." Alana smiled and looked to Drakkar. "I guess those stories had more truth than we knew."

"Wanderers?" Targrove asked.

Drakkar nodded. "Something like the Forgotten. Banished from Cave, but not so violently as the Forgotten. They were given a choice to remain silent in their beliefs, or leave."

Targrove scratched the back of his head. "Let me guess. Not really a choice, was it? Did they die mysteriously if they didn't leave?"

"Yes," Alana said quietly.

"Every city, every people, has a story like that. I figure the few I met that didn't were either lying, or just hadn't lived long enough to see it happen."

Alana met his gaze. "It is kind of you to say so, but it does not lessen the indignities of our past."

"The shadows make us who we are," Drakkar said. "None of us would be here without them."

"Easy to say when you don't live in them." Targrove focused on the ground. "Harder when you see the consequences on the battlefield."

"Harder when you see the consequences on the face of hungry children," Drakkar said. "It is why Cave became a haven for pirates all those years ago. Alana and I are old enough to remember the last famine."

Alana clicked the box closed and held it close to her chest before reaching out to Targrove and embracing him. "Thank you. I know what happened in the war was never your intention, nor Charles's. Drakkar has told me many things from his travels with the Steamsworn. May the sands find you well, Targrove. You are welcome in Cave."

Targrove held on to Alana for a moment, and when they separated, tears had gathered at the edges of Targrove's eyes. "That means a great deal to me, Nameless. I will not disrespect your gift."

Across the street, Tatsu climbed to the top of the wall and shouted. "Word comes from Midstream! Forces close from the northwest. Mordair's allies are moving."

"Where the hell were they hiding?" Targrove spat. "Archibald's had his eye on that entire area."

"I need to speak to the council," Alana said. "Find me there if you need me." With that, she sprinted down the street.

"Could they have had more tunnels?" Drakkar asked, watching Alana shrink into the distance.

"Aye, it's possible." Targrove clenched his fists. "Well, now they'll have to deal with Theo. And if they thought *I* was a force to be reckoned with." He laughed, and it was one of the more unsettling things Drakkar had heard in quite some time.

CHAPTER ELEVEN

ALICE WATCHED THE graceful shadows in the canopy above. It was a strange feeling, being so awed by the massive creatures, and knowing they could kill in an instant. She'd been close to Shadowwings before, but Acidwings were quite new.

Of course, that paled in comparison to the creature they were currently riding. Alice ran her fingers over the edge of the thin saddle, feeling the light material between the structure of their Tree Killer's wings. Wings that were tied down to prevent any accidents, but gleamed an iridescent green when the sun reached them between the leaves and branches far above.

"I still can't believe William stayed in Karn to sketch a fountain," Furi called out from behind them. Her mount was keeping pace with their own.

Alice grinned at her. "He did seem particularly taken by it!"

"So," Mali called over her shoulder. "How do you like riding on the back of a Tree Killer?"

"It's … different." Alice couldn't keep a tremor of excitement from her voice, or perhaps fear. "Our friend lost his leg to a Tree Killer in the desert. So it's … it's a little unsettling." She turned to get a look at Furi, who rode a Giant Stick.

Furi waved, apparently far more comfortable with her mount than Alice was with the Tree Killer she shared with Mali.

"What happened?" Mali asked.

So Alice told her as they wove between the mighty trunks of the Forest Giants, Acidwings gliding above them as unseen things crunched through the leaves and underbrush. She told her of the old ironwood tree and how the Tree Killers had blended into the bark and sand instead of the greens and browns of the forest. And she told her how the tree had come alive, and what had happened to Jacob.

Mali cringed. "That's a rough way to end up a Biomech."

"Do you … I mean, does Karn hate Biomechs, like a lot of cities in the east?"

Mali laughed and shook her head. "No. We've known quite a few. You see them quite a bit with the pirates, or smugglers, as some of them prefer to be called. I guess they have a dangerous trade."

"No berserkers in your stories?"

Mali glanced back and raised an eyebrow. "Like those tall tales from the war? No, can't say I've seen one of those. We didn't have Biomechs in Karn until well after the war."

"They were real," Alice said. "Tinkers used the wrong metals for their implants, and it poisoned their minds." She didn't miss the shiver in Mali's shoulders.

"That's … well, that's terrible. Kind of puts a new perspective on some of the old tales."

Furi came up beside them in a wide clearing, the lumbering gait of her Giant Stick easily catching her up to the others. "Did I hear you talking about Biomechs?"

Mali nodded. "Alice was telling me about Jacob."

"You should ask Smith to show you his biomechanics if you really want to see something."

"Oh, yes," Alice said. "He's had an extraordinary amount of work done."

"I'd like to see that." Mali looked down at the brass watch mounted in her leather wrist cuff. "We'd best be turning around. I wanted to keep you away from Arun and the elders while they discussed letting Belldorn land here. They can be … weird when outsiders are here, but their meeting should be done soon. Are you hungry?"

"Starving," Furi said.

Mali tapped the back of the Tree Killer's head, and it slowed to a stop. Furi's mount stepped up beside it as if it wasn't worried one bit about being next to something that considered Giant Sticks dinner. Mali rifled through one of the saddlebags before tossing something wrapped in paper over to Furi. She handed the same to Alice.

Alice unwrapped it and found a tightly rolled cylinder of bread and meat and cheese. "What is it?"

"Flattened fried fish and a white cheese. I'm not entirely sure what the sauce is, but it's good and salty."

Furi took a bite and leaned back in her saddle. "Mali, that's fantastic!"

Alice tried it and wasn't quite as enthusiastic about it as Furi. When Mali had said it was salty, that was a vast understatement. Alice wasn't sure if she could make it any saltier by eating a handful of salt. But food was food, and the farther into the roll she got, the more she had to admit it was pretty tasty.

The richness of the cheese helped offset the saltiness of the sauce, but any bite that was missing cheese was still overpowering. The crunchy texture was quite pleasing, though.

Mali handed her a gourd with a cork in the top. "Water. For the salt."

Alice chuckled. "Thank you. It's a lot more salt than I'm used to."

"Is Ancora one of those cities that doesn't like to use spices? Or do you preserve your fish in some other way?"

"I wouldn't say that, but we definitely use less salt." Alice twisted the cork out of the gourd and took a long drink. It had a subtle flavor to it, almost fruity, and it was welcome.

"Finish up your snacks and we'll be on our way. It's only about thirty minutes back to the city from here."

THEY DIDN'T WIND around the forest nearly so much on the way back. Instead, Mali found a wide trail, and they stuck to it. Either the path was often traveled by carts and crawlers, or it was constantly trampled by the local wildlife. Whatever the case, Alice wasn't complaining about the even terrain and lack of bushes she'd had to be mindful of on the journey in.

Soon enough, the treeline broke, and they could catch glimpses of the city in the distance. Alice didn't see the ruins and remains of what they'd traveled through before. It was an entirely different area than Jakon had led them through.

Without a compass, or some form of navigation, Alice quickly realized they could be lost inside the woods for a long time. But she hadn't seen Mali use any tool to help navigate.

"Mali, how do you not get lost in here?" Alice gestured to the dark expanse of the forest under the canopy.

"The trees are marked if you know where to look." Mali pointed up. "You can see it right beneath the lowest branch of many trees."

Alice squinted at the closest branches, still some fifty feet above their heads. She didn't see anything at first, but as they passed the second Forest Giant, she could just make out a pale scar.

"Is it the diamond shape?"

Mali nodded. "If you really look, you can see the left side has been scraped away a bit more. That points us to the city. They only go a few miles out into the woods, but that's enough for most people. Farther than that and you'd need a compass. Farther than that and it might help the Children of the Dark Fire as much as it helps us."

Alice found the marking one more time before they stopped appearing. And once that happened, they could easily see the city through multiple paths.

Mali led the way into the city, toward the fountain they'd seen earlier, passing several families and a few merchants setting up stalls near the city square. None of them appeared too concerned at a Tree Killer walking nearby. William was still there, his notepad in hand and his pencil moving across the page.

"Should we tell him we're here?" Alice said.

"William!" Furi shouted in answer.

He fumbled his pencil and looked around before finding them and waving. He gathered his things and started walking after them.

A few more minutes brought them to the stables, where Mali and Furi both handed their reins over to two kids who didn't seem nearly old enough to be that close to a Tree Killer. It was a jarring thing to see, considering Alice's main experience with the creatures had been watching one nearly kill Jacob.

The three of them trailed Mali, sticking close to their Karn guide as she turned down an alley. The cobblestones weren't as even here, and Alice found herself tripping more than once.

William listened to their story about the woods, and he didn't seem to have the slightest regret about not following them on the saddle of a Tree Killer.

Beyond the alley, the streets evened out once more, and between two of Karn's soaring towers sat a modest building. Perhaps it would have been three stories high in Ancora. Windows stretched up into a pointed arch, letting light into a space lined with seats and benches that had an echo of Bollwerk.

Mali stopped outside the doors and waited. "We shouldn't interrupt them. I see a few people left inside."

"Is it another thing we just shouldn't do as outsiders?" Furi asked. "Like a tradition or something?"

Mali shook her head. "No, I just don't want your presence to have an impact on their decisions if they aren't final. I don't want them to turn your allies away. It's not fair to you, or to us. Arun will do what he can."

It wasn't the biggest boost of confidence Alice would have liked to hear, and she could tell Furi felt much the same. The Skyborn dug her toes into the street and sighed before turning her attention back to the building.

A few minutes passed before the doors creaked open, giving them all a glimpse of the chamber beyond. It wasn't as ostentatious as Bollwerk, or as humble as Canopy, but the grand stone statues gave Alice an ominous feeling, and that was from a distance. Maybe it was the idea of the elders denying them access, or maybe it was the history of the place, but something had unsettled Alice.

Arun led the group coming through the doors, waving to them as he made his way over. "Well, I have bad news for Jakon."

Alice's chest tightened.

"I think that pirate is going to have to fly back here with a few barrels of mead. That …" Arun scratched the side of his head. "*That*, of all things, is the council's price."

"Price for what?" Mali asked.

"For using Karn as a port." Arun grinned, and Mali raised her hand as if she was going to slap him.

"Your humor is terrible," Mali muttered.

"So Lady Katherine can land here?" Alice said, finally wrapping her head around Arun's banter. A rush of relief untied the knot in her stomach, and the looming statues looked more like a bastion now than a threat.

Arun inclined his head. "Indeed. I would say she will be welcomed here. The merchants are ready to sell to travelers, war or not. So, of course, hosting a fleet is appealing to them, and they have much sway with the elders." Arun sighed and rubbed his hands together. "There is more, friends of Jakon. I need to tell you of the control center that lies to the south."

"What control center?" Furi asked.

"For the Great Machines," Arun said. "Long ago, it was a central hub, another forest city. That was before the dark times came and it was overrun."

Mali stood up a little straighter. "You got their permission to speak of it?"

"I did, Mali. The elders are not so foolish as you may like to believe. At least not in all things."

"You found one?" William asked. "An actual control center? Several writings say they were all torn down and their functions moved inside the Great Machines themselves."

Arun shook his head.

Alice prompted him when he didn't continue. "Part of a war?"

"No." Mali eyed Arun before turning to Alice and Furi. "It is a place of death and ghosts. You will need an airship. No mount can enter those woods."

Furi frowned. "Why?"

"It is the highest concentration of parasitic fungus we know of. Whatever enters does not return."

"People return," Arun said. "But you can't take mounts into the dead zone. They'll spread the spores. You'll see them when you get there. Burn your clothes before you journey back."

"They are poison to people as well," William said. "Many varieties are, anyhow. Caution will be needed."

Furi's eyebrows climbed a little higher. "Why would we risk going there, then?"

"Because it was a control center for the Great Machines," Alice said quietly. "And the Children of the Dark Fire live inside of one."

Furi cursed and crossed her arms. "We could learn something about them. Maybe more than the dead one in the desert taught us."

"It is not all good news," Arun said. "Your friend, Eva, is on her way. There is a battle brewing around Midstream."

Alice stiffened. "We need to get back to Ballern. If Mordair is starting the fight, we have to be sure the Skyborn are ready. Be sure the Stormborn are united."

"We need to get to Kura," Furi said. "This is what she's been preparing for."

CHAPTER TWELVE

G LADYS STOOD BESIDE Theo at the top of the watchtower. The old tinker's wheelchair unfolded with a hiss and a pop, standing her upright so she could see as easily as anyone else through the binoculars mounted in the windows.

Theo turned and eyed George. "If you mean to reach the shelter before this begins, now is the time. Half a mile is a long way under fire."

"They don't have a bomber," Gladys said. "All I see is two transport airships. Everything else is on the ground."

"That doesn't mean they aren't dangerous." Theo's words were calm, a simple statement of fact.

Gladys bit her lips before steeling herself. "I won't ask my people to fight for me if I'm just going to run away."

George thumped the end of his spear on the floorboards. "I am with you, Princess. For sand and blood."

Theo harrumphed and turned back to the window. "I knew I liked you. Stay on your transmitters. Get your skiffs prepped and ready to flee in case things get dire."

"The Guard is working on it now."

"Good, good. If we're lucky, every last one of those fools will drive straight into that line of Tail Swords. I doubt that will happen, but one can hope."

Theo clicked the transmitter in her collar. "Helena, I see two groups of armored crawlers heading this way. Only one looks to bear Fel's markings. I don't recognize the markings on the others."

Helena's response came back, short and clipped. "Understood. Dividing forces."

Gladys leaned forward and put her eyes up to another pair of mounted binoculars. The dark gray and violent red of Fel's colors were easy to pick out. She swiveled the scope to the east and found the other group. Her heart hammered in her chest. A star formed from the quills of a Stone Dog. There was only one group she knew of who bore that symbol.

"Rana."

"Rana's dead," George said.

"I know that." She leaned into the scope. "I know that *very* well! But those are his flags, George. Those are his people."

"Perhaps they come to offer assistance?" Theo asked, frowning as she watched the two groups of crawlers slowly edge toward each other, finally merging into one long front. "Or perhaps not."

George rubbed at the side of his face. "Then is this Mordair's doing? Or did the remaining warlords think this an opportune time to strike?"

"You can ask them if any survive." Theo's voice fell to an ominous whisper. "But I wouldn't be too hopeful about that. Mordair has long influenced the warlords, George. Through money and favor he has made them an extension of his will through the years."

Gladys clenched her fists. "We need to get down there and fight. I won't let my people fight alone."

Theo made a sound deep in her throat. It wasn't a laugh, but it wasn't agreement either. "These are old tactics, Princess. Warlords have used them for decades. The biggest threats are likely already inside the city proper. What you see unfolding before you is the bait. But they do not understand how much that bait is about to cost them."

"What do you mean?"

Theo turned to Rikken. "Bolt the door and guard the hatch. They will come for Gladys, and they will be forced to come through the windows or the floor. Your father will not be happy if his friends end up dead. Or you, for that matter."

Rikken nodded and stepped closer to the hatch after throwing the heavy bolt in the door to the stairs. He rested the shaft on his shoulder, blade angled at the floor as if he meant to stand there for hours. And for all Gladys knew, that's exactly what he planned.

"If that hatch so much as twitches, run them through. The airships are in range." Theo smiled. Actually *smiled*, and the expression showed Gladys a darkness in the old tinker she hadn't seen before.

But it was there in all of them now, wasn't it? Knowing they might need to kill to stay alive. To protect their people. Gladys's chest tightened. There were times she wished she wasn't a princess, that she didn't have to make decisions that would put so many people in harm's way. She already knew what question Theo would ask next.

"At your command, Princess. Are you ready?"

Gladys closed her eyes and stepped up to the binoculars before clicking the transmitter on the small table beside the window. "Helena. Execute."

Helena didn't answer. Instead, two dunes flanking the path of the crawlers flattened out as the Titan Mechs hidden inside them stood. Sand cascaded down those monstrous forms as they turned toward the airships.

Each raised an arm, twisting one of Jacob's modified traps mounted to their framework. Flashes of light illuminated the recesses of the launchers. The burners had been lit. She knew what came next, and as much as she didn't want to see it, she watched it unfold. It was her order that had triggered this.

A volley of four javelins fired from each Titan Mech. Three found purchase in the airships.

"Fifteen degrees up," Theo said into the transmitter.

The Titan Mechs adjusted their angle of attack and fired again. This time, seven javelins found homes in the hull, the gas chambers, and the cabin.

"Again!" Helena's shout came back across the speaker.

As the third volley hit, the first group detonated, triggering the rest in a cascade of flames. Fireballs erupted from the ships, burning so hot the support lines crumbled in under a minute. The entire gas chamber separated from the eastern transport, while the cabin and everyone inside it fell into an inferno.

The second tried to limp away, but the last volley of firebombs caught the deck in its arc. Whatever had been on board had been far more volatile on the second ship. An explosion ripped the hull to splinters, slicing up through the gas chamber so its futile retreat turned into a sudden crash onto the sands.

It would have been smart of the armored crawlers to run at that point, but they'd apparently not been watching the carnage behind them. Instead of fleeing, they charged forward. Gladys couldn't turn away as they reached the riverbed and saw what waited within.

Some tried to stop. Some tried to drive through the clusters of Tail Swords. None of the crawlers broke the perimeter. Flashes of black chitin met the incoming crawlers. Swords struck forward, impaling the engines and releasing great gouts of steam. Claws sheared through the armor plates of the crawlers, the power of the Tail Swords unmatched by thin metal.

"Round them up," Theo said. "*If* there are any survivors, I'd like to speak to them."

"Understood."

Gladys turned away from the carnage in the riverbed. The impact of the collision with the Tail Swords triggered a frenzy. If any escaped the wrath of those creatures, it would be few.

The door behind Gladys shuddered, and her sense of horror at what she'd just witnessed shifted. Theo had been right. Mordair and the warlords sacrificed many for one chance to reach her in the watchtower. But how had they known she was there? She almost snarled as the answer came to her. They had spies in Midstream. And not just Archibald's spies.

She lifted a pair of throwing knives from her vest.

Moments later, the hatch in the flood creaked open. Rikken's strike was like that of a Tail Sword. Swift, inescapable, and deadly. She heard the choked cries behind the wood as Rikken stepped forward, glancing through the hatch.

"Two more," he said as a bolt sailed up through the opening, narrowly missing his head.

Gladys slammed the lock open in the door and sprinted down the stairs, barely registering George's muttered curse. If he'd been standing by the door, he could have stopped her, but he wasn't.

She took the stairs two at a time, and her boots crashed into the landing. Rikken was right. Two more attackers stood on the third floor of the watchtower. But now *she* blocked their exit.

"Put down your weapons, and you can live."

The first started to pivot their bolt thrower from the hatch to Gladys, but the second grabbed their arm.

"No. It's done." She struggled to hold the other's arm down. "You saw what happened to those airships."

"I did!" the first shouted. "I saw what these monsters did to them! Just like Rana said."

Gladys narrowed her eyes. "Rana is dead. Rana has *been* dead for quite some time now."

"You lie!" The first tried to pull away, and as he did, Gladys realized he wasn't much older than her. He was a child, but life hadn't let him remain one.

The older woman with him forced his arms into the air so he could fire at nothing but the ceiling. Gladys took her chance. She hurled two throwing knives at the boy. Or more particularly, just above the boy's hands. The first cracked the wood on his bolt thrower, but the second cut the string.

It lashed out wildly, cutting the side of his face like a whip before he dropped the weapons.

"She cut me!" His shout was filled with as much disbelief as anger.

George had caught up at that point, and Gladys could see Rikken's spear in the hatchway.

"Rikken, stop!" Gladys's voice carried, rife with authority she didn't always feel. But Rikken held. He didn't relax, but he didn't strike.

"George," Theo called. "I would appreciate a hand down the stairs."

George scowled at Gladys and then made his way up, grabbing Theo's wheelchair and clipping it into a guide rail in the wall. Once that was set, it was an easy thing to slide her down to the next floor.

"Stand down, all of you." Theo patted Gladys's arm as she rolled past. "Now, who are you? Obviously not Rana's people, because those fools all know he's dead."

The woman almost deflated, running fingers through her dark hair as she tossed her bolt thrower away. It clattered across the floor as she sagged against a dark brown chair. "We're from Fel. From … things aren't good there. We've had a lot of hunger and the river's been poisoned. Many of us fled after that."

Theo raised an eyebrow. "The river's been … what kind of damned nonsense is that? No one can poison a bloody river, girl. It would wash away in short order."

"But he told us."

"*Who?*" Gladys said, unable to keep a growl from her voice.

"He said he was Rana. He had the flag, and the tattoo."

Theo cocked her head to the side. "What tattoo?"

"The metal flames."

Gladys felt sick. "That wasn't Rana. That was one of the Children of the Dark Fire."

"No." She shook her head and took a step back. "No, that can't be. He led us out to the forest. Showed us where you killed everyone by the Red Woods."

"Mordair did that," George said. "You have fallen for a lie, miss." He clicked the transmitter in his collar. "Helena, imprison any survivors. They have been manipulated by the Children of the Dark Fire." He turned his attention back to the woman. "Archibald has been sending food to Fel. The city has been cleaned up. The bodies cleared from the walls."

Horror spread over the woman's face.

Rikken dropped through the hatch, landing with his spear held across his chest. "Princess, I would request you restrain them if you wish to speak to them more."

Gladys nodded, and neither of the surviving attackers resisted. "Who was that man?"

The woman glanced at the body on the floor. "My brother-in-law. He … he introduced us to … to the man who wasn't Rana."

George cursed under his breath. "We need to go back to Fel, Gladys. If more of that cult remains, they must be countered."

Gladys nodded, but kept her focus on her attackers while Rikken bound their wrists. It left the boy's face to bleed, and Gladys cringed at the wound. "Get them medical attention before taking them to prison. Let them rest, have some food, and we can decide what is to be done with them."

"She means to poison us," the boy growled.

"Rana would have killed them," Theo said, ignoring the accusation. "As would Mordair."

Gladys studied her prisoners for a moment before she responded. "Then I suppose it is good I am neither of those men."

CHAPTER THIRTEEN

ALICE LAUGHED WHEN Eva almost snapped at the transmitter. "This ship is the absolute worst."

Hearing Lady Katherine's chuckle in response was oddly disarming. "I am quite certain you did not contact me to complain about the ship."

"No," Eva grumbled as the engines rattled and a small burst of black smoke emanated from the port side. "Alice, Furi, and William got the alliance for you. Jakon may have had something to do with it, but he was gone by the time this flying garbage can got me there."

"Eva," Kat said. "You're telling me we have a new dock?"

"Well, a new place to deploy to." Eva nodded to herself. "They don't have any airship docks to speak of. You'll need to anchor and deploy via lines or supply ships. Ships that can land on the ground will be welcome too."

"None of those are an issue. Is everyone with you now?"

"Alice, Furi, and William are."

"Good. Well done to the three of you. What are your intentions now?"

"Get back to the docks," Alice said. "We need to make sure our allies are ready now that we know Midstream is safe."

"Theo has always been formidable. She is one of my best tinkers, and Belldorn would not be the same without her. As to your plan, that is good. I can think of no better option. Prepare that city for what is to come. And perhaps I will see you in Karn."

"The transports?" Eva asked.

"Well tested. There are some final details to be seen to, but we will be on our way soon enough. Our allies are gathering now."

"I'm here if you need anything, Kat. You can find me on the docks until I can rendezvous with the nearest transport."

"I will keep you apprised of our status. Your ship … your *proper* ship, will be waiting for you. Until then." Lady Katherine disconnected with a small hiss of static.

"This is happening." William's voice was quiet, as if he were merely speaking his thoughts aloud. "There's going to be a battle in Ballern."

Furi reached out and squeezed William's arm. "There is. Is there anything you want to hide? To keep safe if anything happens to the store?"

William rubbed his forehead before nodding. "Definitely. I'll keep the shop closed tomorrow and move out the most valuable items. And, of course, anything from the old presses that has to do with the Children of the Dark Fire and the things they've changed."

Eva glanced back at William. "Don't close the shop. Don't do anything to raise suspicions. It could be dangerous for you and for all of our friends."

"It's only been closed one day off my regular schedule so far." He bit his lip. "I can't very well move crates of books out without people taking notice."

"You can if we help," Furi said. "Let us talk to Kura. We can get her all the information she needs. She'll understand how important your collection is. Alice and I can come back at night to help you move things out."

William rubbed his chin and glanced between the pair. "It *is* common for deliveries to go out at night. It could work."

Alice adjusted her seat on the hard metal chair. She rather missed

The Ray's plush chairs in the moment, but she had more important things to consider than her comfort. "If you can get the books to Belldorn, they would be well protected. The Crown Library is quite a fortress in itself."

William sat up a little straighter. "Would they let me? I mean, let me visit something like that?"

"William," Eva said. "They would let you visit that library even if you weren't bringing them crates of priceless books."

He hesitated. "There's so much we don't know." William's voice trailed off. "It's so hard to learn something new about a place when generations have been taught something else. The damage the Children of the Dark Fire have done, trying to teach people what really happened in the Deadlands War ... what happened *before* the Deadlands War. I can't believe Belldorn could be so generous with that much knowledge."

Eva pushed two levers forward before dragging a third through a series of hard stops, each denoting gears for different functions in the old airship. "Don't mistake my words, William. Belldorn has its share of issues. They just aren't as bad as you've been led to believe."

William inclined his head. "Any help you can offer will be most appreciated.

"We know a few smugglers too," Alice said. "They're especially good at transporting goods you don't want anyone to find."

"That could be the perfect option for the more sensitive titles and manuscripts."

"Eva, could you take care of that?" Alice asked.

Eva sat up straighter. "What, me? I don't want to talk to him about that. Do you know how much trouble he's caused Mary over the years?"

"Or we could just ask Mary. I'm sure she'll be close enough once the carriers have deployed. Especially if Kat's onboard."

"Never mind," Eva muttered. "I'll talk to Jakon. Have everything ready by five in the morning, William. Jakon likes things dark."

Furi leaned forward on her jump seat. "Be sure to tell him I'll be there, too. He doesn't know William that well."

"He's sold me a few things in the past." William's lips quirked up in a small smile. "Granted, I had my suspicions when everything he offered had no provenance, but that's a risk you take with walk-ins."

The docks grew larger in the windscreen as they reached the border of the Gray Woods. Airships choked the skies in a flurry of activity. Some of Fel's warships drifted to the north while others came in to dock and likely refuel.

A frightening thought flickered through Alice's mind. The fight wouldn't just be on the ground in Ballern. They were going to be fighting from the bays all the way out to the Bones, too.

✧   ✧   ✧

FURI WATCHED WILLIAM leave after Eva secured their airship on one of the lower docks. The shopkeeper muttered to himself until he was well out of earshot. Furi suspected he'd have every title he wanted to save mentally cataloged by the time he made the short walk back to the store.

As crowded as the skies were, Furi expected the line for the lift to be dreadful. Instead, they found almost no wait, quickly hopping onto the second lift to pass their way. No one spoke as they rode up three floors with a pair of Fel soldiers.

One of them was in uniform, and while Furi couldn't be entirely sure the second was a soldier, she carried herself like one. Her posture was a little too good, her clothes too sharp. And if Furi was being honest, she didn't look like someone from Ballern.

The doors to the lift squeaked as they exited into the warehouse district. The soldiers continued on, talking about the weather, of all things. Furi led the way to the southernmost walkway of the docks, passing some of the fancier restaurants mounted to the framework around them before entering what amounted to an alleyway full of small bars and patrons who had no desire to be recognized.

One thing the Skyborn had always liked was their privacy. There wasn't much worse in the world than a nosy neighbor. Or at least there hadn't been until Fel had shown up.

Furi caught snippets of a conversation as they passed a small bar with a brightly polished countertop. She slowed her pace to listen a bit longer.

"All I know is those girls have been missing two days now."

"For what? Flying a Stormborn flag? Ridiculous. Even if we don't like them, doesn't mean someone else can't support them."

"Unless it was the Steward who made them disappear …"

The last came as little more than a whisper, but it was enough. Furi knew that barkeep. She knew how loyal he was to the crown. For him to so much as speak one negative thing about what the nobles had done, or had even endorsed, was quite a rare thing.

There weren't any more small shops as they crossed onto the Bones themselves. Instead, a few tiny tents peppered the walkways until even those vanished, and Furi turned left, taking them past a section of rusted railing where few cared to walk.

She heard Alice's sigh of relief when they returned to the plated walkways. Metal that masked the grates beneath, and hid the sheer distance to the city below.

"Furi," Eva said.

Furi slowed, glancing back. "What is it?"

"Do you really intend to help William?"

"Yes. He has some of Lady Katherine's books now, and she's going to want them back."

Eva nodded. "Be careful, please. Where will you stay tonight?"

"Not on your ship," Alice muttered.

Eva chuckled at that. "Plan on The Ray, then. I'll speak with Jakon and make the plans. If you don't hear from me, plan on finding him on the lower docks."

"We won't need to do that," Furi said. "We can stay with William until Jakon is ready for pickup. *Then* we can sleep. Besides, if we really need a place, Alice can stay with me on the docks."

"Probably best to have options." Eva nodded.

Furi increased her pace, stepping deeper into the warehouse district until they came to the school. She pushed open the door, surprised to hear so many voices inside. The voices weren't raised or angry. Regardless, it made her anxious, even tense, not knowing who might be waiting there.

But it wasn't an ambush or an enemy inside that classroom. It was Kura and a dozen Skyborn she'd grown up around. Some of them were old now, and some were only her age, but she knew them from the docks and markets, and a handful had even been friends with her grandparents.

Kura looked up when Eva let the door slam a little too hard. "Furi, Alice, Eva, come here, come here. Please." Furi had known Kura almost her entire life. And one thing her teacher wasn't good at was hiding her emotions from her students.

"What's wrong?" Furi stepped around the gathered people until she was beside Kura. Alice and Eva waited closer to the back of the seats.

"Everything is wrong, Furi. More kids have gone missing."

"I heard a barkeep talking about that. For waving a Stormborn flag or some such thing?"

Kura crossed her arms and clenched her fists. "That was someone else, Furi. Those women were at least adults. We have missing *children*."

"Mordair took them!" an older man snapped. "Sure as you're standing here in front of us, we saw those Fel soldiers take them. We all just watched like fools, like we didn't know what to do."

"Take them where?" Furi asked.

"We don't know. Onto one of the warships, and then they left. We've no idea where they went."

"Alice?" Furi said. "Do you have any idea?"

Alice shook her head. "I don't. I'm sorry. All I know is when people went missing in Fel, they were already dead."

A low roar sounded from outside the classroom. Like a cheer at some great gathering, but it was darker, angrier.

"We can't fight them," a young man said, placing his head on a desk.

"That's all we *can* do," Alice whispered from the back.

The door crashed open behind them. "They … we know where the missing Stormborn are." Jakon's voice was strained as he heaved for breath. "Gods, Kura, they hung them from the docks."

Furi's heart stuttered in her chest as she pushed her way to the door.

Jakon grabbed her arm. "You don't need to see it."

"Where are they?"

His grip tightened for a moment before he let go. "By the warships. Where they hung the flags."

Furi ran out the door, and the screams of the Skyborn grew immediately, unshielded by the walls of the classroom. She didn't need to ask Jakon where the bodies were. She knew that now.

Every face on the docks stared at them. Looking toward the blood-soaked dresses of two young women with gaping wounds where their throats should have been. The screams threatened to break her. The cries of their families, so much more violent in their raw grief and rage.

Furi's fingers strangled the cold metal railing. Skyborn moved to grab the bodies and Fel soldiers beat them to the ground. More moved against them, but the soldiers were ready. It didn't look real. So close. So horrible. This was her *home*.

"Jacob saw this in Dauschen," Alice said, her voice so calm Furi rocked away from her. "I saw it in Fel. Mordair's going to start the real killing soon. These will not be the last, Furi."

"I'll kill them," Furi snarled.

"Kid, no," Jakon said, holding his hands up. "This isn't the time."

"Not the *time!*" Furi jabbed her finger toward the bodies. "Look at them! They're dead. They're as dead as Beck and almost every last one of my friends from the Nightingale. This stops now, Jakon. You fight with us, or you run. But you get the hell out of my way."

She shouldered past him, her boots crashing on steel as the echoes of a brawl broke out across the docks. "You always called this city a powder keg, Jakon. Mordair just lit the fuse."

Jakon cursed under his breath. "I'm with you."

✦ ✦ ✦

FURI PAUSED WHEN she threw open the door to the school. More people had joined Kura in the short time Furi had paced around the warehouse district, reminding herself Jakon was right even if she didn't want him to be. She found people who had spoken against the Stormborn, and others who had spoken in support of them.

"Furi," Kura said, gesturing to her. "Come, please, tell our friends what you saw in Belldorn. What you saw outside the Red Woods."

Furi didn't let her frayed nerves stop her. She stepped up beside Kura, clenching her fists as she turned to the gathered crowd, meeting one gaze after another. "I saw the fate of the Skyborn. I saw what happened to those who let Mordair and those like him stay in power. Those women hanging from the docks saw it, too. And it will be your children. Your parents. Your grandparents. Every dissenter will join them on those ropes if Mordair isn't stopped.

"That bastard may have bought the loyalty of a few, but the Skyborn are loyal to themselves. And I tell you now, our best hope is the Stormborn. Our allies are coming. Stand with us, or get out of the city. War will be in Ballern, and if you aren't fighting for our home, you're still going to die for it."

"You can't know that!" one of the dissenters cried out. "You can't ask us to sacrifice our families."

"I can't," Furi said. "But if you don't, you'll all be gone, or living in terror under the fist of a Mordair. Alice can tell you what that was like. She lived under the rule of Newton Victor Burns. How well someone of the old blood must have been treated, or so you would believe."

Furi ground her teeth. "But you all know who Newton was. Brother to Gregory Mordair. Butcher of Gareth Cave. Newton Victor Mordair was his true name. That story has not been wiped from our minds by the Children of the Dark Fire, has it? At least not yet. Give them and Mordair time, and you can try to live in some inane bliss that will only cost you everything you value in this world. Alice."

Furi raised her arm to her friend, and Alice bowed her head. Her words weren't loud, but they landed with the crash of a landslide. It was one thing to hear the rumors of what had happened across the Crystal Sea. It was quite another to hear Alice speak of the crumbling walls, the stampede of invaders swallowing her home and friends, and the ruin of the Lowlands left behind. The death sentence handed down to a boy, a child apprentice of a legendary tinker.

Alice raised her chin, a fire returning to her words as she ended with one last sentence. "You can let Mordair and that cult consume your families, or you can fight."

There were no words of agreement in that place. There was only the cry for battle, an echo of the growing riot outside, and a call to arms for all the Skyborn. For should the day not be lost, the Stormborn must rise.

✧　✧　✧

Patrice stood in the throne room, watching the small, bright fires on the docks far above. Embers sometimes fell, and she knew it would be homes and businesses burning right alongside the relative peace of Ballern's docks.

"This was premature," she said, the barest hint of distaste bleeding into her words.

Footsteps echoed in the room as Mordair joined her at the window. "I think not. The nobles supported the idea of destabilizing the Skyborn. Our sources are not wrong about Belldorn's intentions, Patrice. Ballern must be primed for this encounter."

Patrice turned and studied the hard lines of Mordair's face. She couldn't deny the man could hold a crumbling city together, but Ballern was not that. Ballern had small cracks, small divides. It wasn't like Fel. It was a different world. And the Skyborn far outnumbered the fisherfolk he'd once brought to heel.

"How long should we allow this to continue?"

"An hour at most." Mordair sifted through a small bowl of seeds before plucking one out to eat. "Then we can pull the soldiers back to the warships. Keep a constant guard at every entryway. A show of force on every gangplank, every walkway outside the residential areas. Tear down every flag that isn't from Fel or Ballern. I don't want a hint of the rebellion's flag, or the Skyborn's flags."

Patrice hesitated. "The Skyborn flags *are* from Ballern. This city can't exist without those people."

"It will be different, certainly, but I prefer my cities without parasites, Patrice. Now go. Relay my orders to the captains on the docks." He didn't so much as glance at her, instead watching the fires far above.

"As you wish, Steward." Patrice took her leave.

✧　　✧　　✧

THE RIOTS RAGED for nearly five hours. No one was sure how many died, but Alice knew it would be far more before the week was over. She stepped through a pool of drying blood on her way to the lift, Furi following close behind.

Fel soldiers lined the distant walkways, blocking paths that were normally open to all the Skyborn, but leaving much of the southern docks unguarded. She caught sight of more than one restaurant that had been burned down to its metal bones. It reminded her too much of the Fall. Too much of the destruction she'd seen in the Lowlands, even if it was a much smaller scale.

Alice took a deep breath and tried to focus on their task. Jakon had agreed to help transport whatever rarities William wanted to send to Belldorn. That meant Alice and Furi needed to get to William, and there was no telling how long the current calm would last.

The fire brigade worked to extinguish one of the last fires on the level above them. Embers drifted past, not far from where the bodies had been hung. Alice was relieved to see the dead had been taken down as night approached.

Alice caught a glimpse of soldiers headed their way as they stepped into the lift. She closed the door and Furi slammed the switch to get them moving. Alice didn't miss the shudder that ran through Furi.

"Are you okay?"

Furi shook her head. "No. No, I'm not. Those fires could have burned the docks down, Alice. I've seen worse, but not by far."

"I know, it was bad."

"And those Fel soldiers, blocking the fire brigades until their own ships were safe. It's just … they let people *die*. They didn't just kill them, they let them die in fires and stampedes and chaos." Furi looked up with tears in her eyes. "How could anyone do that to another person?"

Alice's voice was quiet. Barely audible above the rhythmic hum of the lift. "They don't see anyone else as people. We're all just obstacles. Threats."

The lift came to a stop with a rattle of the gate and a reverberation of the cables above them. Alice pulled the door open as Furi wiped her eyes. They hurried across the street side by side, apparently having the same idea of getting off the larger thoroughfares. The alleys were tighter, and more importantly, darker.

They didn't see but one other soul on the way to William's bookstore, the citizens likely taking shelter and most of the guards occupied on the docks. The door didn't budge in Alice's grasp, so she tapped on the window. One light flickered in the back, the only indication someone was still there.

William's shadow appeared a short time later, hurrying forward to unlock the door and usher them inside. "I am so glad to see you two uninjured. What happened on the docks? I've heard so many rumors here. Even the markets closed when the fires started."

"They hung two bodies from the docks," Furi said. "Two women who had been making Stormborn flags."

"So it was true." William ran his fingers through his hair and gestured for them to follow him to the back. "Is Jakon still coming?"

"As far as we know, yes."

"Good, that's good. I can't help but think about what would happen if they reached the store. Everything in here is fuel for the flames."

William led them into his office where the wall of books with the gilded griffins had been before. Nearly all of them were gone, but what caught Alice's attention was that a section of the bookshelf swung back into the wall. William ducked through the opening, and Furi followed.

Alice took another look around the office and then joined them in a space that wasn't meant for three people. The far wall bore a ladder that stretched some nine feet into the air. Boxes and small crates were crammed into that space. Alice noticed several more of the gilded griffins there, but also far more loose paper. Manuscripts, she realized as she picked one up.

"You have another Yan Wu manuscript?" Furi asked when she glanced at what Alice was holding.

"Four, in fact. None as significant as the one you brought me, but there is history there unchanged by the Children of the Dark Fire. Yan may have had a few biases, but nothing so severe as that cult." William gestured to the bottom shelf. "I put four crates on the floor. I'll hand things down to you, and you can arrange them for transport. Then we can move the next set of crates in."

Alice bent down and pulled a crate out, surprised by how deep into the wall it sat. Jacob would have loved it, like a drawer that just kept going. Leather lined the interior, which would both help keep water out and provide some modicum of protection against harsher environments. Not fire, though. Nothing would stop a fire from devouring those books.

William climbed up high enough that he could reach the top shelf. Furi followed close behind, staying just a few rungs off the floor. William slid the first armful of books off in one go, and Alice immediately had a nightmare vision of the books and her friends ending up in a tangled mass on the floor.

But Furi took the books from William without hesitation, and without losing her balance. She pivoted slightly to lower the stack to Alice, and Alice in turn placed them in the crate. By the time she finished sorting the spines into a uniform arrangement, Furi had the next stack.

They continued like that, both pristine leather and crumbling bindings passing through Alice's fingers as she loaded up title after title.

"We should be using gloves for these," Furi said.

William grimaced. "We should, yes, but gloves are slick, and time is short. Whatever minor damage we inflict is worth the price of saving them. Come now, down a rung and we can begin the next crate."

Alice shifted two shorter books to the side and slipped a manuscript scrawled on a square notebook into the gap. No meaningful space remained in the first crate, so she slid the lid on top of it and grunted as she picked it up, waddling through the doorway to get it out of the way.

Furi already had the next batch of books in her arms before Alice pulled out the second crate. Alice hurried to get it ready, and the cycle started again. She thought at the speed they were moving, the room would be cleared in an hour. But the shelves were deceptively tall, and the hours fled deep into the night before the last manuscripts found a home in the last crate.

"Looks like you could use a trundler."

Alice screamed at the voice behind her, spinning, ready to strike at whoever had tried to ambush them. But instead she found Jakon, wearing an infuriating smirk on his face. Alice's desire to strike him didn't lessen in the slightest.

"That was uncalled for, Jakon," Alice muttered.

"I'll take that crate if you like," the smuggler said.

"That would be wonderful. Do something useful with yourself instead of standing there watching us."

Jakon gave Furi an awkward smile at Alice's comment. "I think I hit a nerve."

"We're all on edge." Furi rubbed her hands together. "You saw what happened on the docks, Jakon."

"That's why I'm here. Not much use fighting for a history that's entirely lost, is there?"

William slid around Furi and shuffled past Alice until he could reach a hand out to Jakon. "I appreciate you taking this to Belldorn. More than I can say. Whatever your price is, I pay it gladly."

Jakon eyed the extended hand before shaking it. "William. It may be best if you leave Ballern for the time being."

"I can't abandon my city now." William looked at Furi. "I can't leave my friends and customers to fight this on their own."

Jakon offered a kind smile. "Furi tells me you're the most studied expert in the history of the Children of the Dark Fire."

"That's probably true, but it's more of an unhealthy hobby." He flashed an awkward smile, apparently somewhat taken aback at the praise.

Jakon raised an eyebrow and glanced at the stack of crates. "Sure. Regardless, you're going to be a target. People who have sold you some of these books are not going to be your friends. Some will likely be interrogated, and I'm sure you know where that will leave you. Harboring banned books is more dire a crime than flying the flag of the Stormborn."

William closed his eyes and blew out a breath.

"Can he go with you?" Furi asked. "Can you take him to Belldorn?"

Jakon shook his head. "Not all the way. I can't do much else if I'm across the Crystal Sea. But I can get him to Karn. From there, one of the supply ships can take him to the carrier and on to Belldorn."

"Go," Furi said, and the pleading in her voice hurt Alice's chest. "You should be at the Crown Library. You should see it." She gestured to the crates on the floor. "You can contribute to it. They control access and the humidity for their rarest books. They'll be safer there than anywhere you could keep them in Ballern."

William pinched the bridge of his nose before crossing his arms. He didn't speak for a time until he slowly raised his gaze to meet Furi's. "I can't let the past burn with our city. There might be more I can help with from Karn while I'm there. I'll go with Jakon."

Alice felt far more relief at William's words than she'd expected to. She could only imagine how Furi must have felt. Judging by the way she crushed William in a hug, she was rather happy with the outcome.

CHAPTER FOURTEEN

J ACOB STOOD AT the controls to a Titan Mech as the rain started to fall in earnest. It made the loading ramps slicker than he'd expected, and another pilot had already dropped a load of barrels into the mud. After that, Jacob took over.

At first, he'd done it so he could show the other pilots how to angle the feet of the Titan Mech, creating as much friction as possible on the slick surfaces. But when he realized how exhausted the others were, he decided to take over the controls himself. It would at least buy them a short time to rest.

Smith joined him from across the carrier, taking on another Mech as they started loading the center holds and stacking several warehouses' worth of supplies. They had enough food to feed the army of people who would be living on the carrier for the two-day journey and the battle to come. The workshops' exteriors had been finished with tall blast shields, set up around those designed for explosives work.

But closer to him, relatively speaking, at least, were the landing zones for the supply ships and transports. Most came and went, but others, those that would be making the journey across the Crystal Sea with them, remained in place, creating a maze like the alleys of a small city.

Smaller transports and crawlers roamed the deck, hauling fuel and supplies to each designated storehouse. The transmitter crackled on his console.

"Jacob, ramp's down on the southwest corner."

Jacob rolled his eyes and hit the button to respond to Smith. "On my way. I'm going to anchor it. If Frederick wants to yell at me later for punching holes in his deck, that's fine, but this is slowing us down."

It was the third time a ramp had slipped in the mud. It was an utterly ridiculous waste of time, constantly coming back to reposition it so it *probably* wouldn't fall. But of course, the ramps still fell.

They'd already retrofitted bolt cannons onto the Titan Mechs. Jacob waited for the next pair of crawlers to mount the ramp beside him. Once they were on the deck, he threw the wrist switch to the right, spinning the hand of his Mech 180 degrees.

"Frederick agrees," Smith said through a burst of static.

Jacob frowned and clicked the transmitter. "Did you just ask him? You did, didn't you?"

"It is best to keep him informed, Jacob. I know it has been a long day, and a trying one at that, but Frederick needs to know of any changes to the carrier."

Jacob knew Smith was right, but it still irritated him that Smith would ask permission for a single bolt in the loading ramps. He took a deep breath and tamped down his annoyance. Jacob knew he didn't always know best, but there were some things so obvious it was infuriating when they were ignored.

After securing the Titan Mech against the carrier, he slowly shifted the levers for the hips. Once the angle was right, he used the smaller lever to make minute adjustments to the position of the arm, getting it as close to center as he could before clicking the button for the bolt cannon.

The crack of the anchoring bolt through metal echoed around him, even through the thick glass canopy of the Titan Mech. Jacob shifted the arm to the side and nodded. The bolt was nearly flat against the ramp. Nothing should get caught on it, and the long slab of metal shouldn't slip into the mud again.

That done, he righted the Titan Mech and made for the next ramp. That one would be trickier, he knew, as the entire surface would be covered in mud because they hadn't anchored them in the first place, thinking the weight would be enough to hold them steady. Jacob sighed and eased the levers for the Mech's legs back and forth, passing three more construction crews along the ramp as they finished the barracks and mess halls.

Soon it would be time to make the journey to Ballern. Soon, there would be far more dangerous things to worry about than angering Frederick over a single bolt.

✧   ✧   ✧

ONE OF THE things Frederick *had* done that Jacob was quite impressed with was set up a network of speakers not unlike those Ancora used at Festival. When announcements came that the entire carrier needed to hear, they were nearly impossible to ignore.

"Clear Bay 9. Supply ships incoming from Canopy. Gather the spider-mount feed and be ready."

Jacob looked up into the rain. The clouds had broken in the far west, and the sun turned the droplets into fiery jewels. Descending from the shadow of the storm clouds were two massive supply ships, far outweighing any of the smaller vessels currently docked on the carrier.

He clicked the transmitter. "Smith, that has to be Samuel. None of these ramps have fallen since we anchored them, and the last of the walls is up on this end of the carrier. I'm going to take a break and find him."

"Go. We all need a break. I will ask Frederick to send out those pilots who have had a chance to rest."

Jacob didn't wait to hear more. He popped the canopy as soon as the Titan Mech was fully crouched, leaving the glass partially closed to act as a very heavy umbrella. He slid out the side into the rain, taking it slow on the slippery steps of the Titan Mech's leg.

Once he hit the mud, he frowned at the steps. They needed to add texture to them. He hadn't considered that in the build. Neither had Charles, for that matter. Of course, they'd been designed for the desert, and the desert saw far less rain than the coasts.

Jacob turned away from the Mech and followed a small crawler up the carrier, hurrying to hop on the luggage rack in the rear. "Are you going anywhere near Bay 9?"

The driver looked back, raising his goggles. "Jacob! Good to see you, lad. I'm going to Bay 7, so it'll be a quick walk to Bay 9."

"Good to see you, too. I thought you'd be in Bollwerk." Jacob grinned at the driver, Walter Jones, as the rain and wind caught his hair and they headed toward the nearest throughway.

Jones nodded. "I was. Even picked up that princess friend of yours. Things have been hectic in the desert, lad."

"So I've heard. Have you talked to Archibald?"

"Briefly. I was graced by His Majesty's presence for half of lunch yesterday."

Jacob laughed at that. "Are you flying out to Ballern with us?"

"Partway, yes. I'll be on the supply ships running back and forth to Belldorn. Apparently, we have a place to disembark that's not on Mordair's doorstep, so I hope that helps us prepare."

It was a sobering thought. On one hand, it didn't much matter where they disembarked, because the destination would be the same. A battle at Ballern.

They bantered a bit more as the crawler passed one of two hospitals set up on deck. *Hospital is a loose word*, Jacob thought, *considering the front of the narrow structure is open to the elements outside of a thin tarp.* But that's how most of the structures were on the carrier. The simple construction served two purposes. They could be built at speed, and they were remarkably light.

Airships that had appeared so small from the cockpit of the Titan Mech loomed up around them. Long supply ships and a dozen brigs lined the higher-numbered bays. Jones turned just past one of the new ships from Bollwerk as it settled onto the deck, slowing as he reached the walkway between the bays.

"I think this is your stop, Jacob."

"Thank you! I'll see you in the skies."

With that, Jacob hopped off the back of the crawler and hurried toward the supply ship that was tethered to the deck. He didn't know why he was hurrying, exactly, as he couldn't get any more soaked than he already was.

◊ ◊ ◊

"Easy, girl. Easy!" Samuel tried to calm the Stalker in the stall beside Bessie, but the mount was entirely done with being cooped up. And the problem with that was that once one spider started getting impatient, almost every other mount insisted on moving too.

The bolt to the stall slid open, and some absolute madman stepped inside with the rapidly stomping legs of a creature large enough to break bones, or worse.

"Easy." Drakkar's deep voice rose above the frantic drumming of legs all around.

"Drakkar!" Samuel barked. "Get out of there. It's not safe!"

But the Cave Guardian kept moving forward until the Stalker's rear legs thumped into the back wall, and it had nowhere else to go. Only then did Drakkar stop and pull a large black carapace out from under his cloak. Samuel recognized it immediately. An adolescent Water Beetle.

Drakkar moved slowly with the beetle outstretched in one hand and his empty palm hovering above it.

The Stalker shifted slightly from one side to the other, studying Drakkar and his peace offering. The Cave Guardian lowered the Water Beetle so the Stalker could easily snatch it from him, or easily take his arm off. Or at least, that was what Samuel was thinking.

But the mount gently plucked the beetle away and started eating it while Drakkar patted the Stalker between its eyes. The Cave Guardian looked up at Samuel, and as impressed as the Spider Knight was, he was a little annoyed at Drakkar's smirk.

"I'm glad you're not dead," Samuel muttered. He climbed down from the side of the stall where Bessie had retreated and made his way into the hall. Few of the other spiders had stirred since Drakkar calmed the Stalker.

Samuel wasn't sure what hit him, only that he'd been walking forward one moment, looking over his shoulder, and the next something, no, some*one* had plowed into him, flattening him against the wall. "Jacob! What are you … how did you?"

Jacob grinned at him. "I heard the supply ships were coming in from Canopy, and I heard what bay you were docking in."

Samuel gently pushed him away. "You're soaked!"

"Well, it's raining." He gestured to the rear of the ship.

Drakkar laughed as he stepped into the corridor and offered Jacob his fist. Jacob wrapped his fingers around it in the greeting of the Steamsworn. "It is good to see you, Jacob."

"You too, Drakkar." Jacob pulled the Cave Guardian into a hug before stepping away and glancing at the pair. "Where is everyone else?"

"Upper decks, mostly," Samuel said. "The spiders travel better if there aren't too many people in close proximity." He pointed toward the bow. "It was Nora's idea to use the seating area for more storage here in the stables. It worked out alright, but I think everyone up top is ready to get out of the ship for a while. It's a bit cramped."

Jacob combed his wet hair back with his fingers. "Not a long while. We'll be leaving for Ballern soon enough."

"At least we will have the deck of the carrier to move around on." Drakkar adjusted his cloak before reaching for the staff leaning against the stall. "These cargo ships were not built for the comfort of so many people."

"How many joined you? Did Nora come?"

Samuel shook his head. "She stayed behind in Ancora. She'll be working with the Cave Guardians to keep the city safe. Not to mention a couple volunteers I think you know."

"Who?"

"Reggie and Bobby. As many run-ins as I had with those two on my patrols, I never dreamed they'd end up volunteering for the guard."

"Right," Jacob said, his voice trailing off. "I mean, at least they weren't pickpockets or anything."

Drakkar flashed a grin at Jacob, but the joke appeared to pass Samuel by. "Targrove was with us for a time in Canopy. He's likely back in Midstream by now, but I believe he may be joining us in Ballern. Time will tell, I suppose."

Samuel blinked. "Do you actually like him now? You don't exactly sound worried about the idea."

Drakkar shrugged. "It is … complicated."

"Everything's complicated these days," Samuel muttered. He yawned and stretched, watching a line of riders walking past the rear loading ramp. "They must have dropped ropes."

Jacob followed his gaze. "No, there are ramp stairs closer to the bays for the supply ships. Some of them are pretty tall, so they're probably using those."

Samuel smiled. It was hard to reconcile who Jacob was now with the kid he'd known. Sometimes that younger mind peeked through, but more often, Jacob showed confidence and an instinct to help. Samuel only hoped that would be enough for Jacob to come through the war intact. He laughed to himself when he realized that meant mentally, because Jacob had already managed to lose a leg.

"What?" Jacob asked, narrowing his eyes.

"Nothing, nothing. Just thinking about your leg."

If the word *suspicious* could be defined by a single look, it would have been Jacob's face at that moment. Samuel threw an arm around Jacob and led the way into the rain.

✧ ✧ ✧

"No." Mary crossed her arms and stared at Kat, who now stood in the cabin of the Skysworn with no escort, no guard, and apparently, no sense.

"No one will search for me here, Mary." She said it with an infuriating calm. "I will travel with you, in the Skysworn, until we reach Karn. Once there, my guard and their own guard can blend our patrols."

"We don't *know* the people from Karn, Kat. If one of them wants to kill you, you'll be making it far too easy."

Kat splayed her fingers, then quickly pulled down her middle and index finger. A mechanism in her wrist clicked and the barrels of a bolt launcher sprang from the roughly woven cuff of her shirt. "Frederick has armed me with enough gadgetry and concealed armor to see to that. We've fought together before, Mary. I wasn't always a monarch."

Mary almost growled at her. "That was ten years ago. You're out of practice."

"If it's that much of an issue for you, I will contact Eva to do your job for you."

"Sometimes I hate you," Mary muttered. "Fine. Stay with us on the Skysworn. But after Karn, you shouldn't stay with us. You absolutely do not need to be on the front lines in Ballern. I have no idea how bad this is going to get, and we need to be ready for the worst."

Kat inclined her head. "I accept your terms."

Mary pinched the bridge of her nose and kept muttering to herself as she made her way belowdecks and hauled another barrel of ammunition for the chainguns deeper into the hold. She'd let Smith place it where he liked once he got back to the ship, but for now, it was out of the way.

A loud scrape echoed behind her, and she smiled when she saw Kat, the Lady of Belldorn, grunting and dragging another barrel into the hold.

Mary leaned back as an old memory crossed her mind. "Do you remember that time we rolled down the mountainside in a barrel?"

Kat barked out a laugh and rocked the barrel onto its side, rolling it across the floor with ease. "I don't think I could survive that at my age."

"I know I couldn't." Mary grinned at her as she helped Kat stand the barrel back up. "Just … try not to climb into any barrels while you're in Karn, okay?"

Kat eyed Mary for a moment. They'd known each long enough that Kat would understand Mary wasn't talking about an actual barrel. After they'd dropped one into a flooded mountain stream and climbed inside, there wasn't any more control. They were at the mercy of the violent drops and sluices that made their way down the mountain. As kids, they had thought the barrel would be enough protection. Luck had kept them alive.

"I'll be careful, Mary." Kat leaned over the barrel and hung her head, only for a second. "I can't leave my people in a time of so much turmoil."

"Good." It was all Mary said before turning away and moving a crate around aimlessly. Kat didn't need to see her face. She didn't need to see how worried she was about her friend, and the tears in the corners of Mary's eyes would have betrayed her in an instant.

CHAPTER FIFTEEN

J ACOB NEVER IMAGINED what an event the launch of the carrier would
be. During loading, he had thought it looked as though half the city
had joined them for the journey across the Crystal Sea. But when it came
time to launch, he understood how wrong he was.

When he was younger, he had thought Festival was the most people
that could possibly be fit into one space. But the streets and fields
surrounding the carrier dock were choked with people. So much so, they
had to wait to pivot the final ramp up onto the deck until some of the
crew could clear the ground around the Titan Mech.

It was as if fifty Festivals were taking place at once, but the stage
would be flying away at this celebration. He wished Alice were there to
see it. He wished Alice were there to *talk* to. It had been two days since
he'd last heard from her, and he didn't want to think about how long it
had been since he'd seen her. Word had come through Mary from Jakon
that Alice was helping smuggle important manuscripts out of Ballern.
That certainly sounded like Alice.

But everything else was left vague, as if they were worried about being overheard. There weren't any real details. He'd heard rumors of
violent protests in Ballern, but no one seemed to know more than that,
and if they did, they were keeping it quiet. Jacob supposed he could
understand that to a degree.

Choosing the right time to deliver information to allies could be
almost as important as the information itself. Archibald had gone into

great detail on that belief in his writings in *The Dead Scourge*. Jacob wondered if the Speaker of Bollwerk still believed that. He laughed to himself. Of course Archibald did. The man was a walking bag of secrets. Though he was curious how many of Archibald's secrets Frederick knew.

"Jacob, how are you?" The voice was old yet commanding, and it took Jacob a moment to place it.

"Targrove!" Jacob turned to find the old tinker standing beside him at the railing near the carrier's edge. "What are you doing here?"

"Going to Ballern, of course. Well, more precisely, Karn. Once I heard we had a new alliance with that ancient city, I couldn't stay away."

The turbines in the deck whined, and Jacob leaned on the railing. He glanced down the entire stretch of the aft deck, and other than a few crew, no one else stood along the safety lines.

"Aren't you worried about standing so close to the edge?" Jacob asked.

Targrove laughed. "I know almost every tinker who directed this build, Jacob. I have a great deal of faith that we will be fine. At least for the launch. As to whether or not we'll make it across the Crystal Sea? That remains to be seen." It was a fair point, but Targrove didn't sound worried about it.

Jacob turned back to the view around them. "Do you think Kat organized all of this?" He gestured to the gathered crowds and banners as two long lines of streamers flew from two of the towers.

"The fanfare? I suspect so. It is good to keep the morale of the city up. War is hard on everyone, lad. This war is no different."

"Jacob!" He turned toward the voice, finding Smith standing on top of the stairs to control tower A. "Are you joining us?"

"You should go," Targrove said. "This is a momentous thing."

Jacob smiled at the old tinker.

"Meet me in the workshop when we're airborne." Targrove returned his smile. "I'd like to take a closer look at those exoskeletons you've been working on."

"Definitely! I could use some help."

Targrove nodded as Jacob hurried over to the stairs, taking them two at a time for the first few stories before his lungs told him he should slow down. His breathing was heavy by the time he reached Smith, and his knee certainly let him know he'd been climbing stairs.

"Don't die on me now." Smith patted his back and led him into the pilot house.

He could still see the crowds lining the streets of Belldorn, but the thunder of their cheers and the whine of turbines were muted in the pilot house. Frederick stood at the helm, and Jacob was surprised to see him there. He had assumed Frederick would be in the control tower at the bow, instead of the aft, leaving tower A to the pilot.

Mary stood on the far side of the pilot house with Lady Katherine. They both offered him a nod as he stepped up beside Frederick.

The older tinker took a deep breath and glanced at Jacob. "I suppose now is the time we find out how right we were."

"Did I ever tell you about testing the glider packs?" Jacob smiled at Frederick. "Charles had me jump off a roof. This seems a little more planned."

Frederick laughed and clapped Jacob on the back. "He always was a little brash when it came to practical testing. If he could see you now, Jacob." Frederick smiled and stepped away, gesturing to the levers for the turbines. "Take us up."

Jacob shivered at the idea. That Frederick would let him take the controls for the maiden voyage of the carrier. The bronze alloy felt cool in his grasp. He clicked the transmitter to speak with the second control tower. "Raise turbines to half on a count of ten."

"Understood," came the crackling reply of the pilot.

Jacob counted down from ten, Frederick watching his every move, and at each number Jacob edged the throttles a little higher, the whine of the turbines joined by a roar of air. An unending gust sent grass and small plants flying from beneath the carrier, enough air to push every streamer and banner back into the city streets as the carrier squealed and rose from its low dock.

It wasn't like a launch in an airship. It wasn't even like a launch with a far-less burdened carrier. The rise felt smooth, with no rattle or stressed metal to be heard. Jacob kept his eye on the levels, making sure the carrier held at no more than five degrees. Anything above ten degrees could risk a failure where the two halves joined.

"Pressure is good," Smith called from the panel on the opposite side of the pilot house. "Mary, radio the Porcupines. We will be ready to dock with them in five minutes."

Jacob stepped back, watching as the towers of Belldorn grew shorter, and then vanished below the line of the deck. "Frederick, you want to take care of docking with the Porcupines. I … haven't practiced that part."

Frederick grinned and stepped forward. "Of course."

Jacob made his way to the rear windows. He could just see the nose of one of the Porcupines as it moved to the west. The docks for those monstrous warships were constructed on booms to the port and starboard sides of the carrier. Jacob thought he'd watch the docking sequence, and then head to the workshop to talk to Targrove.

He hesitated and then made his way over to Mary and Lady Katherine. "Mary, have you heard anything else from Alice?"

Mary offered a small smile before nodding. "She helped Furi and William get several crates of books out of Ballern with Jakon last I heard. I don't know much else than that."

Jacob glanced at Lady Katherine. She didn't appear to be listening to anyone, instead staring out the side window as the first Porcupine approached its docking point.

"She's with Kura, too," Jacob said. "Her and Furi know the docks better than anyone."

"We'll see her soon. If you want to use the transmitter on the Skysworn tonight, come by any time. You know how to get to it."

"Thanks, Mary." Jacob paused. "And, umm, Lady Katherine?"

She turned and studied Jacob. "Yes?" There was a slight quiver in her voice, and it was only then that Jacob realized Lady Katherine was remarkably uncomfortable on the carrier.

"I just wanted to say thank you. For listening to us. For letting us help. I don't want to see what happened to Ancora happen anywhere else."

Lady Katherine smiled, her voice evening out as she apparently found some comfort in the distraction of a simple conversation. "Jacob, that is a lovely thought. But I don't know if we'll ever truly achieve it. You're talking about something that comes with every war. Even if we cannot stop it entirely, I suppose we can still mitigate the damage."

"Even if it's a little, it's worth it. Belldorn's losses were bad enough."

"On that, we agree."

Jacob nodded to the Lady of Belldorn before leaning closer to Mary. "Targrove is here, too. I'll be in the workshop with him if anyone needs us."

"Tell Smith. He hasn't stopped talking about that walking armor you've been working on."

"The exoskeleton?" Jacob asked, his voice rising a bit.

Mary leaned back and looked up as though some great burden had been mentioned. "Yes. Please. Take him with you."

Jacob grinned and made his way across the pilot house to Smith. "I'm heading to the workshop with Targrove for a bit. Want to join?"

"Yes, I do. Let's make sure nothing happens with the Porcupine docking clamps, and then head down."

"Perfect."

✧ ✧ ✧

ANOTHER TWENTY MINUTES passed before both Porcupines were anchored. It was a jarring thing, seeing those massive warships attached to the distant sides of the carrier. Jacob knew quite well how large those ships were, but at that distance, they didn't appear much larger than mere supply ships.

He led the way down the stairs, leaving Frederick and company to work the controls for the time being. The workshop waited in the nearest quadrant of the carrier, but that didn't mean it was close. Jacob and Smith wandered past four brigs, several crew standing on the bridge between the gas chambers, watching the organized chaos on the carrier's deck.

Now that the Porcupines were anchored, far more people could be seen near the railings. They were high enough that no one would have to worry about falling over them. And if that ever became a worry, the ship would be crashing, anyway. Jacob hoped never to see that happen, and they'd done all they could to make sure it wouldn't.

Jacob and Smith turned to the left at one of the larger intersections, passing a pair of Titan Mechs that stood motionless outside the workshop. A few tinkers worked on the shoulder joint of the first, which told Jacob it was the Mech whose hydraulics had failed during the assembly of the carrier. Thankfully, there was enough empty space that a skilled tinker could still easily perform repairs without having to disassemble the entire mechanism.

Heavy canvas flaps felt rough between Jacob's fingers as he pushed his way inside, the scent of oiled leather and superheated equipment blossoming as they entered. There weren't many tinkers at work: two operating the forge, and one hunched over the arm bracket of an exoskeleton.

Jacob grabbed a stool and dragged it closer to Targrove, causing a metal-on-metal squeal that made Jacob cringe. Smith was far more considerate, lifting his stool and gently setting it down on the opposite side of the old tinker.

Targrove raised the lenses from his right eye and leaned back, crossing his arms. "This is a masterwork. How much of the exoskeleton did you salvage from the workshop?"

At first Jacob was surprised Targrove hadn't greeted them in any way, but then he remembered how Charles used to get when he was deep into a project. Or how he himself got, for that matter.

"We took quite a bit, but the gears were all locked up. I had to rebuild it from his schematics. I added some ratchets for pivoting. They lock so the wearer won't get broken in half by the forces. The rest I polished down and reassembled."

"This metal looks new …" Targrove's voice trailed off.

"This one is. The original had a lot of salvage, but I couldn't reuse all the interfaces. They'd aged too much."

"They got sticky," Smith said with a nod. "Had to use my biomechanics to get a few parts unstuck for Jacob."

Targrove harrumphed. "I'd call that a bit more than sticky. Tell me about the ratchets."

Smith pointed to the parts in question. "It's a two-way ratchet. It took some work, and I can't figure out how to build it without the pilot manually forcing the switch."

Targrove leaned closer to the upright exoskeleton, studying the hip joints. "Have you considered adding a claw to the exoskeleton itself? Leave the ratchet to spin freely, but within a threshold that would still be safe for the pilot?"

Jacob stared at the old tinker. "But that's … so simple."

"You don't always need it to be fancy. You just need it to work." Targrove dusted his hands off. "Come now. Smith, strip the housing off those ratchet joints. It might let a bit more sand and debris in, but that's something we can worry about after we're done."

"Why do I suddenly feel like an apprentice again?" Smith asked.

"I'm not dead." Targrove raised an eyebrow. "So, you'll be an apprentice for some time yet."

Smith chuckled as he stood up and started working on the first joint.

Jacob moved to the other side and began removing some of the plating he'd installed. It would give them far easier access, which meant they could start testing it even sooner. And if there was one thing Jacob had learned as a tinker, testing was the fun part.

Owen stood on the deck of the stolen ocean liner. It looked as though it would be more at home on the bottom of the sea than transporting a small fleet of fishing vessels across rough water, but the hull held. She'd held together one day already, and one more was all they needed.

Trevor cleared his throat nearby to catch Owen's attention. "You want to discuss the plan again?"

Owen nodded, walking over to join Trevor and the gathered captains of the fishing vessels. "We've made it through one storm, friends, and the skies look clear over the Crystal Sea. It should make the transition as gentle as possible."

"I've spoken to most of those who have joined us, Owen." Fiona waited for him to meet her eyes. "Some have lost their desire to fight."

Owen inclined his head. He knew that would happen to some degree. It is one thing to join in the battle cry at a rally. It is quite another to stare that battle down on the horizon. "That will not be an issue, Fiona. If we all chose to fight, it would be obvious to Fel's fleet what was happening. Our goal is to make precise, targeted strikes against the ships themselves. Sinking an ocean liner would be a victory, to be sure, but even disabling one for a day or a week could prove just as effective.

"If they have no wish to fight, or take that risk, all I ask is they sail into the waters around the docks. Stay with the other fishing vessels. The presence of more of our ships will lower the suspicion of those of us who act as tender boats between the ocean liners."

Trevor started to interrupt, but Owen held up a hand to ask for silence. The ship bobbed over a large wave, sending a spray of water up above them and scattering a small cluster of Sky Needles.

"Some who wish to fight should still head for the docks. Mingle in the markets of Ballern. Be ready should things escalate. You may be the only chance the rest of us have to escape if we're cornered. Those who intend to board, you know how to break a ship. Four of you are ship-builders, and I've worked in the yards for enough years to know the same. We need at least five saboteurs. The rest can sort itself out."

"You'll have more than that," Fiona said. "You'll have far more than that."

Owen didn't stop the smile that lifted the corners of his mouth. He'd worried more of the fisherfolk might change their mind on the journey to Ballern. But what Mordair had done was as unforgiveable to them as it was to Owen, and that gave them a bond stronger than any tyrant could hope for.

✧　✧　✧

DRAKKAR SAT AT one of the many long tables in the mess hall. The light metal wasn't the most comfortable thing he'd ever experienced, and its ability to maintain a chill was far from appealing, but the gathering in that space made him smile.

Spider Knights from Ancora mingled with dragonriders from Canopy, exchanging stories of trials and hunts and even the care of their mounts. But they were not the only riders in that place. Three Cave Guardians were spread throughout the room, and Drakkar knew that was but a tiny fraction of the numbers who had ventured to Ancora and Midstream, and even Belldorn. The conflict had spawned a new camaraderie between them, though he wished peace could have done the same.

They were all outsiders to each other, strangers on a floating fortress, bound for a war none of them wanted. Well, Drakkar thought that last bit was mostly true, but a few of the Spider Knights sounded more than ready for a battle. It might be the typical blustery Ancoran attitude that many of its soldiers shared, but there were far more who were reserved, and they were perhaps older.

Drakkar suspected those were the soldiers who had seen the Fall with their own eyes. The aftermath might have been terrible, but to watch a city be ground away beneath an unstoppable tide was quite another thing.

"Drakkar!" Samuel's voice was plenty loud beside the Cave Guardian that he certainly hadn't needed to elbow Drakkar to get his attention. "I told Tatsu how disappointed you were that we wouldn't be riding Dragonwings."

He narrowed his eyes and glanced from Samuel to the dragonrider. "It is exhilarating, but I've no need to move like that above a mountain."

"Nothing like it," Tatsu said, raising a glass to Drakkar. "I can see how it isn't for everyone. Like those Jumpers, for instance. Now that is truly a disconcerting mount."

Rin broke away from his conversation with one of the Spider Knights to comment on Tastsu's claim. "Agreed. I'm glad we'll have them for the forest and the dense city streets, but give me a Dragonwing. At least it has wings while you're flying through the air!"

Several Spider Knights erupted into laughter.

"We brought a handful of Dragonwings," Tatsu said as Rin went back to his animated conversation. "If you feel a need to take wing again."

"I'm rather fond of the Stalkers." Drakkar took a sip of his water and smiled at Tatsu. "They can be fast enough when they need to be."

"Not fast enough to outrun a Dragonwing." Samuel smacked his metal mug on the table, letting it ring out until a few eyes had turned his way. "Did I ever tell you all how Drakkar saved me from a pack of Stone Dogs?"

"Oh no," Drakkar muttered under his breath.

"Grab your drinks and listen close, because it's quite the tale." Samuel snatched Drakkar's water away and put an ale in his hand instead.

The Cave Guardian grinned at the Spider Knight. "I wonder how you know that tale, considering you were unconscious most of the day."

That got a raucous laugh from the gathered crew, but many of them leaned in, listening to Samuel recount the story. And while Drakkar cringed at some of the embellishments, such as the ludicrous idea he'd caught the quills of a Stone Dog in his bare hands to protect Samuel, most of the story was true.

As annoyed as Drakkar had felt when Samuel first started that story, the feeling faded as he watched the faces around them, slowly realizing the brilliance of the Spider Knight's timing. Many at that table might have been outsiders to each other, but they all understood what it was like to fight for your friends and family. And if a Cave Guardian could put his life on the line for a Spider Knight, maybe fighting side by side wasn't such a strange idea after all.

CHAPTER SIXTEEN

URI STOOD ON the edge of the Bones, looking out to the Crystal Sea. They only had another day and a half before the carriers from Belldorn and Bollwerk would be in range. A day and a half to prepare their allies on the docks. The closer they came to that moment, the more Furi worried just how badly the Children of the Dark Fire had poisoned the minds of her fellow Skyborn.

Footsteps sounded behind her, light shoes on thin metal that told her it wasn't a soldier, and likely not Jakon, who liked to wear his boots no matter the weather. The wind picked up, sending a chill through her as she turned to find Kura.

"Furi, are you coming to join us? Jakon has an idea about using the lower docks on the Bones."

"I'll be there. I just needed some air."

Kura hesitated. "Are you okay?"

"I will be. It's …" Furi clenched her fists. "We all trained in Fleet. We can all fight, but I don't think we all will."

"Furi, there are times when you have to accept what is coming, and make peace with the idea of meeting whatever that may bring." Kura offered a small smile.

"It's bringing a fight to our docks. To our home."

"No, Furi. I'm afraid it's bringing things much worse than that … and much better. You have seen the face of war. You have watched your friends and family die in it. But you have not seen it ravage your home."

"I thought you said it was better. That's … that's awful, Kura."

"Hope comes with the fight, Furi. Hope comes with the struggle. We may not all live to see what changes this war brings to our home, but I can hope for the best. And hope is something that left these docks a long time ago."

Furi grimaced and looked away as pressure grew around her eyes. The idea that such a simple sentence could upset her like that. It was maddening. It was maddening because it was true. Long before Mordair came and the queen died, Ballern had been rotting from the inside. Some may be willfully ignoring it, but the signs lurked on the docks and in the gilded halls of the nobility.

"The nobles have sided with the Children of the Dark Fire." Kura waited to say more until Furi turned to meet her gaze. "And what will the Stormborn bring to those who have cast out the Skyborn, Furi? What can we fight for while they still hold power?"

Furi released her grip on the chilled railing of the Bones as her sadness kindled something else. Something hard and cold and unyielding. "They want to worship the Dark Fire? It will be their funeral pyre."

✧   ✧   ✧

ALICE STOOD AT the back of the docking bay, watching Eva fly into the narrow gap on the Bones. She flinched at the minuscule clearance. The docks had long ago been built up too much to allow larger vessels to dock on the lower, older levels, but Eva hurtled into the space at speed.

She glanced at Jakon standing beside her, and a mixture of admiration and concern twisted in her gut at the sight of the maniacal smile on his face.

"Furi!" Jakon called out. "*This* is what I told you about."

Alice had only a second to register that Furi and Kura had joined them, and then Eva's clunky old transport ship crashed into the bay. The springs screamed as they compressed, sending shards of rust tumbling off in every direction before the docking clamps engaged, locking Eva's ship into place.

The side of the lightly rusted transport slid open, and Alice released the gangway. It wasn't as rusted as the clamps, but it was bad enough that she wouldn't be excited about walking across it.

Eva, apparently, shared no such compunction. She walked onto the aged metal and put her hands on her hips, looking over the edge before shaking her head at Jakon. The pair laughed. Literally *laughed* as Eva stood on that death trap.

"They're mental," Alice whispered as Furi stepped up beside her.

"We've known that for ages." Furi grinned.

Jakon gestured for them all to come closer. "See? Look at these old clamps. They work as good as new."

"That might be a slight exaggeration." Eva raised an eyebrow. "Don't you think?"

"A bit squeakier, maybe. And, well, yes, there was a lot of rust flying about, but nothing to compromise their integrity, and it *worked*."

"You were docked and disembarked in under thirty seconds," Kura said. "And you were both the pilot and the soldier running for the gangway."

Jakon clapped his hands together. "Exactly. That gives us time to get more soldiers off the ships and defend the lower docks while the larger ships take the top of the docks. Give them nowhere to run."

"We could still lose people here." Alice pointed to the decks above them. "If one of those warships comes down, it could crush the Bones."

Kura crossed her arms and took a deep breath. "It's worth the risk. They'll likely deploy the warships once they realize the carriers are coming. And the carriers won't make it here before one of the scout ships slips through our own lines."

"Listen." Furi gestured to the nearly empty docks all around them. "No one even came to check on us. There's too much going on for this to draw attention. That was a hard impact, not exactly quiet, and no one is here. I always hate to say it when this happens, but Jakon's right."

"Thanks?" Jakon laughed quietly. "I know where to get more of these old docking clamps for the bays that don't have them anymore. We have, what, a day to get ready? It's enough time. We can work in shifts. Keep our numbers low to avoid suspicion as much as possible."

"I can tell Mary and the others. I'm sure they're anxious to hear from us as it is. Let me contact them."

They all turned toward the sudden crash of boots on the walkways. A small girl with a smear of soot on her cheek ran up to the group, glanced among them all, and held a folded piece of paper out to Jakon. She bowed slightly and ran away as fast as she'd come.

"More allies?" Furi asked.

Jakon shook his head as he unfolded the paper. "No, Furi. More information. We have the location of the carrier. It's being used as a secondary dock to the south of Ballern." He rubbed his cheek and grimaced. "Our allies will need to swing wide to the south to get to Karn if they don't want to engage."

Eva nodded. "Alice, use the radio on the transport. Tell Kat and Mary we're working on the docks and we know the location of Ballern's carrier."

Jakon stepped closer. "Tell them we'll be ready."

✧   ✧   ✧

ALICE SAT IN the cabin of Eva's transport. The transmitter wasn't as well hidden as the one in the Skysworn, but the obviousness of it was somewhat obscured by a tangle of wires and tubes hanging through a panel that had likely been removed a long time ago.

With the dials set, she clicked what looked like a broken button. She wasn't sure if the carriers would be close enough yet for the collar transmitters to receive a signal, but she wanted to try. "Jacob?"

No response came back, which either meant they still weren't in range, or Jacob was too tied up to answer. It was always a gamble reaching out to him when he was so busy in the shop. He hated missing her call, but she didn't want him to drop some vitally important project because they hadn't talked in a day or two. Or had it been three now?

Alice sighed and leaned back in the captain's chair. She watched Jakon waddling down the dock with another half of a docking clamp. She couldn't help but chuckle at the chef-turned-smuggler. Or was it the other way around? He might have known where to find more of the docking clamps, but he failed to mention they needed to be assembled. She supposed dragging scrap metal around was less suspicious than fully assembled clamps.

It wasn't a major problem, but it meant they had to recruit more help to assemble them in time for Belldorn's arrival. Except it wasn't really just Belldorn. It was the Stormborn. Ancorans, Cave Guardians, and soldiers from Archibald's own guard who were on those ships.

There were times watching history unfold didn't feel quite real to Alice. As if she knew some pivotal moment was occurring all around her, things that would be written about for decades, but in a way, it felt like any other day.

She took a long, slow breath and leaned forward to click the transmitter one more time. "Jacob?" She sat up a little straighter when the silent buzz she'd been met with before turned into a hiss of static and a rhythmic thump.

"Alice? How did you … are we that close already?"

"Apparently so. How are you? It feels like it's been ages since we talked. Did you get my messages? They were supposed to be relayed, but

I had no real way of checking in. It's been a little crazy here."

"I did, yes. It came through … well, I guess you know where it came through."

She did, but she doubted they needed to be so coy about naming their friends at this point. Mordair knew who his enemies were, and even if he learned Kura's name, the battle was too near to stop it.

"You saved the books."

Alice grinned at Jacob's words. "Yes, they'll be safer across the seas. Kat will take care of them better than anyone."

"I've seen her around, you know? It's strange being with them. Theo's assistant is with us, too."

Targrove and Lady Katherine were traveling on the same vessel? The thought was somewhat strange considering the vast difference in their stations, but then again, the carriers were massive. She remembered skimming by Ballern's carrier, and even if the new carriers were half that size, they would hold thousands of soldiers.

"I was supposed to contact Mary first," Alice said, "but I wanted to talk to you. I better find Mary's frequency and let her know what's happening."

"Don't worry about that. She's right here next to me in the workshop, yelling at Smith. Mary!"

A few seconds passed before Alice heard Mary's voice cut across the line. "I don't need you interrupting me, Jacob. You've been around Smith too long, and I sure as hell don't need another Smith to deal with. What?"

"Alice wants to talk to you, and you weren't monitoring the transmitter on the ship, so she contacted me instead."

"Because I wasn't monitoring the transmitter? Of course that's why. What other reason could there possibly be?" Alice could hear Mary's sigh over the speaker after that remarkably shocked comment. "What is it, Alice?"

"They located the carrier. South of the city, along the river. Not far from the Gray Woods, as I understand it."

"River delta," Mary said. Someone else responded, but the transmitter didn't pick up their voice. "We know where that's at. I'll inform the others."

"Who else is there?" Alice asked.

But it wasn't Mary who answered. It was Jacob. "Me and Theo's assistant. Mary just dragged Smith off. Probably to see Kat."

"Would you like some privacy?" Targrove's voice was barely audible over Jacob's transmitter.

"No, it's fine. We don't have much time as it is. Alice, have you been told where the landings are? The full extent of what's happening?"

"Yes. And as you know, I helped secure one of those sites."

Jacob stumbled over his words. "I know, I mean, yes, but, but did …"

Alice almost felt bad at the sheer awkwardness she could trigger in Jacob on a whim. A very large part of her hoped that never changed. "Jacob, Jacob, it's fine! I was joking."

His sigh of relief caused her to laugh again. "I should have known. It's just … you know, things are stressful. I'm not trained to help lead a big project like this. If anything goes wrong, I'm going to be partially to blame, and it's a lot of pressure."

Alice smiled as she watched Eva and Jakon walk by, the latter gesturing wildly about something that Alice only hoped didn't involve directions. "Jacob, you've clearly done well. Stop doubting yourself and deal with the problems as they come. You don't need to invent your own." She quieted as she followed that up. "Time will bring you enough problems to solve."

He paused. "That sounds really smart. It'd probably help if I could actually take that advice instead of worrying about putting an extra bolt in the carrier without Frederick's approval."

Alice leaned forward and groaned. "I just realized it's something my mom used to tell me all the time. If you tell her I quoted her, I will end you."

"Noted." His voice had a light note, a hint of a laugh. "I have to go. We're testing the exoskeleton again, and between the three of us, I think we almost have it done."

"That's great, Jacob. Go then. I'll see you again soon."

"Love you."

"Love you, too."

CHAPTER SEVENTEEN

S MITH CROSSED HIS arms and leaned against the Skysworn's landing gear as he eyed Mary. "All I'm saying is just because a high-impact landing worked with that flying brick Eva was piloting, doesn't mean it will work for all of our landing vessels. And you *know* how narrow the access points are on the Bones."

"I didn't leave Kat with Frederick and Targrove just to hear you worry about *clearances*, Smith. You think the clearances on the Bones are tight? Do you remember—"

"Pirate's Cove," Smith muttered.

"—Pirate's Cove?" Mary echoed. "That was like slipping between the teeth of gears, and you want to complain about an airship dock?"

"I am only voicing a concern. Those supply ships are large. The gangplanks will have to be set at an angle or they risk hitting their gas chambers."

Mary raised an eyebrow. "If only we had a tinker who could do the math to figure out how long the gangplanks would need to be for that."

Smith overheard Rin talking to Drakkar. "Are they okay?"

"Yes. They sometimes fight like an old married couple. It is … yes, they are okay."

Smith barked out a laugh and smiled at Drakkar.

The Cave Guardian raised an eyebrow and leaned in conspiratorially toward the dragonrider. "And they have excellent hearing."

"Stuff it, Drakkar," Mary muttered. "Smith, can you do the math? Or do I need to ask your boss?"

"Theo's assistant?" Smith asked, standing up a little straighter. "He would be quite disappointed if I could not make such a simple calculation."

"I meant Jacob," Mary said as Jacob walked out of the hold.

Smith stared at Mary, slack-jawed, as Drakkar burst into laughter.

"Whoa." Jacob raised his hands in the air. "Don't drag me into this."

Mary nodded her head slowly. "I hear Jacob's got an old Mech design of Charles's almost ready for the battlefield. Sounds like it's one of the more impressive things—"

"I will make the necessary calculations and get them to Kura and Jakon." Smith pinched the bridge of his nose. "The docks will be prepared."

"Thank you, Smith. I can't tell you how happy I am to hear that." Mary winked at Jacob.

A brief metallic squeal sounded, and Rin flinched. He fumbled with his collar and clicked the transmitter. "This is Rin. Can you repeat that?"

"We have a scout ship pilot secured," Tatsu said. "Meet me at the hospital. They aren't unscathed. Rin, you need to be there."

Rin frowned at those words, a small knot forming in his gut. "I'll be there, Tatsu."

"Five minutes."

"On our way. You'll get there before us."

Smith eyed Rin, noting the crease in his brow and the clenching of his fists. "What do you think Tatsu wants?"

"I don't know, Smith, but he's rarely so vague. He means to shock someone, and I've no idea if that means me, or whoever the pilot is they recovered. Judging by the stress in his voice, it may not be good."

"We had best go and find out." He glanced at Jacob. "You are welcome to join us." When Jacob hesitated, Smith offered him a kind smile.

"You can return to the workshop if you would like. I know you want to finish that exoskeleton."

Jacob turned to Rin. "Let me know what it is when you get a chance. Like Smith said, we're almost done, and it could be a valuable resource."

Rin nodded and stepped away from the worktable in the bay while Smith followed him. Mary stayed close at their side. While part of Smith wanted to ask if she was sure she didn't want to find Kat again, the other part of him knew Mary would do what Mary needed to do.

THE WALK FROM the Skysworn's bay to the hospital wasn't a long one, but it felt like it, knowing a dragonrider had managed to recover a pilot. This was their fifth encounter with a scout ship, but their first captured pilot, and it wouldn't be long before Ballern realized their ships weren't returning on schedule.

The carriers might have been designed to endure a battle in the sky, but it was one aspect of those behemoths Smith hoped they'd never need to test.

Rin had been right about getting to the hospital after Tatsu. Two Dragonwings sat on a low railing meant for tying down clippers and strikers. They didn't seem concerned by the small crowds of people walking past them, instead focusing on satchels of Sweet-Flies on the ground.

Smith and Mary followed Rin into one of the few structures on the carrier that had solid walls. Or at least had three solid walls.

A nurse eyed the group and pointed to a hallway without asking a single question.

Rin nodded to her and led the way through a handful of barriers formed from thick translucent plastic. The conversation was easy to follow from there as only two beds currently held any patients. And a single bed was flanked by a pair of dragonriders.

Smith's steps slowed when he recognized Allie, one of Canopy's most prominent leaders. She had a woven helmet tucked beneath her arm, and stood along the wall while Tatsu knelt by the side of the bed, holding someone's hand.

But it wasn't Allie who caused Rin's steps to slow, or Tatsu. It was the sight of whoever was resting in that bed, her face scarred from old burns and her ribs wrapped in a bloody bandage.

"Ling?"

The scarred woman turned to Rin, her jaw dropping as she pulled her hand away from Tatsu and reached for the other dragonrider. "I thought you were dead. How are you all here?"

"Us?" Rin said with a laugh, stepping forward and gently taking her hand. "That's a long story."

"Then tell me."

Rin blew out a breath. "Captured by Belldorn, but released in time. I joined with Canopy and have been living in the forest city for years. Tatsu had more sense than me, so Belldorn released him earlier. That's Allie, who's been with you and Tatsu. She's a great leader of Canopy."

"One of many leaders," Allie said.

Ling's brow furrowed as tears gathered at the corners of her eyes. "It's true, isn't it? What the Stormborn are saying? Ballern is lost."

Rin took a knee next to Ling's bed as she pulled away. He glanced at the medic. "Is she ... will she recover?"

The medic inclined her head. "She will, but she'll need time to heal. We have plenty of space here. She's not going anywhere for at least a week. Isn't that right, Ling?"

Ling grimaced and relaxed back into her pillow. "Who am I to argue with the medic?" She met Rin's gaze. "Why are you here? What is this ship?"

Rin bowed his head. "You're on a Stormborn ship, Ling. It's an alliance between the Steamborn and Skyborn, Bollwerk, and Belldorn, and even the fisherfolk from Fel."

"Steamborn? The Ancorans have come to fight Ballern?"

Rin sighed. "Ling, no. They've come to fight Mordair. The Steward. He's … he's not a good man."

Ling's face broke down. Her voice cracked. "I know, Rin. I saw what they did on the docks. I watched them hang Kallie and Bin."

Rin didn't respond. He only stared at Ling, but Smith could see the redness in the dragonrider's eyes. Those were not random names Ling had spoken. Rin knew them.

"They were our friends," Tatsu whispered when he caught Smith and Mary staring. "We grew up together. Joined Fleet a few years apart."

"They'll come for the Skyborn, Ling. If we don't stop them, all our friends and families are going to hang from those docks."

Ling's knuckles whitened as she snatched up Rin's hand and squeezed it. "What do you hope to do against a fleet? What can any of us do?"

Rin hung his head before steeling himself. "You can give us the codes to check in. We've had to attack more than one scout ship, and Ballern is going to notice."

"You … killed them?"

"We didn't want to, Ling, but one report of this carrier could give Mordair time to prepare for what's coming. War is war. If we learned one thing in Fleet, it was that."

Ling closed her eyes, the muscles in her cheeks flexing. When she looked back at him, her expression had hardened. "The Queen's Crest. Is it true what they say? The Children of the Dark Fire?"

Rin's jaw tensed and he cursed under his breath. "Ling, you need to rest."

"Tell me what you know, and I'll give you the codes for three shifts of strikers." Ling winced as she unzipped a satchel at her hip.

"She wouldn't let us remove that," the medic said. "I don't know if it's a weapon, or—"

Tatsu grabbed the wrist of the medic when he reached for Ling. "She is our friend, sir. I trust her with my life."

Ling held a small pamphlet out to Rin. "Tell me the truth, and take it. I remember the promise we made on the last day of the last year."

"As do I." Rin placed his hand over Ling's. "The Queen's Crest represents the Children of the Dark Fire. They control the nobles. They changed our history to hide the fact the Deadlands War was almost entirely their design. I've stood in the Crown Library in Belldorn, Ling. Our friends have some of the original manuscripts written by Yan Wu. Our past is not what you think it is."

Ling turned Rin's hand over and left the pamphlet resting in his palm. "Then I will stand at your side. With those who were wronged, and with those who I helped wrong." Pain contorted Ling's face, but Smith didn't think it had anything to do with her physical discomfort. "Call me Stormborn."

✦   ✦   ✦

RIN STORMED OUT of the hospital. A cursory glance showed him what he needed to know. Ling had given them a schedule that only an officer would have access to. Ling had risen through the ranks of Fleet, only to find out everything she'd fought for had been a lie.

"Rin!" Tastsu called out. "Rin, stop!"

He turned to find Tatsu, Smith, and Mary racing after him. He tried to keep his voice measured, but rage won out. "They hung Kallie and Bin! I hadn't seen them in ten years, but they were still my friends."

Tatsu slammed a hand down on his shoulder. "They were my friends, too. Where do you think you're going?"

"Watch over Ling." Rin hesitated. "I … I don't know what I'm going to do."

"Allie stayed with Ling. Figures she can answer a whole lot of questions that we apparently aren't staying to help our friend with."

Rin's fists tightened.

Smith reached out and took the dragonrider's shoulder momentarily. "You cannot fight them alone, Rin. You need to take a step back and focus on how to use what Ling gave you."

"Listen to him." Mary squeezed Smith's arm. "He's kept me out of more trouble than I care to admit. Keeps me alive to get into more trouble later."

Rin took a deep breath, concentrating on the cool air, trying to let it calm the heat running through his blood. It didn't help much, so instead, he unfolded the pamphlet from Ling. "Thank you, all of you. I know you mean well."

Tatsu stepped around so he could read the pamphlet, too. "We're going to need a Ballern transmitter."

"We have them," Smith said. "Recovered after the battle in Belldorn. Both of the control towers have one installed. Frederick thought it would be better than trying to steal one from an active warship every time we needed access."

Rin let out a short, humorless laugh. "That's … sound logic. Come with me. We can send in the first report and get the tower on a schedule to transmit the next few shifts. After that, we'll be at Ballern's gates. After that, it will be far too late for Mordair to stop us."

CHAPTER EIGHTEEN

JACOB HELPED FORCE the last of the new inserts into the exoskeleton. Targrove had insisted on having a set of his own, and who was Jacob to say no to that? And, if he were being honest, the idea of working side by side with Targrove wasn't something he could walk away from. It reminded him of Charles even more than restoring the exoskeleton did, and there was a kind of peace in that.

"Are you sure we didn't make these inserts too wide?" Jacob asked, looking at how much room Targrove's boot had to shift.

"Trust me, lad, if we ratcheted that tensioner down as tight as you wanted, the pilot would lose all feeling in their foot in half an hour."

Jacob shrugged and swung the rear cage for each leg closed.

"That's good. Now let me try to lock the rest in place. If this old man can operate your exoskeleton, well, then you're on to something." Targrove cast him a grin and threw the bolts home on the cages. For the back bracket, Targrove pushed a spring-loaded lever that closed the hinges.

But it was what Targrove did next that had Jacob worried. A burner sparked in the tinker's hand before dropping into an armored boiler outside the left thigh.

"What are you doing?" The question came fast, and he didn't quite keep the concern out of his voice. Testing an idle exoskeleton was one thing, but standing inside it under pressure was far riskier.

"A proper test." Targrove twisted the shoulder joints, nodding at the quiet click of the ratchets before testing the pivot of the hips. They resisted at first, until steam started to trickle from the valves and releases. Then the old tinker moved with ease, turning one foot out before taking a step forward.

He picked up an anvil and chuckled, moving it from one exoskeleton hand to the other. That anvil weighed more than Jacob did, and possibly more than Smith, but Targrove handled it with little effort. They both cringed when Targrove dropped it from a few inches off the mount, denting an anchor. Jacob was a bit annoyed that he'd probably need to hammer that out and re-level it, but the thought was gone in a moment as Targrove stepped forward.

"Wait!" Jacob started after Targrove, almost having to sprint to keep up with the sudden stride. The exoskeleton let the pilot cover more ground, and even though Targrove wasn't technically running, Jacob had to in order to match his pace.

And then they were outside, away from the workshop, and Jacob's concern for the old tinker turned into something else. A fierce warmth that he'd felt a few times before, when he'd helped build the nail gloves with Charles, or improved the glider packs on his own, or when he was alone with Alice. It was an unbridled joy in a time of darkness, and his own shouts were matched only by Targrove's whoops from the pilot seat.

Jacob was well and truly out of breath by the time they circled the bay and returned to the workshop. He worried how much of a toll that run would have taken on Targrove, but the old tinker appeared to have barely broken a sweat. His worries about the exosuit taking too much effort to pilot evaporated in a moment.

Targrove's gnarled fingers undid the latches on his own, each release working as Jacob had designed it, allowing for a single pilot to enter and exit unassisted if needed. The old tinker hopped down to the ground, wincing at the impact, but his smile returned a moment later.

"Look," Targrove said, rolling up the hem of his worn leather pants. Beneath, his leg had only the faintest redness, but no bruising or abrasions. The insert had worked as he claimed it would, and it was a subtle reminder that Jacob still had a great deal of things to learn. "The test now is to see how fast it can cool down."

Jacob slid a pair of heat-resistant gloves on and hurried to the front of the exoskeleton, checking over each connection in the boilers. They'd all held, and the vents released small puffs of steam as the valves normalized the pressure.

"You might want to stand back a little bit." Jacob undid the safety on the main evacuation valve and then pushed against the spring. As easy as it was when the system had no pressure, he had to lean into it when it was fully pressurized. But as soon as the valve passed the point of resistance, a billowing cloud of steam shot toward the workshop's roof. The shoulder joints returned to an inert position as the boiler cooled and the pressure fled.

Targrove crossed his arms as he leaned in to study the joints. "I don't see any undue wear. Granted, it was a quick test, but I think we're ready to try weighing it down with armor."

"I'm almost done getting the anchors on." Jacob turned back to the workbench and grabbed a handful of wide metal clasps. The thin metal was easy to bend in the jig Targrove had configured, creating a gap just large enough to be forced over the braces of the exoskeleton. But that was only half of the issue.

The other was anchoring the clasps in such a way that the armor plates could still move, slide over one another, and tilt out when needed. If that failed, it could lock up the exoskeleton's movement. Depending on what the pilot was engaged in at the time, that could be a very bad thing.

Jacob positioned a scaled-down bolt cannon over the clasp and on top of a light armor plate. A loud metallic crack sounded when he pulled the trigger, sinking the rivet through both layers alike. He turned it over and eyed the flattening of the rivet. It wasn't quite as flush as he would have liked.

"That'll do, Jacob. A little more movement is a good thing in this case."

Jacob nodded and handed the plate to Targrove. The old tinker started on the legs, which was likely the best call, since the upper extremities of the frame could still be hot from the boiler. After a failed test at fastening the armor the day before, Jacob had decided to bevel the sides of the plates. Without a flat edge to get snagged on another plate, the movement was both quieter and smoother on his test joint.

Targrove snapped the armor into place as fast as Jacob could hand it to him. At most, Targrove had looked at Jacob's layout for the plates twice, and yet the old tinker put each piece exactly where it needed to go. The longer, gently curved pieces fit over the thigh and the shorter angled plates protected the ankle.

Targrove held his hand over the boiler to check the heat before shaking his head. "I think it's best if we stop there for now." He glanced at the clock on the workbench. "Should be landing soon as it is. Did you notice the trees on our little jog around the bays?"

Jacob blinked. "The … what?"

"Maybe we should step outside. This isn't the kind of sight you should miss because your head is so deep in your work." Targrove squeezed Jacob's shoulder before leading the way outside.

Jacob didn't see anything out of the ordinary at first, other than some distant mountains, and even those were just foothills. He shivered when a cold breeze ruffled his hair, wondering if perhaps they were higher than he thought, and those weren't foothills at all.

But then he turned toward the bow, and all thoughts of mountains fled, because the distant mountains were dwarfed by trees. Trees that, for a moment, he thought might rival those of Canopy. But as he and Targrove walked toward the edge of the carrier, he could see that even Canopy's trees would pale in comparison.

"The Forest Giants of the Gray Woods," Targrove said. "I've been all around this world, Jacob, and there is nothing quite like them."

Jacob slowly pulled his gaze away from the lush green and soaring trunks in front of them to study Targrove. "Have you ever been across the Silver Gulf?"

Targrove raised an eyebrow. "The Silver Gulf, Jacob? Aye, that I have." He paused and turned back to the vista ahead of them. "What is it you want to know?"

"What's it like?" He didn't know what to ask, exactly. Maybe it was a silly question, but he could always hope. "Is it … are the people kinder? I mean, do they have as many wars there?"

"I'm afraid if there are people, there are wars." Targrove offered a sad smile. "But it is not all bad, Jacob. There is always a light to a shadow, a sheath to a blade, as it were. It's another world across the sea, but it's not so different than Bollwerk to Ballern, or Belldorn to Ancora. You'll find more folks who look like Alice, though."

"The old blood?"

"Indeed." He let out a low chuckle. "A rather pretentious term, don't you think? A trivial name for a group of people."

"Some folks put a lot of stock in the old blood. The Children of the Dark Fire, Ballern, there are even superstitious Ancorans. Alice has some stories about that. I remember this one older lady wanted a lock of her hair for good luck."

Targrove let out a sharp breath. "I am not too surprised by any of that. You know what I think you would quite enjoy across the Silver Gulf? The food. They have more cows and chickens than any city this side of the sea. They built great protected farms for them, though the price is still prohibitive to many. If you know where the pirates are, though, you can always find a bargain."

"Maybe Smith and Mary can take us there one day."

"Might I recommend adding Jakon to that trek? He and George are the best chefs I've had the pleasure to meet. And Jakon is far more attuned to the ways of the pirates than a Royal Guard."

Jacob grinned at Targrove before focusing on the Forest Giants. They soared higher now, and the deck of the carrier tilted slightly as the pilots edged their way closer to Karn.

"ARE YOU SURE this is okay?" Jacob asked, following behind Smith.

"It is fine." Smith grunted and lifted the entire exoskeleton, walking it up the ramp to the hold on the Skysworn. "If you mean to come with us to Ballern, this will give us something to do while we're waiting for orders."

Jacob wrung his hands. Excitement warred with apprehension at the idea they'd be flying to Ballern soon. But the carrier had found a place to anchor, and they now hovered close to the ground, with the towers of Karn off the starboard side.

"How long do you think we'll have to wait before we can leave? Before we'll know something?"

"That will depend on Owen and the fisherfolk." Smith powered down his biomechanics now that the heavy lifting was done. "If any suspicion is raised on the sea docks, it could cost those people everything."

Jacob glanced back down the loading ramp and nodded. It was a mad idea. He'd seen the boats the fisherfolk used, and he'd seen the docks outside Ballern. The boats would blend in well enough if they could make it across the sea. Whether an ocean liner was taking them most of the way or not, the very idea of deploying one of those tiny vessels onto the

Crystal Sea made Jacob's spine tingle.

"Now, what do you say we close the loading dock and let Mary fly us to Ballern before she chews her own arm off?"

"I heard that!" came a half-amused, half-annoyed shout over the horn.

Smith grinned and started closing the ramp. "Time to go."

✧   ✧   ✧

ALLIE STOOD BEFORE the open bay door as they floated away from the deck and made for the city. The only thing standing between her and a very long fall to the earth below was a cargo net. The Forest Giants and blue sky made a striking backdrop to her address.

"All of you, listen well! Karn has offered us their welcome, and we mean to repay them in kind. We'll take the spider mounts into the Gray Woods, and the bulk of our forces will head for Ballern. Capture anyone fleeing Ballern if you can, but if they are hostile, do not hesitate to strike them down."

Allie gestured to the columns of gathered Spider Knights and dragonriders. They looked one and the same now, each wearing the familiar riding leathers Samuel had grown so accustomed to in his service to Ancora. Nora had sent nearly every last set of leathers they had in storage to be sure everyone would be protected.

"Company A will lead the way to Ballern with Company B bringing up the rear." She turned to eye the last column of soldiers. "Company C will venture deeper into the Gray Woods, heading west. You will be the eyes and ears on the ground for Karn, as they are withdrawing the majority of their own scouts to reinforce the city. This will give you access to their hides and their defenses, should you need them. Questions?"

"What's in the west?" Tatsu asked.

Samuel almost laughed because he knew Tatsu was well aware of what waited in the west. And apparently, Allie had the same thought at his rather obvious prompt because she scowled at the dragonrider.

"As I'm sure you're all aware at this point, the Children of the Dark Fire are based to the northwest, as well as being present in Ballern. Should they move against Karn, by their own whims or by Mordair's instruction, we will meet them in the woods.

"Fight well, all of you." She paused before raising her fist into the air. "For the Stormborn."

Allie's gesture was met with a roar.

✧   ✧   ✧

KAT WALKED BESIDE Targrove as they made their way across the carrier toward a small transport. As cold and windy as the journey had been, it wasn't quite as unsettling as a fleet of airships taking off all around them.

"I'm rather surprised Mary let you go alone," Targrove said.

"She knew I'd have a very old and grumpy tinker with me. That's protection almost as good as Mary herself."

Targrove grinned at her. "Theo will be jealous, you know. She rather enjoys the times you come to visit the workshop. But I am quite sure my grumpiness is not the main reason for our reunion."

An armored crawler sped past them, its treads like thunder on the carrier's deck. No one raised a hand in greeting or salute, and Kat was glad to know the aviator hat provided some semblance of anonymity. The enormous copper-framed goggles felt ridiculous on her forehead, but they were certainly distracting.

Kat sighed and nodded to Targrove. "You're right. Mary thought we'd been seen too much together on the carrier. If there's an assassin on board, they could have recognized the pattern of our movement."

"Of course, the Skysworn is rather infamous in Belldorn, isn't it? Not the most subtle place to hide."

"Perhaps not, but certainly one of the best defended. Smith takes his security very seriously. Almost as seriously as the maintenance on that ship."

Targrove hooked his thumbs into the pockets of his leather apron and smiled at Kat. "Well, you'll be happy to know who taught him that particular neurosis."

Kat gestured for Targrove to lead the way onto the shuttle, and she followed him up the ramp. It wasn't as small as it had first appeared, perhaps half the length of the Skysworn. It had room for at least twelve passengers to be seated, but Targrove and Kat were the only ones there when the doors closed and the pilot launched the ship.

They passed over the last bays of the carrier, and Kat watched the view in the windscreen shift from the flat grays and worn brass of the airships on the deck to the lush green forest that surrounded Karn. The pilot didn't take them far, angling for a wide square where other shuttles were dropping soldiers and supplies. Below, an even larger supply ship had set down.

The pilot turned to face them as the shuttle settled to the ground. "My Lady. Master Targrove."

Kat blinked at the man, recognition slowly rising from the back of her mind. She'd seen him before, in Belldorn, working the docks.

Targrove's hand shifted almost imperceptibly, but Kat knew the tinker was armed, and likely ready to make a mess out of their pilot.

"Mary asked me to bring you down," the tinker said. "Am I to assume she didn't mention that fact?"

"Who are you?" Targrove said.

"Name's Jones. Walter Jones. And I am unfortunately related to Archibald."

"You mean you're one of his spies?"

Jones sat up a little straighter. "Well, if you want to be technical about it, sure. But I meant he's my blood."

Kat relaxed as Targrove's hand fell away from his pocket.

"Now, Mary said to give you some directions from the square. Are you familiar with the old church in the southeast of Belldorn? With the stained-glass windows that come to an arch?"

"I am," Kat said, unable to keep a hint of curiosity out of her voice.

"Good, good. The council building of Karn looks something like that. Quite a bit shorter than the towers. But you want to follow this street straight ahead until you reach the fountain, and then take a left. You can't miss it from there. Ask for Arun."

Targrove's eyes widened a hair. "You're Archibald's cousin! I remember you. Theo and I had drinks with you and some of your compatriots at The Fish Head several years ago. My, that must have been nearly a decade past now."

"Indeed. And if I'd known I'd been drinking with the late great Targrove at the time, that would be a secret I would have been quite terrible at keeping."

Targrove chuckled and glanced at Kat. "I grew my beard long. It made a better disguise than that aviator hat."

Kat flicked the insulated flap covering an ear, her voice taking a light tone. "You wound me, Targrove."

"Well, times change," Jones said. "I'll have you know I'll speak of this to no one. This flight was off the record, and the only other person who knows about you being here is Mary. Which likely means Smith and Jacob know, too, if I'm being honest. But … well, pirates."

"Pirates indeed," Kat said. "Thank you for the transport, Walter. And do take care of yourself."

"And you, My Lady."

Targrove stood to leave, patting Jones on the back before heading to the rear of the shuttle and pulling the release for the loading ramp. Kat followed down before taking the lead through Karn, a city she knew little about except for the stories of Yan Wu and legends that predated the Deadlands War.

The shuttle left behind them, blending into the churning cloud of supply ships and brigs now taking to the skies. They might have made it to Karn without anything worse than a few skirmishes with scouts, but that would all change soon enough, Kat knew.

Targrove's pace slowed when they reached the fountain. He stared at the water cascading from one level to the next, but he said nothing.

"What is it?" Kat asked.

"Just remembering. There were stories of Karn in the Deadlands War. Stories of grand fountains and towers to rival Belldorn. I always said I'd come back, but I didn't. I saw old pictures once. A tinker from Karn, who found himself in the middle of the Deadlands War, showed them to me. Showed me this fountain. But it didn't run with water. It was cracked and dry."

Targrove pointed to a jagged line in the center column. "In the photo, this was broken, and that boy couldn't talk about it without tears in his eyes. War nearly destroyed the people who live here, Kat. And here we are, bringing war back to their doorstep."

"Mordair will come for all of us, if he's given the chance. You know that. Karn would be no better off then."

Targrove sighed and turned to Kat, his piercing gaze meeting hers. "Let's find Arun."

Kat started to the north, following the street Jones had told them about. To say the directions were all they needed was an understatement. The road ended at an intersection, and across the street, the council building crouched between two massive towers. Even if the guards hadn't given it away, the sharp peaks of the windows' arches would have.

She took a deep breath and walked to the nearest guard. "Greetings, soldier. I seek an audience with Arun."

"No one is allowed to enter except ..." The guard hesitated and stared at Lady Katherine briefly. Then he stepped to the side and gestured to the door, giving her a full view of his uniform's dark green and brown panels. Heavy stitches crossed every seam, but Kat was sure they were for show, given how little the panels flexed. "Please, Lady of Belldorn, you will find Arun awaits your arrival."

"What gave me away?"

"You speak like the academics who visit us, but your gait is like the nobles, and you asked for Arun. But I know you are not a noble because they treat us all without respect. They have no honor."

"At least it wasn't the hat." Targrove gave Kat a broad smile.

"My thanks to you, guard. Be well." Kat led the way to the door, pushing through and holding it for Targrove. She'd been so focused on her interaction with the guard that the interior of the council hall took her by surprise.

The support columns in that cavernous space were no plain things, instead carved with impressive detail and style to look like the guards of Karn, standing watch over everyone inside that building. It was strange that a building only some three stories tall could feel so imposing within.

Imposing though it might have been, it was also stunning. Each statue was detailed with long, sharp lines, forming the arms and shields and even swords. All of those tapered down together, from the shoulders to the feet, giving the illusion that the statues were larger than they truly were.

Kat's boots echoed on the polished stone floor as they passed the first line of statues and stepped into something that shared characteristics with many city councils she'd visited. If Archibald removed his long benches and replaced them with ragged stone, he might not be far away from what waited in Karn.

"Welcome, Lady Katherine."

Kat turned toward the voice, finding a woman standing there who didn't quite match her own height. The woman tucked a bit of dark hair beneath a beret. Kat could have mistaken her for a Ballern soldier, one of many of those who had been imprisoned and released over the years in Belldorn.

"Thank you for your greeting. Could you direct me to Arun?"

"I could, but he can be rather boring."

"Mali," a man's voice boomed, rising in volume as if the woman's name itself were a curse.

Mali gave a small bow and took on a formal tone. "Please, this way. It is rare they let us pirates into the council hall, so I have to entertain myself."

"You must be William's friend." Targrove gave her a knowing look.

Mali leaned to the side a bit and studied Targrove. Apparently satisfied with her appraisal, she started walking across the floor, gesturing for Kat and the tinker to follow. "William's here. Or he was, at least. I understand he's already taking his books up to the carrier."

"The Lady of Belldorn need not concern herself with the shopkeeper, Mali." Arun tapped an obsidian fountain pen on the table before setting it down beside a leaning tower of maps and ledgers. He stepped around the table and placed his hands on his hips before gesturing widely. "Welcome to Karn, my friends. I do hope you find our fair city to be of benefit to your campaign."

Kat offered a broad smile. "I hope we can forge an alliance that is far stronger than a mere benefit, Arun, to both of us. Thank you."

"You should know not all the elders were supportive of allowing your forces here. I'd recommend keeping a guard with you."

"I have all of the guard I need, Arun."

Arun eyed Targrove. "If that is true, I highly doubt this man is a tinker."

Targrove chuckled at that, and Kat fought to keep a straight face because if Targrove was anything, it was most assuredly a tinker.

"Come, please. I would like to share our maps with you. There is much you likely do not know when it comes to the Great Machines, and this battle will not end without the Children of the Dark Fire engaging in it."

Kat followed Arun the few steps to the table. He pulled one map to the side and unrolled another, setting heavy gray metal cubes on the corners to weigh them down.

"Have you spoken to your advocates? The ones known as Furi and Alice?"

"Wasn't Jakon with them, too?" Targrove asked.

Arun harrumphed.

"You'll have to excuse him. He's not that fond of pirates. Except for me, of course." Mali gave Targrove a grin. "We only tolerate them in Karn to keep a supply of … goods."

"Yes, well, Jakon had to leave on an errand before a decision was made, so I would hardly call him an advocate." Arun picked up one of several bronze markers from the border of the map and slid them toward the center.

Kat glanced between the two residents of Karn. "Regardless, I haven't spoken to them at length."

"Not to worry, My Lady, I will provide the pertinent details. Should we find ourselves in a battle for Karn, I would like all our allies to know what to expect."

Kat leaned closer to Arun, looking at the small square illustration on the map beside one of his markers. Two words were clear. *Control center.* The other, northwestern marker, sat next to a similar illustration, but this one was far larger. It wasn't written in the standard language, but Mokuskrit. That didn't matter because Kat knew enough to recognize the lines and angles for what they were.

"The Great Machine." She traced a path from one to the other, and in the middle sat Karn, flanked on all sides by the Gray Woods, but unsettlingly closer to the Great Machine than she'd believed. "Are the distances accurate here? The maps we have in Belldorn show this area to be quite a bit farther from Karn."

"No more than a day's ride through the woods. The Children of the Dark Fire control most of the immediate area close to the lake and outside the forest. It is possible they will flee to Karn if the battle reaches the Great Machine."

"We will not leave you undefended."

"We are never undefended, My Lady, but your support is appreciated. A favor for a favor, as it were."

"You know of another control center." Targrove's eyes didn't rise from the map. "I've been to one in the desert, but it was inside the Great Machine itself."

Arun nodded. "I am familiar with the dormant god in the Deadlands. The Children of the Dark Fire speak of it at length. The control center for that machine fell into the sea long ago. Swallowed by a storm that is believed to have destroyed Pirate's Cove as well."

"You know about Pirate's Cove?" Targrove rubbed his chin.

"I used to talk too much," Mali muttered. "I'd only been there twice, and didn't get to explore nearly enough."

Targrove rubbed his chin. "I don't recognize you, so that makes a kind of sense. Not that many strangers come through Pirate's Cove, so they normally get quite a bit of attention."

"You've been to Pirate's Cove?" Mali's brow furrowed.

The wide smile on the old tinker's face probably wasn't the most reassuring expression, but Targrove didn't elaborate. "If this control center is better preserved, it could have schematics, manuals, or even tools that could help us infiltrate the Children of the Dark Fire."

"The young scholar, William, thought much the same," Arun said. "It is not a safe place to go. If you wish to send your people there, I must tell you about the dangers of those woods."

"Death and ghosts," Mali whispered. "Nothing but death and ghosts."

✧　✧　✧

"THIS IS A mount I could grow accustomed to." Drakkar smiled as the Stalker tilted slightly from one side to the other, her wide gait keeping pace with the Jumpers, without feeling like he was going to fall from the saddle at any moment.

"You know you're only matching our pace because we're armored, right?" Samuel called after him.

Drakkar laughed. "And yet my mount feels no slower than she did in Canopy."

They started up a hill lined with the bulging roots of the Forest Giants. Jumpers and Stalkers alike did not hesitate to start over them, but Drakkar had to admit he did not enjoy the view down into the tangled roots below. A fall there would certainly be fatal.

Armor plates clanged together as they navigated the uneven terrain. All but two of the Stalker's legs bore armor. Those remained exposed, allowing the Stalkers to launch stiff hairs from their abdomen that were almost as imposing as those of a Stone Dog, if far less venomous.

The Cave Guardian ran his fingers through the bright orange strip of hair on his mount's back. The spider seemed to enjoy that, regularly vibrating anytime someone scratched the area.

Samuel and Bessie passed them, scampering over and under the larger gaps in the tree roots. Drakkar glanced back, watching the Spider

Knights and dragonriders following them. It was strange knowing how recently the dragonriders had begun their training on the spiders, because they moved as naturally with their new mounts as they had with the Dragonwings. Their experience with their airborne mounts had proven valuable.

The line of mounted soldiers stretched farther than Drakkar could see beneath the Forest Giants. Memories rose of the first time he met Charles, and how skeptical he'd been that the old tinker could possibly have Cave's interests in mind. And now he was marching with allies that might never have set foot in the Gray Woods if it hadn't been for Atlier.

Drakkar turned his attention back to the terrain ahead of him, keeping pace with his Ancoran friend, a dragonrider, and a ruler of Canopy.

CHAPTER NINETEEN

J ACOB COULDN'T STOP bouncing his foot as he watched Mary from his jump seat. She deftly brought them up through the airship traffic around Karn, rising above even the Porcupines before slowly accelerating to the northeast. Even at that height, some of the Forest Giants threatened to scrape the bottom of the Skysworn.

Smith's voice echoed over the horn. "Pressure is stable. Thrusters primed."

"Hold on." Mary gave Smith a second to get seated before flipping the lock and engaging the thrusters.

As quick as that, Jacob's intense study of the Forest Giant branches around them ended, instead blurring with the speed of the thrusters as the turbines spun ever faster.

With the tallest of the trees behind them, Jacob had a clear line of sight to the Gray Mountains far in the distance. Ships from the other carrier would be headed there. Some of them had likely left already, preparing to approach the docks above Ballern.

Jacob leaned forward. "Mary, do you think we can find Alice once we dock?"

"I'm pretty sure I couldn't stop you from finding Alice after we dock if I wanted to." Mary glanced back at Jacob and smiled. "I'm not sure we should all go, though."

"Agreed." Smith's voice sounded tinny over the horn. "Mary and I are more easily recognized. Jacob should be safe enough to visit the warehouse district. Assuming that is where Alice is, of course."

Mary nodded. "It sounds like they'll be working on the docking clamps all day. Little doubt that's where everyone will be."

That's all Jacob needed to know. He could head for the Bones and if Alice wasn't there, he'd try the transmitter. They wouldn't be at the bookstore if William were already gone. Maybe the market with Jakon if they had the docking clamps finished.

He'd know soon enough.

✦　✦　✦

THEY HAD ALMOST two hours to spare before they'd arrive at the docks, so once Jacob grew used to the view of the Forest Giants and distant mountains, he made his way to the workshop belowdecks.

Smith had wedged himself between two large copper pipes and Jacob could hear a wrench clanging against something deeper inside the ship. He choked back a laugh when Smith started cursing at length. The tinker normally had an incredible amount of patience when it came to maintenance, but deadlines could fray anyone's nerves.

Jacob focused on the small crate of armored plates for the exoskeleton. The largest of them were already fitted to the lower torso, forearms, and chest, but the joints needed more delicate work. Those would be more like the overlapping pieces he and Targrove had fashioned for the hip joints, only on a smaller scale.

That scale created issues of its own. Jacob needed to reduce the chamber of a bolt cannon to fire a much smaller rivet. A simple prospect as far as the idea went, but a bit more of a mess once he started trying to load the springs.

As his third attempt resulted in another spring launching into the rafters above him, Jacob joined in Smith's lengthy cursing.

Of course, the older tinker wasn't nearly so subtle about his own laugh when he caught the spring and handed it back to Jacob. "Problems?"

"I could ask you the same thing," Jacob muttered.

Smith grinned. "Oh, I knew I'd pay for that design when I installed it. Only place for the valve to go without running another fifty feet of pipe. Figure I can endure some frustration to avoid that. What seems to be the issue you're having?"

"The striking plate. Every time I push it down, it tilts and the spring slips past." Jacob held it out for inspection.

Smith took the palm-sized bolt cannon and turned it over, eyeing the barrel and the square metal striking plate inside. "Double the thickness on the plate. Give it enough height and there will not be enough space to turn, no matter how thin or heavy a spring is used."

Jacob blinked. "That's … that's an easy fix." He took the bolt cannon back when Smith handed it to him.

"Seems you might need a bit more rest. We didn't get much sleep finishing that carrier."

"I couldn't sleep if I wanted to. This is just as good. Once this exoskeleton is done, we can use it like we do the Mech arms."

"Sleep is still needed, but … wait, you mean use the exoskeleton like a wearable crane?" Smith rubbed his neck. "That is an interesting idea. It wouldn't have the load capacity of a Mech arm, of course, but for smaller jobs, it could be an impressive tool."

"I thought the miners might be able to use it too. It'd be easy for them to haul their breathing units around if they could mount it on one of these."

"They likely would not need so much armor for that."

Jacob let out a quiet laugh. "I know that. But I also know where we are."

Smith didn't say any more about that, and Jacob was glad. He knew

Charles had designed the exoskeleton as a weapon of war, and until their war was done, it was best to be prepared for what might come.

✧　✧　✧

AFTER IMPLEMENTING SMITH'S idea for the bolt cannon, Jacob was finally able to get the rivets and clips anchored to the last of the armor plates. He finished the torso and forearms, but the upper arms would have to be done later. Jacob didn't want to untie the exoskeleton from the wall and have it fall over. It was heavy enough it could damage something on the ship, or someone.

He tucked the remaining plates into the wood crate and slid it into the hold next to the exoskeleton.

"Grab a seat," Mary called over the horn. "Cutting thrusters in ten."

Smith simply put an arm out and braced himself on the wall, but Jacob unfolded a jump seat beside the workbench and belted himself in. He'd experienced the force of the thrusters often enough that he didn't want to try Smith's technique.

Everything on the ship lurched forward as the thrusters cut out, inertia causing tools and rivets to clink together across the workbench before settling back into place. The sunken groove all around the work surface caught every stray bit before it could fall to the floor.

Once the ship settled onto an even plane, Jacob gathered up the remaining loose bits from the bench and dropped them into a jar, sealing it before adding it to the crate beside the exoskeleton.

"Smith, if you're going to vent the boilers for the turbines, you might want to do it now. I can see the docks on the horizon, and they're busy. Very busy. We don't need to draw extra attention to our arrival."

"Understood. I'm sending Jacob up."

"What, why?" Jacob asked. "I can help. I've seen you vent the thrusters before. Giant cloud of steam, very hot. You know I'm a tinker, right?"

"You can help if something goes wrong. That is the rule. I have re-fined the thrusters, but they are still far more dangerous than any conventional engine. Don't forget that."

Jacob sighed before nodding to Smith. He walked past the gun pod in the floor and headed into the narrow corridor that led to the ladder. In moments, he found himself squinting against the wind, trying to clip on to a safety line. The gusts finally settled enough for him to make a more coordinated effort.

Mary might have slowed down, but they were still moving faster than most airships. Jacob slid along the safety line until he could reach the door to the cabin. Only once it was open did he disengage his clip and step inside.

"Take a look." Mary held up a pair of binoculars.

Jacob took them without a word, leaning into the windscreen as he tweaked the focus on the binoculars. A thick black and gray haze resolved into a swarm of airships. But they weren't all the dark gray of Fel, and they certainly didn't all bear Belldorn or Bollwerk's colors or designs.

"Are those all Ballern ships?" He didn't hide the concern in his voice.

Mary nodded. "Looks like they pulled some of the fleet back from the carrier. Hopefully, they're only here for a rotation, because that is far more resistance than we'd been expecting."

Jacob narrowed his eyes, studying the scale of what he saw. Two of the ships in the distance looked like destroyers. The same kind of ships Furi had served on. Porcupines could make short work of them, but Fel's warships were docked there, too.

"Perhaps a strike on the carrier would be the best course of action," Smith said over the horn. "It could draw much of the fleet away."

"Or draw more of the fleet to Ballern," Mary muttered.

"It is a risk, either way."

"It is, but the plan is still for the best." Mary nodded to herself. "Seize the docks. Not even Mordair would be fool enough to bomb Ballern's docks while they float over his head. Regardless, we aren't going to the Bones, Smith. We'll dock with the smugglers."

IT WASN'T LONG before the traffic around Ballern's docks didn't feel quite as bad as it had appeared. Once they were inside the perimeter, the brilliance of the design of the airship docks truly shone. Gaps between the levels showed clear markings of the clearances for the entire lane, as well as signaling multi-direction traffic with arrows painted on the level above.

Those who knew the docks well, like Mary and Smith, could fly through the heart of that tangle of steel and copper and avoid the worst of the outer traffic. The interior was another matter as they drifted by, showing the bustling paths and streets of various shopping districts.

Near the center of the docks, the levels could almost be mistaken for one another. It wasn't until they passed out of an area full of citizens dressed well enough to be nobles that signs of disrepair made an appearance. Instead of freshly painted supports, old murals had been chipped away by time and weather, and perhaps a few airship collisions.

But as the shine fell away from the surrounding docks, Jacob knew that meant they were getting closer to their destination. Mary guided them around a corner, and Jacob had to do a double take as The Ray came into view.

"That's our spot. Right next to our favorite chef."

"Are you talking about Jakon?" Smith asked, his voice rising. "I do not believe I have ever heard you utter such a kind word about him."

Mary glared at the horn before letting out a breath that was *almost* a laugh. She let the rear of the Skysworn drift forward, turning them sideways before guiding them into a bay next to Jakon's ship. The docking clamp squeaked as it closed around the bow of the Skysworn.

Jacob hopped up and grabbed his glider pack, checking to make sure he still had the large air cannon concealed in the back. This close to Fel, he didn't want to be going anywhere without it.

"You get into trouble, you run," Mary said. "The less information Mordair has, the better."

"I will. See you soon." He exchanged a nod with Mary before rushing out the cabin door. Smith waved as he gathered rope to tie the Skysworn down, opting against additional docking clamps.

And between one step and the next, Jacob found himself plunged back into the busy walkways of Ballern, heading for the Bones.

But it wasn't the walk through an area he wasn't familiar with that bothered him. The air buzzed with energy and crowds, which set his nerves on edge. It was a sensation he'd encountered before, the kind of dread preceding a battle or a judgment that could turn his life upside down.

Jacob wasn't sure what caused sensations like that. Maybe it was the snippets of conversation he caught, the Skyborn whispering a little too loudly about Mordair and the Stormborn, or perhaps it was the guards, normally absent on the lower docks from what he understood, now nearly as thick as those who lived there.

At least it wasn't Fel soldiers. Most of Ballern's fleet was made up of the Skyborn, and while some of them would surely follow orders, even under the command of the Steward, more would join the Stormborn. They had to.

Jacob passed another lift, this time circling wide to the south side of the docks, avoiding the densest crowds and taking a path through some of the smaller bars near the Bones. Beyond that stretch of specialized cooks and bartenders, he found himself in one of the tent cities on the docks. There his steps slowed, a divide on terrible display the likes of which he had not seen since Ancora.

Instead of a wall dividing the Skyborn, it was the blood-red flags of Fel emblazoned with a Tail Sword. The very idea that Mordair could have injected his own symbols into the Skyborn, to have earned that level of loyalty from a people he would grind to so much dust, sent a bolt of anger through Jacob's chest.

Past the next intersection, he found the scraps of a Stormborn flag, torn and tattered and burned. But it wasn't merely the flag that had met with the flame; it was the tent it had belonged to, smoldering in the brisk breeze on the docks.

Jacob clenched his fists and rushed past until the tent city fell away behind him, and the tiny lift that would take him to the edge of the Bones came into view. It was best not to react to something like that. Not when he didn't know who was watching. No one waited there, so far out on the Bones, away from everything else, but Jacob still hurried to close the creaky gate and force the lever down.

He closed his eyes and took a deep breath, trying to focus on what good they'd done. Kura had influence over the Skyborn—they weren't all lost because of a few Fel flags.

The lift squeaked to a stop and Jacob opened the gate, finding not an empty stretch of abandoned docks, but the hurried buzz of two dozen hands preparing the docks. Rust and decay were the most prominent features on that level, having been eclipsed by the sprawl of the upper levels. Two people turned toward Jacob when the gate squealed closed. They exchanged a quick word before one left and the other headed for Jacob.

Jacob couldn't see her face until she lifted the large, furry hat from her head. Kura raised a hand in greeting.

"Jacob, it is good to see you. Am I to assume Mary and Smith have reached the docks as well?"

"Yes, they're docked by The Ray. Have you seen Alice?"

"Many times." She gave him a knowing smile. "She's working on the north side of the Bones. Helping Furi install some more of these antique docking clamps Jakon is so proud of." The bite in her closing words told Jacob the chef might have overstated the condition of said equipment.

"Thanks, Kura." He started to walk away, and then hesitated. "Kura, in the tent city …"

"We call it the Bones, Jacob. All of it is the Bones. Some choose to live in the portables. Though you can still refer to an individual home as a tent, if you like."

It was a small thing, naming the cluster of tents *portables*, but Jacob supposed that was more respectful than just calling them a tent city. He could have sworn he'd heard Skyborn call it the same, but his memory could be shaky when he was stressed. And there had been little more than stress in his life of late.

"I saw some of the portables burned out. One of them had a Stormborn flag. And … and a lot of others flew Fel flags."

Kura gave him a small smile. "Jacob, there are dissenters among the Skyborn. No one people are entirely united. But the things you saw were for show. Fel soldiers have been offering gold in exchange for displays of loyalty on behalf of the nobles. Or so they say. If it was on behalf of the nobles, why would they ask to fly Fel's colors? But the truth of it is buried, I am afraid."

She shook her head and took a deep breath. "Much of it is show, Jacob. Do you think someone who wished to burn the flag of the Stormborn would have left enough of it to recognize what it was? I assure you they would not. Go see your friends. Soon, you'll have more dire threats to concern yourself with."

It was an oddly reassuring dismissal. "Thanks, Kura."

Jacob walked past her, hurrying down the wider path until he cleared a support column and could see the far end of the Bones, and the cluster of people working on the clamps there. He couldn't make anyone out at first, and he had a hard time not looking down, catching glimpses of the city proper a long way below them through the grated floor.

For a time, he was confused how a single person was able to lift a docking clamp on their own, but then he noticed it was only one half, and the walkway was lined with disassembled parts. As Jacob walked closer, two figures fumbled with the halves before driving what he guessed was a friction pin into the hinge.

After a few more steps, he could make out their faces, realizing one of the people he'd seen was Eva, and the other Jakon. He didn't say anything as he passed them. Startling someone as they held heavy equipment over the edge of an airship dock wasn't exactly good etiquette.

A tray filled with friction pins caught his attention and he couldn't help but smile. It was nice to be right, even when it was over such a small detail. Jacob didn't recognize the pair working on the second clamp, but as he neared the end of the far docks, he couldn't miss Alice's fiery hair peeking out from beneath her gray hat. It almost looked like a beret on her head, except for a wide cuff of shaggy fleece.

Furi pointed at him a moment before Alice turned around. Jacob had about two seconds to ponder how long a fall off the edge of the docks would be before she nearly tackled him in a hug.

"Jacob!"

His momentary panic about their towering height and questionable railings melted away as he squeezed her as tight as he could.

"I'm so glad you're here. We could really use a hand finishing up these clamps." Alice hesitated as she pulled back and grinned. "And it's really great to see you." She grabbed the sides of his face and kissed him before hurrying back to Furi.

"Hi Jacob!"

"Good to see you, Furi. Rin and Tatsu were on the carrier with us, but I didn't see much of them."

"In the workshop?"

Alice chuckled under her breath. "It's like she knows you."

"Well, you've talked about him quite a bit, too, Alice. That makes it easier to guess."

Jacob picked up a friction pin and turned it over in his hand. "Furi's right. Targrove was on board. Between him and Smith, I think the exoskeleton is just about done."

"The what?" Furi asked.

Alice forced a spring into the gap behind the docking clamp. "It's that small Mech he's been on about."

"I haven't been *on* about it. It's not like I'm obsessed with it or any-thing."

"Uh huh."

Jacob took a knee beside Alice. "It looks like you're about done with this one."

"You're right, but there are another dozen between the last few here and the docks to the west."

Jacob whistled and leaned to the side, looking west as if he could see clear to the other side of the dock.

"Did you have any issues on the flight?" Furi asked. "I've been wor-ried. I don't know if Alice has been worried. She sure doesn't act like it."

Alice scowled and went back to locking the second spring into place.

"She's just better under pressure than the rest of us." Jacob grinned at Furi. "The flight was good, really. Did you hear from Rin or Tatsu?"

Furi shook her head.

"They captured one of the scouts. I think she was about their age. Her name was Ling?"

Furi cursed under her breath. "I knew Ling. We served together in Fleet. Is she … I mean, did she hurt anyone?"

"She gave us the codes and schedules for the scouts. She might be the only reason the carriers haven't been attacked in earnest yet."

They focused on the docking clamps for a time, getting them mounted to the edge before testing the springs with a long piece of light metal. When everything passed the test, Jacob remembered something else Furi and Alice might be interested in. "I got to talk to Kat, which was nice. She finally convinced Mary to come to the docks and leave her behind."

"Did Mary leave her with a full company of guards?" Alice asked with a laugh.

"She probably would have if Targrove wasn't with her."

Furi dragged another spring over for the next clamp. "Targrove? Wow."

Alice raised an eyebrow. "Targrove's guarding Kat? Have pity on the next assassin that tries to kill her."

"Let's hope that amounts to zero assassins, yes?"

Alice swatted his arm. "Of course, you know that's not what I meant. But I mean, Targrove has *seen* things, Jacob. I certainly wouldn't want to cross him."

Jacob worked on assembling springs into their housings as they talked. He'd had the same thought about Targrove. He considered the old tinker a friend, but Targrove had a ruthless past. One born of the Deadlands War. Jacob had seen what that war had done to his friends. He only hoped the war with Mordair wouldn't do the same to his own generation.

CHAPTER TWENTY

Owen studied the schematic one of the shipbuilders had brought with them on the ocean liner. It would be accurate for two of their targets, but the other battleships featured much older layouts. The kind Owen had visited almost daily when his father had been a shipbuilder. Before the darker times came to Fel and took so many of his family.

"That's as deep as we need to go." Trevor tapped the far end of the schematic, near the fuel bunkers.

"Oh, that's all?" Fiona muttered.

Trevor flinched at her scathing tone. "We drop the parcels there, and we get out."

Owen leaned forward, bracing both hands against the heavy wood table, his voice dark and exhausted. "It's not good enough. How long will it take them to work through those bunkers, Trevor? Two days? A week?"

"We can't very well stuff a bomb directly into the furnace, can we?" Trevor's response had a trace of fire in it, a symptom of the frustration many of them felt. "Put it on the conveyor, if they have one, but that's as close as you should get. At least if we plan on coming out with all our limbs attached."

"You'll be missing more than your limbs if you're standing next to one of these bombs." Fiona grinned, and Owen had to admit the expression was rather unsettling. "You need to get these in the hands of the stokers."

"The ships don't have stokers anymore," Trevor said, an edge of irritation in his voice. "You should know that."

"And *you* should know how to hide a simple bomb in solid fuel." Fiona scowled at him. "Instead, you nearly set us all on fire, didn't you?"

"That's enough," Owen said, drawing the attention of both of his allies. "It was an accident, and as much as Trevor might be irritating you, can you not see how thankful he is for the help you provided? Without your skills with bombmaking, we would have been forced into far less efficient means of sabotage."

"Like sticking a rod in the gears of the turbines?" Fiona raised an eyebrow.

Even Trevor smiled at that.

Owen chuckled at his initial idea. "Yes, like a rod in the turbines." After a great deal of laughter from Fiona and Trevor at that suggestion, Fiona explained to Owen that the newer ships were armored against so simple an attack.

He traced the path back through the schematic, from the points of entry to the lifts and staircases, to the cargo holds and boilers themselves. "We each take two bricks of solid fuel. Carry it in your pack. Get your story straight. If we're lucky, we won't encounter more than two patrols of guards. Plan on being far less than lucky."

"I still think you're discounting a larger issue," Fiona said.

Owen took a deep breath and nodded. "I know. You made it clear our entire plan could be delayed if the furnaces have cooled. I think you're overly concerned. They'll keep the boilers warm, ready to run or drive the main cannons should the need arise."

Fiona crossed her arms. "I only hope you're right."

"And you're sure we should only be targeting the battleships?" Trevor asked, the anger in his voice having fled for the moment. "Leaving a means to move their goods and supplies on the water is still an advantage in some conflicts."

"I'm sure." Owen nodded. "Supply lines are vital, yes, but we won't need to worry about that if our allies are hit from above and below simultaneously. Ground the warships and, if nothing else, we'll know their line of sight."

"I think you're still underestimating my bombs, Owen. One of these makes it into the furnace, they aren't going to be worrying about their cannons."

Owen eyed Fiona. She'd assured him the blast radius would limit the risk to bystanders, but comments like that worried him. "But you're sure this isn't going to send shrapnel into the market? I don't want innocent people hurt."

"I can't promise that, Owen. Too many things to consider. Too many things that can change an explosion. But I can tell you, the boilers are away from the docks, based on reports. Every ship is docked by the bow."

"That will have to be good enough." Owen sighed and looked at the schematics once more. "Draw up your maps. Nothing obvious. We deploy the fishing vessels an hour before dawn. Stagger the launches. Make sure everyone under your command knows what their task is."

Fiona let out a long breath. "We're almost all fisherfolk, Owen. We know how to cause distractions."

"I've broken up enough brawls at my pub to know that's the truth." Trevor held his hands up when it looked like Owen was going to snap. "Don't worry, we'll talk to everyone. We're all ready to see Mordair suffer for what he did to Fel."

Fel, yes, thought Owen. *But they hadn't seen Dauschen and Ancora. They didn't fully understand what Mordair was willing to do to a city. The time had come for Fel's King to pay his due.*

✧　✧　✧

OWEN PAUSED AS his hand grazed the clip Jacob had repaired on the side of the speeder. The boat rocked up and down as it moved over the waves of the Crystal Sea. The Gray Mountains rose along the western horizon against a bright moon, and south of them, he could just make out the glow of the city in the early morning darkness.

He'd been in those waters before, for a long fishing expedition many years before. That was a different time. A different world, for all it mattered now. Mordair ended the long expeditions, calling them a waste of resources. Owen could still remember the speech that damn fool gave. Even some of the fisherfolk started to believe it was about the resources, as Mordair claimed.

In a way, Owen supposed, it was.

Piercing light breached the eastern horizon a few minutes later, revealing the strange color in the water where the rivers and sea met. The salt water shone as dark as an endless abyss, while the fresh water from the glacier-fed rivers flowed with a light green hue.

As glad as he was that Vaughn and Hefina were safe in Ancora, he wished they could have been there to see that view. The first time Owen had laid eyes on those waters was something he'd never forget.

The view meant something else, too. It meant they were getting close. The estuary was only an hour from the docks with the speed of the currents in that region. Owen glanced off the port side, seeing only two other fishing vessels on the water. One he was certain was Fiona, but the smaller boat he didn't recognize.

Nothing looked out of sorts with their loose formation. Nothing to raise the suspicions of any guards on the docks. Owen adjusted the bearing to avoid a shallow stretch of rock that was notorious for sinking ships in the Crystal Sea. He wasn't sure if the draft of all their vessels would clear the rock, but it was an avoidable, and potentially costly, error.

His bearing took him across the northern bay. They could have docked there. In fact, three of the fisherfolk who weren't carrying explosives intended to do just that. But hauling the heavy blocks of solid fuel through the entire city was too likely to get them noticed. It was one thing to be moving under weight, but it was quite another to be pouring sweat in the relative cool of the morning.

The airship docks and towers of Ballern proper resolved in short order. With the height of the sun, he could make out morning traffic all along the docks, both for the airships and the Crystal Sea. But the vessels on the sea were all dwarfed by Fel's great ocean liners. Even at such a distance, while the trawlers and hunting ships of Ballern looked no larger than thumbnails by the shore, the warships held a threatening presence.

Time swept by on the water. Owen was lost in his thoughts, wondering just how bad an idea their attack was. He considered whether some of his allies might defect to Fel, warn the ships once they made land. Except it wasn't Fel here, not really. It was Mordair, in a distant city, playing Steward in the wake of an assassination. More than one person had called Ballern a powder keg. Owen intended to put a far more literal meaning to that expression.

✧   ✧   ✧

FIONA HAD TOLD him security at Ballern's seagoing docks wasn't anywhere near as robust as what used to guard Fel's docks. No matter how many times she'd repeated that on their journey across the Crystal Sea, part of him worried things would have changed.

But the simple truth of the matter was Ballern's docks *couldn't* be secured like Fel's as the city stood now. In Fel, there were only three paths in or out of the city, gated and fully staffed by guards. It was an easy thing to check every vessel that came in from the open water. The only exception was the fisherfolk, but the caves frequented by the fisherfolk still had a guard station between them and the city proper.

Ballern, however, had opted for efficiency instead of caution. Perhaps it was because there weren't many empires with a seagoing fleet that were of concern, but seeing Fel's warships in the water told a different tale. Caution should have been their priority.

For the moment, Owen didn't care what the true reason was. All he knew was it provided him a level of access to the market and docks he scarcely could have hoped for. Trails of smoke rose from Fel's ocean liners, darkening the sky above him as the swells nearer the stone docks rocked his speeder.

The smoke told him the furnaces were still lit. The thickness of it told him he'd been right to reassure Fiona. If he had to make a wager on it, he'd guess that some of Fel's soldiers had taken up residence. Part of him hoped they'd have time to escape after the ocean liners were sabotaged. Another part of him felt they'd made their choice and could live, or die, with the consequences.

Owen shook that dark thought away. Those soldiers were still citizens of the same city, whether they'd had their differences or not. But memories were a hard thing to break, and he still remembered what those soldiers had done to his brother. At the order of the king or not, they still had the blood of his family on their hands.

His knuckles whitened as he crushed the steering wheel in his grip. Owen pushed the throttle forward and angled the bow into an oncoming wake. As soon as the ship nosed down again, casting a salty spray all around, he spun the wheel to the starboard side. The speeder sliced through the water past the looming shadow of another ocean liner-turned-warship.

Beyond, the water was open but for a cluster of fishing boats that wouldn't have looked out of place in Fel. And if they wouldn't have looked out of place in the north, the vessels of the fisherfolk would blend in just fine.

Owen guided his boat to the stone docks before entering what might once have been a slip for an ocean liner, but had long since been broken down into smaller slips and lanes for the more diminutive vessels. The rolling blue water gave way to pale stone, and in the distance was overwhelmed by colorful tents and banners flying over the market.

It was easy to find an empty slip, and Ballern's docks had ample coils of rope stowed beside every cleat and mooring post Owen could see. That was certainly different than Fel. Any rope left unattended in Fel would be gone and up for sale in the night market by the time the sun dipped below the Black Mountains.

Owen eased back on the throttle until his fishing vessel gently bumped against the padded dock. He took two quick steps to reach the edge of the boat and hopped onto the dock itself. The rope felt smoother than he'd expected, but even with that reduced friction, he figured it would hold to the cleat well enough for the bow line. Owen added an extra loop just to be safe.

He finished tying the boat down with an aft line and one spring line before returning for his leather backpack. With that secured, he gathered up a speargun, torn net, and a large cooler filled with Sea Claw tails to complete the evidence for his story, should he need it.

Owen glanced at the clock on the dashboard before eyeing the sun's arc. It gave him a rough idea when the others would be making land. Given the time, he needed to start moving. It might be easy for one Fel citizen to slip aboard an ocean liner without notice, but a group of them all attempting to do that at once could raise far too much suspicion.

He'd be the first to board the ocean liners. He'd be the first to know if they were doomed to failure, or if they would be celebrating a victory in the market under the nose of their bastard king.

Owen marched toward the farthest ocean liner.

✦　✦　✦

EVERY FOOTSTEP SOUNDED like thunder on the metal gangway, threatening to fray his nerves. But no one stopped to check Owen's cooler or so much as batted an eye at his speargun. Apparently, his choice to blend in had been a good one, as the guards at the top of the ramp didn't stop mocking the Ballern citizens below them for even a second as Owen passed them.

The tarnished letters of the ship's name caught his eye before he stepped onto the deck. The Serpent had been a fishing ship, and a grand one at that, before the king of Fel had converted the ocean liners into engines of war. In an odd way, that had worked out fine for the fisherfolk, driving demand for their own catches. Or at least it had been fine for those who didn't end up on the walls.

Polished wood met his boots, but no matter the care that deck had been shown, it couldn't hide the old stains of oil and guts of a fishing vessel. It was more surprising the smell hadn't lingered. The ocean liners used to haul in catches large enough to feed half the city, and the mess had been something to behold.

Owen adjusted the straps of his pack, fumbling with the spear gun over his shoulder and cooler in one hand as he made his way toward the center of the ship. There were lifts closer to the gangway, but they only led to the officers' quarters and the cargo hold, and either of those could lead to a curious gaze, or worse.

Instead, he followed the length of iron walls and portholes of the top deck, passing only one guard who appeared to be on patrol, and was apparently far more interested in the bustling dock below. Owen turned when he reached the center of the deck, skirting the edge of a large panel that once covered the fish holds. But *The Serpent* was a warship now, and all that hold would contain was weapons meant for much larger targets than fish.

Owen glanced back before reaching for the lift. The worn iron lattice squeaked as he pulled the gate open, but there were few people on deck to take any notice of it. Inside, with the gate closed, Owen set his cooler down and unsheathed a stout knife. He jammed the blade into the corner lift's control panel, wincing at the short shriek of metal. He didn't think the controls had been updated in decades, and pressure at the right angle was enough to pop the lock that prevented access to the bunkers and boilers.

The lever moved swiftly down, passing the block at the cargo hold before clicking into place. Owen withdrew the blade and sheathed it, then kicked the cooler into the corner and wadded up the net before placing the speargun on top. If it was there when he left, he could grab it. If it wasn't, well, he could still run. Every other path out was more likely to be well guarded.

Owen took a deep breath as the lift slowed and came to a jerky stop. He frowned at the change in the air. Gone was the sea breeze, replaced by the thick scent of oil and coal and burning fuel. Solid fuel might have been the choice for most of the ships, but every ocean liner Owen had worked kept an emergency supply of coal on hand, too.

The lattice slid open with little effort, and the control panel clicked, releasing the lever so the lift could return to the higher floors. But Owen had done enough things in his life that required a hasty retreat, and placing an explosive in the engine room of the ship he was on seemed like it would require the same. He jammed his knife into the guide for the gate. So long as it stayed open, the lift couldn't rise.

That done, Owen turned to the narrow hall lit by flickering lanterns. It always unsettled him, knowing the flame of any single lantern could ignite a bunker of fuel and send a ship to the depths of the sea. They might have had sophisticated fire suppression units installed on every vessel in the fleet, but the logical side of his brain wasn't what took hold in the deep sea.

Heat emanated from the next hall, indicating the smoke uptakes were nearby. That meant the emergency coal bunkers would be close, and more importantly, his target would be too. No one waited by the high walls of the bunker, and the first row of emergency boilers sat cold.

The floor rumbled beneath his feet as he crossed the threshold of the engine room. Owen spared a glance backward to make sure no patrol had entered the area. That wasn't too surprising considering how deep in the ship he was. A cursory look told him he was alone for the moment, and he stepped closer to the bunkers of solid fuel.

Trevor had been right. There weren't stokers there. Not any human stokers, at least. Instead, a long, scorched conveyor belt led from the bunkers to a turntable. From there, the bricks of fuel collided with a myriad arrangement of guides until they came out the far end in a uniform line, the apparent randomness ending in the simultaneous placement of bricks on the belts.

The belts themselves moved slowly, dropping a single brick into each boiler as Owen watched. They fell into the fires one after another, not quite synchronized, but certainly better timed than a single stoker could have accomplished.

Owen didn't hesitate after that. He took the explosives out of his pack and slid them onto the turntable. The colors weren't a perfect match, but close enough in the dim light of the furnaces and lanterns, no one would notice the difference in them.

He watched the conveyor for another minute, trying to time how long it might take for those bricks to reach the boiler. As slow as they'd seemed at first, he doubted he had more than fifteen minutes to get off the ship and safely into the market.

Something hit the ground hard, a clang of metal on metal that rivaled the roar of the engine. Owen heard a muttered curse before the long handle of an ash shovel appeared behind the row of boilers.

They might not have had stokers, but *of course,* someone had to be shoveling the ash out of the pit. Owen didn't like the idea of leaving someone in the engine room to die, but he didn't exactly have a choice. Tipping off anyone on that ship could ruin their sabotage, get them imprisoned, and likely get them all executed.

But the ash shovel vanished, and a shadow walked around the corner of the boiler.

It was a kid. A *kid.* Not much older than Vaughn, if he had to guess.

"What are you doing down here, mister?" The kid brushed his hair back, leaving a streak of ash on his forehead as he squinted at Owen.

One thing the fisherfolk had learned to do as Mordair's iron fist closed around their city was to have a story and stick to it. Another thing they'd learned was to improvise when that story collapsed like so much dust in a strong wind.

"I used to work on this ship. Long time ago now. Back when she was a fishing vessel."

The kid scoffed at him. "Mister, this hasn't caught fish in twenty years. You don't look that old."

"You'd be surprised," Owen said with a small laugh. He almost sighed when the kid's posture relaxed, and the ash shovel wasn't held across his body like a weapon. It took everything he had not to look at the conveyor.

"Well, you might want to get out of here. Nothing but dirt and heat by the boilers."

"Can't forget the oil."

The kid cursed under his breath. "Got that right."

"You the only one down here?"

His eyebrows drew down, and he tilted his head to the side. "What do you want?"

Owen hesitated, and another idea came to mind. "Captain said to find a young sailor down here and send him topside. They're needed on the bridge. If you're the only one down here, that must be you."

The kid rolled his eyes. "Great. My cousin is such a needy brat. Give him a captain's hat and he thinks he can boss me around. I'll tell him this time, mister." He dropped the ash shovel, letting it clang against a bunker, and dusted his hands off.

"Should probably hurry, even if he is your cousin." Owen worked to keep his voice casual. "Not good to keep the captain waiting."

Owen gestured to the hall and the kid mercifully went. He spared a look at the conveyor, cringing when he saw the first brick entering the outer corral of the turntable. He looked at the kid and risked pushing the brick back about two feet. It might buy him five minutes, or one minute, but he'd take what he could get.

That done, Owen hurried after the kid, passing him in the hall before dipping in by the elevator. He pulled the knife out of the gate, obscuring the view as he did it. Owen picked up his cooler before the kid stepped in beside him.

"Going after some big fish?"

Owen hefted his speargun. "This? No, it's just for Sea Claw. Good fishing to the east."

The kid pushed the lever up. "You going to the deck, too?"

"I think so." Owen winced at a squeal of gears as the lift whisked them up. "I was going to drop these in the big cooler, but I think I might take them to the market to cook."

"Good soup in the market. So I hear. I don't get out of the bunkers much, though."

"I'm sure they'll let you out soon enough. They have to rotate shifts eventually, don't they?"

He harrumphed and squinted as the lift reached the sunlight of the deck. "I'll tell my cousin you said so."

"Good luck." Owen turned to the port side and started for the gang-way. The kid headed for the starboard railing and vanished toward the bow. That was enough, Owen told himself. It was already a risk, and doing anything else put far more than one kid in danger. But he couldn't leave him down there. At least now he had a chance. And maybe he'd do something with that chance one day. Owen only hoped it wouldn't be meeting Belldorn on the battlefield.

✧   ✧   ✧

Owen released a long-held breath as he passed the final pair of Fel guards. Their gray uniforms and red sigils were a disease infiltrating the docks of Ballern. Soon enough they'd scatter. Soon enough, their attention would be elsewhere, and Mordair wouldn't know which way to look.

The idea made Owen smile. He turned down the third row of vendor stalls, as it was most populated with stewpots and sizzling pans. The cooler full of Sea Claw tails was a bounty for any chef, but the first two he came by sent him farther down the row. Finally, someone was more than happy to trade soup for Owen's full catch.

"I've had more than one vendor tell me you're the best on the docks," Owen said.

The chef raised an eyebrow. "Generous of them. Usually they only say that if they need something that's hard to find. One of them running low on sake again?"

"Why are we *out here*?" the chef's partner asked in a low growl. "We should be on the docks, Jakon. That's where the fight will be."

"Hush."

The young woman stood up a little straighter and glared at the chef. "Did you just tell me to hush?" She snapped before her voice lowered to a whisper, but Owen could still make out most of it. "You won't help the

Stormborn. You won't help me. You're walking away from the Skyborn, Jakon. How could you?"

Jakon closed his eyes and sighed.

"You're part of the Stormborn?" Owen asked, whispering as he leaned toward the pair.

"She is. I'm the hired help."

The woman crossed her arms and scowled. Three boys swooped by, each dropping a folded note into the chef's hand.

Jakon studied them, smiled, and handed them over to her. "There. Can you stop yelling at me now, Furi? You have the word of the guilds they'll stay out of your way."

"Why are you talking to me like this?" Owen asked. "You spill secrets like so many sweets."

"I have no secrets from the fisherfolk of Fel, my friend," Jakon said. "You shouldn't have brought northern Sea Claw to market. The color is wrong before they're cooked. At least, for those who might be looking."

"How … no one notices things like that." Owen glanced between Jakon and Furi. "You're the … you're the captain of The Ray, aren't you?"

Jakon gestured widely. "Indeed, sir. My generosity is known to the edges of Fel. Isn't that wonderful, Furi?"

"I have to get back to the docks. I hope you won't leave us, Jakon."

The chef didn't answer, instead stirring his stewpot, but Furi didn't leave.

"Owen!"

He turned toward his name, finding Trevor and Fiona making their way toward the food stall. "All is well?"

Both of them nodded. It was almost in unison, and not the most discreet thing he'd ever seen.

"What are you three up to?" Jakon asked, a crooked smile crossing his lips.

Owen glanced at his watch. "That obvious?"

"To the trained eye, perhaps." Jakon shrugged. "But the overconfidence of a king can be all the distraction one needs."

"Is this a problem?" Fiona leaned on the table, trying to look angry until she caught a whiff of the stew. "That smells amazing."

"Please, have a bowl. If you mean to fight, you'll need the energy."

Furi sidled up beside Jakon. "You're the fisherfolk Alice talked about, aren't you?"

Owen froze as he took the bowl from Jakon. "How … I've been across two continents, and all I seem to run into is friends of Alice and Jacob."

"You support them?" Furi asked.

He nodded. "I support anyone who stands against Mordair."

Furi glanced around and leaned on the table. "The docks are going to get ugly. The Stormborn are coming. If you want to be in the real fight—"

Thunder tore through the market, bringing the entire assembly of people to silence as smoke and debris and fire exploded from the far side of The Serpent. A secondary explosion ripped through the port side hull, cutting into the warship beside it as black plumes and flames reached for the clouds.

Owen sipped at his soup and watched. The gray and red uniformed soldiers of Fel ran toward the ocean liner. There wasn't anything they could do other than evacuate the sailors at the front of the ship.

"Better than a rod in the gears." Trevor took a long sip from his bowl, not quite hiding the smile on his face. "This really is a wonderful soup, Jakon."

The chef slowly turned back to face the fisherfolk, his eyebrows a bit higher than they had been.

Fiona grinned at him before leaning in conspiratorially to Furi.

"We'll be on the docks here if you need us, lass. You won't be in this fight alone."

The deep growl of failing metal pierced the air as the stern tilted away from The Serpent, finally succumbing to the combination of the bomb and the pressure of the water. It didn't have far to sink in the bay, but it would be joined by its sister ships soon enough.

"Well, I think it best if you depart, Furi. It would appear things are well in hand on the docks."

She nodded and gathered up a sack from beneath the table before sprinting away.

Jakon watched her go before turning back to Owen. "How many?" He gestured toward the billowing smoke with a small tilt of his head.

"All of them," Owen said. "Mordair owes a debt."

"He'll still have his airships. That is threat enough. What about the ocean liners in the north?"

"He has more?" Fiona asked, bracing a hand on the table. "I hoped the rest had been lost in the battle with Belldorn."

"Some were. Others are docked on the far side of the mountains."

Owen cursed. "This is still good. This weakens him. Belldorn can handle a fleet of airships. Targets on the sea are more problematic."

"So you say." Jakon stirred his stewpot as the market slowly started churning with buyers again. "How long?"

Trevor studied his watch. "Any minute. Fiona?"

"Five minutes. Assuming the others didn't run into trouble."

"Well then …" Jakon sat down on a stool and ladled himself a bowl of Sea Claw stew. "I guess we should watch the show."

And what a show it was. There was little left of the back half of the second ship, shrapnel and embers pinging across the edge of the dock. Owen hoped there hadn't been more kids on that one because anyone near the aft deck was gone in an instant. That was the breaking point for the market. Shoppers and vendors both started packing and leaving as fast as they could. Evacuations started immediately on the remaining ships, but they didn't finish before the last of the bombs reached their boilers.

The third blew down into the sea so hard that the stern rose up before crashing into the water. It was a perfect execution, completely disabling the ocean liner while putting the least number of bystanders at risk.

But the final explosion shook the city. Fireballs and shrapnel poured into the sky, arcing and sizzling in the water and the first two aisles of the market itself. The ship had clearly been storing explosives because there was nothing left but a fiery hull. Anyone on board was dead, and Owen's heart felt heavy in his chest.

War was ugly, but Mordair's debt must be paid.

CHAPTER TWENTY-ONE

"WHERE WERE OUR *scouts*?" Mordair asked. There was no rage in his voice, only the slightest emphasis to his question. That fact wasn't enough to keep the room from flinching away from him. "You tell me communications have been sparse, and yet you raise no alarm. And now …" He gestured to the billowing cloud of smoke outside the window.

"Steward." Jonas calmly laid one hand atop the other on the long meeting table. "It was *our* suggestion to send more scouts and position more patrols along all the docks of Ballern."

Mordair slowly cocked his head to the side, hiding the anger boiling behind his words. "Is it not *your* tower upon the docks that serves as Ballern's greatest lookout? Were you not bragging of your impenetrable observations in the same breath you claimed to have demanded more scouts?"

Jonas saw the trap, and his mouth snapped closed.

"Did any of you bear witness to the unquestionable wisdom of the Archduke of Willett? Perhaps the Children of the Dark Fire recall?"

The hooded cloak in the corner gave one small shake of their head.

"No? Baroness, what of your … recollections?"

The Baroness of Auxley steepled her fingers. "It is as you say."

"*What* is as I say?"

Her jaw flexed before she answered. "No one in this room demanded more scouts. A handful of missed check-ins is no cause for alarm."

Patrice sat up straighter at that claim.

"Something you wish to add?" Mordair asked.

The Red Hand nodded. "Perhaps under normal circumstances, a missed contact would be no cause for alarm. Did you not think, *in this case*, with the queen assassinated, and an invader lusting for the blood of your people, a missed check-in could be *everything*? We have a word for that kind of thinking in Fel. Treason."

"Ridiculous," Jonas muttered. "Threatening the Baroness for agreeing with you." He bit off his words. "You are not above *anyone* here."

Mordair slammed his hand down on the table. "You will double guards in your tower, Jonas. Take the most loyal of your soldiers and station them twice as thick. Consider yourself under siege, because in short order you will be. And if another check-in is missed by so much as five minutes, I want to know. If you think the Lady of Belldorn didn't have a hand in the bombing of our fleet, you are a fool."

Jonas opened his mouth to respond, but Mordair cut him off.

"Now go! All of you. Rally your guards. Send them to the docks. If they came for the ocean liners, they will come for the airships. These are your orders. Fulfill them as you deem fit."

The entire table left without a word, leaving Mordair and Patrice alone with the hooded form in the corner.

"Lane," Mordair said.

"Yes, Steward?" the hooded figure looked up.

"All is prepared?"

"Of course, Steward." Lane inclined his head. "The airships of Fel will not be fired upon at the Great Machine. But should a craft flying another's flag pass our docks and arrive at the Great Machine, they will be left in ruin."

"Even if it is Ballern itself."

"Indeed."

A cold smile crawled its way across Mordair's lips.

CHAPTER TWENTY-TWO

Alice wiped a bead of sweat from her brow. She wasn't sure how many docking clamps they'd assembled at that point, but judging by the rust and grease slicking her gloves, it was a lot. Jacob grumbled over a bent spring as he used a screwdriver to remove the mounting bracket for a third time.

"I don't think it needs to be perfect, Jacob."

His shoulders slumped and she couldn't help but smile at his apparent defeat. "I just don't want them to trap an airship."

"Pretty sure that's the point of them."

Jacob narrowed his eyes, but Alice caught the crack of a grin before he turned back to the spring. He tested the lever and nodded to himself, finally reassembling the clamp before dragging it to the edge of the docks.

Alice stepped closer and held the bulk of it up while Jacob bolted the bracket to the mounting plate on the dock. He was almost done tightening the last bolt when they heard it. An explosion that rattled the Bones beneath their feet.

"What the hell was that?" Jacob hopped to his feet and turned in a slow circle.

Alice saw it first, a billowing cloud far below, close to the docks on the sea. "One of the ocean liners? Something close to the market, for sure."

They started moving in that direction, trying to get a better look at the smoke and fire in the distance. They walked south until the path ended, finding Kura and some of the other Stormborn near the railing, watching the smoke rise higher.

"Is the fleet here already?" Kura asked. "I didn't think they'd closed the distance."

Alice leaned forward, looking out through the gaps in the dock, scanning the skies for anything that might be a Belldorn airship. "They aren't here."

"Well, someone's here," Kura spat. "And now Mordair's going to be on alert."

"Not the best timing," Jacob said.

Kura balled her fists. "That's an understatement."

Alice turned toward Kura. "It might not be all bad. If Ballern turns their attention to the sea, more of Belldorn's ships could slip through before Ballern realizes what's happening."

"It doesn't matter, Alice. No one can fire on the airship docks without risking a total collapse, which means Fel's warships have the advantage. They can sight an attacker from where they are, but Belldorn can't fire on them until they leave these docks."

Alice bit her lip. "Then the raids on Fel's warships … that's the only way to stop them?"

"That or destroy the docks, and no one wants that. Not even that fool Mordair."

It wasn't long before another explosion tore through the sea docks far below. Movement intensified on the docks above them, and Alice had little doubt the same thing was happening closer to those ocean liners.

She clicked the transmitter in her collar. "Skysworn."

Mary's voice came back fast. "What is it?"

"An attack on the ocean liners. There's a lot of movement seaside and on the airship docks. If you're close, it could be a good time to come visit."

"Understood. We're testing a new valve Smith installed. We rendezvoused with Kat and her Porcupine. I wouldn't say we're close, but we aren't terribly far. And the clamps?"

"Done."

"Stay ready. Tell that fool of a tinker not to get his other leg blown off."

Jacob's mouth hung open a bit. "Did she just …"

But Mary was already gone.

Heavy footsteps sounded on the Bones behind them, and Furi raced across the walkway, stopping a few feet from Kura, her breath ragged from exertion. "It's the fisherfolk from Fel. They're attacking the ocean liners."

Kura grimaced and rubbed her neck. "First things first. Get food while you can. You don't want your energy failing you at a critical moment. We have stores in the warehouse—some of Jakon's meal bars. They aren't the best tasting, but they last."

"We'll bring a load down here for everyone working on the docking clamps."

Kura shook her head. "No, Furi. Check in with the guilds on the dock. Make sure they are *ready*. If Mordair knows what he's doing, he'll split the earthers between the sea docks and our home. Things are about to get rough in Ballern."

Another explosion rumbled from far below, echoing off the mountains before fading to nothing.

Alice reached out and squeezed Furi's arm. "Let's go. Show us where the stores are, and we can get them prepared for anyone coming through the warehouse."

Furi glanced between Kura and Alice before nodding. She placed a hand over Alice's and then turned away, leading them toward the nearest ladder.

✧   ✧   ✧

ALICE BARELY NOTICED the cold metal in her grip as she hurried up the ladder behind Furi. No thought of falling from Bones crossed her mind as the ladder swayed ever so slightly in the wind. They had a purpose, and her focus on that was absolute. This was what they'd been preparing for. If the battle bled over into the city proper below, if fires razed the shops, William would already be gone, the evidence and history in those books protected by their allies.

They crested the lip of the next level and a gust of wind sent Alice's hair into a storm around her face. She grumbled and pulled it up, using a clip on her collar to pin her hair beneath the cap. The wind brought the scent of fire and oil to her nose, and she spared a glance back at the billowing cloud of smoke.

That dark pitch would reach the docks soon. Ash and cold embers from whatever lives had been extinguished on the sea.

An awful thought flickered across her mind. It was a better death than what the Lowlands had been given in the Fall. Alice shook those darker thoughts away and followed Furi down the length of the Bones. Crowds had gathered there, and it was a struggle to pass them. Every second they were delayed raised the level of her frustration.

But there was no fast path through the people. A strange mixture of panic, awe, and confusion filtered through the masses. Furi didn't hesitate to push her way through, and there were times Jacob helped force someone out of their path.

They reached a wider section of the docks, and the crowd mercifully thinned, leaving them to sprint past empty shops and bars with pots still sizzling on their burners. The center lift had no line, with all the attention on the burning ships below.

Something else caught her eye as the gate closed and the lift rose. "Did you see the warships?"

Jacob gave one sharp nod. "Their flags are out."

"Their flags are always out," Furi said.

"Not their battle flags," Jacob said quietly.

The lift slowed and Furi pulled the gate open. "We can't worry about that now. So they know someone attacked the docks. They can't know what else is coming."

"I hope that's enough." Alice hurried after Furi, jogging side by side with Jacob as they made their way to the warehouse district. To the north she could see the warships, destroyers, and more looming all across Ballern's docks. But Mordair's soldiers were scattered. Only a handful guarded the gangways, while others worked their way through the panicked crowds, shouting orders she couldn't make out.

"They don't know what they're doing," Furi said. "They aren't organized in the chaos."

"They will be." Alice spoke with certainty. Their enemy may be somewhat disorganized at that moment, but she knew what Mordair was capable of. Even if she hadn't lived through the Fall and seen the aftermath at Dauschen, she'd lived through the attack outside the Red Woods, too. It had been precise, brutal, and ruthless. Furi had seen it too, and Alice had little doubt Furi's understanding of Mordair was just as keen.

Furi opened the door to the warehouse and hurried inside. Jacob followed, and Alice made sure to shut it behind them. They weren't the only ones who had returned there.

Eva stood over the transmitter, and she didn't look happy. "I'm telling you. This is the time to strike. Tell Kat."

"They should have timed the strike on the ocean liners, that's all I'm saying." Mary's voice crackled over the transmitter. "It's infuriating …

but we'll do what we can."

Eva took a deep breath and glanced up at the newcomers. "The tinker is back. Docks are ready?"

"They are," Furi said. She didn't stop to say more, instead pulling a large crate off the shelf. She had two more on the floor before Alice could so much as offer to help.

"Understood." It was the last thing Mary said before the transmitter fell silent.

"She's right," Eva muttered. "They should have coordinated that attack."

"It's good enough." Alice pulled several trays of dry bars and snacks out of the crate, setting them beside Furi's pile. "The fleet is close by, isn't it?"

"Not far, no. And they haven't been attacked yet. At least not in force."

"Fel's warships are still docked. Owen may have split their attention. This could be *good*, Eva."

"I know, Alice. That's what I was trying to explain to Mary, but any part of *any* plan that doesn't go perfectly is an abject failure to our dear *captain*."

"She's probably just trying to keep Kat from getting assassinated." Jacob shut his mouth as soon as he caught the glare from Alice and Eva both. Furi, however, apparently found this to be quite amusing. She actually *laughed*.

"Come on," Furi said. "We don't need to be bickering among ourselves. You have two guild leaders in this room."

Alice turned to look at the group behind them. She didn't recognize most of the faces, but she trusted Furi to know the Skyborn who had become Stormborn.

"Take what you can carry," Furi said. "Jakon made these. They're dense and will keep your people fed for the coming battle. If we lose ground we may lose access to our stores."

One of the guild members bounced a small package of food in his hand. "Tell that smuggler we said thanks."

Eva waited for the guilds to leave before she said more. "The Spider Knights are moving through the woods. They'll come from the southwest and cut off any ground reinforcements heading for Ballern. That means the Stormborn have to hold the docks where they are. Until the fleet arrives, we're on our own."

"We need to get back to the ship," Alice said. "I want all of our weapons on us from now until this is over. And the glider packs. If we're fighting on these docks, I want a glider pack."

Eva nodded. "Jacob, Furi, do you need anything from the ship?"

Jacob shook his head. "No, but we're coming with you."

Eva looked up at the pair of Skyborn in the corner. "You two. Make sure anyone who comes here has food and weapons. We'll be back soon, but I have no idea when things are going to get bad out there."

One of the men nodded, but the other just looked pale and so nervous he might pass out. Alice hoped the other could take care of him.

✧　✧　✧

RETURNING TO THE ship meant passing through the crowds again. It reminded her of the crowds at Festival, the revelers watching the dance, entranced by the music and food and drink. Only here it was different. The docks were filled with fear, nervous glances, and a boiling mix of anger and righteous delight.

Worse than any of that was Jacob. Alice didn't like seeing him look so ready, so alert. He looked as though he could take on the world, his eyes focused and brows drawn as they slipped from one cluster of people to the next. Her heart sank as the reality of it all sank in: he looked like a soldier.

Alice stared ahead, keeping her attention on Furi and the crowd. Jacob didn't need to see she was upset. He was too good at noticing that, and the last thing any of them needed to be talking about was how this wasn't the life they should be living. How they should still be home in Ancora, worrying about Cork or whatever assignment from Miss Penny Jacob had blown off again.

Now was the time to be soldiers. They needed to focus on the task at hand, because far more lives than theirs hung in the balance. The battle was coming, and they could greet it with tears, or teeth.

CHAPTER TWENTY-THREE

OWEN STOOD IN the entryway to the docks of Ballern and watched the ocean liners burn. There was a small satisfaction there. More than small, if he was honest with himself. Mordair had started this war long before, but soon it would end. Soon his reign of slaughter would be over, and if the price of that was more blood, so be it.

Trevor walked toward him, casually sipping a bowl of soup as he grinned at Owen. "This is the last of it. Have to say, that chef is good."

"How can you eat more right now?" Owen asked.

"I don't intend to die on an empty stomach. We should have beer in our stomachs for that, though this soup is a good substitute."

Owen raised an eyebrow.

Fiona held up her hand. "He owns a bar, Owen. What do you expect?"

That got a laugh out of both of them, though Trevor didn't look terribly amused.

"More guards." Owen watched as another Fel squad marched into the market, headed for the burning ocean liners. The evacuations would be done soon, which meant the interrogations would follow in short order. "If we mean to do this, it needs to be soon."

Trevor took another sip of soup. "Wait until the time is right. We want as many soldiers by the ships as possible. Pin them in. Strike too early and we'll get ourselves trapped."

Owen studied the southern end of the docks. Two dozen fisherfolk milled around the remnants of the vendors who had come back to gather their wares. Ten more lingered far too close to the ships for Owen's comfort, but they didn't look out of place.

They had more fisherfolk in the alleys just outside the market, and if the northern landing parties had arrived without issue, they'd enter through the eastern archway. So many ifs. Too many variables. But this was for Vaughn. For Hefina. For all the fisherfolk who would suffer under a return to Mordair's rule, and for those who already had.

Raised voices drew all of their attention to the slip nearest the wall.

"This is it," Fiona said. "That's Argyle, without a doubt."

Owen took a deep breath to steady himself as the scene unfolded. Argyle gestured to the ship with a large hammer. To someone who didn't know better, it could have been mistaken for an elegant workman's sledge, but it wasn't. The double-headed tool was a war hammer. Traditional among the fisherfolk to protect their homes.

It looked small for a sledge in Argyle's fist as the man was nearly seven feet tall, but Owen knew the style of hammer. It was at least five feet long. Good for reaching through windows, or across nearby ships.

A second soldier grabbed the arm of the first, letting Argyle and the other fisherfolk pass. Argyle shook his head as he reached the gangway for the second ocean liner, the least damaged of them all. He cast a smile over his shoulder before the war hammer came down on the dock, shattering the anchors for the ramp and sending it into the sea.

"This is it." Owen cursed under his breath. "Now. Go go go."

Trevor dropped his bowl of soup, leaving the contents to splash across his boots as the vessel shattered.

Owen pulled a whistle from a pouch on his vest and raised it to his lips. A piercing cry echoed out from the instrument—two pulses, a brief pause, and three more. It meant there was a threat in the area. Except this wasn't a warning for dangerous creatures in the water. This time, *they* were the threat.

The fisherfolk on to the south drew blades and hammers from the Sea Claw traps slung across their backs. Others revealed weapons they'd stashed in close-knit baskets that served as fish traps in the rapids near Fel.

There was no warning before the first of the fisherfolk reached the Fel soldiers. There was ash and fire in the air, and then there was blood on the earth.

Violence exploded in the market like a tinderbox, but confusion gave the fisherfolk the upper hand. Owen leveled his speargun at an archer who had stepped up onto a table, the snap of the overstretched bands trying to pull the weapon from Owen's hands when he fired. But his aim was true, and the archer stared down at the shaft stuck in his chest, trying to pull it out before he fell backward to the stones.

They didn't fight alone that day. They wouldn't die alone. The Skyborn of Ballern joined in the fray, a wild mix of mercy and ruthlessness as they cut into the Fel soldiers.

"Join the Stormborn or die!" became the battle cry on the bloody stones of the docks. And it turned more than a few of Mordair's sailors. The patches of Fel's Tail Sword dropped to the ground, torn away from uniforms as sure as the flags from the bearers.

Those loyal to Mordair formed a line across the docks, exactly as Owen had hoped. They could only engage a handful of the fisherfolk at a time, and if Owen was going to bet on anyone in a brawl, it would always be the fisherfolk.

But that fight was no brawl. No skirmish in a pub left dozens dead on the floor. A sword lashed out in Owen's peripheral vision, and he barely raised the speargun in time to parry it. But the blow did its work, severing the bands of the weapon and turning it into little more than a metal club.

"Fight!" Fiona roared beside him. She stumbled one step as a guard hit her cheek with a flagpole. He should have followed up. Fiona lunged, landing a hammer strike that collapsed the man's jaw. He didn't have much time to scream before the killing blow fell between his eyes.

The spray of gore stunned Owen's attacker, taking him off guard, and Owen took the opportunity to sink a broken blade into the soldier's neck. A swift boot to the chest sent the man off the edge of the docks, still scrabbling at the wound in his neck. Owen drew a sword from his backpack, short and meant for close quarters, but it would do the job.

Blood pooled around the bodies, forming rivulets between the paving stones of the market. Some of Fel's soldiers stopped on the opposite side of the tables as reinforcements flooded in through the archways, as if those heavy wood benches would keep them safe.

"For the fisherfolk!" Owen shouted, kicking the nearest bench into an archer's kneecaps. He hurdled the table, landing a vicious kick in another guard's ribs, before missing the next completely. A strike from Owen's sword sent the man reeling. An ax whistled as it cleaved the air, splintering the table as Owen rolled to the side.

Trevor lunged beside Fiona, a narrow Fel sword cutting through flesh as quickly as it slid through the air. More soldiers poured through the archway, slowly pushing the fisherfolk back.

Owen gritted his teeth as he engaged another pair of soldiers, feeling the sting of metal when a blade scored a hit on his triceps. Even if they lost here, it wouldn't be the end of the battle. Even if they lost here, Mordair would know who had taken half his fleet to the bottom of the sea.

The ground took his breath away as a poleax tripped him up, and he saw death above him. She wore a dented helmet, her eyes a radiant amber. Until a blade sprung from her throat, and a feral child threw her to the ground.

It was hard to recognize the face, so covered in blood and ash. But it was the child from The Serpent. The child he'd almost let die. A child who should never have been so good at killing.

Owen climbed to his feet as that kid waded back into the battle, a scream on his young lips.

"For the Stormborn!"

✧   ✧   ✧

SAMUEL TRIED TO adjust his position in Bessie's saddle, but he had the sad realization that no matter how he sat, he was going to be sore. There came a point, after so many hours, saddles just weren't comfortable. It was annoying how little the dragonriders were complaining.

He stole a glance at Tatsu, who looked as comfortable on his Stalker as he did on a Dragonwing.

"If you keep fidgeting, you're going to fall off."

Samuel turned to find Drakkar wearing a wide smile. "I'm ready to be out of the saddle for a bit, alright? Is that so terrible?"

Drakkar's smile didn't fade. "You should try riding a Stalker some time. It is quite refreshing, and smoother even than our best-trained Walkers."

Bessie chose that moment to shake her rear leg, clearly annoyed by being weighed down with armor, and almost rattling Samuel's teeth out in the process.

While he tightened his grip on the saddle, leaning back into the most padded portions, something in the trees caught his eye. It wasn't much, a glimmer of light before it was gone. It could have been the eye of a Tree Killer, but he didn't trust anything in the Gray Woods. They were in the enemy's territory, and there was much they didn't know.

Samuel tapped on Bessie's back, slowing her down until she was side by side with Drakkar's mount. "Something above us. Have you seen it?"

"I have seen many things, Samuel. It is a strange place, these Gray Woods."

"Not arguing that. I was worried it could be a Tree Killer. I know there are a lot of them in the woods, but don't the Children of the Dark Fire ride them, too?"

Drakkar kept his eyes focused on the canopy.

Rin wheeled his Jumper around, slowly climbing over the roots of one of the giant trees to avoid becoming an obstruction. He came down on Drakkar's flank. "Did you see it, too?"

"Did you hear me from over there?" Samuel gestured to the far side of the formation where Rin had been.

"No, but I saw you speaking and thought it might be because of the canopy."

Samuel nodded. "Like a flash of light?"

"Yes."

"The Spider Knight thinks it might be a Tree Killer," Drakkar said.

Rin shook his head. "Too bright. It was metal, no doubt. Something's following us. If I had a Dragonwing I could be on it in an instant."

Samuel smiled at Rin. "Oh, we don't need a Dragonwing for that."

"Samuel …" Drakkar started.

But the Spider Knight was already pulling the quick releases for Bessie's leg armor. One at a time, they fell to the ground, the spider flexing her joints in relief.

"I'll make it fast. Grab my armor, would you?"

He couldn't quite make out Drakkar's response before he gave Bessie the signal. She might have been a tiny bit slow with three armor plates still anchored to her saddle, but it wasn't enough to keep her on the ground anymore.

Bessie leaped onto the nearest Forest Giant, and scampered toward the canopy, branches and wide leaves narrowly missing Samuel as she darted in and out of the thickening cover. The shadows of the forest gave way to the sun overhead as they passed the level where he'd seen the light.

Samuel directed Bessie to the west. She scuttled out onto the nearest branch, pumped her legs twice, and launched them forward. Samuel leaned into the saddle, the momentum keeping him mounted as well as the restraints could. Bessie's legs spread wide, changing angles ever so slightly before they hit the next tree.

Something crackled nearby, and it took a moment for Samuel to realize it was his transmitter.

"To the Stormborn and our allies. The battle has begun in the markets of Ballern. This is your call to arms. May we all find peace in the end."

"Kat?" Samuel whispered under his breath. "What the hell was that? Are they deploying the airships?"

But the thought left him as Bessie pushed through the hanging leaves, and Samuel found exactly what had been stalking them. He had a second to evaluate what waited in front of them, his reaction slowed by his split focus on the transmitter. Huge black eyes sat in a red face with short mandibles beneath long outstretched antennae. Ridged, brilliant green wing covers ran the length of its back, catching the sunlight as it shifted through the branches.

Samuel rapped behind Bessie's right eye, and the spider sprang into action. The spray from the Bombardier slammed into the branch where they'd been, and while Samuel braced himself for the terrible burns he'd heard tales about, nothing reached him but a foul, musky stench and a wave of heat.

The beetle hadn't been alone. On its back sat a cloaked form, dripping in the gray robes of the Children of the Dark Fire. This wasn't a chance encounter. This was an ambush.

Samuel pulled an oval silver whistle from a pocket beneath the armor on his thigh. He covered the end holes on the face of the engraved whistle with his index finger and pinky and blew hard. Two shrieking notes, unmistakable in their high pitch, then a pause, followed by two more. The pattern repeated as Bessie scampered down the trunk of the Forest Giant.

The Spider Knights would know the signal, but the dragonriders might not have remembered their training. Samuel clicked the transmitter in his collar. "Drakkar! Bombardiers in the canopy, scatter!"

But it wasn't only Bombardiers in that place. Bessie leaped without warning. Samuel struggled to stay upright, leaning deep into the saddle, and the spider's violent movements saved his life. A Tree Killer's scythe cut the air above him.

Bessie hit the branch and bounded into the air again, landing squarely on the Tree Killer's back. The rider never had a chance. Bessie's fangs punctured the rider's cloak, tearing it away to reveal the bloody armor plate beneath, and an empty face on a limp body.

Samuel ripped his halberd free from the loops on the saddle and thrust down between Bessie's legs. The Tree Killer spasmed twice and lost its grip on the Forest Giant's bark. Bessie felt the shift and hurled herself away, twisting in the air as Samuel cursed at the sudden movement and held on with one hand.

Another blast from a Bombardier splattered across the bark above them, the spray singeing the exposed flesh of Samuel's wrist and cheek as if boiling water had been thrown at him. With horror, he realized how far away that Bombardier was. At least seventy feet, and that stream of superheated liquid had hit with force. The Stalkers would be like Pillies in a pond.

Bessie moved to the opposite side of the tree and raced to the forest floor. Samuel could do little more than hold on and try to keep his halberd from hurting her at that point. But the Spider Knights' mounts were trained well and had learned to regroup on instinct. She sprinted into the towering arches and valleys of the Forest Giant's roots, the impact of Bombardiers and other weapons hitting the wood above them.

Samuel crouched low, and Bessie shot back out onto the path, racing toward the nearest group of Stalkers. Superheated blasts from the Bombardiers dug pits into the dirt, sending sprays of burning mud into the air and scattering the Stalkers.

But the Bombardiers weren't the only mounts with a long-range attack. A Stalker spun and raised its abdomen, raking its leg across the spear-like hairs in rapid succession. A scream came from the canopy above, and a rider fell to the earth on the back of their Bombardier, the hairs of the Stalker embedded in both.

The still forms of the Tree Killers and Bombardiers weren't the only casualties on that field. Two Stalkers lay broken against a knot of roots, their legs curled beneath them and their riders motionless. Samuel flinched away from the second. She was not merely still, but half her upper body had been melted away. The Bombardiers shouldn't have been able to do that, and a cry told him it hadn't.

"Acidwings!"

Samuel caught sight of the orange stripes of Drakkar's mount and urged Bessie closer. She scampered to the left and right, dipping into another cluster of roots before exploding out the top, arcing through the air to land beside Drakkar.

"They have Acidwings!" Samuel said. "How are they controlling them?"

Drakkar, far more collected than Samuel, pointed to the canopy. "That is a simple answer, my friend. They are not."

Another cloaked form fell from the highest branches, screaming as their body smoked before the impact silenced them. Bombardiers, empty of riders, scattered through the canopy. Acidwings attacked some of them, but the thick wing covers gave the Bombardiers good protection against the worst of their attacks. Their riders weren't so fortunate.

A pitch-black Stalker wove through the edge of the Forest, coming to settle in beside Drakkar. "What word?" Allie pulled her hood back, exposing a blistered forearm.

"Tree Killers and Bombardiers set an ambush in the canopy," Samuel said. "Some wild Acidwings are attacking both sides."

Allie nodded and turned to the pair of riders closing from behind. Rin, mounted on another Stalker, and Tatsu's Jumper, hopping along the roots beside him. "You were right, Tatsu. There are Tree Killers here, too. If they are anything like the Deadlands species, they'll shelter until the threat is gone before attacking again."

"Which means we should be gone before that happens," Drakkar said.

Allie studied the scene ahead, swooping Acidwings and Bombardiers dueling in the skies while the spider mounts raced away beneath them. "We must divide our forces. They are a threat to Karn as much as to our allies in Ballern.

"Drakkar, take Samuel and Company A to Ballern. Rin and Tatsu can show you the best way through the city."

She turned to look at the dragonriders, as if silently asking if that was acceptable. It was a sign of respect, and yet another reason Samuel found himself liking the people of Canopy more and more.

"It's time to go home." Rin looked up to Tatsu. "Best path forward."

"Quarter mile north puts us on a wider path. Canopy isn't as dense. We could be spotted by airships, but an ambush by the Bombardiers would be easier to avoid."

Rin nodded. "Samuel, round up the Spider Knights. We need as many as we can for the infiltration of Ballern. You're better on the city streets. The dragonriders know the woods better. They can reinforce Karn."

"I'll escort them," Allie said.

"Good." Tatsu eyed her wound. "Get that arm dressed before it gets infected. I'll be sure Samuel does the same."

Rin's brow drew down. "What about the dead?"

"How many did we lose?"

"Three, from what I've seen. Though more were burned."

Samuel wondered if it was anyone he knew. Anyone he'd trained with in Ancora or even Canopy. He almost didn't want to know. They'd lost three allies. Three was a number; it wasn't a face. It was easier to fight on when the dead were only numbers.

Allie grimaced. "Anyone injured, get them back to Karn with Company C. Whoever is able, we'll scout the Gray Woods with guides from Karn. Leave the dead."

"Here, in the woods?"

"Yes, Rin. And should I fall in this battle, you will do the same. It is not such a bad fate to return to the earth. Though I admit I would prefer not to be … melted." Allie grimaced as she said it. "You all have your orders."

Samuel clicked his transmitter. "All Spider Knights, head north until you reach the next road. We'll take it all the way from Ballern. Company A will continue to Ballern. Company B, return to Karn. Company C, we need half of you back in Karn as well. The rest can follow us."

Shouts went up in the deeper woods around the Forest Giants. No one argued with the idea of moving away from the Acidwings. Two of them had struck the head of a Bombardier and now greedily slurped at the remains with long proboscises. Samuel was glad to put the vision of that ambush gone wrong behind him.

They moved farther into the shadows.

✧   ✧   ✧

JACOB CHECKED THE straps for his glider pack for a second time. He went over Alice's as she finished slipping half a dozen air cannon magazines into her belt. Bolt gloves covered both of her hands, and Jacob tried not to think about why she had so many cartridges in the leather thigh bag she'd found in the lockers.

It was the same reason he had bombs and Bangers and Burners stashed across his own pockets, he knew. The idea of another fight, another battle looming, was exhausting in itself. But giving up was a far worse prospect.

Eva studied the glider packs and smiled. "They're really quite impressive, Jacob. Better than anything I ever had with the Skyriders."

"Smith mentioned something about the Skyriders," Jacob said. "Did you really use gliders a lot? Do you still have them? I'd love to see them one day."

"Our patrols all wore them, yes. Once the brigs came into service, most of us joined a proper crew. I'd be surprised if Theo didn't keep a few of those old gliders around. They weren't so maneuverable as yours, mind you. But they were silent and hard to see. Are you all set?" She turned back to the console.

Furi was ready, but she took the time to go through her weapons again. She slipped knives, bolt throwers, and a slender crossbow into the extra space of her glider pack.

Eva pounded her fist on the console. "Not yet, you fools."

Jacob hurried to the windscreen to see what Eva was looking at. A flag some twenty feet by twenty feet snapped in the wind. It was Fel's flag, with a ragged red X painted across its entirety. Beside it, a Stormborn banner glittered as its sequins caught the light.

"It's like lighting a fuse while you're *standing* on the bloody thing," Eva growled. "Come on. We need to get back to the lift. If this goes wrong, it's going to go very wrong."

"Should we move the freighter?" Alice asked. "Clear up space on this level?"

Eva shook her head. "Look to the north. I see two of Fel's destroyers already backing out of the docks. It wouldn't take much to trigger an attack once the docks aren't in the line of fire. And an unmarked freighter might be just their kind of target."

They followed Eva to the gangplank and hopped back onto the docks. Furi closed the hatch behind them, and they were off, heading for the lift.

It didn't take long to run into the Stormborn, and the whispered conversations had grown louder. They weren't rumors in the back of the little bars and tents along the Bones anymore. They were blatant, with many emboldened by the attack on the sea docks, and more than one skirmish breaking out with the Fel soldiers.

"The real fight's in the market!" a young woman said nearby. "Let's go. They won't fire on the docks, and those rebels are going to need help down below."

"They're right, aren't they?" Furi asked.

Eva pulled the lift open when they reached it. Three other Skyborn were inside, but Eva didn't bother to whisper her response. "It may be where most of the fighting is now, but it will move. I've seen it before."

"For the Stormborn," one of the other women in the lift said.

"For the Stormborn," Eva echoed. They rattled to a stop, and she pulled the gate open, some of the people following them onto the docks, and others continuing up. They stepped into a crowd who were no longer simple observers.

Jacob saw blood on the ground by the nearest bar, enough of it to know someone had been gravely injured. To the north, a line of Fel soldiers blocked every path leading to the warships. And before them, the Skyborn rallied.

There were more than words exchanged as the volume rose, and Eva led them through the masses. When they reached some of the dwellings, several people stepped out of their homes with weapons in hand. Swords, axes, crossbows, and a strange, hooked blade that would have been at home on a fishing vessel.

A scream cut through the air, and Jacob watched in horror as a girl fell from above. There was no time to react. No time to help. She slammed onto the platform behind the Fel soldiers.

One gray uniform turned, looked down at the girl pleading for help, and ran her through with a sword.

The response was immediate, unrestrained, and utterly ruthless. Five Fel soldiers died in an instant. Enough bolts and blades penetrated their torsos to bring down a horde of Red Death. Blood ran freely as the line broke, and the Stormborn were unleashed.

"Keep close!" Eva shouted.

Jacob and Alice already had their air cannons primed. They stayed back to back, flanking Furi. Running into that chaos was a quick way to die. They could do more from where they were. Fel soldiers might have expected attacks from swords and bolt throwers. They'd never see an air cannon coming. But they'd damn well hear it.

Jacob tracked the nearest soldiers across the chasm. They'd been cut off from both sides of the street. He eased the trigger back and the air cannon thundered, a cloud of red viscera rising across the dock.

Alice's air cannon echoed Jacob's. The damage might have been less spectacular, but the soldiers were no less dead because of it.

Furi shouted into their ears. "If they deploy all the soldiers on those ships, we're all dead. We have to stop the warships!"

"The transmitter." Eva leveled a bolt thrower at a guard rounding the nearest corner. "We need to get to the warehouse. Contact Mary. Tell them to come *now*!"

Jacob cursed and fumbled with his collar. "Skysworn. Skysworn, come in." He ratcheted the slide for the air cannon and took aim again. "Skysworn!" The air cannon thundered in his hands and sparks flew as one of the far railings deformed beneath the shot, sending another soldier reeling but alive.

"What is it?" Mary asked, her words hurried.

"Fighting on the docks."

"We know, the fisherfolk."

"No! The airship docks. Skysworn, the airship docks are—" He didn't finish the question before the first of Fel's battleships fired. A large clipper over the sea vanished in a ball of black smoke and orange flame.

"What was that?"

"Fel's firing on airships outside the docks. Whatever you're going to do, do it now!"

Mary let out a string of curses. "Hold the docks. Hold the damn docks!"

Not all of Fel's warships pulled away. Some remained, and Fel soldiers poured down the gangways, spilling out into the Skyborn's home. Armed with poleaxes and spears and shields, they were prepared for close-quarters fighting. They had the tools to put down anyone who challenged them.

Jacob ground his teeth. The Battle of Ballern had begun.

CHAPTER TWENTY-FOUR

MARY RAN HER fingers through her hair, clenching her jaw so tight she thought her teeth might shatter. They were out of time. She sprinted down the deck of the Porcupine. Kat and Arun were still on the bridge, as far as she knew, and they couldn't wait to act any longer.

She reached the middle of the ship in short order, boots cracking against the wooden deck, before she pulled the armored door to the bridge open. Two more doors were inside, but they were open.

Arun tapped the map in the Gray Woods outside Ballern as Mary raced across the bridge. "They encountered the ambush here. Not far from the city at all."

"And there are no other major roads from the north?" Kat asked.

Arun shook his head. "Only the east. Anything else would have to come through the woods themselves, and that is not something I would expect of the Children of the Dark Fire."

"Kat, I have news from Jacob about the docks." Apparently, Mary hadn't kept her voice as steady as she thought, because Kat broke off her conversation immediately and turned to face her.

"Bad?"

Mary nodded. "They're fighting with Fel's soldiers stationed near the Bones. It may have spread more already, I don't know. But we need to act."

Kat looked back to Arun. "We'll leave a Porcupine near Karn, guarding the northwest. If anything comes down that road, it won't have an easy time of it."

"A generous offer, but it may serve you better." Arun rubbed his hands together and studied the map before returning his gaze to Kat. "We can defend ourselves well enough, Lady Katherine. You need your ship in the north."

Kat smiled and clicked the transmitter in her collar. "Archibald. We have news."

✧   ✧   ✧

RIN HUNKERED DOWN on the back of his Jumper, Hilda, as if she were a Dragonwing that might soar into the air at any moment. Of course, without her leg armor attached, his mount might very well soar into the air at any moment.

The Stalkers moved fast below him, but even their impressive speed was no match for the Jumpers. As silent as those huge mounts could be at a casual pace, the Stalkers raised a thunder as they ran through the Gray Woods. If there were Tree Killers and Acidwings waiting to ambush them, they'd all decided not to attack the armored stampede.

Rin matched Samuel tree for tree, leaping ahead to scout the path for additional ambushes. Far below, Tatsu followed beside Drakkar, their allies bunching up close behind them. The tight formation might not be best in the case of a volley of arrows, or other wide attack, but the churning dust and detritus turned the mob to shadow, and it was a terrifying sight to behold.

Over and over, the message from the transmitters replayed in his mind. Ballern's market was a battlefield. The docks had erupted into violence. The place he'd called home for so many years was crying out to every Skyborn who'd ever set foot on the Bones. And he'd be damned if he'd let it burn.

The leather in Rin's fist creaked as he grabbed the saddle harder when Hilda launched them off another branch. Wind pulled the hardened leather helmet hiding his hair, and he wondered how Hilda would move with no armor at all. She might well have rivaled Bessie.

Rin glanced toward the Spider Knight. Samuel still had his halberd drawn and raised in the air, shifting and moving with Bessie as if they were one body. It was a dance, Rin had come to realize. A dance of violence and death that few could match. The Dragonwings gave their riders speed and an advantage in height, but here in the Gray Woods, the spiders ruled the ground.

The tight quarters of Ballern would be no different.

Rin grunted as they slammed into another tree. The branch beneath them bent as Hilda scampered across it, and instead of jumping again, she took him back to the ground. There was only a second to wonder why, and then the forest gave way to grassland, and the walls of Ballern rose before them in the distance.

Airships circled the docks far above. Smoke curled near some of the largest gas chambers, telling Rin instantly where some of the fighting was. It certainly hadn't been contained to the warehouse district. Some of the visible flames were on the highest levels where a few nobles lived. They might not have been earthers, but they were the worst sort of neighbors.

But for those flames to be seen miles out, they had to be massive.

Samuel and Bessie slammed into the ground beside him, kicking up dirt and crumbling leaves that had fallen from the Forest Giants. The Spider Knight had to shout over the roar of the Stalkers and Jumpers behind them.

"What's the best way to the market?"

"Shouldn't we head for the docks first?" Rin asked.

"No. Leave that to Mary and Kat. We need to help on the ground." Samuel sounded like an officer in that moment, and Rin wondered just how many battles the Spider Knight had seen.

Rin glanced toward the pale white stone of Ballern, some of its tallest towers peeking over the wall, crowned in brilliant golds and silvers. "Straight through the main gates. Turn when you see the largest archways."

"For the Stalkers, fine! What about us? We don't need the ground, Rin."

The dragonrider leaned back in his saddle as though Samuel had slapped him.

"The shopping district. Just inside the wall." His words came fast as he pictured an entirely different path. "Most of the buildings are only three to four stories, and they aren't smooth."

Samuel grinned at him. "Now that sounds like home. I'll tell you about the Lowlands sometime!" He clicked the transmitter on his collar, and his voice drifted away, only to come across as a staticky buzz a moment later.

"Stalkers, take the main street east until you see the huge archways to the marketplace. You won't miss it. The fisherfolk and the Stormborn are already fighting. Jumpers, if you dropped your leg armor, follow us! Otherwise, stay with the Stalkers."

Rin looked behind them, struggling against the wind. Four other Jumpers hopped to the outside of the Stalkers and scurried toward them. When he turned to face the city again, they were almost on it. Roads of stone and sand passed beneath Hilda's feet.

The dragonrider leaned close to her saddle again, tapping on her head to guide her directly to the gates. Rin worried the western gates might be closed, but people were running through them, away from the city. If the western districts were evacuating, how bad had it gotten on the ground?

Rin steeled himself and pulled ahead of Samuel. Hilda didn't slow as they closed on the crowds running from Ballern, but the flood of citizens spread around them like water, scattering to the wind when they saw what was coming.

There were only two expressions on those peoples' faces. Terror and shock. As many refugees as Rin saw fleeing the gates, he knew there were countless more inside the walls. People who would sit and wait, watch and listen as the city was torn down around them, not quite believing what had come to their city until it was too late. The best he could hope to do was end the fighting faster.

Mordair might have removed the queen, but he had ignited a revolution among the Skyborn.

The pack of spider mounts reached the soaring gates of Ballern and passed through. One moment they were on the dirt and stone of the main road, and the next they were in the city proper. A quick glance told Rin there were no guards in the tower, no one to lower the gate. Most likely either dead or having abandoned their posts.

If that changed now, it would be far too late to stop the march of the Spider Knights and the dragonriders. Rin grimaced when he saw the dead on the streets of Ballern. Not cut down or slain, but trampled by their own neighbors. He'd seen the like when riots had gripped the villages outside Belldorn in response to Lady Katherine's increased patrols.

Rin tapped on Hilda's head, and the spider leaped without warning, wide feet grasping the stone and window ledges of the nearest building. He leaned forward and clung to the saddle until they crested the top of the building. It wasn't hard to tell where the market was after that.

The ruined warships still spewed smoke so high into the air that it drifted over the walls themselves. He focused instead on the family he knew was inside those walls. Not the family he was born to, but the Skyborn themselves. Kura, Furi, even that damn pirate, Jakon. They were worth fighting for as chaos enveloped the city. And if he had to, he'd die to protect them.

Samuel sounded a piercing trio of notes on his whistle, and the Spider Knights roared behind him.

✧   ✧   ✧

DRAKKAR STAYED CLOSE to Tatsu. The man had grown up in Ballern, and he would know far better if anything was out of sorts inside the walls of the city. Of course, everything was out of sorts. Chaos ruled the streets, and picking one threat from another in that jumble of bodies was a near impossible task.

He could no longer see Rin or Samuel as they'd gone over the buildings to the south, but he could plainly see the soldiers forming a line near the fountain ahead. "Tatsu!"

"I see it!" Tatsu turned to Drakkar from the back of his mount. "That is one of the roads that leads to the palace. The other is by the largest fountain, past the lifts. If they do not attack, do not attack them."

Drakkar urged his mount to stick closer to the buildings the Jumpers had gone over. It kept them farther from the line of soldiers, but not far enough to avoid a well-placed bolt or throwing knife. It might be safer to engage, but it would also guarantee a battle in the middle of far too many bystanders.

They passed the first cluster of guards without incident. The Stalkers' claws cracked against the stone streets as the armored company moved deeper into the city. But whatever had kept the soldiers from attacking Tatsu and Drakkar was lost by the time the rear lines flooded through the gates.

Shouts and screams echoed behind them, and Drakkar glanced over his shoulder. Two of Ballern's guard had engaged a Jumper. It was a mistake quickly ended by a charging Stalker. One minute they had spears raised to strike, and the next they were lost to the churning legs of the spider.

Whatever signal had gone up, it was enough to trigger the defenses ahead of them on the street. More soldiers lined the path on either side, and an armored barrier waited by the distant fountain. A shadow moved behind the slits in the metal, and Drakkar shouted a warning when something like a miniature ballista bolt whistled past his shoulder.

He didn't have to see what happened behind him to know it had found a target. The crunch and scream were unmistakable. Drakkar reached into his cloak and pulled out one of a dozen collapsed spears. Cave may have had a long and troubled history with tinkers, but their weapons lingered.

It was little more than a weighty orb of dark metal, until he clicked the release and hurled it at the line of soldiers ahead of them. The wild spin of the orb stabilized, and as it did, the tips of the spear exploded from either side. Perhaps they'd been invented for portable fishing gear, but they'd found a deadly new purpose in the Deadlands War.

The spear took a soldier in the chest behind the barrier, and Drakkar angled to the gap in the line when the fallen man's comrades jumped away. They might have had a good formation, but it broke in an instant. If they'd fired again, they could have taken out far more Spider Knights, but they tried to angle their shields toward Drakkar, focusing on their most immediate threat.

A bolt sailed past him, crashing into the shop next to his mount and sending chips of rock up to ping off the spider's armor. The Stalker flinched as a shard bounced off one of her large black eyes. One thing Drakkar had learned in his time with Samuel was that spider mounts were quite docile, until they weren't.

The Stalker's pedipalps reared up, and her fangs rose into the air, each the length of Drakkar's arm and twice as thick. She came down hard on the first ballistae, shattering the wooden brace behind it and snapping the tensioned string.

It sprang like a whip, slicing through a Ballern soldier's armor like so much paper. The spider's fangs struck fast, leaving ruin in their wake. Wounds so large they looked like cannon fire instead of a bite. The Stalker spun, crushing soldiers beneath her clawed feet as they tried to fight back with swords and crossbows, but as fast as the attack had started, Hilda surged down the road at Drakkar's direction.

Drakkar leaned to the side to check Hilda's injuries. She'd been fast, but blue blood still dripped from two of her legs. She wasn't slowing down yet, but she'd need attention soon, or exhaustion could get them both killed.

Another line of soldiers flowed out from the shopping district to the south, but they weren't alone. Fel loyalists clashed with Skyborn, so distracted by their pursuers they never saw the line of Spider Knights that ran them down.

A Stormborn flag hung from the wall, the burning remnants of Ballern's flag beside it. Drakkar readied another spear.

OWEN STARED DOWN at the blank eyes of another enemy, rolling off him and leaving the dagger embedded in the corpse's chest. They couldn't keep this up. Argyle's war hammer had slowed. Fiona's blood-soaked leathers bore stains from more than her enemies.

The ground shook when an explosion ripped through the far ocean liner yet again. Owen started when he saw a plate of metal spiraling through the air. "Eyes up!" he shouted as he got to his feet and ran, feeling the wave of heat from the latest blast overtake him before slowly subsiding.

Trevor dueled with a Fel guard, each wielding a whip-thin sword as though they were in a fencing tournament and not trying to kill each other. Owen feared Trevor didn't hear his warning, but Trevor lashed out, catching the thigh of his enemy before running toward Owen, leaving the man to be crushed by flying debris.

Another wave of soldiers marched through the archway, heavily armored and trailed by two dozen archers. Owen's shoulders slumped.

Fiona stepped up beside him, tightening her gauntlets before smashing them together. She drew a broad ax from her back and eyed the incoming forces. "If it had to be today, I'm glad it was with you lot."

Owen closed his eyes. He'd see Vaughn and Hefina again one day. In another life. But for now, he could fight with his friends. He could fight for his city. And he could die for his family.

His voice boomed as adrenaline coursed through him, forcing his body to do the unthinkable as he charged forward. "Mordair will *burn!*"

The first line of soldiers kneeled as the fisherfolk rallied, closing the distance. The archers nocked their arrows, drawing longbows and crossbows back as they took aim.

But another voice cut through the air. An accent Owen had come to know well. The voice of an Ancoran screamed like the damned. "For the Stormborn!"

A cascade of Jumpers crashed down on those archers, hurdling Ballern's walls from the west, and plowing through bodies like bales of hay. Halberds struck and swept and retreated as fast as their wielders could move. And what soldiers dared to strike back found themselves beneath the Jumpers, buried in fangs and claws as the spiders scrabbled over the ruined market.

Only one of the spiders fell to the archers. But the rider took up behind the glistening silver armor of a Spider Knight, her cloak snapping in the wind as embers from the burning warships floated across the scene.

Owen looked at Fiona, her knuckles whitening on the handle of her ax, and she screamed, "For the Stormborn!"

The surviving fisherfolk echoed her call, and they ran toward the archways. They could see it when the lines broke. When the gray uniforms of Fel scattered and tried to retreat. But they had no exit. Their ships burned. The fisherfolk waited in front of them. And a cadre of Stalkers closed on them from behind.

Some surrendered. Some died on the ends of spears and fangs. But the market belonged to the Stormborn.

The nearest of the Spider Knights circled around, joining the cluster of fisherfolk.

"My name is Samuel. Spider Knight of Ancora. If you are able, get to the airship docks! The battle here may not be done, but we will hold them on the ground as long as we can." The Spider Knight rubbed something in his collar, and Owen couldn't hear the words.

Samuel scanned the market. "Get the injured to the bookstore to the west. They're setting up a hospital there now. Use it until we can secure a better facility." He looked out to the ruined warships on the water. "And well done!"

CHAPTER TWENTY-FIVE

FURI BOUNCED ON the balls of her feet as Kura dialed in the transmitter. Blood drenched her teacher's sweater, but Kura didn't move like she was injured. Furi had little doubt it was someone else's blood.

"Take it," Kura said.

Furi leaned down and clicked the button. "This is the Skyborn. Fel's airships are pulling away from the dock. Ballern and Fel have set a perimeter and their carrier has been sighted to the northwest. Fighting on the docks is getting worse. We need you *here*."

The transmitter crackled. "Understood, Skyborn. Fleet is en route. Get guides to the landing bays and make ready."

"Is that Lady Katherine?" Furi asked, staring at Kura.

Instead of answering, Kura leaned past Furi and clicked the transmitter. "At once, My Lady." Kura turned to Furi. "Get back to Jacob and Alice. I want you with them. They don't know the docks like you do."

Furi's words came out rushed, almost panicked. "I can help guide the landing parties, Kura."

"I know you can, but this isn't the time. You're the one who told me about Jacob and his weapons. Keep the tinker *alive*."

Furi grimaced and clenched her fists, wanting to argue but trusting Kura. "He doesn't just make weapons."

Kura stood straighter. "I need you to go."

Furi's jaw flexed before she nodded. "We aren't done talking about this." She stormed out of the warehouse and headed for the nearest ladder. If Jacob and Alice were taking the lift up two floors, she had an idea where they should be. She only hoped they were still alive.

✧   ✧   ✧

TWO FLOORS UP, the fighting wasn't as dense, but Jacob remained in a crouch, hurrying past the homes and bars of the upper level with Alice at his side. Eva stayed close behind. The docks were far larger there, spread out to eclipse even the Bones beneath them.

Columns of thick smoke from the levels below shifted both sides of the conflict in various directions. Without a breathing mask or air tank, no one would dare to run through those clouds. Not to mention the conflagrations closest to them would be hot enough to scorch their bodies.

While the upper levels had their dangers, they put them above most of the destroyers, and that was exactly where Jacob wanted to be. If there was one thing they'd learned how to do in their time with Smith and Mary, it was sabotage an airship.

The ring of metal on metal echoed around them, some distant and muddled, and others immediate as a bolt careened off a tin wall at Jacob's side.

He slowed when they reached the corner of one of that level's nicer homes. It gave them more shelter than the canvas-covered bars and food stalls. Ahead, where the docks extended out over the destroyers below, they lost most of the cover between districts.

"How far is that?" Eva asked, going down on one knee as she studied the walkway.

"Close to one hundred feet before we have cover again," Jacob said.

Alice reached out and squeezed his arm. "If it gets bad, we can go over the side, take the gliders down a level."

Eva blinked at that. "I don't have a glider."

"We can carry you." Jacob rubbed the back of his neck. "We both have the newer braces and brackets. These packs can take far more weight than just two people without collapsing."

"And steering?"

Jacob let out a low grunt. "It should be fine."

"We need to work on your approach to reassuring people," Alice whispered.

Alice's comment broke the tension in the air for only a moment before another explosion sounded in the distance. Jacob leaned around the corner, finding an airship in flames over the Crystal Sea as it dove toward the water in ruin.

"Throw a firebomb," Alice said. "As a distraction."

Jacob's back straightened as he turned to look at her. "Here? We could burn someone's house down."

Alice slowly raised an eyebrow. Probably waiting for Jacob to remember the choking columns of smoke as he rethought his reply.

"Right. Firebomb. Uncontained, it's going to be a huge flash, but it won't last long."

"It doesn't need to last long. We only have to make it to the shops right there." She pointed to the stretch of metal structures. So close, but far enough to make them easy targets for a skilled archer.

"Alice!"

Jacob looked around, trying to see where the voice had come from. Alice found them first.

"Furi! Where did you come from?"

"The walkway below this level. They used to use it for … never mind. Look behind you on the floor!"

Jacob turned and blinked at the square beneath his feet. Looking into the distance, he could see one after the other every fifty feet or so, and he shuddered when he realized how easily they could have been ambushed from underneath.

Alice shooed him off the square and pulled at the small rings recessed in the edge. It opened in silence, the metal barely making a whisper as it revealed a short ladder to what looked like little more than a crawlspace.

"Move!" Eva ushered them forward.

Alice dropped through first, hurrying down the ladder rungs until her boots met the wide grate below. Jacob followed, surprised the walkway had so much more space than it had appeared from above. He could easily stand, and he thought even Smith might be able to clear the hanging struts and supports without hitting his head.

Eva wasn't nearly so cautious. She pulled the hatch closed, and then let herself drop to the walkway, her boots slamming against the grate before she struck off to the east.

At first, it wasn't so bad being between levels, but the long drop to the city below had Jacob looking any direction but down. He might not have been bad with heights, but there was a point when almost anyone's head would spin when they stood on the precipice, glider or not. Especially when the only thing holding you back was a rusted railing and a grated floor that had certainly seen better days.

Their distance from the fighting didn't hide the carnage entirely. Chaos enveloped the level below. Stormborn banners fluttered in the wind opposite the flags of Fel and Ballern. Uniformed Skyborn still fought on the side of Ballern, and it tightened Jacob's chest to see it. How could anyone fight for Mordair after all he'd done?

"Hurry!"

Jacob looked up and found Furi's head poking through another hatch above them some twenty-five feet ahead. Eva's steps quickened, leading the trio to the next ladder. A cold breeze came in from the north, carrying some of the smoke and ash toward them as they reached the next level. It wasn't enough to choke them, but the far line of Fel soldiers broke and scattered.

"Every block has those walkways," Furi said. "Some of them were built over, or only have one entrance, but if you see a hatch, you can hide under it. I never see anyone on them."

"How did you find us?" Alice asked.

"I know the docks better than most. Beck might have known them better … before he died. I knew if you were going to attack the destroyers, this level made the most sense. Another level up, and the wind would ruin your aim. Another level down, and you'd be too close if there was an explosion."

An airship burst into flames to the north, spiraling down into the mountains.

"We have to hurry. Belldorn is coming. Kura will be waiting for them at the docks, so whatever you mean to do, we need to do it now."

Jacob glanced between the homes at the long stretch of docks between them and the destroyers. "Can you get us closer to the column of smoke by the destroyers without being seen?"

"Maybe. Follow me." Furi didn't say more, instead heading farther east, toward the Crystal Sea. Her bootfalls grew heavier as she ran, and the more distance they had from the lifts, the less cautious they grew with the sound of their running.

Furi turned to the north at the second street from the end of the docks. And more than any other, that walkway truly looked like a street. There were no exposed lattices beneath their boots, or questionable railings to make Jacob even happier they were wearing gliders.

The homes were small and humble, but there was a sense of elegance among the neatly trimmed bushes and gardens that lined the walkway. Most importantly, Fel wouldn't have a line of sight on them unless they saw them from above. But few destroyers dwelled in the higher docks. Most remained near the center. Ballern's own warships waited above them.

Jacob only hoped the fact they were staffed by Skyborn might buy them some small edge in the battle to come.

MARY FOCUSED ON the skies ahead as Kat's voice came over the transmitter. Except it wasn't the casual tone of her friend. These were the calm, commanding words of Lady Katherine, leader of Belldorn. It often felt like they were two different people, so good was she at separating those personas.

"No one is to fire on the docks. They are not a strategic target. Any airship that has cleared the airspace is a target, but those that remain docked are not. Should a docked ship fire its cannons, relay that to us, and our ground forces will make those ships a priority target."

Smith's voice echoed over the horn as the engines of the Skysworn roared. "She is putting the entire landing detachment at risk with that command."

"What else can she do, Smith? Ballern's docks are a floating city. It's the same as firing on Midstream or the Lowlands."

"What remains of the Lowlands, Mary?"

Her grip hardened on the levers in her hands. "I know, Smith. Maybe we can stop that from happening here."

It wasn't long before they caught up to the forwardmost line of brigs. The brigs had pulled ahead of the Porcupines, creating a wall of airships in the sky. It wasn't the best formation for the Porcupines to maintain a line of fire, but it was nearly impossible for another airship to slip by undetected.

Gas chambers and cannons glinted in the sun, a backdrop of storm clouds over the Crystal Sea flanking them to the east. The line of airships deployed from the carrier stretched as far as Mary could see, until they finally vanished into the bright orb of the sun.

She eyed the transmitter, hesitated, and then dialed a new frequency. "Warship One, this is the Skysworn."

The signal crackled and then resolved into Archibald's annoyingly composed voice. "Warship One receiving."

"Are you closing on the docks?" There was a long pause, and Mary worried they'd lost the signal. "Warship One?"

"Yes. All forces deployed and confirmed with Belldorn. I am surprised you did not simply ask your friend, Skysworn."

She could have, she supposed. But Kat had enough on her mind. After all they'd been through with Archibald, the least he could do was answer Mary's question. She clicked the transmitter.

"We'll see you in the skies."

Mary saw the smoke before she could see Ballern. The enemy carrier had moved west of the city, and any deployment would take time to return. Kat had given the command to circle out to the Crystal Sea and come in from the east. This served two purposes. They'd be in line with the makeshift slips under the Bones, and an obvious show of force at sea could distract Ballern and Fel from Archibald's forces in the north. It was risky, and they'd lose ships, but it was a good plan.

"Chainguns ready," Smith said.

Mary eased the throttle forward, and they shot out ahead of the brigs, diving close to the water before leveling out. No warships waiting on the sea. Either the fisherfolk had been more successful than she'd hoped, or Mordair had moved the rest of his fleet somewhere else, which left the awful question of where those ships might strike them from. But if he'd moved away from Ballern, all he'd have left were ground defenses and the combined airship fleets of Ballern and Fel. She let out a humorless laugh at that thought.

That meant the battle was going to be in the air, which gave Belldorn and Bollwerk the advantage.

"Brace yourself, Smith. We're going topside." Mary gave him all of ten seconds before she pulled back on the controls and guided the Skysworn upwards at a steep angle. They cut in front of the brigs and several small strikers before reaching the low clouds rolling south over Crystal Sea.

She leveled the Skysworn out as they broke through the cloud bank and gritted her teeth when she saw what waited in the distance. Mary pulled the mounted telescope on the console closer, sweeping it across the horizon and tallying up the ships stationed outside the docks. She cursed and spun the dial on the transmitter before clicking the button.

"Kat. Ballern fleet is at a higher altitude. Say again, Ballern is stationed well above the docks. Come in high or you'll be in range of their main guns."

The transmitter crackled and Lady Katherine answered. "Understood. I'll inform the brigs." With that, she was gone.

"Just the brigs?" Smith asked. "Seems like they ought to warn the damn Porcupines."

Mary pulled farther out to sea and circled wide. "We're going to hit them from the starboard, Smith."

"They are heavily armored, Mary. The chainguns cannot do much against that kind of plating."

"They can get their attention. And that's good enough. I want those ships focused on us and the brigs until the Porcupines get in range."

"Better suited to a striker."

"The day I can't outmaneuver a striker is the day I retire."

"Can't retire if you are dead."

Mary grinned and pushed the throttle forward.

✧   ✧   ✧

JACOB STARED DOWN at the deck of the destroyer beneath them. Every person he could see wore a Fel uniform, but that didn't mean every one of them was loyal to Mordair. He pushed the thought aside. To do nothing could leave them in a worse spot than they were already in.

Furi leaned outside the torn tent that hid them from view to anyone in the west. "Still clear. Wait ..."

Alice sidled up beside her. "What is it?"

"Ballern uniforms. Fleet uniforms. Look at the central lift." Furi gestured toward the thick column of metal that housed a cluster of lifts.

"They're fighting," Alice said. "They're fighting Fel."

"Some of them are. It looks like others are just ... watching?" He didn't keep the slight confusion out of his words.

Eva harrumphed. "I'd rather have them watching than helping Fel. Now get those bombs ready, Jacob."

He nodded and turned back to the four compound bombs. "One might be enough to take out a destroyer if we get it in the smokestack, or close to the boilers."

"So use two," Alice said.

"Exactly. We'll have ten seconds after we lock the shell closed. It's a lot of time, but it's not *that* much time. Which way do you want to run?"

"How big of an explosion will it be?" Furi asked. "Can we even get away?"

"I wouldn't be throwing it if I didn't think we could get away. It should be pretty contained. The destroyers are armored, so it should disable them without doing anything spectacular."

Furi blew out a breath and took a burner and a casing from Jacob. "Click it. Close it. Lock it."

"Throw it," Alice said. "Don't forget that last bit."

Eva held her hand out for one of the compound bombs. "You two drop the bombs on this destroyer. Furi and I will move to the next and you drop at my signal. As soon as it's done, we run south. Soldiers will come this way to investigate, and none of us needs to be here for that. Get back to the ladders and back down to the warehouses. Understood?"

No one argued. Jacob handed the last bomb to Alice as Eva and Furi hurried to the west, hiding behind various buildings and homes as they went. Once they were in position, Eva raised her hand.

"That's the signal," Alice said. "Let's drop these and go."

"On three." Jacob held the burner in one hand. "One. Two. Three." They both clicked their burners and closed the shell to the compound bomb, locking it before taking aim at the smokestacks.

Alice was a better shot, so she took the farther target. The bomb sailed in an arc before making a quiet click as it ricocheted down the exposed mouth of the smokestack.

Jacob did the same, and as soon as he was sure he hadn't missed, they ran. Mentally, he counted down from ten, trying to figure out when the bomb would detonate. He spared a glance to the west, relieved to see Furi and Eva sprinting across the walkway two blocks down.

Alice shouted when the first bomb exploded, followed closely by the second. The walkway shook so hard Jacob feared it might fall out from under them, and his foot slipped, sending him down to the grated floor.

He rolled and cringed at the enormous fireball engulfing the railing where they'd thrown the bombs. Alice grabbed his arm and dragged him back to his feet a second before another explosion ripped through the docks to the west.

"Run!"

They ran full out, heading to the ladders and arriving just before Eva and Furi.

"Nothing spectacular!" Eva snapped as she ushered everyone down the ladder. "I need to have a talk with you and Smith about what *words* mean, Jacob!"

They paused for breath on the next level and headed east, watching one of the destroyers drift out to sea, a magnificent ball of fire. The other caught on the docks, crumpling a section of the walkway before the airship squealed to a stop. There were no giant flames to light the wreckage, but Jacob doubted it would be going anywhere.

Two destroyers down. Far too many to go.

✧　✧　✧

MARY FOCUSED ON her target as two massive explosions shook the skies closer to the airship docks. The nearest destroyer came into range of the chainguns, and no one had yet fired on the Skysworn. Mary wasn't sure how long that luck would hold out, but she figured it would definitely be gone as soon as they attacked. She eyed the decks with a pair of binoculars before turning to the horn.

"Deck's clear. Ready to fire."

"Guns are loaded. Fire at will."

Mary flipped the guard off the trigger, let out a slow breath, and opened fire with the forward chainguns. Sparks and flame came to life across the hull of the destroyer. She maintained the staccato bursts of fire for a full ten seconds before easing back, still feeling the vibration of the chainguns lingering in her hands.

Then it was a matter of waiting, and they didn't have to wait long. At first glance, Mary thought the cannons were swinging toward them, but the bow of the airship followed and she couldn't help but feel relieved.

"The Porcupines are going to have a wide target with that ship turning toward us, Smith. Hold on." She forced two levers to the right, and the Skysworn pulled away from the destroyer like a Sea Claw in water. Mary dove, cutting low enough that the destroyers would have to unbalance themselves to target the Skysworn, and no sane captain would do that.

It didn't stop the smaller arms from focusing on them, and streaks of fire crossed the windscreen before Mary jerked the Skysworn to the north, checking for any pursuers through the port windows. A handful of small strikers appeared between the destroyers, sweeping down from the clouds, narrow gas chambers and gray hulls telling her they were Fel.

"I would have preferred Ballern," Mary said under her breath.

"Ballern's strikers are just as fast."

"I know that, Smith, but they aren't as well armed, are they?" Mary's annoyance bled away when she caught another glimpse of the destroyers. Flashes of light and black clouds appeared between them a second before the report of cannon fire reached the Skysworn. The Porcupines arrived.

Three of the huge destroyers had already made the mistake of exposing their broadsides, but more strikers appeared around them, spreading to the south and east as they moved to meet the incoming fleet. Mary saw two options. Circle back between the destroyers, or engage the strikers on the open sea.

"Smith. You might want to strap in. We're going back into the line of fire."

"Mary, are you sure—" But his question cut off as she split two levers, one to engage the smaller stabilizing thrusters near the aft deck, and the other pushing the throttle higher. The Skysworn nosed up, the ping of bolts from the first wave of strikers catching the hull.

As maneuverable as those small ships were, they couldn't change directions fast enough at that speed. Something slammed closed on the lower decks, and Mary heard the whir of the gun pod.

"How did you get into the pod that fast?"

"I jumped. And yes, it hurt."

Mary shook her head and eased the hull in a slow rotation, giving Smith a clear line of sight to the strikers as they passed. He didn't miss his chance. Short bursts of fire and dark shadows whipped out from beneath the Skysworn.

Strikers were fast and hard to target, but it didn't much matter how fast a ship was if it flew straight into a hail of chaingun fire. Two ships went up in smoke, trailing fire before one exploded in a brilliant ball of flame and the second crashed into the Crystal Sea.

Mary finished the ship's rotation and leveled out, heading back toward the destroyers. Thunder shook the Skysworn as a Porcupine opened fire, its shot leaving trails of smoke in the air. Some of those trails ended in a long arc down into the sea itself. Some ended in the ruin of a destroyer, two of its gas chambers rapidly deflating as the aft deck careened into the waters.

It took time for the main cannons to reload, and that meant Mary had time to get them through the battle. She wanted to be closer to the docks. No one would fire on the docks, and every ship there would be safer beneath the Bones.

They reached the airspace around the destroyers, and Smith didn't let up. Chaingun fire tore into another ship, but the strikers scored a hit on the Skysworn's armored gas chamber. Mary breathed a sigh of relief when the metal plates held together.

"Mary! Cluster of skirmishers to the north."

She cursed when she saw what Smith had warned her about. Apparently, Ballern wasn't going to be sitting this battle out, Skyborn or not.

Skirmishers were nowhere near as agile as the strikers, but they were armed with much more powerful weaponry. The sleek forms cut through the air, two pontoons to either side that bore armored gas chambers. But it was the center she worried about. A cannon above and below, and bolt throwers that launched ballistae bolts running down either side of the ship.

The genius of the design was the angle of those bolt throwers. You couldn't flank them when they were in formation. Always six ships in formation—three above, three below in a staggered line.

Mary clicked the transmitter. "Skirmishers in the north, behind the destroyers. Warn the brigs!" She didn't wait for Kat's response, instead spinning the transmitter back to the general frequency.

"Take them from above," Smith said. "That or retreat, right now."

The Skysworn nosed higher, taking a sharp angle into the air that would nearly put them in the low cloud bank. But the situation shifted violently from one moment to the next. Another line of strikers punched through the clouds above, essentially giving the skirmishers a roof of protection, and the brigs came in range of the destroyers.

Mary cursed as the skies exploded all around them. Ships splintered in the sky as Belldorn's flak cannons found their mark. Brigs flanked the Ballern destroyers, but even as they did, more skirmishers launched from Ballern's docks. The Skysworn shook when something detonated beside them. Mary wasn't sure if it had been a striker or an explosive, but shrapnel pinged against the windscreen and detritus cartwheeled through the air, trailing smoke.

The line of skirmishers shifted as a large salvo from Belldorn's Porcupines erased the center pair. One moment they'd been holding formation, and the next the top craft pancaked onto the lower and both fell.

"Strafe starboard!" Mary shouted as she angled for the hole left by the ruined Ballern skirmishers. She kept the closest destroyer behind the Skysworn. None of the cannons of those skirmishers would dare fire on their own warship.

A brig beside them caught a ballista bolt through the windscreen. There was a chance someone on the bridge survived, but if the controls were ruined … it wouldn't matter much. Mary clenched her jaw as the brig tilted and dove into the sea below, taking its crew of twelve into the depths.

The Skysworn shook from bow to stern when the destroyer at their back suffered a direct hit. Cannons and towers erupted off the ship's flank, sending metal and burning wood to shower over the Skysworn's deck.

Smith cursed over the horn, and Mary didn't want to think what that explosion must have looked like from the gun pod.

"Get ready!" Mary leaned closer to the windscreen, eyeing the angle of the bolt launchers while trying to give Smith the best possible position. The best angle was a terrible idea for keeping out of the line of fire, but sometimes terrible ideas were the best option.

The Skysworn lurched to the left, rolling slightly as Smith unleashed a hail of fire on the eastern skirmishers. Sparks burst across the armor before a large flash ripped along the supports. A pontoon dropped from the lower skirmisher when another small explosion took out the braces, and Smith moved to the next.

Mary clamped down on the trigger for the forward chainguns. Three skirmishers down in one sweep. Now that was a story she'd be able to tell Eva until the day they died. Mary roared as the chainguns cut through the bottom of the upper skirmisher, but the move had been risky. Too risky.

The Skysworn shuddered, and the steering levers ripped out of Mary's grip as the entire ship lurched away from the skirmishers. Glass shattered behind her as a bolt caught the ceiling, trailing fire into the cabin.

"Smith, fire!"

"Where?"

"Cabin!"

The chainguns below her silenced, and the Skysworn dove. If she couldn't pull out of it, she could at least skim across the water, give them a chance to survive the impact. Metal crashed against metal when the hatch to the cabin flew open.

Smith ripped off his safety line as he pulled on two arm-length gloves. Normally used for handling the searing pipes of the boiler, he'd found another use for them altogether. Smith wrapped his arms around the fiery bolt and tore it out of the roof.

Singed leather and burnt hair joined the smell of superheated metal and ash choking them in the cabin. A moment later, Smith heaved the bolt back out the window. Mary tilted the Skysworn to the starboard side, and the flaming projectile bounced off the deck once before tumbling down to the sea.

"Mask!" Smith shouted.

Mary fumbled beneath the console and grabbed a pair of filtered masks. It wasn't as good as what many of the miners used beneath the mountains of Belldorn, but it was a lifesaver, nonetheless. She threw one to Smith before pulling the other over her nose and mouth, snapping the goggles into place.

Smith cursed as he bent the door to a locker open, coughing as he retrieved two wide glass orbs from their padded shelf. He slammed one of the fire extinguisher orbs against the ceiling, and the second against the floor of the cabin, and in a flash, the air filled with a choking white cloud.

Mary couldn't see a thing, not the console in front of her, not the sea before them. All she could do was hold the ship steady as the cloud dissipated. When it finally did, she found two strikers bearing down on them, and two skirmishers in pursuit.

"Smith…"

He took a deep breath and closed his eyes. "Run, Mary. We have to try."

Bolts peppered the bow of the Skysworn, their speed failing with the damage to the ship. The strikers neared. It would be seconds before they were close enough to puncture the Skysworn's armor.

The transmitter crackled to life. "You better be on this frequency, Mary!"

Mary slammed the button down. "Jakon? This isn't the best time!"

He snapped back at her. "Next time I ask for one barrel of pickled eggs, I only want *one* barrel of pickled eggs!"

The Ray punched through the cloud cover above them. The sides of the ship unfurled, rolling its cannons out like the spiral of a sleeping Walker. But The Ray's fangs were far deadlier than any Walker.

Flames and steel exploded from that bank of cannons, shredding one skirmisher and both strikers in pursuit of the Skysworn. For good measure, Jakon punched a hole through a flanking destroyer's secondary gas chamber. A devastating blow when the secondary was all that was left.

"Can you get back to the carrier?" Jakon asked over the transmitter.

Mary watched her pursuers fall from the sky, the flames only diminishing as the ships slipped beneath the waves of the Crystal Sea. "Maybe. I don't know. Smith?"

He shook his head. "I do not believe so."

"Then head for the southwest corner of the docks. I'm at your side, Skysworn."

Mary bit the inside of her mouth. She wouldn't shed a tear in relief. It didn't matter if no one but Smith was in that cabin to see her. She wouldn't shed one damn tear at Jakon's help.

Smith grabbed her from behind and held her tight, and Mary couldn't stop the tremor in her lip, or the tears on her cheeks.

✧ ✧ ✧

ARCHIBALD WALKED THE bridge of Warship One. Circling around to the north had cost them precious time. Precious time he hoped would buy them an advantage even Mordair couldn't counter.

He turned when heavy footsteps sounded behind him. "Natalia."

The tinker nodded. "Titan Mechs are ready to deploy. We have them loaded on the supply ships."

"And the defenses for the supply ships?"

"Also completed. Each is armed with a pair of chainguns, and the standard array of bolts. They couldn't carry as much ammunition as I would have preferred, but it should be enough to get to the ground."

Archibald looked across the bridge, studying the pilots as they coordinated the route to the docks. "Give them an opportunity to surrender. Especially Ballern's fleet. Mordair may have nurtured some loyalty among the Skyborn, but I doubt that loyalty is without cracks."

"How do you mean to do that?" Natalia asked.

"Target their largest destroyer. Once it burns, raise the flags."

Natalia glanced away before returning her focus to Archibald and nodding. "It will be done. Shall I send the supply ships now?"

"Yes. The Spider Knights may have things at a stalemate in the city proper, but the Titan Mechs should drive the point home. Close the city off and we'll clear the skies."

She turned and walked toward a bank of consoles. Archibald heard the crackle of a transmitter before the tinker started giving the orders to deploy the Titan Mechs.

"What would you think of this, Charles?" Archibald whispered under his breath. "The war we should have ended in the Deadlands."

CHAPTER TWENTY-SIX

"F IRE ON WILLETT'S tower. Lift the restrictions."

"Sir?"

Mordair turned to the man who dared question his order, and his voice boomed. "Fire on Willett's tower! Do not stop unloading the cannons until it crumbles! Do it *now*! And when that falls, implode the eastern gas chamber of the docks."

The soldier stared at the Steward, wide-eyed.

"It's fine." The Baroness of Auxley stepped toward the soldier. "The archduke would be willing to sacrifice his tower. It's been abandoned for this battle."

The soldier bowed and hurried off.

Mordair raised an eyebrow. "I do not need your pandering, Baroness."

"You asked that soldier to murder an archduke, Steward. Find a more subtle way to ask impossible tasks of *your* people."

Annoyance flickered through Mordair's thoughts, but he supposed she had a valid point. He hadn't had enough time in Ballern to bend its people entirely to his will. Having the leaders of Ballern pay him heed had worked well enough, but it wasn't the same as Fel. There were still uprisings in Ballern. Perhaps the Children of the Dark Fire could assist with that when they returned to the city.

"You are dismissed, Baroness."

She left without another word or show of respect. The Red Hand stepped up in front of him when the door banged closed and they were alone.

Patrice slapped him hard enough to rattle his teeth. "How dare you? They are innocents in this!"

Mordair barked out a laugh, gently rubbing the sting from his flesh. "Innocents? You kill innocents regularly for me, Patrice."

"I kill those who are a threat to your power," she hissed. "I do not kill innocents, Gregory. There is a *difference*."

Mordair narrowed his eyes, his voice flat. "You approved of Newton's plan to bring Ancora low, did you not? Did you believe innocents would not die when the walls fell, and that city was overrun?"

Her teeth audibly ground together like chalk squeaking across a blackboard. "You go too far, and it will cost you. We could have remained in this fortress for months. Made true preparations with the Children of the Dark Fire."

"I have made more preparations than you know, Patrice. Deploy the fleet to the north. The barricade across the Gray Sea will stand."

Patrice glared at him. He could only imagine what frustrations must be running through her mind, but the goal was in sight now. She would understand in time. They would all understand, and secrets were not secrets once the wrong ears heard them.

SAMUEL STOOD BESIDE Bessie. She kept tapping Drakkar's mount with her pedipalps as if she wasn't quite sure what the massive Stalker was. The Cave Guardian's mount, thankfully, appeared entirely unbothered.

The market had been cleared, and the fighting outside the archways had slowed dramatically once the airships engaged in the sky. Seeing the Fleet of the enemy at your doorstep could change the momentum of a battle in moments. The Stormborn formed perimeters on the ground, close to the lifts and gates of the city, and now that they'd secured the hospital, more of the injured were being treated.

Samuel patted Bessie between the eyes and looked up at Drakkar. "Feels like we should join the fight on the docks."

"In time, yes. But the spiders are doing more to keep Ballern and Fel in check than I would have thought."

Samuel looked off to the west, where spiders marched up and down the streets and clung to the stone walls of Ballern. They might not have the entire city under guard, but their presence was known.

Perhaps most surreal was the bard who had climbed a table in the market and started to play for those left in the aftermath of the battle. Samuel wasn't familiar with the songs, but he did hear some of the Stormborn say the huge beard and broad armor belonged to Grimhelm the Bard.

The fact the man's lute also housed a bolt thrower amused Samuel quite a bit.

"What do you make of that?" Samuel asked, gesturing to one of Ballern's destroyers circling the docks as its cannons swung low.

Drakkar sat up straighter in his saddle. "Samuel, they're going to fire on the city."

"What? But I thought—"

It was all the warning anyone had. The report of the cannon reached them a split second after a nearby tower showered the area in stone splinters and debris. Many of the spider mounts ran before their riders could gather their wits enough to do the same.

The tower started to fall and Samuel scrambled to get back on Bessie. "Drakkar, run!" A glance showed him the soaring structure tipping forward as Drakkar's Stalker sprinted away. The minaret fell through the top floors, sending clouds of debris toward the sea and into the city.

It looked so far away, and then it was on the archways, an avalanche of screaming Ballern citizens and broken stone and wood. Something heavy hit him, and then, nothing.

✧   ✧   ✧

JACOB AND ALICE were almost back to the warehouse when the first explosion hit the city. Furi's gasp said everything any of them could have. A tower fell, scattering debris and death as it went, flattening buildings and people and leaving a cloud of dust and dirt in the air.

It was a vision like the ruin of Dauschen, and the horror of that place came screaming back into Jacob's mind, freezing him in place.

"We have to go!" Alice shouted, pulling on his arm. "Eva, Furi, now!"

"They can't fire on the city!" Furi screeched. "They can't—the people! Oh gods, the people!"

The same destroyer that had fired on the city shifted to the east, and Jacob could see the cannons moving. Fire pelted the ship, but it didn't change course, didn't try to evade the attacks, only took aim at its next target.

"They're firing on the docks." He grabbed Alice and slowed her down as they reached the warehouse district. Ahead, Kura and several Stormborn stared down at the ruin below. The fighting above them ground into silence as the full horror of what had happened settled in.

But Mordair wasn't done. Mordair was never done.

"Eva, get back!" Alice screamed.

Jacob crushed the transmitter in his collar. "Ballern is firing on the docks. Get everyone off the Bones. Now!" But the warning was too late. Everything was too late.

He stared down the barrels of the cannons as they opened fire. The armored gas chambers of the docks dented, and then failed. Great plumes of dust and air blew out from the sides, and the Bones fell.

"Kura!" Furi cried out.

"Jump!" Jacob shouted as loud as he could. They could jump now, or die. "Alice, jump!"

Eva turned and stared back at them in horror as the lattice walkway beneath their feet crumpled. Alice dove, tackling Eva and knocking her off the side of the docks. Two seconds. Three seconds. An eternity, and then Alice's wings opened.

But Kura and the others were already gone. The warehouse falling toward the city below.

"Furi!" Jacob's voice cracked as he grabbed her. "Jump!"

She did, and he followed right behind her, his foot slipping with the sharp angle of the failing docks. Another walkway fell in front of them, narrowly missing Alice and Eva, but the stabilizers held, and while her wings shuddered, she stayed aloft.

"Dive and pull up!" Jacob shouted, hoping Furi could hear him. He did the same, trying to catch sight of Alice, trying not to be crushed by the falling debris. There was a time it would have been exhilarating, but it was only terrifying as people and metal showered down around them. He tried to look up, predict where to go and what to avoid, but they were too deep in the debris field. It was little more than a game of dice now.

He grabbed the lever on his glider pack and waited, tucking his legs together and keeping his arms tight until Furi finally opened her wings, and did exactly what he'd said. She pulled up hard, snapping forward and catapulting herself out of the worst of the debris field.

Jacob held on another second, not wanting to hit Furi, or the largest chunk of the docks whistling through the air toward him. If the glider packs had still been Charles's design alone, they wouldn't have held up to the forces Jacob was about to put on his.

He slammed the lever down, and his wings snapped open. He moved his hands to the controls as fast as he could and pulled up with every ounce of strength he could muster. Jacob's vision grayed as the same forces that threatened to rip the wings from his back tried to steal his consciousness.

Bits of metal and wood pinged off the reinforced wings, and he felt several sharp edges cutting the skin of his face. He dove again, keeping his head down to protect his eyes as much as he could before pulling up a second time. Jacob risked a glance back, and his heart hammered at the vision that unfurled behind him.

A huge section of the docks was gone. Not gone, though, not really. They had crumpled into the city below. Fires raged below as dust turned everything to an eerie shadow. How many people had been on those docks? How many people had been in the city below them?

He couldn't do anything about that now. Jacob scanned the air around him and Furi. The worst was below them now, and they couldn't land on it without taking unimaginable injuries. The city wall lay shattered, stone piled along the shore and down into the Crystal Sea itself. They had to go west, or possibly south, if the market wasn't buried.

Jacob caught sight of Alice in the west, and moved to follow.

✧   ✧   ✧

ALICE WIPED THE blood from her eye and glanced down at Eva. The makeshift lash she'd fashioned from her belt took some of the strain off Eva's grip, securing her to the glider's harness by her forearm, but Eva was in far worse shape than Alice. Whatever that last explosion had hit them with had cut more than the glider's wing. And the spreading crimson stain on Eva's shoulder turned Alice's stomach with worry. Her grip still felt tight on Alice's wrist, and she hoped that grip would last.

"Eva, can you hear me?"

"Yes. Just… dizzy, Alice."

"Where's the hospital in Ballern?"

"Ballern? We should go to Belldorn."

"Later, tell me where."

Eva's head rose a hair and Alice didn't miss the tremble in her arm. "Something about a bookstore. That's what they said. But the hospital's near the west gates. West. That's right, but it should be left, shouldn't it?"

Alice gritted her teeth and tilted the glider west. There were a couple hundred feet of debris, but then the road cleared. All the glider had to do was *not* tear.

The descent was too steep, and Alice knew it, but she also feared Eva needed to be in the hospital immediately. But even if they found it, what if they were full? How many beds could they possibly have?

She shoved the growing panic of those dark thoughts to the back of her mind. None of it would matter if they crashed into the stones like a dropped boulder.

Alice kept the glider teetering between a dive and even flight. They passed over the worst of the debris, and the first fountain rose up to greet them, far faster than she would have liked.

"Eva. Eva! I need you to run. I can't hold you up and control the glider at once. Can you?"

"I can. Just … fuzzy. I can run, Alice."

Alice ground her teeth and pulled back hard. If the wing hadn't been torn, they would have risen. Instead, their descent only evened out, leaving them flying into a crowd with terrible speed. Three people leaped out of their path, dodging Eva's legs before Alice shouted, "Now!"

She snapped the wings closed and released Eva's belt in the span of a moment. The ground threatened to break Alice's ankles as she sprinted forward, feeling as though someone had shoved her hard from the top of a staircase. Alice maintained her balance for all of three steps before falling into a roll.

Eva followed close behind, showing far better coordination than Alice expected before Eva fell to her knees on the stone. She put her arms out to push herself up and collapsed to her side. Alice hurried over to her.

"The hospital! Where?" she pleaded with the shocked faces staring at her.

One boy, covered in gray dust, pointed to the northwest. "The short square tower."

"Thank you."

"Alice!"

She looked around, and when her name came again, she glanced up. Jacob and Furi angled down toward her, sweeping up at the last second so they could land gracefully at her side. Tears coated Furi's face, and the Skyborn wiped at her eyes.

"We have to get her to the hospital. She's bleeding."

Jacob slid closer, kneeling beside Alice. He pulled back the edge of Eva's shirt by the wound and grimaced. "I've seen worse."

"Help me carry her." Alice said, moving to stand on the opposite side of Eva.

"Alice, you're bleeding too."

"I'm fine!" she snapped. "Now, let's get her to the hospital."

Furi kept a hand behind Eva, ready to catch her if she slipped.

"There's a triage at the old bookstore."

Alice recognized the voice, but she wasn't sure why until she looked up. She was surprised to see Patrice standing there in the crowds. The woman had always seemed more suited to the nobles when she'd seen her in the bookstore.

"It's closer."

"Thank you." Alice hefted Eva over one shoulder while Jacob took the other.

Furi moved around them, taking the lead, moving people out of the way so they could reach the bookstore faster. Eva mumbled something under her breath, and Alice's heart hammered in her chest. She'd seen people die from far less severe wounds. Even if the initial trauma didn't take them, infection could be as bad as a bolt to the head.

They fought through the crowds for three blocks before turning left and finally reaching the bookstore. The interior had beds set up from front to back, with barely enough room to walk between them.

"Help!" Alice said.

A young woman hurried over. She didn't look old enough to be a doctor. She didn't look old enough to see what was happening in the city outside. Alice almost let a laugh escape her lips at that ludicrous thought. The woman was probably five years older than Jacob and Alice.

"We'll take her. How long has she been injured?"

"She was in the explosion when the docks collapsed."

The woman paused with her fingers on Eva's wrist as she checked her vitals. "Then … it really happened?"

"I'm afraid so."

"Right … right." She raised her voice. "We're going to have a lot more patients, Chin!"

An older doctor in the corner called for his assistant, telling them to round up any nurse or doctor who wasn't already at the hospital. A kid ran through the doors at a sprint.

The young woman turned back to Eva, pulling out a pair of shears to cut her shirt away. She grimaced and packed a thick square of linen into the wound. "Chin, we need the steamer. She's got a deep wound."

"I'll get it," Chin said. "Check for breaks!"

"What's her name?" she asked, glancing at Alice.

"Eva."

She focused on Eva, checking her legs and feet over for any obvious injuries before returning to her torso and head. "I'm Tu. It's nice to meet you, Eva. Can you hear me?"

Eva didn't respond.

Tu checked Eva's eyes and pulse again, her voice calm when she spoke. "You three might want to leave."

"Is there anything we can do?" Alice asked.

Tu closed her eyes and took a long breath. "If you can, help the injured. Get them here, or the hospital. People are going to be in shock, and they won't know what to do."

"You *were* listening to me," Chin said as he hurried over to the bedside with what appeared to be a boiler with a long handle and a blue-tinted glass vessel on the side. "Get the dressing off, and we'll flush the wound."

Furi took a step closer to Jacob when Tu exposed Eva's injury and started flushing it with a clear liquid.

"Looks like a piece of metal is in there," Chin said. "Take the pliers and pull it straight out. Same angle as the wound itself. It missed the largest arteries. She was lucky."

Alice almost deflated with relief. It didn't mean Eva would definitely be okay, but she had a much better chance than bleeding out in her hospital bed.

Tu dropped the length of metal into the used dressing before Chin leaned forward, lowering a nozzle so steam from the boiler could penetrate Eva's wound.

"What is that?" Jacob asked.

"Carbolic acid. A bit nasty, but it keeps the wounds from going bad. Helps keep the infection at bay with these deeper wounds." Chin glanced up. "You're a tinker, aren't you?"

Jacob nodded.

"I thought you looked a little too interested in that steamer." Chin smiled. "We'll take care of your friend. Tu is right. The best thing you can do is bring us more patients. Help who you can. Try not to dwell on those you can't."

Tu started dressing Eva's wound as they backed away, finally stepping into the street as more of the injured slowly made their way to the hospital to the north and the triage at the bookstore.

"Come on," Alice said. "We aren't doing any good standing around here."

✧   ✧   ✧

ARCHIBALD STARED OUT the windscreen of Warship One. Carnage. It was the only word for it. Mordair had fired on the docks themselves. Brought nearly a quarter of them down onto the city itself. The entirety of the eastern districts was lost in smoke and debris.

Distantly, someone asked for orders.

Archibald's knuckles cracked as he clenched his fists. Mordair had never been one to observe the rules of war, but this was beyond monstrous.

The transmitter in his collar crackled. There were only two people who knew the frequency, and not many more who knew he always wore it.

"Did you see it?"

He knew it was Lady Katherine, but it didn't sound like her. There was no emotion in her voice. Just raw shock. But when she asked again, that shock grew into something like Archibald felt. A cold, fiery thing.

"Did you *see* it?"

Archibald clicked the transmitter in his collar. "I saw it. I saw all of it. Move to the west. Cut them off if you can."

"Cut what off?"

"Fel's airships are moving to the west."

"It wasn't a Fel airship, Archibald. I received the report directly from three different brig pilots. That was one of Ballern's destroyers. They just …"

How could any of Ballern's soldiers slaughter their own people like that? Part of him knew every sailor on that destroyer should be interrogated, stand trial, and be made an example of. Another part of him wasn't ready to drag this into a hollow spectacle.

"Sir?"

Archibald lowered his gaze to his commanders. "Target the destroyer and Fel's warships. Nothing lives."

His commanders exchanged glances before turning to the rest of the crew.

"Full to starboard. Ready all cannons. Chainguns primed!"

The Speaker of Bollwerk strode back to the captain's chair and sat down, pulling up the horn for the launch bays. "Natalia. This is Archibald."

No one responded for a time, but voices came and went over the horn until Natalia's words came back louder than any other. "I'm here, Archibald. Do you wish to abort the launch of the Titan Mechs?"

"No. I want them on the ground. Help with the rescue where you can. Put down any armed resistance. Without hesitation. The nobles' guard has been seen at the palace. Get there. Find them. Bury Mordair. Ready the firebombs."

"Understood."

Archibald clicked the transmitter in his collar. "My Lady. I intend to destroy any airship that leaves the docks not flying a white flag. I would suggest you give the order to your fleet to do the same."

She didn't respond for a time, but her words came back heavy. "Agreed. Every ship at my disposal will be in the air. Nothing will escape to the south."

Warship One swept to the east until they had a direct line of sight on the Ballern destroyer.

"Cannons in range," his commander said.

Archibald looked back to the windscreen at his commander's words. "Fire at will."

"Deploy stabilizers on the port side. Starboard cannons, fire at will."

It was nearly impossible for one to feel the cannons fire on the massive warship, but rarely were they all unleashed at once. The floor vibrated beneath Archibald's boots, and the sky burned with cannon fire. The first three hits spelled the end of the Ballern destroyer. It raised a white flag as it lost maneuverability.

"White flag present."

"Fire chainguns." Archibald's words were flat.

Natalia's voice sounded over the horn. "We are ready with the firebombs at cannon four. Confirm deployment?"

Archibald almost snarled. "Fire at will."

It wasn't hard to tell which projectile was the cluster of firebombs. A trail of smoke that burst into a second sun in the sky. A second sun that slammed into the Ballern destroyer and spread like flame on fuel.

The white flag burned, and the gas chambers failed, dropping the destroyer several hundred feet to the water below.

In the south, the skies darkened with streaks of cannon fire from the Porcupines and black clouds from the flak cannons of the brigs. Archibald had seen death in war before.

Never had it felt so deserved.

CHAPTER TWENTY-SEVEN

Something stung his face, and Samuel bolted upright. Light assaulted his eyes, and not even the clouds in the skies could dim it enough to avoid the pain.

A hiss sounded behind him, and a furry gray cloud suddenly appeared over his head, chasing away the horned helmet. Samuel struggled to make sense of what he was seeing.

"He's awake! Keep digging for more survivors."

The cloud resolved into Bessie's underside, and she skittered around stones and boulders, getting a better look at him. Samuel patted her between the eyes, frowning at the puffs of dust and dirt that rose from her hair as he sat up.

He could see scratches on her legs, but very little signs of damage. A small drop of blue blood oozed from her right rear leg, but that looked to be the worst of it.

Samuel scratched just beside one of Bessie's fangs, and the spider finally decided he was going to live, and sprinted off toward another cluster of Jumpers. That gave him time to take in what had happened, and why soldiers from Fel and Ballern and Belldorn were all digging in hills of rubble.

It was only then Samuel noticed the unmoving Stalker beside him, the orange hair of its legs stained with blood and its head lost beneath a stone nearly the size of a speeder. *Orange hair ... why does that seem so ...*

"Drakkar!" Samuel screamed, scrabbling to his feet as he raced to the crushed spider. His shoulder twinged as he lifted stones and hurled smaller rocks away from the Stalker.

There was too much weight. He'd already seen what had happened to that Stalker. There wasn't enough left to call it a spider. What would that weight have done to a man? It didn't matter. He wouldn't leave his friend trapped on the docks of Ballern.

Drakkar had risked so much to drag him from the caves of the Fire-worms. Samuel couldn't leave him under that rubble. Not now. "Drakkar!"

Another body joined him, digging through the rubble, and distantly Samuel noted the horned helmet etched with a cloaked figure like death itself.

"Here!" the helmeted man shouted. "All of you, here, now!"

Samuel didn't understand why the man was calling out until he saw the hand, stained gray and white with the dust of the collapse. He joined four other soldiers as they leaned against a stone, leveraging it away from the body underneath. Samuel was afraid to look back as the ground shook and dust billowed up before the stone rolled twice and splashed into the sea.

"Grimhelm has a live one!" Samuel knew that face, but names were fuzzy. It took too much time to remember. "Get him to the medics, now!" Owen. Owen from Fel. "*Now!*"

Tears flooded Samuel's vision as they carried Drakkar away. He tried to follow, stumbled, and a strong arm caught him.

"Easy, lad," the helmeted man said. "That a friend of yours?"

"Yes. Drakkar."

"They'll take care of him." Dark eyes in the shadows of the helmet narrowed. The helmeted man reached up and turned Samuel's head before wincing. "Looks like you could use a trip to the medics, too. Get yourself bandaged up and help us look."

"Who are you?"

"I'm the bard, of course." The man smiled, a kind expression that was entirely out of place in the ruin of Ballern. "Go. See to your friend. And yourself."

Samuel followed the men carrying Drakkar. They didn't go far, only to the opposite side of what had been the market. To the place where the wounded cried out, and the dead stared with unblinking eyes. He sat beside Drakkar as they stripped the Cave Guardian's cloak and dressed two deep wounds in his back.

They said something about a head wound, and Samuel wasn't sure who they were talking about. They poured cold fluid over his head before poking him with something sharp and wrapping his head in a bandage. Someone said not to move until the medic cleared him, and that he could do. He needed to gather himself. He needed to make sure his friend was safe. And he prayed the rest of his friends were in better shape.

✧ ✧ ✧

"Tatsu!" Rin called the dragonrider's name again, and Tatsu finally turned to him.

Tatsu shook his head. Another one lost. How many people just died under Mordair's watch?

"Take them to the alley and move on." Rin's heart stuttered when he saw the small, broken form in Tatsu's arms. He closed his eyes and took three deep breaths, trying to ignore the grit that coated the air and stuck between his teeth.

He turned his attention back to the line of soldiers standing guard outside the palace. Only three had abandoned their posts to help with the search and rescue. Rin guessed the others were loyal to Mordair, or so conditioned by their training in Fleet their duty knew no bounds.

Regardless, they were useless to him now. Rin picked up the makeshift stretcher formed from a broken flagpole and a bloody banner wrapped around it until it would hold enough weight. They were on the edge of the attack, and the injured were just now reaching the block with the hospital.

Worse, worried families choked the street, slowing everything down, looking for their loved ones. Rin could understand they feared the worst, but the congestion was going to cost them lives.

"Move everyone back!" he shouted to the nearest soldiers who had abandoned their fight. "Keep a perimeter clear so we can get to the hospital."

The ground shook beneath his boots and he worried about another collapse. But when he turned, he saw what was coming. Two Titan Mechs ducked through the city gates, heading east. Rin's shouting might not have gotten the crowd's attention, but the enormous machines certainly did.

"As soon as those Mechs pass," Rin said, "hold the people back!"

He didn't recognize the pilots, though that might have had something to do with the distortion on the windscreen, or the sheer height of the Titan Mechs. But it didn't look like Jacob or Smith, and he cursed again at the broken transmitter in his collar.

He should have felt lucky. The length of metal that had crushed it could have just as easily killed him. Rin bent down and gently slid a wounded woman onto the stretcher. Finally, one of the palace guards broke away, coming to offer aid.

Or so Rin thought. The only warning he had was the shout of an officer to stay in formation.

The sword came fast. Its long blade clanged against the handle of the stretcher, narrowly missing Rin's neck before it took a chunk out of his vambrace. The soldier reared back to strike again. Instead, he froze when a knife cracked into the side of his skull.

Tatsu appeared behind the soldier, ripping the blade out before slitting the soldier's throat. He dragged the man to the palace entrance and dropped him at the boots of his fellows. The dragonrider stared them all down.

No one spoke, but one guard nodded at Tatsu.

Another tense moment passed, and Tatsu turned away. He grabbed the other side of Rin's stretcher, and they started for the hospital. "I leave you alone for two minutes, and you almost get yourself skewered."

"I'm slower on the ground."

"Oh, I know." There was irritation in his voice, but also a mild amusement.

Rin gave Tatsu the smallest smile. "Thank you."

✧   ✧   ✧

MARY LEANED AGAINST Smith and watched the end of an era as Ballern was buried beneath the ambitions of Mordair. "What if Eva didn't…"

"Don't," Smith said. "We do not know anything. We can try the kids, if you want."

She shook her head. "No. If they're hiding, the transmitter could give them away. We don't know what's happening on the ground."

The hinges on the door to the cabin squeaked and Jakon stood as a silhouette against the afternoon sun. "Maybe it's time we find out."

Mary took a deep breath and climbed to her feet. "Are we secured?"

"Tied you off myself. The Skysworn isn't going anywhere unless the entire dock collapses." Jakon glanced outside and cringed. "Allow me to rephrase that."

"It's fine, Jakon." Mary chuckled and rested her head on Smith's arm for a moment. "We can help with the search and rescue."

"I can do more good moving stone than I can repairing the Skysworn. That can come later. For now, let us see to Ballern." Smith followed Jakon out of the cabin, grabbing a belt of tools from the lockers along the deck before strapping it over his leather apron.

Mary took a pack of medical supplies and a long pry bar. "You might have your biomechanics, but the rest of us need leverage."

Smith offered her a smile, and they continued out onto the docks, heading toward the lift.

Looking east turned her stomach. These weren't the docks she knew. There should have been bars and restaurants bustling with people. Tiny homes peppering the walkways that led to the warehouses. But they were gone.

The docks simply ended, dropping away to nothing.

She stayed close to Smith and Jakon as they reached the lifts. Several people just stood at the railings, staring down at what was left on the ground while airships battled to the north. But it was no longer Fel and Ballern combined. Ballern's destroyers all deployed flags of surrender, as did a handful of Fel's.

But the cloud of ships wasn't uniform in their surrender. Some still took aim at Bollwerk's mighty warship and the brigs of Belldorn as they wove in and out of the ranks. Fel's attackers were shot down in short order, but several escaped west.

It did little to dull the losses Mary knew Belldorn had suffered. They'd sent landers and brigs both to settle into those new slips, and Mordair had dropped the docks on them. How many families had been broken in that slaughter?

The gates closed behind them, and Mary looked away, focusing on her friends. "Where is Fel going? Fleeing west?"

Jakon grimaced. "If Mordair's truly formed an alliance with the Children of the Dark Fire, he could be heading for the Great Machine. The city within the Great Machine is armored. You've seen the remains of a Great Machine. Now imagine it well maintained and protected by a fleet."

"Maybe he's still in the palace?" Mary said. "We could go there."

"The palace guards will have every floor locked down after what we just witnessed. Loyal to Mordair or not, they'll work to protect the other nobles sheltering there. Every other citizen will be forced out, or restricted to the lowest floors."

Smith looked down as metal creaked and squealed in the lift, the rails clearly not as straight as they had been before the destruction of the Bones. The crowds below grew louder as they neared, calls for medics and lifts drowned out by the heavy footfalls of a Titan Mech making its way east.

There was no fighting there. At least, none that Mary could see. There was only dust and dirt and blood. The door squealed open after they came to a jarring stop, and Mary started outside, her boots crunching on pulverized brick.

Smith stepped up beside her. "Follow the Titan Mech. I can do the most where the debris is heaviest."

"I can't wait anymore, Smith. This is … this is …" Mary clicked the transmitter in her collar. "Eva, come in. Jacob, Alice? Drakkar, Rin, Samuel, *anyone!*"

No response came. Mary's heart hammered in her chest. Dread worked its way into Mary's bones as the silence continued.

The transmitter crackled to life. "Mary? Mary, it's Furi."

"Furi, where are you?" Mary almost crushed the transmitter between her fingers. "Have you seen Eva? Have you seen the others?"

"Eva's okay, but she's in the bookstore with the medics. They're taking good care of her, Mary."

Furi said more, but Mary didn't hear her. All she could do for the moment was sob in relief. She'd feared the worst. Smith put his arm around her, and she leaned into him.

Jakon switched the dial on his own transmitter. "Furi, what about the others? Kura? Jacob and Alice?"

"Kura fell," Furi said quietly. "Jacob and Alice are with me. We're in the market, but I wouldn't call it a market anymore. I thought you were going to leave us."

Jakon grimaced and looked away. "So did I. But I couldn't do it, Furi."

"Getting soft in your old age." It almost sounded like a joke, but there was only sadness in her voice.

Jakon blew out a short laugh through his nose. "Maybe I am. We'll get Mary to the bookstore, and then Smith and I will join you in the marketplace."

"Send Smith, now. We need him. It's … it's bad, Jakon."

"On our way, kid."

✧   ✧   ✧

THERE WAS ONLY one comparison Jacob could make to what he saw in that city of ruin. The Fall of Ancora had been worse in some ways, but this was all done by the hands of people. There was no stampede of invaders. There was no argument that the result was worse than the intent. This was cold, brutal, and deliberate.

He was sure he'd heard the transmitter over the chaos of the search and rescue, but he couldn't make much out with the screams all around and the thunder of the occasional cannon in the air. He'd reach out when things quieted.

For now, he focused on moving what he could, using levers and fulcrums to magnify his efforts. Some stones shifted, some levers bent, but Alice and Jacob kept their focus. His arms felt like they'd been lifting barrels all day before he heard another voice.

"Jacob!"

"Did you hear that?" Alice asked. "Someone called your name." When the stone at the end of the lever rolled to the side and came to a rest, she turned and squinted.

"Alice!"

Armor crashed against stone, sounding like a calamity to rival the screams and impacts of the people digging through debris.

Alice grabbed Jacob's arm and spun him around. He had a single moment to register who was in front of him before Samuel crushed him and Alice in a hug.

"I didn't know if you two made it. I thought … you were on the Bones, and … and …" He pulled them tighter. When Samuel finally released them, Jacob couldn't help but notice the blood on his upper arm and torso, mixed with streaks of dust and dirt that had been washed away from much of his bandaged forehead.

"Are you okay?" Alice asked.

Samuel looked down at his bloodied clothes. "Most of it's not mine."

"Have you seen Drakkar?" Jacob asked.

Samuel nodded. "He's near the wall with the medics. They talked about moving the injured to the bookstore or the hospital. I don't know if that's going to happen. Medics setup a tent to keep the worst of the dirt out so they could tend the wounded."

"You were on the ground, weren't you?" Alice reached out and dusted Samuel's back off, frowning at the dents that peppered the Spider Knight's armor.

Samuel took a deep breath. "We were. Bessie's okay. She's over by the Jumpers on the wall." He pointed through the archways to the market. "Drakkar's mount didn't make it. A lot of knights didn't make it. Can't focus on that now. Let's help who we can."

Jacob didn't ask anymore. The stories could wait. The people buried in the rubble couldn't, and they still had a chance to save some of them.

"Help us look for survivors, would you?" Alice reached out and squeezed Samuel's arm. They continued for a time, shifting rubble and stone as the search continued.

Sometime later, shadows stalked through the city to the west. For a moment, Jacob didn't understand what he was looking at. But the shadows resolved into Titan Mechs, and they were headed straight to the collapse.

"We need to clear out of here," Jacob said. "Keep a few spotters to look for people, and the rest need to get out of the way."

Alice followed Jacob's gaze and cursed. "Archibald. How many did he bring?"

"I don't know." Samuel bounced on the ball of one foot. "But sometimes I really like that old bastard." The Spider Knight moved to organize the search and rescue at the edge of the debris field, clearing a path for the Titan Mechs while allowing several volunteers to scout ahead in the rubble.

The transmitters emitted a burst of static before a familiar voice echoed between Alice and Jacob. "Looks like a couple Ancorans and a half-dead Spider Knight up ahead."

Jacob couldn't stop the smile on his face. "Frederick! I thought you'd be on the carrier or a warship."

"I was, but all my tinkers can do my job. Redundancy is key, you know. One of Targrove's more annoying, but useful, rules."

"We have searchers in the debris, but we can't move the biggest boulders."

"I'm not sure the Titan Mechs can move the biggest of them, Jacob. I seem to have picked up some strays by the hospital, though. Maybe they can help."

Frederick's Titan Mech swept past them with a nod from the tinker. A second followed close behind, but the sight that waited beyond that filled him with relief.

"Mary!" Alice cried out, rushing over to the captain of the Skysworn.

Mary gestured for Jacob to come closer as she kissed Alice on the head. Smith wrapped all three of them up in a hug that could crush bone. Mary broke the silence when Smith released them.

"Furi called for Smith at the market. I knew it would be bad, but this is awful."

Stone ground against stone behind them, and when Jacob turned to look, Frederick's Titan Mech hurled a broken piece of an archway into the sea. In the distance, far to the northeast, more Titan Mechs moved along the coastline, digging through rubble, searching for those who might have survived the impossible.

Alice reached up and held his cheek. "They're for more than killing, Jacob."

He held her gaze for a short time, studying the flecks of black across her bright blue eyes. "Thank you." Jacob leaned forward and kissed her softly. "We need to go help Furi. Frederick can handle this."

When he turned away from Alice, he found Smith with a wide grin on his face. Mercifully, the tinker didn't say another word as they passed through the surviving arches to the market.

CHAPTER TWENTY-EIGHT

Archibald braced himself on two outstretched arms, leaning over a table filled with maps of both Ballern and the terrain around the city. Red magnetic squares marked the perimeter of where the worst of the collapse had landed. Triangles in the same color marked the escaping warships of Fel.

Mordair had moved fast. Whether his decision to destroy the docks was well thought out, or the actions of a panicked madman, Archibald couldn't be sure. One thing he was certain of—Mordair had already had a plan to move his forces.

He clicked the transmitter in his collar, dreading the conversation he was about to have. "My Lady. We need to speak."

Lady Katherine answered so fast she must have been around people she trusted implicitly. "What is it, Archibald?"

"The brigs you couldn't track past the cloud bank. Our supply ships located the wreckage along several ridges in the Gray Mountains. Whatever they found besides the destroyers, it didn't end well."

"I assumed so, though I am sorry to hear of their loss. How much of Fel's fleet escaped? Do we have an idea of how many destroyers evaded us?"

"Perhaps half? I cannot be sure of an exact number. We can only hope the destroyers that surrendered on the docks don't change their mind."

"Disable their cannons and secure the engine rooms if it has not been done already. It will matter little from there. The Skyborn who are loyal to the Stormborn should provide assistance."

"They lost a great deal, Kat. This could break them."

"Bollwerk has never suffered a loss like what happened in Ballern, Archibald." Her voice remained quiet, but her words held a terrible weight. "You have not seen the resilience of a people wronged. Even should they break, they will answer the call to fight Mordair. I have reports of Ballern destroyers joining Fel in the retreat."

"I as well. Only two, but it is worrisome nonetheless."

"They've run from a city I would never have bombed to a machine I would see destroyed to break the Children of the Dark Fire."

Archibald's lips tightened as he considered the other reports that had come in. "There is another issue, Kat. Armored transports have been seen fleeing west from the north side of Ballern. Mostly Ballern's armored crawlers, but there are some of Fel's among them. They fly the black and red of Fel. It could be Mordair himself."

"I doubt that very much, Archibald. You think Mordair would trust a Ballern transport enough to risk his life in one? Or be bold enough to reveal himself with his own flag?"

Archibald rubbed the back of his neck and stepped away from the maps, looking instead through the windscreen at the ruin of Ballern's eastern districts. "Perhaps you are correct. I thought to deploy our bombers, but it may be an unnecessary violence."

"Archibald." The transmitter crackled. "Send them a message. If they ride with Fel's colors, they are the enemy of all our allies."

He crossed his arms and glanced to the starboard windows. The carrier was close enough that the bombers could be on that caravan in under an hour. To delay would put them in the airspace of the Children of the Dark Fire, and he didn't know enough about their fortifications to risk that.

Archibald took a deep breath. "It will be done. Send word to your forces. They have one hour to abandon any pursuit of those crawlers. Anyone left nearby will not survive when the bombers finish their task."

"Understood. I will inform Karn as well."

CHAPTER TWENTY-NINE

"I WAS NOT sure if you would return." Mordair climbed into the rear seat of the striker, the regalia of his position as Steward abandoned for a worn cloak that would have been at home on the docks.

Patrice eyed him. "You take no one's counsel but mine, Gregory. And even mine is sometimes ignored. If I leave you to your own devices, you may do something more foolhardy than turning an entire district into a graveyard."

"You worry too much for the lives of your enemies."

Patrice reached up and pulled the canopy closed once Mordair was settled. "I spoke with Lane. The Children of the Dark Fire aren't what I would call thrilled with your attack on Ballern."

"They will be far less thrilled with my plans for the Great Machine, I am sure."

"You're going to get us killed, Gregory." She squeezed the throttle until her knuckles whitened. "And do not think I've forgiven you for that slaughter in Ballern. It is one thing to execute civilians to keep the order, but what you did was as foolish as Newton's antics in Ancora."

"Perhaps I will offer up the Battle of Ballern as a tribute to my late brother. I am sure Lane and the others could fabricate a wonderful tale about Newton's great sacrifice, and our righteous vengeance. Nothing resonates with the lost like the glory of war."

Patrice released the anchor for the striker and let the nose rise for a few feet before pushing the throttle forward. It might have been an older

Ballern model, but the ship held steady as they streaked to the northwest, slipping past one of Bollwerk's great warships and a shadow that rivaled it. They were hidden in that lone striker, a ship that would raise little suspicion from any observer.

"They built a carrier," Patrice said. "I'd heard the reports, but it's not the same as seeing it with your own eyes."

Mordair leaned forward, pulling slightly on Patrice's seat. "Their tinkers are skilled. I will grant you that. But we still have Ballern's carrier. They may have avoided engaging with the entire fleet at Ballern, but it won't be so simple at the Great Machine. Even as we speak, the carrier is moving over the Gray Woods. It should arrive shortly after we do. Archibald and his allies will find it hard to push through our lines. We only need time, Patrice, and time we can buy."

The world below disappeared in a white haze as the striker reached the cloud bank.

CHAPTER THIRTY

OWEN STOOD SHOULDER to shoulder with Fiona, Trevor, Jakon, Rin, and Tatsu. The palace was the last building to be secured. That meant the nobles were inside, and possibly anyone else who had been coordinating quick raids on the rescue efforts.

Broken bottles and stones littered the area around the guards, but they had only retreated far enough that the overhanging balconies provided some measure of protection.

Jakon stepped forward, and the guards visibly braced themselves for conflict. "I'm speaking to you as someone who calls Ballern home. Let us into the palace, or we will kill you. These are fisherfolk from Fel, dragonriders from Canopy, and you likely know me as the captain of The Ray. Stand. Down."

Twenty soldiers stared at Jakon, but he saw several of them fidget. One of their spears hit the ground, and the woman walked away, muttering about the search and rescue being more important than the nobles.

Four more followed her.

"Are you sure we should let them leave?" Owen asked. "If they have loyalty to Mordair, they're a danger."

The iron-banded doors behind the guards creaked open, drawing dust and dirt into the immaculate halls beyond. "Guards, leave your post."

Jakon blinked at the woman in the doorway as a few of the guards left without further prompting. He knew the Baroness of Auxley well enough to see the slouch of her shoulders as opposed to her normally rigid posture. Dark circles hung below puffy eyes, and he never thought he'd find that kind of defeat in her down-turned gaze.

She met his eyes. "Mordair is gone." Her words were reserved, a cold acceptance behind them. "Some of the archdukes joined him in exchange for empty promises of wealth and power in his new empire."

The soldier farthest from the baroness drew her sword and charged. One thing Jakon had always prepared for was an unexpected attack, and the bolt flew from his wrist as if he'd been carefully tracking a stationary target.

It took her in the neck. There were few people who would keep fighting when they knew they had a mortal wound. Most would try to save themselves. And the soldier was no different. Her sword clattered to the ground as she tried to stop the blood.

Another soldier lunged and slid a blade between her armor plates. Whatever he hit, she went down like a sack of flour the moment he tore the blade out. He pulled his own armor off and threw it on the ground before ripping the patches off his shoulders.

"For the Stormborn!" He stepped back in line, standing guard behind the baroness.

She glanced at the rest of the guard, two more of them now abandoning their armor in the dirt, before turning to Jakon. "Those of us who remain are giving our fortunes to the city. Rebuild what you can. Show them a better path."

"I'm no leader, Baroness."

"Our leaders are dead, Jakon. Don't let our city die with them." The baroness removed the tiara from her brow and dropped it on the dead soldier at her feet. "Guards. You are all dismissed. Let any who wish to enter the palace do so at will."

Jakon stepped closer to the guards. "If you would, please escort the nobles back to their homes. Keep them safe. We will need them to confirm their generous gifts." Most of the guards dispersed, heading into the palace to gather the remaining nobles and taking others into the streets, back to their homes.

The Baroness of Auxley cast a glance over her shoulder at Jakon and the others, a small smirk on her lips. "No leader indeed, pirate." With that, she disappeared into the halls of the palace.

"We'll stay with the guard, Jakon," Rin said. "Tatsu and I grew up with many of them. We may be Stormborn now, but we all grew up Skyborn. We all endured our time in the fleet."

"You don't need my permission, Rin. Do what you think is best."

"The fisherfolk and I will return to the recovery efforts," Owen said. "None of us are afraid of some honest work."

Jakon nodded. "I'll join you as well, once I see to the docks. Word is there are still small skirmishes above." But even as he spoke, the flags on the palace changed. The familiar colors of Ballern gave way to a white flag with an iridescent embroidered circle in the center.

"What does that flag mean?" Owen asked.

"It means Ballern has surrendered. It is well and truly done."

Owen watched as Jakon's expression shifted. The pirate's brow drew down, and his posture stiffened as he turned to the gathered crowds around him.

"Stormborn! Skyborn! Keep the paths to the hospital and medical facilities clear. If someone is lost, help them. If there are bodies to move, clear them. We'll see to the dead, name them, and burn them at dawn before the Carrion Worms appear, as is our custom.

"Dragonriders and Spider Knights, check the rubble before the Titan Mechs get to it. Be as safe as you can, but be fast. We have more missing than I can imagine, and precious little time to find them." He clapped his hands together. "Spread the word and go. I want every guild that pledged themselves to this fight to join us in the recovery. Find them and get the message out."

Two guild leaders relayed Jakon's orders, sending their people out into the rubble. Many more followed.

"You've seen this sort of thing before," Owen said.

"No. Not like this. This is worse. This reminds me of the stories the Ancorans tell. And that is something I never wished upon my worst enemy."

Owen turned to Fiona and Trevor. "Come, we have work to do."

✧   ✧   ✧

JACOB WASN'T SURE how many shifts they'd taken, or if it was two or three days that had passed in that blur of dirt and blood and anguish. But he alternated between running the Titan Mechs with Frederick and repairing boilers and pumps for the medics.

The hospitals might have been well equipped, but no one could be prepared for that kind of demand. Tools and systems that were meant to run intermittently were forced to run dusk to dawn, an abuse that broke more than machines.

Night fell on the docks again, and he thought that meant two days had passed, or possibly three. The only real rest was in the dark, when they'd had time to shower and scrape the blood and dirt from their hands. A time when he could crawl beneath a blanket with Alice and try to forget the things he'd seen that day.

Even when he could block out the ruin of Ballern, visions of Ancora and Dauschen came back to haunt him. But Alice was there. She reminded him there was light after the darkness. He just had to make it to the other side.

In the morning, he'd help Smith with more repairs on the Skysworn.

It might have been heavy work, but there weren't any bodies that had to be moved, and for that, he was grateful. He tried not to think of the funeral pyres and the way their flames danced across the glass of the Titan Mech. Tried not to think of the stench that followed, or the slow approach of Carrion Worms.

Those were the things that waited in the sunlight. Now it was dark, and Alice was nearby. The rest could wait a few more hours.

✧ ✧ ✧

JAKON STOOD AT the ragged end of the Bones, one hand on the remaining railing as he looked down at the rubble far below. The Titan Mechs had made progress, but there was more to be done. He didn't want to imagine how many souls were lost in the rubble, and every passing hour made it less likely to find survivors.

For what it was worth, they'd cleared a great deal of stone and metal, finding nearly fifty survivors in the worst of it. Fifty. Jakon sighed and rubbed his eyes with his palms. He wished Kura were there. She had always been a voice of reason in the Skyborn. She knew how to guide the energy and anger of the docks while focusing her own like a blade. That was the power of a natural leader. A power he wasn't sure he could conjure himself.

Jakon turned to face the crowd gathered near the central lifts for the eastern docks, summoned by the messengers deployed that morning. He wasn't a leader, but he wouldn't let his city burn.

"I won't lie to you. Not about this." He projected his voice as best he could. The wind was with him, and that would help. "Hard times are ahead for Ballern. Hard times for the Stormborn. I hope you all understand that's what we are now. The Skyborn died at Mordair's hand, just as he brought ruin to Fel and Dauschen and Ancora."

Jakon didn't mention the base at the Red Woods, or even those lost in Belldorn, but the memory of all of them dwelled behind his words. "I'm a smuggler. It's no secret. I've carried goods and people from every city on our continent across the Crystal Sea, as far as Ancora.

"I've met the worst we have to offer. And the best." He eyed Furi in the front row of the gathered people. "I've called you friends, I've called you rivals, but we are all one beneath the nobles."

Mutters of agreement rose to a quiet buzz.

"The nobles don't fully understand their mistakes yet. They've pledged their fortunes, but only in a bid to save their lives. A bid *we* will honor because we are not like them. We will not sell our city and our people to the Children of the Dark Fire."

Jakon clenched his fists and took a deep breath. "The Battle of Ballern may be done, but this is a war, friends. This is a war that will not end until Gregory Mordair lies dead at our feet, and the Children of the Dark Fire burn in the flames they worship!"

He waited for the roar to calm. It might not have been Kura's way, to incite them like that. To call on their need for justice. Their desire for vengeance. But it was his way. It was the pirate's way. And before anything else, Jakon was a pirate at heart.

Slowly, the cheers receded. He watched Furi wipe her eyes as she pulled a flag from her backpack, unfurling the mosaic of a Shadowwing and holding it high.

Jakon took a deep breath and gestured to the palace far below. "Our queen was not who many of you believed her to be. She allied with the Skyborn, fed us information that allowed us to resist the whims of the nobles when they would have ground everyone on the docks beneath their heels. You must spread the word, the truth of it. We will march on the Great Machine, and our price will be paid. For the Stormborn, and for the queen who was taken from us." His voice cracked with raw anger. "For the families who were broken and for the blood in our streets. We will. Not. *Bend!*"

It was a moment. A point in time he knew he would look back on as the start of a great victory, or the end of the city he knew. He could only hope it was the former, and work to make it so.

Furi ran forward and threw her arms around him. Her voice raw as she turned and screamed to the crowd. "For Kura! For the Stormborn!"

And they echoed with a roar.

CHAPTER THIRTY-ONE

JACOB SAT ON one end of Drakkar's cot while Alice sat opposite him so they didn't dump the Cave Guardian on the ground. A week had passed since the collapse of the Bones, and while most of the injured had been transported indoors, several tents had been erected in the area that had once been the markets.

"I still think you should have asked to be moved to the bookstore," Alice said. "At least you'd have more than you can read while you recover."

Drakkar shook his head. "No, Alice, I would rather offer that up to those in more dire need. I do not mind the elements, and the sound of the waves hitting the stones of the dock is soothing."

"Books are more soothing."

The Cave Guardian smiled. "Tell me what the world outside the tent is like. Have the tinkers agreed on a plan with the engineers? A way to start rebuilding the city?"

Jacob thought back to the one meeting between Frederick and two of the city engineers he'd witnessed. "I … well … I don't know if I'd call it an *agreement*. There was a lot of yelling, and an older engineer almost attacked Frederick when he insulted him."

Drakkar raised an eyebrow. "How did he insult the engineer?"

"He said something like, 'If that's how you propose to build a tower, I'm surprised the rest of the city hasn't fallen down.' "

Alice cringed. "We really need to send him to cotillion. He'd learn some manners there."

Jacob laughed at the idea of Frederick being forced into a cotillion. It certainly wasn't something you saw older people at, unless they were instructors. "They did at least agree on where to start rebuilding. From the perimeter as the debris is cleared."

"How's your back, Drakkar?" Alice leaned forward, eyeing the bandages wrapped around his chest and back.

"Better. There is still pain, but when the medics tell me I am free to go, I will leave without concern. How is Eva? Have you visited her recently?"

"She's our next stop."

Drakkar settled back in his cot and sighed. "That is good. You should go, my friends. The medics are making their rounds, and they can be quite short with visitors."

Alice held out her fist, and Drakkar wrapped his hand around hers.

Jacob did the same. "We'll see you soon."

They left the tent before saying more, passing cots and medics who eyed them, but didn't comment on their presence. Maybe they'd grown used to the pair over the past week, or perhaps they'd learned who their closest allies were.

Alice took Jacob's hand and blew out a long breath. "Drakkar looks so much better."

"I know. I was really worried about him for a few days there. Let's hope Eva's doing better, too."

Alice squeezed his hand tighter and guided them into the alleys outside the archways. Those narrow paths weren't as empty as they had been before the attack on the docks, and nothing was truly private on those streets.

It was strange hearing the conversations about Archibald and Lady Katherine as if they were larger-than-life figures. Archibald was thought of as a warlord among the Skyborn. A king who ruled with an iron fist in the Deadlands. After all, how else could he keep a city alive?

Whispers of Lady Katherine having crossed the sea echoed through the alleys. Stories of a ruthless monarch who killed at will and without remorse. Claims that the survivors of Belldorn had been turned into spies for the enemy. That they weren't the same people who they'd captured.

"That part's kind of true," Alice whispered to Jacob as they passed one such opponent of Belldorn.

Jacob glanced at the people, older citizens who bore no threat from Lady Katherine, and yet here they stood, trying to nurture a kind of mad paranoia. "If Kura hadn't worked to teach the Skyborn better, this entire city would be against their own best interests. The damage done by the Children of the Dark Fire runs deep."

Alice nodded. "It's rather sad, isn't it? I was always excited about what we found in the Crown Library, but this has to be why it means so much more to Furi."

The narrow street leading to the bookshop-turned-hospital felt smaller with the crowd of people filing past. The doorway wasn't cut out to handle the traffic, but after a few minutes Jacob and Alice managed to slip inside, the bell silent as the door hadn't closed.

Eva's bed had only moved once, farther back into the bookshop. It left beds closer to the door open for those more in need, and those who couldn't bring themselves to the medic. The initial flurry of patients might have subsided, but the doctors and medics still had far too many patients for their current staff. Volunteers had taken up a great deal of the day-to-day cleaning and meal preparation, which helped the medics see more than they could normally handle.

Jacob expected to see Mary at Eva's bedside, but she wasn't. Instead, she was tucked behind the counter that had served as a register, standing beside Smith. He pointed down at something, dragging his finger in a long arc.

"What are you two doing?" Alice asked. "How's Eva?"

Mary gave her a smile. "She's good, Alice. Sleeping again, but she's doing better."

"A map?" Jacob leaned on the counter, eyeing the large map draped over a desk and flowing onto the floor. "The detail on this is amazing. Some of the larger Forest Giants are even noted individually. How long did *that* take to illustrate?"

"It is impressive, to be sure." Smith looked up. "I saw your glider on the workbench this morning, Jacob. Trouble sleeping?"

"A little. I wanted to get the wings re-covered. I don't like being on the docks without a glider."

"A lot of folks are going to feel the same way after last week."

"I know." Jacob rubbed his wrist. "I asked Frederick to distribute the schematics to the local tinkers. It'll give them a way to make some extra income as the reconstruction moves forward."

A thin silhouette appeared in the hall, carrying a small pile of books while trying to adjust his glasses. Jacob stared in confusion, knowing the man was currently embedded in Karn.

"William?" Alice asked. "When did you get back?" She narrowed her eyes. "And what happened to your cheek?"

William smiled as he walked into the light, rubbing the bright pink skin that ran from his ear almost to his nose. "Took a trip with Allie on her Dragonwing. If a dragonrider ever tells you to duck, best to be quick about it."

"I didn't think they were going to be flying the Dragonwings in the Gray Woods," Alice said. "That's what Samuel mentioned."

"Not many of them, no. And most of the time we were above the canopy." He gestured to his cheek. "Not all of the time, obviously. The Dragonwings are good for scouting from above, but most of Karn rides on Tree Killers and the dragonriders are still on spiders."

He let the small pile of books thud on top of the maps. He lowered his voice, not enough to be a whisper but enough that only those closest to them would hear. "Did Mary and Smith tell you why I'm here? I thought Furi would have been here by now."

"No, we didn't even know you *were* here," Alice said.

William blinked at that before turning to Smith. "Didn't you contact them?"

Smith opened his mouth to say something and snapped it closed when Mary glared at him. He clicked the transmitter in his collar. "Furi, we need you at the bookshop. Come quick, if you can."

The same message echoed out from Jacob and Alice's transmitters.

Alice stepped around the counter and studied the map. "We came by to check on Eva. What did you need us for?"

"Let's wait for Furi. It'll be faster if I don't have to repeat this." William sorted through the books and opened one before sliding it to the upper right corner of the map. He placed a plain courier's envelope beside it.

The transmitter hissed with static. "Almost there. I was helping Jakon with the soup this morning."

"Where was that?" Jacob asked.

William glanced up. "They moved the market indoors for the time being. The nobles who own the old theater opened it up. A little piece of normalcy in this … awfulness. It's only a block past the fountains to the north. I spoke with them earlier."

The bell to the front door chimed behind them, and Furi made her way to the counter. Her hair was tied back and sweat gathered on her brow, heavy breathing giving away the fact she'd hurried over. "Did you tell them?"

William glanced at the others. "I was waiting for you." He slid closer to the table, and Smith stepped back, giving William more space to cover the map in books and reach the corners. "You know where the Great Machine is, do you not?" William looked to Furi. "The one the Children of the Dark Fire call Great Machine Alpha?"

"The Valley of the Roots. But that's not on any map. Well, at least not *labeled* on any map."

"I haven't heard that name before." Alice studied the smaller map in the book William had opened.

"You wouldn't have," Furi said. "It's a nickname the locals use. It's in the middle of a forest. And a dangerous forest, at that. Things live in the trees there. Things that don't like visitors."

Smith crossed his arms. "Sounds about like the Gray Woods, honestly."

"You're right, but it didn't used to be." William tapped on the small map. "Look at this. This section of the woods was changed by the Children of the Dark Fire in later editions, but here there's another city on the map. Now, if you compare that to the topography of *this* map." He slid the book lower, revealing a coastline that nearly mirrored that of the smaller map.

"You think that entire area is all part of the Valley of the Roots?" Furi asked. "That's enormous. You could fit Ballern in that space."

"I don't *think* that's what it is, Furi." William picked up the plain envelope and pulled a photograph from the sleeve. He laid it where everyone could see. "This is what Allie and I found."

Heavy fog obscured part of the photograph, but towers rose from a building. A building with the rough outline of a trapezoid, like what they'd seen in the Deadlands.

"It's the Great Machine." Mary turned the photo. "It looks almost the same as the one in the desert. How close did you get to it?"

"That was as close as we dared, even riding on the Dragonwing."

William pointed to blurry shadows in the sky. "It's well defended with small craft, and perhaps most problematic, with a vast array of wildlife."

William pulled a second photo from the envelope. The fog had cleared to a degree, and what waited below sent a shiver down Jacob's spine.

"It looks like a hive. A nest of … what are those?"

"I'm not sure, Jacob, but they live side by side with the Children of the Dark Fire." William ran his finger along the bottom of the image. "These are homes. I can only guess it's where the lowest caste of the Children of the Dark Fire lives, because I spoke with enough of those cultists to know there is a sprawling city inside Great Machine Alpha. I don't think Ballern was Mordair's ultimate goal. This was."

Clouds of shadow and light rose from the smokestacks along the Great Machine. Steam and soot, blown out with such velocity that they blurred in the image, looking more like a dark flame.

William placed a third photo, showing a long line of armored Walkers. Ranks formed closer to the forest, which was southeast, judging by the coastline.

"Are they marching on Ballern?" Furi asked.

"That was my thought as well," William said. "But Arun pointed out the camouflage in the ranks. It is no raid for this city. They are coming for Karn. We believe they know about the alliance there. That Karn is hosting the forces of the Stormborn. Lady Katherine is already making preparations."

"Of course she is." Mary's brow furrowed. "They're trying to divide our forces again. Put our full strength behind Karn or Ballern, and the other will fall."

"Or they are merely buying time," Smith said.

"But this is where we need to be." Jacob placed his hand over the Valley of the Roots.

"Mordair has the rest of his fleet and nearly a fifth of Ballern's surviving fleet at his disposal." William pinched the bridge of his nose. "It's as fortified as Ballern, if not more so. And you cannot just fly an airship into the Great Machine."

"The old stories say the Great Machines are armored." Furi frowned and glanced at Alice.

"Immune to weather," Alice said. "Immune to bombs. I remember the passage. The Great Machine in the Deadlands might have been brittle with age, but if this one's been maintained …"

"Lady Katherine agrees … with Jacob." There was a note of resignation in William's words. "We await Archibald's decision, but I doubt he'll resist if he's come this far."

"He won't," Alice said. "A victory here would rally his city behind him. He won't miss that kind of opportunity."

"I have a few days of repairs left on the Skysworn," Smith said. "How soon do we leave?"

Mary looked to Eva on the bed. "I want to talk to her first."

"Then prepare yourselves," William said. "There is another path. A control center to the south, mentioned by the leaders of Karn, that could teach us a great many things about the Great Machines. The path is dangerous, littered with cordyceps fungus and worse, but there are few I'd rather walk it with."

"Was that a control center in the Deadlands?" Jacob asked Smith. "Where we found the manual?"

"I do not think so," Smith said. "This is something else. If it is from the time of the skeleton, it could hold many things we have long forgotten."

"There are still a lot of Stormborn who want to chase Mordair right now," Alice said. "They're going to want to know about this. And they're going to need something productive to do besides attacking the Great

Machine prematurely."

Mary shook her head. "We can't tell them. It could be nothing. But if it *is* something, and word got to that cult, we could have larger problems than cordyceps. We handle this like pirates. No one talks. Everyone pulls their weight." She closed William's book and handed it to him. "No one outside Kat and Archibald should know."

"Understood." William set the book down and kept one hand on top of it.

Jacob looked down at the map. Part of him was thrilled at the idea of seeing one of the Great Machines operating. That part of him was far outweighed by the dread of what was to come. The war with Mordair wasn't over, and the worst might lie ahead.

Note from Eric R. Asher

One book to go! It feels like it's been forever since the first Steamborn book was released, and it feels like yesterday. Thank you so much for sticking with Jacob and Alice as they explored their world and grew into who they were always meant to be. Stormsworn is coming, and I promise this series will not end in a whimper.

If you'd like an email when each new book releases, sign up for my mailing list. Emails only go out about once per month and your information is closely guarded by hungry cu siths.

(www.ericrasher.com)

Also by Eric R. Asher

Shop ebooks, audiobooks, and paperbacks at ericrasherstore.com

The Theme Park at the End of the World

The Steamborn Series

Steamborn

Steamforged

Steamsworn

Skyborn

Skyforged

Skysworn

Stormborn

Stormforged

Stormsworn

The Vesik Series
(Recommended for Ages 17+)

Days Gone Bad

Wolves and the River of Stone

Winter's Demon

This Broken World

Destroyer Rising

Rattle the Bones

Witch Queen's War

Forgotten Ghosts

The Book of the Ghost

The Book of the Claw

The Book of the Sea

The Book of the Staff

The Book of the Rune

The Book of the Sails

The Book of the Wing

The Book of the Blade

The Book of the Fang

The Book of the Reaper

Dreams of the Forgotten Dead

Garden Gnome Graves

The Vesik Series Box Sets

Box Set One (Books 1-3)

Box Set Two (Books 4-6)

Box Set Three (Books 7-8)

Box Set Four: The Books of the Dead Part 1

Box Set Five: The Books of the Dead Part 2

Mason Dixon: Monster Hunter

Episode One

Episode Two

Episode Three

Episode Four

Want to receive an email when one of Eric's books releases?

Visit ericrasher.com to get started.

About the Author

Eric is a former bookseller, cellist, and comic seller currently living in Saint Louis, Missouri. A lifelong enthusiast of books, music, toys, and games, he discovered a love for the written word after being dragged to the library by his parents at a young age. When he is not writing, you can usually find him reading, gaming, or buried beneath a small avalanche of Transformers. For more about Eric, see: www.ericrasher.com

Enjoy this book? You can make a big difference.

If you've enjoyed this book, I would be very grateful if you could take a minute to leave a review on the platform of your choice. It can be as short as you like. Thank you for spending time with Jacob and Alice.